Catherine's Dream

Praise For *Catherine's Dream*

This is a brilliant and moving novel, one that helps us step into the life and heart of a young woman with a powerful dream—and with all manner of obstacles in the way of her achieving that dream. Not only does this author bring Catherine, her Polish culture, and her journey to life so vibrantly, she takes us into a world in which women had few choices. And yet, this strong character holds on to her dream against the odds, and—well, you'll have to read this page-turning novel to learn how her amazing life turns out.

David Hazard | best-selling author and international writing coach

Catherine's Dream is a gripping novel full of the beauty and loss of a woman finding her way in an oftentimes harsh and cruel world. I found myself immediately on the farm with her, relishing in the new discoveries of a 1920s Polish orchard, the town, and a world far from my own. My heart ached with her, and I wanted to follow her journey all the way through. Beautifully woven with hope, faith, and perseverance, *Catherine's Dream* is a glimpse into history and a story of love and redemption despite the shadows in the light.

Ashley Logsdon | relationships coach/48 Days Eagles

Every once in a while you sit down with a book with no expectations. It fell into your hands unexpectedly, yet within a few pages you're deep into a world, and getting to know characters, you never want to part from. *Catherine's Dream* engrosses, it moves and delights and hurts and pulls you into lives and times that are unique, and real. It's the kind of book you look up from and realize hours have passed, yet you still don't want to put it down 'til "just a few pages more." Catherine is a woman you'd want to meet, and a book you'll want to share. It's just that good.

Nancy Roberts | producer/writer/video and audio editor

Catherine's Dream is well researched and one feels like they are in Poland after World War I. One learns how the following wars bring uncertainty into their life. One sees how women were treated in that time period through Catherine's eyes. Catherine grows through the many trials that come her way. She feels compelled to leave her homeland to marry the man that paid for her ticket. This is a wonderful story of faith, dreams, and romance.

Grace Pettman | author

Thank *you* for the honor and experience of getting to be a beta reader. I've never done this before but I've been fascinated by your determination and commitment to work on this novel, and it's exciting to see it come into existence, so I was eager to read the story and see what it's like to be a part of the process. Great work! Truly . . . it's a beautiful story, and you told it well.

Frances Drost | singer/songwriter/concert artist

With so much against her,
can she reach her heart's desire?

Catherine's Dream

A NOVEL

ROXANNE BOCYCK

NEW YORK

LONDON • NASHVILLE • MELBOURNE • VANCOUVER

Catherine's Dream

A Story of Spirit and Courage

Published in New York, New York, by Morgan James Publishing. Morgan James is a trademark of Morgan James, LLC. www.MorganJamesPublishing.com

Proudly distributed by Publishers Group West®

Publisher's Note: This novel is a work of fiction. Names, characters, places, and incidents are either products of the author's imagination or used fictitiously. All characters are fictional, and any similarity to people living or dead is purely coincidental.

Morgan James
BOGO™

A **FREE** ebook edition is available for you
or a friend with the purchase of this print book.

CLEARLY SIGN YOUR NAME ABOVE

Instructions to claim your free ebook edition:
1. Visit MorganJamesBOGO.com
2. Sign your name CLEARLY in the space above
3. Complete the form and submit a photo
   of this entire page
4. You or your friend can download the ebook
   to your preferred device

ISBN 9781636981543 paperback
ISBN 9781636981550 ebook
Library of Congress Control Number:
2023933532

Cover & Interior Design by:
Christopher Kirk
www.GFSstudio.com

Morgan James
PUBLISHING
Builds
with...
Habitat
for Humanity®
Peninsula and
Greater Williamsburg

Morgan James is a proud partner of Habitat for Humanity Peninsula
and Greater Williamsburg. Partners in building since 2006.

Get involved today! Visit: www.morgan-james-publishing.com/giving-back

To my grandmother, Catherine. May her spirit live forever.

Chapter

1

The door clicked open behind her. Catherine froze, then quickly hid the paper under the ledger book on her desk.

"Did you get those receipts put into the Brzezinski account book?" her uncle asked, as he took off his cap and hung it on the coat rack near the door. She heard Marcin sit down in his swivel wooden chair and shuffle the papers on his desk behind her. She did not turn around but kept her head down to show him she was hard at work lest he subject her to his icy disapproval and criticism, which he was only too happy to deliver at times.

"Well, no. I have not finished yet," Catherine responded, her heart racing. She continued to look down at her desk, pencil in hand. Her eyes glanced toward the paper hidden under the book. An edge of it was showing.

She heard Marcin turn his chair towards her, the irritation rising in his voice. "Why are you not getting your work done? What have you been doing?"

He leapt back to his feet and took the few steps towards Catherine's desk to look closely in the wire basket where he had put the stack of invoices earlier. When he saw how many she had left to enter in the ledger, he looked angry.

"You had plenty of time to get those done."

Holy Mother, I ask your help . . . Catherine prayed he would not look under the large, general journal in which she was entering figures. As he stood over her, she smelled the cigar smoke and vodka on his breath. Vodka made him volatile.

"You're not scratching out those foolish sketches again are you? If I find you've wasted time drawing when I'm paying you to work, I'll send you back to slopping pigs on the farm. Is that what you want?"

Her hand was trembling and to hide it she set the pencil down and pretended to smooth her skirt. During the few minutes he allowed for her lunch break, Catherine had looked out the window at the horse in front of an open-bodied automobile parked just across the street. A vehicle without a horse! She wanted to capture an image of the changing times—from horsepower to automobile power. She was drawing the horse's bridle when the door swung open.

She thought quickly, to distract her uncle.

"Speaking of farms, I overheard in the Market Square there is a large dairy farm near Płaszów on Gromadzko Street. Maybe they could use your accounting and bookkeeping services. That would be a new piece of income, would it not?"

A little of the perpetual irritation left his voice. "I see you had made *some* progress."

Setting the invoices back in the basket, he continued to stand there. "What is that?"

"I'm sorry. What do you mean?" Her eyes searched the desk for something out of place.

He pointed to a folded piece of paper in one of the stacked compartments on her desk.

"Oh," she breathed a sigh of relief. "It's a flyer I took from an electric pole out on the street. Sometimes I use it for scrap paper." By which she meant paper to draw on but didn't dare tell him.

Her answer seemed to satisfy. "Good, you're being resourceful. It was bad enough when my profits went to support the orchard and I had little left over for my own supplies. The orchard we almost lost during the partitioning of Poland. A country with no borders, only wars."

Catherine knew only too well the family almost lost the farm more than once. Last year's apple crop was poor due to a drought. They also had lost a large share of the younger apple tree saplings they'd planted. Her aunt had been in a panic, fretting loudly they would be driven out to live in poverty. Her two older brothers were forced to work at other farms to bring in money.

His arms were folded, and he was staring out the window. The early afternoon sun filtered through the dirty window and highlighted the aged lines of his face. She craned her neck to see what he was goggling at.

Two men had the hood up on an automobile.

"It would be a fine thing if I could afford to purchase one of those. No more horses to clean up after and feed. I could ride in style."

There it was again. His thwarted dream of becoming a wealthy man. The source of his constant frustration and anger.

Catherine glanced down and noticed the corner of the paper on which she had been drawing was sticking out from under the journal.

Marcin looked over at the calendar on the wall. It failed to cover the peeling, water-stained spot on the wallpaper.

"September already. There is so much work to do here, and soon it will be time to harvest the apples." The irritation was back. "I cannot be in two places at once!"

He looked down at Catherine, who stopped entering numbers on the ledger page.

"I need you here to help me. The farm isn't making us money. I cannot afford to get behind on keeping the books for my business clients. If the work isn't done, we don't get paid, and the bank will still want their money."

Marcin continued to hover over her, and she looked up. Why couldn't he go away?

"I do not want to go back to living in a peasant village." He looked down at Catherine. "Do you?"

She shook her head. Catherine knew his frustration came from not knowing Poland's outcome in the Great War, and it made him irrational.

Marcin went to his desk, grabbed another box with receipts and handed it to Catherine. To her relief and a bit of surprise, his expression had softened.

"You think I'm harsh and demanding—I can see it in your face—but I am only trying to help you. Wasting your time drawing will not earn you money or find you a husband. You don't want to be a single, poor, peasant girl grubbing among the pigs and dirt on a farm your whole life, do you?"

"Of course not." She didn't dare tell her uncle her real hopes.

"I didn't think so."

Marcin's voice once again became edgy. "I need to go get a newspaper. There is talk the war is ending and the Central Powers are collapsing. Russia has already withdrawn from the war. All those decades of no Poland, and now . . ." His voice drifted.

She could feel his eyes on her.

"Once you're finished with those—" He nodded at the stack she had been working on and the box he had just given her. "You're free to go. Tell your Aunt Eva I had

3

to stop by the two Jewish businesses in town—she'll know what kind of mood that puts me in. Currently there are thousands of them living in Kraków, and they own everything, including the banks." He grabbed his cap from the coat rack. "Then I must purchase some supplies at the store. Not everything she's in need of, so that will put *her* in a mood."

He smiled a little at her. "You poor girl. Forced to work with your unpleasant uncle."

In a way it was true. She felt like a serf, forced to labor for Marcin, the feudal lord.

When Marcin left, she stared at the stacks of ledgers and box of receipts. She took a deep breath and watched out the window as her uncle untied the horse and climbed onto the wagon seat.

She slid the drawing she had been working on out from under the journal book, opened her bottom desk drawer, and tucked it under a canvas bag.

Yes, Poland was a newly formed government and society, but its economy was fighting hard to survive now in 1918, during the Great War.

Wary Marcin might surprise her by dashing back in for something he forgot, she closed the drawer quickly. A feeling of guilt rose, and she worked swiftly on the stack of receipts to make up for the time she had been sketching.

After the work was finished Catherine stood and stretched her arms up at the tin ceiling overhead. Out the window she saw the late afternoon sun now cast longer shadows on the street. She looked over at the wooden clock on Marcin's desk. It was just past three o'clock. The bicycle she rode to work was in the back hall. Her brother claimed the bike had been deserted on a farm outside of Kraków by a soldier from the War. She wheeled it outside and locked the door. *Free, at least for the evening.*

As she took to her seat and started pedaling, a feeling of independence came over her.

Marcin . . . one day . . . perhaps . . . he would know, though he could control her time, she would not let him rule over her dreams.

She weaved around people walking and held her head high as she rode past the Jewish men who stared at her as she traveled by their storefronts and taverns. Soon the cobblestone road turned to dirt, and the sounds of the city faded away. The roughness of the turf would challenge the rusted old bicycle, and her long-braided light brown hair bounced on her back. She hoped it would not throw the chain today. The rolling hills of Podgorzé surrounded her. Normally, it would take Catherine nearly a half-hour to walk home to the small farm surrounded by apple trees, but the bicycle was much faster.

The smell of fresh manure told her a horse had recently passed this way and was somewhere probably quite near and up ahead. Coming around a bend in the lane, she was relieved to see it was not Marcín, but surprised to see it was Dominik Bukoski, a young man her age from the nearby village of Bukowiec. The person her father had hinted more than once would one day become her husband. Dominik and his father often came to work at the orchard, especially at harvest time.

"Hello Catherine, nice day for a bicycle ride."

Not wanting to be rude she stopped pedaling and coasted alongside of him. Dominik was always polite, sometimes too polite to her. Although he was considerate, there was nothing interesting about him. His face was flat, his voice was dull, and all he ever talked about was slopping or slaughtering pigs.

"Yes it is. It's odd to see you not working but enjoying a horse ride on a country road."

He shrugged his shoulders. "Mama said I need to enjoy myself more. Get away from the farm. She insisted I go for a ride to clear my head."

"I imagine your father didn't like that." Catherine knew his father worked him hard and the bags under his eyes showed it.

"My brothers Lukasz and Szymon are there. Besides, mama said the horse needed some exercise." He patted its neck.

Catherine struggled to keep the bicycle from leaning and started to pedal.

"Have a good evening, Dominik."

The farm hand quickly responded, "You, too. See you in a few weeks at the harvest . . ." His voice trailed off as she left.

Now she pumped the pedals past fields of yellow-brown grass where the poppies of spring blossomed, and a dirt road led to a village on the Vistula River. In the distance were several large rectangular peasant houses with wide, white-washed planks and uniformed square glass windows. She admired the tall, angled, thick brown grass roofs held together with dried clay. They spoke to her of an artistry different from her own, but an artistry, nonetheless. The house where she lived had wooden shingles made from pine slabs, and when it rained the noise always woke her.

Finally, the familiar thin row of white birch trees at the edge of the orchard appeared. She passed an old barn with a straw-thatched roof and siding of weathered wood badly needing paint. With all the work to be done, no one had time and—as Marcin reminded everyone over and over—there was no money to pay workers "just to slather on paint!" The apple trees were laden, almost ready for the picking, and she thought about all the heavy, wooden crates stacked in the barn for the harvest. How her two older brothers, Antonio and Filip, would need to haul them out, and how much swearing there would be.

Was no one happy with their lot?

Catherine crossed the wooden bridge over the stream. The bluish gray jackdaws with their bright blue eyes chirped as they feasted on bugs hiding in tall grasses near the water. Her mother was outside, using an old pair of scissors to gather herbs from the small garden near the house. Climbing off the bicycle, she leaned it onto a tall shade tree whose leaves had started to change. Her father, who was outside talking to her mother, turned around to look at Catherine as mother waved and walked into the house.

"Hello, Papa," Catherine smiled. At the entryway stoop, she removed her only pair of good shoes and put on the worn boots that had been dried in the sun. Hearing her voice, the pigs beyond the house grunted and gnawed at the fence post, as they did if they had not been fed recently. That, of course, would be one of her chores.

Her father's jaw was set. "Marcin stopped by earlier and told me you were distracted today and didn't get all your work done. He thought you took time from your work to draw… Did you?"

She stared, trying to come up with a way to explain herself—not giving too much away, but not lying or deceiving either. Otherwise, Father Jarek would be harsh with her when she made her next confession.

"Don't you understand the good opportunity you have to help us earn money for the farm? Your dowry?"

She did not want to displease her father, but why was everything about money or marriage? And she was confused about his adamance she not "waste" her time drawing. Why could she not draw if it didn't interfere with her work?

"Father, I do understand. But you've seen women from the city who aren't dressed like peasants but in nice, fashionable clothes. Someone designed those clothes. And what about the beautiful artwork in the church? People are needed to be artists—why not me?"

John turned his eyes from Catherine to Dominik who now rode by on his horse and raised his hand at John. Her father signaled back and folded his arms across his chest.

"Because that is not the life God created for you, he wanted you to be a wife and mother, live on this farm and raise a family. Those people in the city you call artists, they came from a different place, they don't appreciate our way of life."

Catherine became quiet, but a wave of confidence was slowly growing.

"Father, may I have some of the money I've earned? I need to buy my own paper to draw on."

John closed his eyes, and one hand went up to his forehead. "Catherine, are you not listening to me?" he said through gritted teeth. "There is no time to draw, and besides, it's a useless pastime."

"But father, I've been by the Polish art school in Matejko Square. The place named after the famous painter Jan Matejko, who created paintings of our history. Are those useless?"

He looked away as he stretched his right arm towards the orchard. "After work, you're needed here for the farm work and in the orchard—also to help your mother with the housework and to cook. Before winter, new blankets must be woven on the loom. There is so much work to do." His face reddened.

Catherine was not deterred. "I know, but I can stay up later or get up earlier. Drawing won't interfere with my work."

But it was too late. He had already turned and walked away.

Chapter

2

The next morning her father sat at the table, staring out the window as he blew on his scalding hot coffee. He turned his head when Catherine entered.

"Father, I've been thinking about our conversation yesterday. There is a bookstore near the cigar shop that sells paper. I just need one book of paper. Surely I have earned one *zloty* coin…"

"I'm sorry Catherine, but all the money you earned goes to me for the orchard. This place is your only dowry and it's like a monster that eats money…." His voice trailed off.

And who will want a poor girl unless he's paid to take her. Say it, Father.

She didn't want to argue with him and fought to keep tears from welling up. They would do no good anyway. "I'd better go gather the eggs." She lifted the empty basket from the table.

"If you see Filip, tell him he can find me at the east end of the orchard by the row of Red Jonaprince apple trees, near the artesian spring."

Walking quickly along the stream toward the barn, she passed under the droopy branches of the large willow trees. She had not allowed her tears to fall, nor would she despite the circumstances in which she felt caught.

Had men always controlled what a woman could own or the simple things of beauty or comfort she wanted to buy—or the life she could live?

9

Catherine was so caught up in her thoughts she failed to notice Laska, the old woman who lived in the village just up the road from the orchard. Laska was straining to carry a basket of wet clothes to hang on the clothesline. Laska always came in the fall to help Catherine's mother serve meals to the workers from distant villages who came to harvest apples and dig potatoes. They would live in huts at the edge of the apple trees for the season, dirty and drinking, and only too happy for the few *zlotys* they earned.

As Catherine passed, Laska saw her stoic expression. "What's wrong, child? What have they said to you today?"

Surely Laska would support what she wanted.

"I'm frustrated about having to create numbers instead of art. To earn money yet not be able to have it." Catherine's face changed from sadness to hope. "I want to draw what I see. I look at things and shapes form in my mind, like a crooked tree or a building in the city."

Laska set the basket of clothes down and looked at her. "We need money to live. Do you know that many artists nearly starve?"

Catherine studied her, noticing how the faded white kerchief with frayed edges softened her sun-leathered face. Most, she liked how Laska's eyes were always smiling. Except for today. Perhaps the grueling chores of a village peasant were weighing on her again.

"But I need paper." Catherine had thought about taking a new ledger book from work, but she would never steal. And besides, Marcin would know if one was missing. So, she just borrowed a page or two from different record books, but even that was getting too risky. Marcin watched over everything.

"Look," Laska smiled.

She reached inside of her apron pocket and pulled out a loose knot of clustered threads. "I do embroidery from the threads I find loose on old blankets and shawls. People ask me, why do I do this?"

She bent over and took a small, worn leather bag from the top of the clothes basket, pulled out a piece of fabric, and showed Catherine a flower she had embroidered on it. "They tell me it's a waste of time, but it makes me feel good to create beautiful things."

Catherine took the piece of cloth in hand, admiring the intricate detail of the little purple and red flowers. "It's beautiful. How can anyone say creating this is a waste of time?" She handed the cloth back.

"I use these pieces to cover up holes in clothing. My art is useful. Pictures on a wall, what good are they?"

The old woman's words stung. Catherine took in a deep breath and looked toward the barn. "Have you seen Filip?"

"I saw him go into the barn with a bucket from the well."

As Catherine walked towards the barn she noticed how the morning sun rays in the clouds behind the barn made a perfect background. Oh, how she would have loved to capture its beauty, but she had no time. There were so many chores to be done before she had to leave for the city.

She walked through the barn door and found her older brother, Filip, feeding the horses. With his short, stout body and thick, muscular arms, he was able to lift the large wooden water bucket with ease.

"Filip, Papa wants you to meet him at the east end of the orchard near the artesian well." Her voice sounded despondent from the conversation with Laska.

Filip set down the empty bucket and scattered the hay in the horse's stalls. "I heard father and uncle Marcin talking about you yesterday. Uncle sounded irritated with you, something about you not getting your work done?"

"I always get my work done. Drawing is something I do when I need to clear my mind from numbers." The conversation took Catherine back to feeling ashamed about drawing.

"What have you used to draw on?" Filip reached over and stroked one of the light brown horses on the neck. Evidently pleased with the attention, its tail swung gently as it ate. "Uncle Marcin suspects you are taking pages from one of his ledgers." Filip enjoyed spreading gossip and his smile showed it. Catherine knew better then to take the bait from him.

"What I would like is my own book with blank paper so my drawings would be in one place." Catherine bit her lip, not wanting to complain. Everyone worked hard to keep the farm going, especially Filip, who they worked like a plough horse. "Father won't let me have any of the money I've earned. So, I find paper any way I can."

Why had she said that? She was sure a lecture or warning was coming.

Filip turned to her, with a slight smile.

"If you need a ledger book, I know where there is a wooden crate of them." Another horse lifted his head and rubbed its chin on the stall door. "Come on, I'll show you." Filip motioned for Catherine to follow him up the ladder to the hayloft. Hesitantly, she set her basket down, knowing her mother would want the eggs soon. They walked toward a small stack of wooden apple crates. Inside one of the crates was a pile of older, used ledgers. Catherine's eyes lit up.

"I came across these last year... this must be where uncle stores his old ledgers." He reached in and grabbed a handful. "Look, some of them are hardly used." Catherine watched as he untied a soft leather covered book. It looked like nothing she had never seen before. The ledger books she worked in were hard covered with taut leather corners. Filip read the writing inside, "This one says 'Karpiński Estate', that's the Estate North of Kraków destroyed last year in the war, what good is it now? Here, take it." He shoved the book in her hands. "Now you can draw to your heart's content."

Catherine felt as if she was stealing. "Should I just ask uncle if I can have it?"

"After the way he acted about the thought of you not doing your work. Do you think he would want to encourage you to draw? Just take it. Do what you like. God knows, there is little enough to be happy about in this life."

She took the ledger from him. The leather was so thick yet soft and supple. Before climbing back down the ladder into the barn she took the book and tucked it inside the elastic of her skirt. As she pulled her shirt over it she paused at the ladder.

I never thought Filip would help me. He usually thinks only about himself.

As they left the barn Filip confided, "Don't worry, your secret is safe with me."

Catherine finished her chores and helped her mother make biscuits. The last thing to do was strip her bed so Laska could finish the laundry. Later her mother would lay a mattress of fresh hay and spread a sun-dried white linen sheet over the sweet-smelling grass and tuck the homespun soft wool blanket of orange, brown, and red stripes over the bed that would later cradle her tired body. She took a deep breath and smiled as she thought about the soft red leather book under her shirt against her skin.

Her thoughts turned to filling the blank pages of the ledger with sketches of country birds, birch trees, and the city streets... she saw in her mind the drawings come to life with vibrant colors, people stood on the street and admired her art. Art that told a story—art that helped others to see the beauty she saw.

"Catherine, did you hear me? Uncle Marcin is here in his wagon to pick you up."

The sound of her father's voice shouting from the next room reminded Catherine of his insistence this orchard and a husband secured her future—not art. He had told her more than once, *"Someone like Dominik would appreciate a girl like you."* She quickly took the ledger and stuck it in her canvas bag under the fresh biscuits to bring with her to the city.

Today she did not have the bicycle, because her other brother Antonio had already taken it to recruit villagers to work the upcoming harvest. As Catherine sat next to Marcin on the solid wood seat of his wagon, a small tension over what happened at the office the day before still lingered between them. Ironically, she welcomed the quiet ride to Podgorzé.

The bright fall sun felt good on her back. The tall brown grasses had lost their summer flowers and the scattered large, leafed oak tree leaves were now a darker green, soon to be replaced by bronze, red and yellow tones. The lullaby sound of wagon wheels and horse hooves on the dirt road made Catherine sleepy. She had been up since dawn and farm chores felt endless.

The sound of the wagon wheel hitting a hole jarred her awake. A quail, startled by the noise ran across the road, quickly followed by another. Aunt Eva said quails meant harvest time.

Up ahead in the distance coming toward them was a Peddler, his wagon full of goods. The morning sun shined above the tree line and cast a shadow of Catherine and Marcin on the road, but it blinded the pudgy driver, and he pulled his cap down to shade his eyes. The mule seemed to struggle as it pulled the over-loaded cart. Marcin lifted his left hand in greeting as they passed, and the peddler responded in kind. Catherine studied the cart with its pots and pans tied to the side of the wagon and clanging as it bumped along down the dirt road. Most of the businesses in town were owned by Jews and they would peddle their goods to the villagers outside of the city. Some might pay with cash, but many would barter with the peddler, trading eggs, grains, chickens. Catherine had witnessed her mother trade apples or herbs from her garden for tea and coffee. Although many peddlers dressed in ragged clothing and talked misery, Catherine knew better; she saw them in town—in front of their shops, fashionably dressed, looking well fed and plump. Some were clients of Marcin's and she saw the money their businesses brought in.

Catherine decided to break the silence. "Laska told me the Jews have opened a tavern in her village to sell vodka." She grabbed the railing on the seat as the wagon wheel dropped in and out of a hole. "Darn it!" Marcin winced.

She peered over at Marcin, who pulled the reins and forced the horses to move to the center of the road.

"Why did the Jews have to open taverns in the villages anyways?" Catherine remembered stories from Laska about fights in the tavern.

"They host celebrations in their village breweries and become even more wealthy. They make vodka from our potatoes, which helps us." He once again steered the horses to avoid another hole in the road. "Doesn't matter if it's weddings or funerals."

"Well, I don't want my wedding to be at one of those places."

Marcin jerked his head back and laughed, "Oh, are you finally thinking about getting married?"

Catherine took the conversation in a different direction. "I think Filip likes to barter with them for a flask of vodka. I found one hidden in the barn when I looked for a pail to pick the last of the berries."

Marcin's bushy eyebrows lifted. "How do you know it's his and not Antonio's? Or your father's?"

There it was again, his constant questioning of her thoughts. She looked ahead, relieved to see the activity of the city.

"Because I can tell when Filip had been drinking, his eyes get red and glossy. His voice gets loud and irritated." *"Like yours,"* she wanted to say.

She felt his eyes on her, and knew he was waiting for her to contradict him again so he could pounce, but she avoided the trap. He was always looking for an argument.

The dull, deep sound of the horses' hooves on the dirt road now echoed sharply as they reached the first cobblestone streets. An automobile turned from a side street in front of them, which forced Marcin to pull hard on the reins to avoid a collision. Catherine grabbed the wood railing on the bench seat to steady herself. Her canvas bag slid off the wagon seat onto the floor near her feet. She quickly grabbed it; thankful the old ledger Filip found for her in the barn had not slipped out.

The ride this morning had been challenging, and coupled with his negative attitude, made him more than normally irritable. She would need to be especially careful about the office today and not get caught making so much as a stray scribble, let alone a drawing—though she had an idea for one since sunrise.

Marcin parked the horses in front of the office and Catherine overheard shouting as she climbed down from the wagon seat. Loud conversations often spilled from the blacksmith shop across the street as the usual customers came and went, but this was a voice she had never heard before—a deep, authoritative, and confident voice. There was something almost mesmerizing about it.

A tall, lissome young man with a head full of loose brown curls, his shouts overpowering those of the shorter, white-haired pot-bellied man he was arguing with. "You are a ferrier!" the older man hollered, "not a silversmith!" His hands tightened into fists. "If I catch you melting silver coins in that forge again, I'll punch you in the head!"

By now, others in the street had heard the commotion and slowed as they walked by.

"But Tata, it's my money, and I can do with it what I want." The younger man pulled off his leather apron and waved his hand into the air toward the group that had gathered, probably hoping a fist fight would break out.

"What are you looking at?" he shouted, throwing his leather apron on top of a barrel outside the shop door.

The older man gave a dismissive gesture of his hand at the younger one who had already gone back into the shop and the small crowd dispersed.

Marcin reached into the back of the wagon to get his leather bag. "Such a lovely man, that Tomasz Kowalczyk. Pity to be his son, Józef. The old man is a drunkard and spends his profits at the tavern. I've heard he gets liquor from the Jews in exchange for his blacksmith services. A terrible way to do business."

So the young man's name was Józef, Catherine took note.

The office was stuffy and stale. Marcin lugged a stack of ledgers to her desk, then dropped a pile of notes in her basket. "Here are the books and receipts I collected yesterday…" Catherine watched as he walked over to the cast iron safe on the floor near his desk, opened it with a brass skeleton key, and put the money he had also collected inside.

Catherine wandered over to open a window and gazed across the street into the blacksmith shop. With morning sunlight pouring in she could see horseshoes hung on the rafters and a big metal pipe hanging from the ceiling directly over a flame on a large, square brick table.

"Catherine, did you hear what I said?"

"Of course, Uncle." She walked to her desk, passing by his.

That's odd, she thought, the account books on his desk are a different color than the ones he gave me. I've never seen those before.

Marcin was winding the clock on his desk. "I said next week I will need you to deliver some paperwork to the Ostrowski Estate in Kapelanka. I will be needed at the orchard to help organize the workers for the harvest, since your father is incapable of…" He did not finish. "I'll write down the directions. Be sure to take this envelope with you, it shouldn't take you long to go there and back on your bicycle. It's only four miles from here."

It was a relief for her to get out of the office and do errands in the city, seeing people whose lives were so different from hers. Going to Kapelanka meant she could ride across the bridge over the Vistula River into Kraków and pass the art school. In her daydreams she saw herself taking classes there, but those were just fancies. For now, here she was, forced to sit at a desk. On top of file cabinets were stacks of papers and books, calling for her to draw on them. She smiled. *But now I have my own book.*

Marcin was unusually quiet, and she hoped he would not mind if she went for a walk during lunch. She would slip out with her bag that contained the small, old, spent ledger with its soft red cover, to go sketch the beautiful church in Podgórski Market Square. Finally, a sketchbook she could take with her! This thought motivated her to take a stack of receipts, open the accounts payable book, and keep her head down all morning, entering figures into the book.

The sounds of the city ticked along with Marcin's clock. The streets were crowded with the rumble of automobiles and carriages. Horses neighed and whinnied, the clang of the trolley bell passed, and the smell of cigar smoke drifting in through the window told her businessmen with their tall hats and canes were walking by. It seemed the world outside this stuffy, cramped office was bustling with important things.

In comparison, Catherine felt her life and work were utterly meaningless. Would there ever be an end to scratching numbers in books? That thought created an empty feeling.

There will be an end to this only if you do something about it, the thought came. Her pencil halted. *But what could she do?*

She felt as if the small flame of a dream were flickering inside her, and everything in her life—keeping these books, her farm chores, helping her mother—all these things were like cold winds blowing and threatening to snuff the dream out.

Soon the basket on her desk was empty and she stood and stretched her back. Marcin looked up as someone entered the office from the street. The poised and statuesque businessman wore a long-flowing black coat, and his expressionless face was defined by a thick white beard and kashket cap over his short hair. Marcin stood up to shake the man's hand. "I've finished the work on time, how about we go and have a cigar to celebrate."

He reached in the cigar box on his desk and handed one to the man whose long white fingers reached for the cigar while the other hand remained wrapped tightly around his rosewood cane.

"I would be happy to go over the books with you. Let's say we go to your place." Marcin grabbed the two ledgers—those Catherine had noticed were of a different color—and motioned for the man to go outside. The man nodded at Catherine, and she noticed his stone-gray eyes. They had a look of cunning.

"Uncle, may I go to lunch?"

"Yes, but don't be long. I will be back in thirty minutes, and I expect you to be here." He stepped outside and closed the door behind him.

As she stood and picked-up her canvas bag, she couldn't help but think about those different colored ledger books. Usually, he would either leave books on his desk or put them on the shelf. He rarely took ledgers from the office. Marcin was always complaining about the Jews, yet here he was going to some secret meeting with one. She knew there was more to the story, but also knew better than to question anything Marcin did.

Chapter

3

The activity on the street made Catherine's heart pound with excitement. The city was so unlike life on the farm. Like all peasant girls, Catherine wore a plain white blouse with puffy sleeves and a black skirt. She noticed many of the women in the city wore shorter dresses and more colorful clothes, their sleeves were narrower and not so puffy, and there were buttons at the cuffs.

Instinctively, she smoothed her hand over the forearm of her blouse, feeling shy about the clothing that gave away her less fashionable, country girl status.

Despite this, the *sense* of the city entered her—the idea life could be richer, more fashionable, more refined. There were concerts here, and formal dances. Passing one of the clothing stores with beautiful hats in the window, she spotted two women. Each wore a black velvet hat with a wide band and full crown. On one, a velvet plum and orange fruit were sewn on the side. The other had a stylish brim with a large silk bow and its crown had a black net with gold embroidery. She squared her shoulders as they passed.

One day I will purchase one and go to wonderful parties where there are eligible young men. I will only marry, she thought, *if I can find a husband to support my interest in art.*

But her next thought was, *And where will I find that living out on the farm— among the pigs, or the apple trees, or the drunken laborers—which?*

The Market Square was not busy today. Normally by the end of the week the Jewish will be set-up to peddle their meats, goods, and wares. At the end of the month Catherine's father, or one of her brothers, will be here to sell apples, potatoes, plums, and other vegetables from the orchard. She found a warm, sunny spot in the center of the Square and studied the majestic structure in front of her—the beautiful St. Joseph's Church in the Podgórski Market Square.

As she settled herself on a bench across from it, she thought it looked more like a medieval castle than a church. It even had gargoyles. At the intersection of the two steeples was a magnificent tower with a clock whose spire rose more than 200 feet into the clear, noon sky. She always wanted to capture on paper its dramatic, inspiring rise.

Reaching into her bag for a potato pancake she would have to eat quickly if she wanted to draw and get back to the office before Marcin. She removed the soft, red leather book from her bag. She ran the palm of her hand over the cover and found a blank page.

Too soon, a clock in some tower blocks away struck the half hour, telling her she was already late in going back. Time slipped by so easily when she was wonderfully lost in drawing. Fortunately, Marcin would not be back when he said he would be. He never was.

Still, she hurried to return, along the way noticing a flyer with the Polish flag and a white eagle in the center nailed on a wooden fence: it said the Government wanted volunteers to fight in the Polish Army against the Ukrainians. An uneasy feeling came over her as she read it. Another War? Would this mean her brothers would be forced to go? They are both over eighteen years of age and were too young to become soldiers in the recent Great War. She had heard stories about young men who are old enough being forced to enlist. She decided to take the flyer and show it to her father.

When she returned to the office, Catherine was surprised to find Marcin already back. There was something strange about him, his breathing heavy and his cheeks flushed.

She stopped in front of his desk. "Uncle, are you alright?"

He continued to stare at the paper clenched in his hand and did not respond.

He must be angry with me because I'm late. Or maybe his meeting didn't go well. Catherine hurried to her desk and sat down, feeling irritated with him—with the whole situation of her life.

With a hint of contempt he asked, "And, how was your lunch today? Did you make time to draw?" He quickly stood and stormed toward her. "Is this one of *my* ledger papers with a drawing on it?" He threw it on the desk in front of her and crossed his arms over his chest. "I looked in your bottom drawer for the accounts payable book for the clothing store on Dabrówki Street and I found this instead."

Catherine squirmed in her chair. She looked down at the drawing of the horse and automobile she had done yesterday. The smell of vodka on his breath warned her of his impending temper. He hastily grabbed the paper and crushed it in his fist.

His breathing became heavier, and the smell of stale cigar smoke combined with the reek of vodka disgusted her. At least he was done browbeating her and would go back and slump at his desk. Maybe sleep off his drinking.

Instead, he pulled open the top desk drawer, his face crimson with fury.

"Uncle, what are you doing?"

He snatched all the papers, and she was relieved most of them were flyers used for scrap paper. Still, she felt her face getting flushed and shrank back from the physical threat she sensed radiating from him, as if she could feel his desire to hit her.

Don't say anything. It will only anger him more.

Picturing her mother's Rosary, she began a silent prayer. *Hail Mary, full of grace...*

Marcin was flipping none too gently through the pages, bending and wrinkling them quite obviously on purpose. "I swear, if there are any drawings on these papers..."

Her body stiffened. She had tucked the leather ledger book with her drawings in her waistband instead of putting it back in her bag. What if he made her stand-up and it slid out?

Marcin stormed over to his desk, muttering, slurring his words. He opened the bottom drawer and stuffed the papers in it.

She sat staring, miserable. *How had her life become this dark hole; would she ever live the life she dreamed?*

"Are there any others I should be aware of? I will search this office high and low, if I find one more of your sketches you will never come back here."

He retreated to his chair, rambling, "I taught you a skill many peasant women would love to learn. You should be grateful, not doing things that are a waste of time behind my back."

He took a cigar from the box on his desk and reached into his vest for his pocket clippers and cut off the tip.

Her eyes searched the desk quickly. Rubber stamps, wooden compartments, an old cigar box. She opened the box and took him a folded piece of paper on which she had drawn a trolley and stood there, shamefaced.

Always quietly obedient and respectful—until now—she said in a hushed but angry voice, "I don't know why you hate me so much."

Marcin looked startled.

"Catherine, I don't hate you." He sat staring for a long moment, then he lit a match and held it to the cigar between his thumb and forefinger. His voice lost a little of the anger. "I'm just trying to help you."

You have an odd way of showing it.

He leaned back into his chair, exhausted, almost out of breath. "Here." He opened his top drawer, "take this envelope to Ostrowski Estate. She will also have a check for me."

"But I thought you said next wee—"

He interrupted her. "I changed my mind. Best you do it today, because next week I will be at the orchard helping with the harvest and I want to cash her check."

"But I don't have the bicycle today."

"Take the wagon. The estate is at the top of a large hill, past Krakus Mound and the Liban Quarry."

The Liban Quarry was west of Podgorzé, which meant she would not go through the city. Disappointed, she took the envelope and left.

The ride to the Ostrowski Estate gave Catherine time to clear her head. She put her hand on her waist and felt relieved to touch the ledger book. No more hidden drawings in desk drawers or cigar boxes. Once outside the city the terrain up to the manor changed quickly. She passed Krakus Mound; a fifty-foot-high summit that had been around for centuries. It was the source of legend and mystery about Kraków's mythical founder, King Krak, who many believe was buried there. This was the first time she had seen it so close. How she wanted to stop and walk to the top of the hill to sketch the view of the city on paper. But her uncle would be waiting for her.

Beyond Krakus Mound was the Liban limestone quarry run by two well-known Jewish industrial families from Podgorzé. The quarry looked so huge, and Catherine had overheard Marcin tell her parents if only he had that account, then

22

they would be rich. To which Catherine's mother replied, "More money only brings more problems."

How was I born to a woman with so little hope of a better life?

As she drew closer to her destination the road narrowed and the trees became dense. Marcin had told her, "There will be a stone wall with the estate name Ostrowski."

In the distance she could see a limestone wall at the end of an intersecting road. On the wall was a carved Coat of Arms, a knight's shield with a hand gripping an axe in the center, with a prestigious herald wreath on each side of the shield. A ribbon mantle that read "Ostrowski 1844" supported the badge of honor, and at the top of the crest was the most beautiful letter O she had ever seen. She wanted to stop and capture a quick sketch to refine later, but there was no time.

Turning in, she traveled down the drive, between majestic elm and ash trees, sunlight filtering through the leafy canopy and dappling the road in front of her. In a moment, the white manor house appeared, regal in its massive four-columned porch.

She stopped the wagon in front of the porch, feeling speechless and, worse, aware that her clothes gave her away as a poor farm girl—realizing the true meaning of being a peasant. People who worked farmland owned by wealthy noblemen.

Still, she squared her shoulders. *I will not allow the richness of this place or these people to make me feel less than I am.*

On the large wooden door was a brass lion's head holding a heavy ring. She pounded the ring several times on the door but there was no answer. To the right was a pathway leading to a large opening where two figures, a man, and a woman, stood in front of a Carriage House. As she approached they were engrossed in a conversation around something the man held in his hand; it looked to be some sort of orange handled knife. A wagon with a large work horse was parked near the barn. For some reason, the wagon looked familiar to Catherine. Also, the voice coming from the young man—where had she heard it? Sensing movement, they both turned to her.

"Hello, can I help you?" the woman asked as she took the blade from the young man, who bent over and picked up a tool. He straightened and walked over to the paddock beside the Carriage House, where a horse was lazing in the sunlight. The man's work clothes were dirty and his brow sweaty; and yet Catherine felt attracted to him. His long legs were set in a strong stance as he opened the stall door, wiped his brow, and ran his fingers through his wavy, dark brown hair.

"Hello, I'm looking for Mrs. Ostrowski. I'm Catherine and my uncle, Marcin Sadowski, wanted me to deliver some paperwork to her."

The woman's blonde hair was loosely pulled into a soft roll at the back of her head, and she had a kindly look. She wore *pince nez* glasses on the bridge of her nose, attached by a chain to the waistband of her long, narrow skirt which fell to the top of her feet. Her shoes looked to be of the finest leather, with stylish curved heels.

"That is me," she replied, smiling.

Catherine reached into her bag and handed her the envelope. "He also said I am to receive a check from you."

The woman took the envelope and slipped a long, thin blade from the pocket of her skirt, though Catherine's eyes were riveted on the young man. The blade was truly lovely, with an ornate, orange colored handle—and the man was lovely, too.

"I see you are admiring my new letter opener. Józef made it for me." She turned her head and smiled at him, though he was busy again with the horse and didn't see.

"Yes, it is beautiful."

Mrs. Ostrowski extended it to her. The blade was smooth and the color of copper. The silver metal design on the handle reminded Catherine of the Coat of Arms decorative wreath carved onto the wall at the estate's entrance. An oval, amber colored stone complemented the crest.

She handed the blade back to Mrs. Ostrowski who once again smiled at her, "My dear girl, you have such lovely, high cheekbones. Has anyone ever told you? Very glamorous."

Catherine felt her cheeks blush. She knew elsewhere in Europe women were co-mingling with each other in ways that horrified the religious. Was this compliment just an observation by a bold, society woman, or . . .

Mrs. Ostrowski turned away, showing no further interest. I will be right back with the check."

She left Catherine and strode quickly toward the manor house.

Left on her own, she watched the handsome young man, Józef, lead the horse into the barn. She wanted to tell him how much she admired his letter opener and decided to approach him. Standing beside the stalls in which she found him working, Catherine watched as he lifted another horses' legs and checked its shoe.

"So . . . you made that blade she used to open my uncle's letter? It is much nicer than the one I use."

He scraped the horse hoof and said nothing.

In the awkward silence, Catherine felt her cheeks flush again. Would he just ignore her? Was he hoping she would go away? Clearing her throat, she ventured again. "How was it made?"

Józef set the horse's leg back down, straightened, and brushed his hands over the back of his pants. Reaching around, he untied the full-length leather apron and lifted the neck strap over his head, tousling his hair.

"I work at my father's blacksmith shop, and I use the forge to melt silver or copper. One day I want to create jewelry." His brow furrowed. "But Tata doesn't approve of my desire to create beauty. He said I have wasted my time and his. He growls at me, 'Work time is not play time!'"

Józef led the horse back into the stall, and his muscular body with its broad shoulders and chest captivated Catherine. She took in every movement. All he had done was to shut the thick, wood stable door, but he might as well have performed a ballet move. She was transfixed by everything about him.

She took hold of herself. This reaction was unseemly for a Catholic woman.

Nodding over at his tools on the floor, he said, "I want to do more than be a ferrier!" He reached down, picked up the black iron horseshoe puller, and held it in the air over his head. "But *this*, I'm told . . . this is where the money is."

Despite his obvious irritation, Józef's voice nonetheless had a soft, deep-chested quality. And then Catherine realized where she had heard it before.

"Is your shop in Podgorzé? There is a blacksmith shop across the street from my uncle's office, where I work, and two men were shouting at each other earlier today . . . was that you?"

Józef crossed his arms over his chest and smiled. "Yes, that was me. I've just returned from some travels abroad and gone to work for my father. We don't see eye to eye, though, if it isn't obvious. Did I interrupt your work?"

"I have a dream, too." The words poured out. "There is something I want to do other than adding and subtracting numbers . . ."

She stopped, not certain if he would laugh at her, but his gentle chestnut brown eyes held her with interest.

"Go on. What is your dream?"

"I want to be more than a woman who works a farm, cooks and cleans." She took a deep breath. "I want to create art."

"What kind of art?" He looked down and refolded the cuff of his shirt.

"I like to draw. It helps keep alive my vision of what's beautiful in this world."

His eyes had not left her face. "And I want to create beauty from vision."

The gray, Lipizzan horse, with its muscular neck and powerful sloping shoulders let out a nicker from the next stall, its ears pricked forward to attention.

Catherine turned to see if Mrs. Ostrowski had come back down the path, but she was nowhere to be seen.

"I think Mona wants me to finish my work with this horse and attend to her." Józef laughed.

"Where did you find such a lovely-colored stone for the handle of her blade?"

Józef put his apron back on, led the first horse to its stall, and led Mona out of the one she was champing about in. "It's amber."

"I've heard of amber. Doesn't it come from Gdańsk, near the Baltic Sea?"

"Some of it. But this amber is found here near Kraków and comes from poplar trees, right here on the estate. Do you know the legend?"

"I don't."

He lifted Mona's right foot and examined it. "According to myth, Phaëton was the son of Helios, the god of the sun. When Phaëton was killed, his sisters cursed the gods and were punished by being turned into poplar trees. Because they were divine beings, their tears of grief turned into amber. I find those so-called tears on the poplar trees here on the estate."

"Here?"

"Yes," Józef smiled, and set Mona's foot down. "Up beyond the northern outskirts of the manor park, near the family mausoleum."

Mrs. Ostrowski now returned from the manor house.

"I'm sorry I took so long Catherine, but my husband just returned from the University in Kraków."

She was carrying a small handbag made of a silver mesh decorated with tiny beads that featured a landscape scene. Opening it, she took out an envelope and offered it to Catherine.

"Thank you." Catherine smiled, nodding her head in a gesture of respect. "Well, I must go." She smiled at Mrs. Ostrowski. "It was nice to meet you both."

She looked over at Józef, who started to remove a worn shoe from the Lipizzaner.

Mrs. Ostrowski had turned and gone back toward the house, and Catherine lingered just a bit, walking more slowly away from the carriage house and horse stalls.

So that was that. Just a few moments with a man who made her heart beat rapidly—and now back to a life of abject drudgery.

Józef called after her. "Before you go . . ."

She wheeled around, imagining he was about to step close and wrap his arms around her.

But he didn't.

"Perhaps we can go to the art school one day together," he said sounding casual, "since we both have an eye for beauty. It would be a shame if we work just across the street from one another and don't see each other again except over horseshoes and ledgers."

Catherine kept walking backwards, trying not to look or sound as eager as she felt. "I would like that"—but she let slip the words, "very much."

Chapter
4

Later, on the ride home with Marcin, Catherine noticed how blue the sky was and the white puffy clouds seemed to float over the hillsides. The sun had drifted down, but it still felt warm on her face. She was thankful for the quiet and thought about the beautiful estate she visited and how she had met Józef. What was this feeling he had caused to rise in her?

As she thought about him, Catherine began to tap her toes to a Polish folk song Laska once taught her.

"You seem quite happy," Marcin observed, without looking at her. "It seems office work agrees with you, yes? Perhaps you've found a career for yourself."

"Perhaps," she replied, to keep the agreeable atmosphere going, and thought, *Dear Heavens, no. Never.*

"Remember, tomorrow is the harvest, so I won't be at the office for a week, maybe longer, depending on how many villagers come tomorrow for work."

She nodded.

"And no more wasting time. You will have twice as much work to do because I won't be there. Do you understand?"

Of course, he had to ruin the pleasantness between them by forbidding her drawing.

"Yes."

"I am counting on you. This future of this orchard is depending on you."

Perhaps you should count on someone else, she thought, wishing she felt bold enough, free enough to say it out loud.

Marcin stopped the wagon and let Catherine off near the path to her house, she was surprised he did not go to talk with her father about what happened earlier.

He cleared his throat. "Tell your father I will be in the barn."

Catherine lifted her bag off the seat and climbed down. *Which means he'll probably talk to Father after all. He can't help himself. He has to report me.*

As she walked toward the house, she smelled cinnamon and apples baking. Inside, she found her mother taking her favorite dish from the oven—rice cooked in milk and baked with a layer of fried apples and spices. On the table were many loaves of bread to feed the workers who would be here tomorrow. There was always so much preparation and fanfare leading up to the harvest season.

"It smells so good in here. And you've been working hard."

Her mother turned around, one hand rubbing her lower back. "Thanks be to God, Laska and Aunt Eva have been helping me to bake all day." She went to the pail and dipped in a tin cup to get a drink of water, fanning her red, overheated face with the other hand.

The feeling Catherine had a moment before was rapidly waning.

"Where is Father?"

"Out in the orchard . . . or maybe the barn."

Heavy footsteps sounded from the entryway and Antonio, Filip, and her father came inside. Unlike Filip who was gruff-looking, handsome and intense, Antonio was tall and plain. His relaxed, slender body and often uncombed, light brown hair spoke of his easy-going attitude. Antonio rarely complained despite the demanding work to run the orchard and farm. Both were ambitious in their own ways, but Filip was unpredictable and impulsive and more likely to win out if there was ever a fight over the property. There was a kind of heartlessness about him.

"Did you see Uncle Marcin at the barn?" Catherine inquired delicately, as her father removed his hat and hung it on a wooden peg by the doorway.

"Yes, he was just coming to the barn when I left. He wanted to sharpen the tools needed for tomorrow's harvest. He also told me about the large check he received from Mrs. Ostrowski." John turned to Mary and smiled, "The harvest is good. Seems when the stork came back in the spring and made its nest on the top of the barn, it brought us good fortune."

Catherine's mother shook her head. "You sound as superstitious as Eva. We have a good crop because God has shown us favor."

John teased. "Well maybe God sent the stork, Mary."

"Is that all Uncle talked about?" Catherine asked, as the men sat down around the table and she and her mother brought them food. *Or did he talk about his vodka rendezvous?*

"That's about it. Why do you ask?"

"No reason." Catherine glanced over at Filip, who gave her a cocky wink and half smile as he stuffed a huge forkful of rice in his mouth.

After dinner, Mary refilled their cups with leftover coffee from the work day. As she did, Catherine reached into her pocket and handed her father the flyer she removed from the fence in the city. He frowned.

"What is it, John?" her mother asked as she sat down.

He set the flyer down on the table and said nothing. Mary picked it up, then raised a hand to cover her mouth, her lips set in a grim line. "I knew all this fighting would only lead to more war."

Filip took the flyer from his mother's hands and looked at it with Antonio, reading out loud, "Polish Legions looking for men to fight for Polish borders in Lemberg."

"What's the fighting about now?" Catherine asked.

John inhaled a deep breath and blew out slowly. "Probably another dispute about who owns what lands. This week we have Ukrainians coming to work the harvest. Maybe they'll know more about this."

Catherine's mother rose and stood before a picture of Blessed Mother Mary holding Jesus. She bowed her head and pulled a rosary from under her blouse.

John shook his head in a way that said, *"As if that does any good."*

Filip looked over at mother and then to his father, he set the flyer down and blotted his forehead with the cloth napkin next to his plate. "Father, I have thought about going to America. Hearing this threat of another war… Well, I've talked with some of the villagers whose family members left and are doing better there than here in Poland. And there is no war in America."

Mary turned quickly; her face filled with anxiety. "But if you leave, who will help your father with the orchard? The farm?"

"Don't forget, Filip," Antonio reminded him, "Americans were sent to fight in the last war. You do not escape war in America."

"Maybe not," Filip retorted, "but there is opportunity to earn better money. To start a new life."

No one spoke, Catherine watched Filip, whose body had stiffened after hearing Antonio's remark about not escaping war. He stood and turned to their father. "I have written letters to Uncle Piotr in Chicago, and he told me about all the jobs in America. He says as soon as you get off the boat there are companies with recruiters to hire you. Right on the spot."

"Yes, I'm aware of my brother making a life in America," John scoffed. His brother Piotr had fled Poland in 1912, before the war. He had come back a year later to take his wife Maria and their two young sons back to America, where he found work at a steel mill in Chicago. He wanted John to come with him, but John's fear of change was too strong.

"He's willing to sponsor me and bring me to America." Filip looked down at Antonio, who was still seated and staring down at his plate.

Mary paused in her prayer recitations and turned toward Antonio.

Filip continued. "He's willing to sponsor you, too."

She glanced at her husband, expecting an outburst. He was not above telling her to keep her mouth shut when he was angry. But John only rose and crossed the kitchen, taking his hat down from the peg. "No more talk of leaving to go anywhere. We need to get our preparations done; tomorrow is a busy day. Those cows and horses won't feed themselves."

Filip clenched his jaw and followed John outside. Antonio rose and went with them.

Catherine stood to clear the table. So many unanswered questions. Would her brothers leave? If so, would she ever see them again?

Why did I bring the flyer home? she chided herself. Even though the news would have reached them eventually, she had touched off a family controversy. But then, Filip already had plans.

She didn't like it when the family was at odds. Normally, the family would be excited about the harvest, especially on a year like this one with such a plentiful crop.

She also didn't like it when her mother looked unhappy. And it occurred to her why the wonderful feeling Józef raised in her faded so quickly when she'd arrived here at home.

I don't want to wind up like Mother—like a beast of burden, overworked and with no joy in her soul.

To clear that thought from her mind, Catherine wet a wash rag in the bucket and squeezed it tight. Eyeing the supper dishes that needed washing, she took the immediate situation in hand. She would *not* think about a future that mirrored her mother's life. It would kill her spirit.

"Mother, I would like to think of brighter things instead of war. Would you tell me again the story about how we came to live on this apple orchard?"

Mary was silent for a long moment, as if torn between staying in her gray mood or turning toward a better one. Then she began.

"I met your father in a village outside of Plaśzow, not far from here. My parents thought him to be a suitable man for me—he was a hard worker in the village, always helping the priest who owned these orchards. As the priest aged, he depended on your grandparents to run the orchard and young men like your father to help manage the workers."

She stopped wiping the just-washed plate Catherine handed her. "Such a big responsibility for such a young man."

Catherine smiled, picturing her father being young and strong . . . like Józef. Since meeting him, her mind returned many times, to the image of him and his invitation. Did he mean it, that he wanted to show her around the town, or was it just an empty pleasantry? Doubt fought against hope.

Mary continued, "Many years ago, priests planted apple trees throughout the land. As the orchards grew the villagers helped to care for them. Eventually the laws changed, and peasants were allowed to own property."

The dishes were done, and Catherine handed her mother the garden herbs from the basket on the floor as her mother stood on a wooden chair to hang them from the ceiling to dry.

"Those changes gave my parents the opportunity to purchase this land. Your great-grandparents were required to work the land for the Lord of the Manor under Feudalism laws. When I married your father, my parents gave him this farm and the orchards as part of my dowry. Because your father had been a hired hand for the orchard, they saw him as a good fit for a husband."

"You mean, you didn't marry him because you fell in love?"

Mary laughed. "Love? That is foolishness. Young people need family members to decide for them who they should marry."

Catherine felt a small sting. Her mind wandered to Dominik. And slammed shut that door. But what if her father pressured her into that match?

"Oh, Catherine," Mary interrupted her thoughts, "don't fret about love and marriage, you will learn to love the man you marry. Just like I did, and every young woman before you."

Mary glanced out the window and stepped off the chair. "Come, there is still a half-hour of daylight, we need to go sweep the huts for the workers who'll be here tomorrow."

The truth was, she was already tired. *Does a woman's work ever end?*

On the orchard there were six huts where the laborers who came from far away villages stayed while they worked the harvest for the few *kopeks* they earned. The roofs were made with straw and dried clay for protection against the elements, and as a small girl, Catherine played in the huts. They seemed so big then; now she realized there was barely room enough for the three single beds, a table with a lantern, a bench, and a bucket.

Later, as Catherine lay in bed staring up at the white wood ceiling, she thought about the conversation at the dinner table and with her mother about marriage. The moon shone through her bedroom window, creating a soft glow. Would part of this apple orchard be the dowry her father offered to a man her family chose for her to marry? Is that man Dominik?

I don't want to live and work on this orchard. I want to be an artist. She turned on her side to face the wall. *I like drawing and creating, not cooking, cleaning, and doing laundry for the boarders.*

She thought about the city and the art school. From outside, she heard the crickets chirp and from the barn the horses rustled. Hearing the horses caused her to think of Józef—kind, mannerly Józef. Would her parents approve of someone like Józef even though, like her, he wanted to create art?

Chapter
5

The next morning was *Dozynki*—harvest time, and everyone was up before the rooster. As Catherine walked to the well there was a mist in the air and her shoes became wet from the damp grass. In the early morning sky, a bright yellow sun was peeking over the horizon. The horses in the barn became restless when she dropped the bucket in the well and turned the handle to retrieve it filled to the brim. The rooster crowed.

Despite Catherine's dislike of farm chores, she welcomed harvest time.

Back at the house Uncle Marcin and Aunt Eva had arrived. Eva was taller than most women and this gave her a slightly angelic quality.

Eva carried honey from her beehives to have with biscuits. Eva was known as the "Madra" or wise one because she had no children, which meant she had more leisure time. She was perceptive about nature and believed her superstitions predicted the future. Today her shoulder-length hair was decorated with a wreath of leafy twigs from the apple trees and colorful fall flowers. She wore a necklace of pink beads with a reddish tinge strung on a silk cord. Eva insisted the amulet protected her from evil spirits and bad people. In her other hand was a small basket with a colorful ribbon weaved around the brim. Inside were a few of the first apples picked. To Eva these apples are sacred and should not be sold at the market. The harvest is not just about work; it is a celebration.

It was time for Catherine to go to the office, which meant she would miss the annual custom of Father Jarek blessing the harvest tools and workers. Eva, Marcin, and her father greeted the workers and as Catherine walked past to the barn to get her bicycle, she overheard Eva talking with Dominik, "We had bonfire on the eve of Saint John's Day this past June to bless the apples, and look, Saint John has blessed us with this large crop."

As she wheeled the bike from the barn, Eva quickly approached her.

"Marcin told me he found drawings in your desk drawer." Her brows furrowed. "Oh Catherine, I feel sorry for you."

No, I feel sorry for you, being married to such an ogre.

Catherine leaned the bike on her hips and folded her arms. "Me, why?"

"Because, you have these silly dreams of becoming an artist. Don't you know in just a couple of years you will be expected to marry?" She leaned closer. "You have to show a man you can cook and take care of a home—take care of him and your children." Eva kept her gaze steady, but her eyes became glazed. "I pray you can at least have children."

Catherine adjusted the strap on the cloth bag hung over her shoulder. She could smell the fresh baked biscuits and honey wrapped in wax paper. Her ledger was safely inside as well, along with the dream she secreted away.

Being a farm wife. Having babies. Why can these women think of nothing more to do with their lives than that?

"Eva!" Marcin walked toward them, angry as usual, this time with a metal-toothed broom in his hand. "Stop talking to Catherine, she has much work to do!"

"I better go, have a good day Aunt Eva."

"I will and remember what I told you." She put her hand on the handlebars of Catherine's bicycle. "Who knows," she continued, "Maybe one of these young men who came here today would be a good husband for you." Her head nodded toward Dominik.

"Goodbye, Aunt Eva."

When Catherine arrived at the office she looked over at the blacksmith shop. The large door was open and there was no sign of Józef. She reached into her bag for the key to unlock the door.

"Looking for me?"

She took in a sharp breath. "Józef! You startled me!" Then she smiled.

"Sorry." He stepped closer and leaned forward, until she was almost pressed between him and the brick building.

The clean scent of his body and his alluring eyes held her.

"Do you want to go with me to the art school today?"

I do. But now I have twice the work to do, so I'll work twice as fast today, and Uncle will be pleased.

"I do, but can we go tomorrow? That is, if my uncle allows me the time."

"Oh, you mean the tall thin man with the round glasses and mustache who works here. My Tata says he is the devil in disguise." He held his fingers up to his head as horns which made Catherine laugh. "All right then, ask him if you must, but what if he says no?" Józef continued to lean over her, his arms crossed.

"I will tell him how much work I have done today, and he will be pleased. I will tell him I want to get some fresh-air tomorrow and have lunch in Market Square."

She could feel his eyes on her again, her cheeks felt flushed.

"Okay, meet me tomorrow at the trolley stop at noon."

Her body tensed. She had no money for the trolley.

"Don't worry," he straightened up and arched his back. "My treat for the trolley ride."

She looked at him with an enticing smile, so thankful and excited by his love for art.

He removed his cap and waved it as he bowed to her, his wavy hair flopped forward. "Until tomorrow, my lovely lady."

"Yes," she said with a smile. "Tomorrow."

Maybe her work today would not be such soul-draining drudgery.

Throughout the day, she eyed the blacksmith shop across the street, and occasionally caught a glimpse of Józef outside while he smoked a cigarette. His long legs crossed as he stood near the rain barrel.

He looked over as if he could feel her stare at him. She reached into her bag and pulled out the old but soft red leather ledger and opened it to a blank page. She took a pencil and sketched him, a more than welcome reprieve from tedious journal entries.

When she met Józef at the trolley stop the next day, he was surprised to see her. "I thought for sure the troll would tell you no. How did you get his approval?"

"I told him several businessmen stopped to pay their bills and about all of the work I finished. That jollied him up."

The bell of the trolley rang as it came to a stop. Józef handed the conductor two silver coins as they boarded. He quickly found two empty seats.

After they sat down Józef turned to her. "And he gave you his blessing?" Catherine felt her cheeks get warm.

"Well, and I told him how we might have a new customer, a blacksmith shop."

"Ha!" He jerked his head back and let out a loud laugh, then he turned to smile at her. "Did you tell him this shop belongs to Tomasz Kowalczyk? Because I don't think your uncle cares for my Tata and vice-versa."

"I just said the word 'new customer' which is music to his ears. Marcin loves his money." *And vodka.*

The trolley crossed the Piłsudski Bridge into Kraków. During the short ride to the art school and museum, she lost herself in staring out the window at the buildings, monuments, automobiles, and there were so many different storefronts. It was indeed a different world from the farm and orchard, one that beckoned her.

"What about your Tata, does he know where you are?"

Józef shook his head. "All he knows is I went to lunch." He leaned close to her, "He thinks I go to the tavern for lunch."

Oh no, please Lord, don't let him be a drinker, too.

"Do you?"

He gave a dismissive wave of his hand. "No, I won't waste my money there."

The trolley bell rang.

"This is our stop."

As they walked down the aisle he leaned over and whispered in her ear. "I've got better things to do with it."

It was a cloudy day and the air felt like rain. They walked briskly and Catherine clutched the strap of her bag to her chest. It would be a short walk to Matejko Square and the Academy of Fine Arts. Catherine was so excited she could barely contain her enthusiasm. In the center of the Square was a monumental statue of a king on a horse on top of a fifty-foot granite pedestal. Catherine strained her neck to look up at it. The king held a bridle in his left hand and a sword in his right hand. On each side of the monument were smaller statues. One was of a warrior blowing his horn and the other of a Polish Knight captured. Yet another was of a peasant who had broken his shackles of enslavement. It reminded her of the story her mother told about her grandparents.

"Here it is!" He stood facing the building with his arms spread apart. Catherine looked up. She had dreamed of this moment. The three-story brick building had perfectly carved stone frames around each window. On the roof were two metal domes with a silver sculpted, winged Pegasus. Despite being anchored to the roof, it looked as if it could fly.

"Let's go inside." Józef held the door for her. Inside was just as beautiful as the outside. They walked around and learned about Zakopane-style homes: dwellings made of logs topped with wood, with slatted, half-gabled roofs and deep, overhanging eaves. Several times, she drew in her breath in amazement; these were the most artistic homes she had ever seen.

When they left, it was still cloudy and gray. The clock at the trolley stop read 1:03 p.m.

I should have been back to the office by one o'clock.

On the return trip, Catherine split her raspberry jam sandwich with Józef, though she couldn't stop talking long enough to eat her half. Before she knew it they were getting off the trolley in Podgorzé.

"Thank you for taking me there, Józef."

"My pleasure, my lovely lady."

A feeling of blissfulness overcame her.

"But before you go back to your dungeon, would thou care to see my shop?"

She looked over at the office. No light shone out through the windows and there was no other sign of Marcin.

But what if a customer comes, then tells him I wasn't there? Her smile dissipated.

Józef reached over and, with his finger, lifted her chin, as if he were going to kiss her. Instead, he just studied her face, smiling.

Her smile returned.

"I promise, it won't take long. My Tata is not here, the wagon is gone."

In the building's dim interior, a light fog of smoke lingered. Józef swung open the large barn-like doors and the smoke began to dissolve. "This is why we always have this open."

Embers glowed on the brick table in the middle of a small half-circled iron cage. Tools and hammers were scattered on the table.

"Tata must have gone out for a delivery."

There were two large windows in the back. A film of soot covered each, preventing light from shining through. The floor was cobblestone like the street outside. There was a large anvil on a metal pedestal surrounded by an iron rack with many odd-shaped hammers hanging from it.

"Follow me, I'll show you how I make beautiful things. I read about craftsmen who used silver and gold to create pieces of jewelry with different symbols. I love the knotwork and spirals of the ancient Celtic designs." He opened a large cupboard and on the shelves were different sized candles and hard clay cylinders. His face turned radiant. "Just like you, I love to create." He smiled at her.

Outside, a wagon and horse pulled-up. "Must be my Tata. Come with me, I'll walk you back to your office."

Catherine looked out the large door. It was Marcin, but because there were automobiles parked in front of the office he continued to drive by.

"Thank you Józef. It's my uncle, I must go."

Running across the street, she quickly unlocked the door, turned on her desk lamp, and rushed to the back to get a drink of water from the silver pail. Then she watched for him to come to the door as she finished her cup of water, her breathing calmed.

Still no Marcin.

Maybe I just thought it was him. She walked to his desk and took another stack of invoices and receipts. The paper they were wrapped in said 'Borzych' and as she sat down, the door opened.

"Hard at work, I see." Marcin carried a rolled-up newspaper tucked under his arm.

She cleared her throat. "Yes, how is the harvest going? I'm surprised to see you here."

"It's going better than expected. The workers who came from a Ukrainian village told us some villagers went to Germany for work. It is more money than what we pay, but the men must work sixteen hours a day and sleep in the fields."

Catherine separated the receipts from the invoices as he talked. Not really listening until she overheard the word "war." She set the papers down and turned around to face him.

"Did you say war?"

"Yes, the Ukrainians said there is tension in Lviv with Russia, Poland, and Ukraine. That is why I came to town, to get a newspaper."

Before he opened the paper, he lit a cigar and stared at Catherine with a suspicious eye.

"Your aunt insisted I come to drive you home. Eva believes there will be a storm. Today, she saw two sparrows dive and chase each other, which to her means something bad is coming. She was afraid for you."

40

He shook his head. "I told her she's crazy, but I am in no mood to argue with her." He opened the newspaper. The headline read:

STRUGGLE FOR LEMBURG BETWEEN UKRAINIANS AND POLES

—RESOLUTION TO INCORPORATE CITY WITHIN

INDEPENDENT POLISH STATE CHALLENGED

Catherine looked out the window and across the street, thinking of Józef. How he made her feel she could be herself, with her own interests and loves.

Chapter
6

I t was the beginning of November, and the harvest was a success. But there was bigger news. Poland had officially declared its independence after 123 years of partitioning by Russia, Prussia, and Austria on November 10, 1918.

From a block over on Wielicka Street came the sound of car horns and drums followed by sounds of people cheering. Catherine and Marcin each got up from their seats and rushed outside. The street was full of people, even the trolleys were stopped.

"Hurry!" a younger man in a straw brimmed hat with a wide black band waved at them as he ran by. "It's a parade! To celebrate our freedom!"

Marcin's long strides made it difficult for Catherine to keep up. In the distance she could see soldiers on horses holding the red and white flags of Poland. People cheered. Flags displayed the symbol of the national emblem, a crowned white eagle.

The elation and wild joy of the people was evident. Some in the crowd carried signs: LIBERTY! INDEPENDENCE! UNITY! Others chanted over and over, "Out of the blue, there was Poland anew!"

A Polish Legion of soldiers marched through the street. Catherine stood on her toes to watch over the shoulders of others as the procession passed. Soldiers and veterans of the recent war marched with their guns while others carried red flags of both red and white. Uniforms of blue with brass buttons and wide leather belts marched in unison. Many had red armbands with a symbol of the white eagle and black leather boots up to their knees which caused their tucked pants to pucker. Soldiers wore round helmets with a wide brim or hats with leather visors and flat crowns. Catherine noticed the stripes sewn on their arms while others displayed medals pinned to their shirt pockets. This was the first time Catherine had seen so many soldiers in one place. Soon the parade ended, and the crowd dispersed. The whole spectacle had been majestic but fearsome.

"Can you believe it? We just witnessed history Catherine!" Marcin's eyes were wide and stunned looking behind his glasses. He grabbed her hands and swung her around in a circle, and she couldn't help but laugh.

For the moment, Catherine allowed herself to feel the celebration that had passed through the streets, despite what it signaled: more conflict. Later, at home, Catherine reported it all to Laska and her mother.

"Even on the street corner, a man played his violin while couples tangoed on the sidewalk in front of his business. The men twirled the women and their skirts flared open and showed their legs. I have never seen a dance like that." Catherine could still feel the upbeat melody that told a story of freedom and independence as these spirits drove the dancers.

Laska was ecstatic about families being reunited in their village. "Yes, Catherine, the war has ended. Freedom at last!"

Despite the good news, Mary's face looked taut, her forehead wrinkled in a deep frown. "But Laska, you heard the Ukrainians who came to work the orchard, they talked about restlessness in Lemberg. Then there was the ad in the newspaper last week from the Polish Legion, looking for volunteers to fight. Even children." She walked to the window and looked outside at Filip and Antonio chopping and stacking wood. "I'm afraid it's only a matter of time before they stop asking for volunteers and force men to enlist."

Catherine did not like to see her mother wringing her hands in worry.

I wish I had some words of comfort for her.

"Well, I must go, it's getting dark," said Laska, retrieving her coat from the rack. Before she stepped outside she turned to Mary. "There will be no more war, it's over."

"I hope you're right." Mary looked at a large wicker basket near the oven. It was empty. "Catherine, would you go fetch wood for my cook stove?"

Catherine nodded and followed Laska outside. She called after her. "Do you think the war is over? What about what the Ukraines said?"

Laska stopped to fix her kerchief. "We finally have our freedom back. There will be no more fighting between Ukraine, Poland, or any other nation. You saw the parade today. The soldiers are home. It is finally over."

"Then why all the recruiting? Do you think my brothers will need to leave Poland?"

"Your brothers are young men, and men need to find their roots. Maybe their roots are elsewhere." She shrugged. "Who can say?" She looked up at the twilight sky. "Only God knows."

Catherine wanted to tell her about Józef, but Laska looked tired and began trudging away down the lane, calling over her shoulder, "Tomorrow we make rugs on the loom."

Catherine went to Filip and Antonio, who still had a pile of wood to chop and stack. She held her arms out to Antonio. "Could you load some wood in my arms?"

Antonio was tall and thin like Marcin, and he towered over Catherine. His big hands easily grabbed two pieces at a time. As he piled the apple wood onto her arms, Filip continued stacking wood between plank boards nailed in rows on the barn wall. Catherine talked loud enough for Filip to hear. "There was a big celebration in the city today. Poland has thrown off the rule by other nations. . . . All the fighting is over."

"*Finally*, good news." Antonio put the last piece of wood in her arms. A wary smile crossed his lips as he wiped his forearm across his beard, his temples wet with sweat. Although he was younger than Filip, with the beard he looked older.

"This means you won't have to go to America," Catherine said, sounding hopeful. "You both can stay here."

Filip stopped stacking wood and turned to look at her, his eyebrows raised. "Oh, because we can believe there is no more war—I heard what the Ukrainians said." He shoved his hair away from his face. "Those soldiers you saw today . . . they're on their way to Lemberg." He scoffed. "That's what your parade was for."

He stood ramrod straight and snapped a sharp salute, grinning at her. "Yes sir, I'll fight for this country and die on some far-off field of battle I don't even care about." He put his arm down. "No thanks."

Pulling a blue rag from his back pocket, he wiped his face. "If anything, this means we need to leave before it's too late. Soon, the army will be coming around in trucks, grabbing men off the streets." He looked over at Antonio who did not respond but bent down to pick up his axe.

Motioning to Catherine, Antonio said, "You better take the wood inside to mother."

Glancing at Filip, Catherine felt a stitch of worry in her chest. She did not want her brothers to leave, but she most certainly did not want them to go to war.

Filip caught her look and when he spoke his face was hard. "Look Catherine, sometimes in life you need to do things you don't want to do. But you know deep down it's the right thing to do."

Inside, her mother was at the table, peeling potatoes. Catherine noticed the dark circles beneath her eyes seemed even darker.

"Mother, if Filip and Antonio go to America, who would help with the orchard?"

Mary stopped peeling and looked over at her. "Don't worry, someone will do it."

Catherine felt her pulse quicken.

Does she mean me?

She wanted to push back against all the expectations she suddenly felt and tell her mother about the art school and how she wouldn't be here to help either. The look of weariness on her mother's face prevented her.

Mary handed her a tin bucket. "Here, go feed the pigs these potato peels before it gets dark."

How I hate the smell of pigs.

"And don't forget the cabbage cores in the wooden bucket by the door."

The month of November was a bountiful and busy month. Catherine enjoyed riding in the back of the wagon with the smell of sweet, fresh apples and the sun coming up in all its glory. Her brothers continued to fill the wagon each week with baskets of bounty, while her father and uncle drove the wagon to the Market Square in Podgorzé.

On the way to the city, as he did so often, Marcin tried to convince John to peddle their goods to the nearby villages, but John was stuck in his ways and did not like change.

"We have always taken our apples and vegetables to the market, why change now? Besides, in the marketplace we get money for our goods, but in the villages they only want to barter."

The word *money* always seemed to get Marcin to agree.

While at work Catherine did not seem to mind the numbers as much, especially since she met Józef. Business had picked-up and Marcin became absorbed in his work instead of his vodka *rendezvous* and other secret meetings. Catherine wondered if it was because her father was in the city more. Either way, she was thankful for the reprieve.

One afternoon, tired of entering long columns of numbers, Catherine felt the urge to sketch a basket full of apples. She put her pencil down and looked out the window.

"It's such a nice day, uncle. You should go outside. Maybe go down to the market to see how Papa is doing?"

Whenever Marcin left to visit her father, he was gone for at least an hour. This gave Catherine time to draw. Marcin seemed to believe when he took all her drawings, he had taken away her desire to draw with it. These days, he was less suspicious and watchful over her.

"No, there's too much work to do."

A thought crossed her mind.

I wonder what he thinks about Filip and Antonio wanting to go to America. Is he worried about the orchard and who will work it?

"All I am saying, Uncle, is you have gotten so much work done already today. Why not enjoy a little stroll?" This was said, knowing a "little stroll" always turned into drinks and who knew what kind of clandestine meetings.

"I feel the cold weather coming on in my knees. Why don't you take a stroll for both of us?"

Surprised at his unexpected generosity, she did not hesitate. Reaching under her desk, she grabbed the new bag Laska made for her on the loom. In it, Laska had even put a hidden pouch for Catherine's sketch book.

Before she could get out the door, Marcin motioned for her to step up beside his desk. Reaching into his pocket, he handed her a coin.

"On your way back, stop and get me a newspaper."

Outside, the street was congested. The fumes from a passing motorcar made her cough. She looked over at Józef's shop and saw him loading farm tools in his wagon. He caught her glance and smiled, then signaled for her to walk down the street as he mouthed the words, *"I'll be right there."*

Removing his heavy leather apron, he stepped inside and shouted something at someone in the shop.

Catherine clutched her bag to her chest.

Could this day get any better?

Strolling to the store with all the hats in the window, she waited, and in a moment Józef caught up to her. He slipped his arm through hers, and they walked together toward the fountain in the square.

"And where are you off to on this lovely day, my noble lady? How did you manage to leave the castle guarded by that dragon?"

Catherine laughed. "Well sir, I am going to get a newspaper for my uncle." For the first time she noticed his dimples and the sparkle in his eye. "Would you like to accompany me?"

"Why, yes I would. It seems I am in need for a walk in the kingdom." He looked over and spied an empty bench near the newspaper stand. He nodded his head. "Let's go over there and sit for a moment." Despite the fact Catherine had sat all day, she was happy to be with Józef.

She left him waiting on the bench while she went to buy a newspaper, the silver coin feeling good in her hand.

One day, I will have my own money. One day when I am an artist, people will come to see my work in galleries and buy pictures to hang in their homes.

For a moment, in her daydream, she saw Józef at her side, beaming at her.

She returned with the rolled-up newspaper in her bag and pulled out her ledger.

Józef looked over and saw her sketching him. He gave her his sexiest smile, spread his arms across the back of the bench, and put one leg over his knee. As she drew, Catherine could feel people stare.

Józef looked up toward the afternoon sun and wrinkled his brow. "Are you almost done? My arms are getting tired."

She smiled, closed her book, and walked over to sit on the bench next to him. One of his arms remained outstretched and she could feel it on the back of her neck.

Sitting up, he held his hand out. "Can I see?"

Hesitant, she handed him the book.

He leaned forward and turned pages till he was past the ledger entries and reached her drawings. There were sketches of Market Square and the church, cars in the street, apple trees at the farm, the horses in the barn, his blacksmith shop; he stopped at the last one and looked over at her.

"You have almost captured me—*almost*."

She looked at him with a question in her eyes.

"I'm more handsome than that."

She laughed, and he moved his arm from the back of the bench onto her shoulders.

Turning her face toward his, he was so close. For a few seconds, she studied the fine curve of his lips, the perfect arch of his dark brow . . . and he was right, if only teasing. He was more handsome than she had been able to render on paper. How was it no farm or city girl had failed to capture his heart by now?

He handed her back the book and as he did his hand laid over hers. Her stomach was in knots. Trying to dispel the energy she felt racing in her blood, she asked a diversionary question.

"Do you like them?"

She could not help staring into his brown eyes, falling into them. His clean-shaven face was radiant as he smiled.

"Like them? Why they're beautiful, just like you."

The trolley bell rang nearby, breaking the spell by reminding Catherine she must get back to the office. Marcin would wonder where she was lollygagging, "stealing" time from him, as he would put it.

"Why are you in such a hurry? Stay. I know a quiet place in the park. We can hold each other there."

"You have no idea how much I would like that," she said, standing. "But we can't. *I* can't. Not today."

She took the newspaper out of her bag and reached for the sketchbook.

"Then when? Can you meet me after your uncle's office closes?"

"I can't then, either. I must get home. If I'm late, they'll ask questions and demand answers."

As she slid the sketchbook into the secret pouch, Józef absently picked up the newspaper she laid on the bench between them. Something on the front page caught his eye, and Catherine saw his body stiffen. She glanced down and saw the huge headline she had not bothered to look at when she bought the paper.

21 NOVEMBER, 1918—

UKRAINIAN FORCES DRIVEN FROM CITY OF LEMBERG

POLISH EAST ARMY CLAIMS VICTORY

"My brothers are thinking of moving to America," she said, feeling her heart sink. "They don't want to go to war."

She waited for him to respond.

"What about you, would you leave Poland and go to America?"

"Me? Probably not. Tata needs my help." He stood and handed the newspaper back to her. "What about you?"

"Oh, well, I never really thought about it." She looked over at the trolley headed toward Kraków. "I want to go to art school." She turned to look at him. "Remember?"

"Of course, I remember. I have memorized everything about you."

As they began to walk, he playfully pushed her shoulder, trying to regain the light mood they had been in. She didn't smile.

"Did I ever tell you the story about the founding of Kraków?"

"No, I don't think you have."

"Legend has it a mythical ruler named 'Krak' slayed the dragon of Wawel Hill, who was a particular nasty creature. This dragon terrorized the townspeople by demanding offerings of sheep and cattle be brought to his cave. In exchange, he would spare the townspeople for their lives."

"Why are you telling me this story?"

"Be patient." Józef touched her arm. "Krak took a sheep stuffed full of Sulphur, which the dragon ate and instantly the Sulphur ignited inside his mouth!" He threw his hands in the air while they walked. "With an unquenchable thirst the dragon went and drank half the river before his bloated belly exploded and the town was freed of his wrath. Krak then married the princess, became king, and built his castle on the dragon's lair and the people built a city around it named 'Kraków' after their savior king."

Suddenly he stopped walking and took her gently by the shoulders. "Catherine, I will have to take you to see the castle so you can draw it."

They were already back at their secret meeting place in front of the hat store.

"Right now, I need to get this newspaper to the dragon in his cave."

He bent down and gave her a soft kiss on the cheek.

"Until we meet again . . ."

Marcin was puffing on a cigar when she entered the office. The red glow of the smoldering tip reflecting on his face almost made her laugh, thinking of the story Józef just told her.

Marcin looked at his watch. "What took you so long?"

She reached into her bag and handed him the newspaper.

"I just lost track of time. The day is so perfect."

"Nothing's perfect," Marcin glowered.

She looked out the window to see Józef walk inside the blacksmith shop.

Some things are.

All afternoon, she worked through the stack of invoices and bill of sales, forcing her hand to enter the figures instead of drawing the image in her mind—one of a young man and woman in a long embrace. She wished she had gone with Józef to the quiet corner of the park.

Later Catherine sat on her bed next to the oil lamp and pulled out her ledger book. She flipped through her drawings until she came to the one of Józef on the bench. She filled in the lighter pencil marks and did not hear her mother come in.

"What are you doing Catherine?" Mary said, making Catherine startle a little.

"If you're bringing Marcin's work home with you, you should be frightened. He wants to own you."

He owns most of me now. And what he doesn't own, the farm and orchards do.

She tried to hide the book, but Mary reached out and took it.

"Those don't look like numbers." Mary turned the pages, and a smile spread across her face. "These are beautiful. You have such talent." She paused on a page. "I love this sketch of the barn, with the hills in the background. And look at this picture of the city. I feel like I am right there."

"Thank you, mother." Catherine reached for the book before her mother came to the drawing of Józef.

Mary sat on Catherine's bed and folded her hands on top of her stained apron. She looked at Catherine, her high cheekbones highlighted by gray temples.

"But what can a young Polish girl do with such talent?"

Now was Catherine's chance. She looked at her mother confidently. "I could go to art school."

Mary's smile vanished, and she gave out a short, mirthless laugh. "We cannot afford to send you there. "We have no money for such a luxury as art school."

The room went silent, and Catherine felt crestfallen.

"What about the money I earned for my dowry? Can't we use that?" She was fighting to keep her thoughts from spilling out. *I don't care to live here on this orchard. I want something more.*

"You know the money you've earned goes toward the orchard, which is part of your dowry. One day we'll find you a man who will be a good provider and take care of the farm. In fact, your father has mentioned Dominik."

Catherine tuned her mother out and held back her frustration.

Mary continued with her line of thinking. "Unfortunately, many of the other eligible young men from nearby villages were sent off to fight in the war, and some never returned." She rose from the bed.

Catherine was devastated. Her mother turned to leave but stopped. "Catherine, where did you get that book?"

"Filip found it in the barn, he said it was an old one not being used anymore." She held up the book and opened it to the first page. "See, it says Karpiński Estate. It was destroyed during the war, where Filip found his bike."

The answer seemed to satisfy her mother.

"It's late, best you turn off that lamp and get some sleep."

Reluctantly she turned out the lamp and slid beneath the covers. The pillow smelled of fresh goose feathers, but the smell of the farm did nothing to ease her mood.

How am I going to go to art school? Am I destined to live on this farm the rest of my life? Young men at nearby villages for my husband? They would not appreciate my art, only my cooking and cleaning skills, and giving them children to work the land. That's all they know or want to know.

She closed her eyes. From the other room, she could hear the murmur of her parent's voices, and in a little while she started to drift off to sleep.

What if she told them the secret hidden in her heart, how she wanted Józef to be her husband?

Chapter

7

A few days later Catherine was surprised to see Eva on the wagon with Marcin. "Good morning, Catherine!"

Catherine smiled. Eva was always so cheerful, so different than her dragon of a husband. "It so cold this morning. Let's ride in the back of the wagon where we can sit close together and let the wooden sides block the cold air."

"The cold doesn't seem to bother Catherine," Marcin quipped—a jab at Eva. No one was spared his temper on a morning after drinking, which was most mornings. "In fact, she's been on her best behavior lately. Always on time. Not even a hint of disagreeableness when I give her work to do."

The two women shared a blanket as they sat on the wood floor in the back of the wagon. Eva leaned toward Catherine and pushed on her arm. "Catherine, do you know what day tomorrow is?"

Catherine slipped her a curious glance. "November 29th?"

"Yes, but it's also Saint Andrew's Day," Eva winked. "On this night a young woman can predict the man with whom she'll fall in love."

Eva always spread superstition and beliefs about fortune-telling. Village women would often come and pay her to hear their fortunes read in tea leaves, secretly, so the priests didn't hear about it.

"If you would like, you could come to my house later and learn who you will marry," Eva said, her eyes lighting up. "We can use my beeswax candle and the key to Marcin's office." She rubbed her hands together. "Maybe you'll meet someone with sophistication from the city, someone who doesn't stink like cows or pigs like the farm boys."

Catherine was aware of the custom to take melted wax and pour it through the eye of a skeleton key into a bowl of cold water. Once cooled, the wax form was held up to a light, to reveal a shadow in the appearance of someone's future partner or it told something about their character.

"What do you say, Catherine?"

"I don't think so." Catherine looked down at the blanket. "When I marry, it will be for love, not because of what a shadow on the wall told me."

"Suit yourself. But if you change your mind let me know."

"Here we are, ladies." Marcin stopped the wagon and jumped down to tie the horses.

The warm office felt good on Catherine's cold cheeks. Today, Marcin would be busy with Eva, which meant Catherine might have a chance to see Józef.

"Not a good day for shopping, Eva. It's cold out there." Marcin walked to his desk and wound his clock.

"The shops will be warm," Eva insisted, as he picked-up the leather bag he used to gather receipts from businesses around town.

"Well, if you're determined, I have plenty of stops to make today. You can shop while I do business."

He looked over at Catherine, who had already started to get the ledger books from the bookshelf. "You'll have plenty to do while we're gone. I want to see all those invoices and receipts filed away by the time I get back."

There went her chance to take lunch away from the office.

After they left, Catherine looked out the window and over at the blacksmith shop. With the cold weather, the big doors were closed.

Her mind was anywhere but on her work. She looked down at the badly worn wooden floor and spun the carousel of rubber stamps on her desk. Marcin's clock ticked.

I might as well get to work. Oh, if only this was my art studio. I would have a large table in the middle filled with drawings. And in the windows, I would put my best sketches. People would come by to admire them. I would have on the finest clothes, like Mrs. Ostrowski....

A quick knock on the door interrupted her thoughts, and it opened a little.

"Józef! What are you doing here?"

"I saw your uncle leave with some woman."

"That was my aunt, Eva."

He stepped inside and walked over to Marcin's desk. "So, this is where the dragon sits?" He sat down, leaned the chair back, and placed his hands behind his head.

Catherine could feel herself blushing.

His eyes caught the box of cigars. Reaching over, he took one out of the box. "Just as I figured, he does blow smoke."

Catherine smiled and shook her head.

He put the cigar back, picked up a pencil, and twirled it between his fingers.

Then he seemed to notice her expression. "What is it?"

"I won't be going to art school."

His light expression disappeared, and he sat up. "Why not?"

She avoided his gaze. "My mother told me we have no money." As she said the words, she felt a twinge of sadness in her chest.

"Well, you don't need art school. Just keep drawing." He stood up and reached into his pocket. "I came to show you something." He walked over to her. "Hold out your hand."

Curious, she opened her hand toward him and in her palm he placed a piece of jewelry made of silver. It was heavy and round. On it was a simple drawing of a bright sun tucked inside a knotted crescent moon with an enigmatic smile. In the middle of the sun was a circle of amber. The design seemed whimsical.

"The solar and lunar cycles are the natural timepiece of the Celts. The winter equinox and summer solstice alignments are important for specific activities: planting, harvesting, hunting."

She handed it back to him. "It's beautiful. It amazes me how you can create beauty from metal."

He smiled. "Like you do with pencil and paper."

"Do you plan out each piece on paper or do you just carve it?" She wanted to push away from talk about art school, which was too painful to think about.

"I usually just create on a hunch what my customer wants. But it would likely be better if I had a drawing to work from."

She picked up his hint. "What if I drew something for you, based on an idea you had or what a customer wanted?"

When their eyes met, the energy between them was palpable.

"I like your idea," he said, winking, and thought for a moment. "I would like to design a piece to tell someone they are not alone. No matter where they are or what their circumstances."

He strolled casually to the window, crossed his arms, and looked out at the street. "Something with a symbol of faith."

He turned around, and when he looked at her she felt a deep connection she'd never felt with anyone else ever in her life. Her skin tingled.

Catherine took a deep breath. "I'll work on something, but not today. As you can see, I have so much work to do." She nodded toward her desk.

"I have noticed how the dragon keeps you busy." He walked toward the door. "Let's meet at our secret spot for lunch." He opened the door, removed his cap, and bowed toward her. "Until then, my lady."

Before she could tell him no, today was not a good day, he was gone.

Her fingers flew in a bid to get her work done as quickly as possible. Drawing numbers did not seem to bother her anymore.

For the rest of the morning, she glanced at Marcin's clock to see if it was noon yet, and finally it was. She picked up her bag, put on her coat and looked out the window.

I had hoped Uncle and Eva would have returned by now. She looked over at his desk. *I'll leave him a note, explaining I've done everything he gave me to do and I went outside for some fresh air.*

Not long after Catherine left, Marcin and Eva returned.

When Catherine returned to the office she was glad to see Marcin and Eva were back. She was about to tell Marcin about all the work she finished but was surprised by his irritated mood.

"Did you enjoy your fresh air with that blacksmith fellow?"

Eva looked down, not saying a word.

"It's not proper for a girl your age to be with an older man. Now I know why you were late from lunch so many times. I knew you were hiding something. I felt it."

"He's not much older than me." Catherine felt a lump rising in her throat.

He crumpled up the note she had left and threw it in the wastebasket. He strode to her desk, flipping ledgers to be sure she had finished her work. It seemed impossible, given the stack he'd left her. But the work was done.

Marcin's eyes narrowed as he held his fingertips together. "Either way, your father will not be happy about this. I think it's best if you don't be seen with him anymore."

"His name is Józef and I'm not doing anything wrong."

Marcin's frustration spilled over. "You are obviously hiding what you are doing, and that is wrong."

Catherine's mind raced over all the money Marcin took in without recording it in these ledgers—money that should be going to her father for the farm and for her dowry.

Who are you to be telling me I'm hiding something when you have secret meetings with clients?

She looked over at Eva for some support, but her aunt just stood there, frozen.

As Marcin glared at her in triumph, Catherine wrestled with wanting to tell Eva Marcin's secrets, but that would end her trips to the city. She would be stuck out in the country, a farm girl forever, or at least until she became the wife of some farmer they picked for her she didn't love.

"Do I make myself clear?" Marcin stood there, with an unrelenting stare.

Catherine looked down at the wooden floor. It was clear she had to be what Marcin and her family wanted her to do and be, whether she wanted to or not.

I hate giving into him. But I have no choice.

Now she understood why Filip wanted to leave; though a voice argued with her. *But he's a man, and it's different for men.*

Brushing past her, Marcin grabbed his coat off the wall peg.

"If you'll excuse me, I need some fresh air."

He slammed the door behind him, leaving Catherine to look at Eva in despair.

Eva continued to stare out at the street and said nothing.

Chapter

8

Ever since Marcin had seen Catherine with Józef he forbade her to leave the office. Of course he had told her father about Józef, and they threatened to not let Catherine come to the city anymore if she continued to see the young blacksmith.

"We will pick a suitable husband from among the eligible young farmers. Someone who will know how to tend and work the orchard."

Catherine could not bear to do forced farm work all day and never have the chance to be with Józef again. She swallowed the lump in her throat and held back her tears. "All right, then. I'll keep my distance from him," she agreed—for now.

One afternoon in early December, Marcin left to do what he called "Christmas shopping for Eva", leaving Catherine, as usual, with a stack of work to be done by the time he returned. Despite the earlier overcast sky, a ray of sunshine burst onto the city streets, bringing with it a flurry of activity. Catherine's back hurt from sitting on the hard chair for so long and she decided to step outside.

The streets were lined with peasants trying to sell their goods. Catherine watched as the Jewish businessmen strolled by each peasant woman, stopping to haggle for the knitted scarfs or colorful striped wool bedcovers handcrafted on a loom. Soldiers on their way to the Ukrainian border to defend Poland's boundaries were also pausing to talk with the peddlers, and the women smiled and flirted as the soldiers investigated their baskets and made comments.

"Would you take two kopeks for this?"

"Four."

"Three."

Further down the street were Christmas trees for sale. Their dark green needles and spacious branches added a touch of nature to a street of cobblestone and brick. A group of young boys stopped to watch as a man stood a tree upright and spun it around. He pulled on the branches confident the tree was fresh. Satisfied, he handed the vendor a marka and lifted the tall tree to carry it away. Catherine's heart softened as she thought about her father putting up their tree on Christmas eve.

I wish Józef would come outside to see me standing here.

It had been a couple of weeks since she last saw him, and her heart ached as she stared at the blacksmith shop. Despite the sunshine, the air was cold. Catherine took a warm hand from her glove and placed it on her cold cheek. She looked over at the shop one more time and seeing no one decided to go back inside.

A sharp, loud whistle followed by the sound of someone running across the street made her turn around. Her hand remained on the door handle.

"Catherine!"

Józef.

She smiled and the cold from her cheeks disappeared as he stood close to her.

He rubbed his hands together. "How have you been? I have missed you."

She stood up straighter. "I have missed you, too."

His gaze dipped to her neckline, and she smiled and tilted her head toward the office door. "I've been busy. The dragon keeps me in the dungeon, you know."

A church bell rang in the distance.

"One day I'll rescue you from that dragon, just like Krak did at Wawel Castle." He stared into her eyes. "I wanted to ask you—"

"Catherine!"

She looked over Józef's shoulder and saw Filip on his bicycle coming toward them. Her heart pounded.

Red faced with exertion; Filip stopped next to her. "Father wanted me to give a message to Uncle." He then realized Catherine was not alone and his eyes narrowed as he looked at Józef. "And who might you be?"

Józef extended his hand. "Józef Kowalczyk. My father owns the blacksmith shop across the street."

Filip stuck out his hand and Józef took it in a firm handshake. Catherine noticed Filip did not let go right away.

He arched his brow. "Are you the Józef who Catherine is forbidden to see?"

Józef gave Catherine a subtle wink. "I don't know anything about that. Why would I be forbidden to see her? Was there something I should know?"

Catherine interrupted. "Józef just came over to say hello."

Filip crossed his arms. "If your last name is Kowalczyk, then you must be related to Tomasz Kowalczyk, the town drunk. I wouldn't want my sister around anybody like that."

Józef reached into his coat pocket and took out a cigarette pack. He offered one to Filip who accepted.

Catherine's cheeks felt cold again and was uncomfortable watching Filip size up Józef.

I'd better go back inside and get some work done before uncle comes back.

Józef lit his cigarette and handed Filip the box of matches.

"I'd better get back to the forge to finish the horseshoes I need to deliver today." He inhaled and let out a fog of smoke.

Filip's face was serious. "What's your rush. Finish your smoke. We can talk. Catherine, go inside. It's too cold for you out here."

Józef caught Catherine's eye with a look that said, *don't worry—I can handle this.*

From inside, she watched the two of them out the window. *Is Filip going to tell Uncle and Father I was with Józef? If so, I won't be coming to the city again.*

She felt a knot in her throat and remembered Józef wanted to ask her something. How could she get the message to him when she was not allowed to leave the office?

She continued to watch; Filip's shoulders relaxed as they exchanged grins between puffs. Catherine sat down at her desk and hid some of the papers Marcin had put in her basket in the desk drawer, to make it look like she completed more work than she had. After a few minutes, Filip came inside.

"So that was the famous Józef who Uncle and Papa talked about." He walked down the hall to get a drink and gulped down the cup of water.

Catherine put her pencil down and turned to face him. "If they would take time to get to know him, they would feel different."

Filip sashayed toward her, he crossed his hands under his chin, looked toward the ceiling and fluttered his eyes. "Oh, Papa, if you only knew how he makes me tingle inside."

The door opened and Marcin charged inside. "Filip, what are you doing here? Is everything all right at the farm?"

Filip looked at Catherine whose eyes pleaded with him not to say anything about Józef.

"Yes, everything is fine. Mother needs you to go to the Jewish market and get her a carp for Christmas dinner before you come home. She also wants some oranges, and a Christmas wafer from St. Joseph's Church."

He handed Marcin the list, who glanced it over. He was in no mood to haggle over a fish, and he handed the list back to Filip.

"I'll tell you what . . ." He walked over to the small safe on the floor next to his desk and dialed the combination to reveal banknotes and coins.

Filip's eyes lit up.

"Instead of me going to the market, why don't you go?" Marcin reached in and grabbed some paper Markas and counted out what was needed. He handed the currency to Filip who stood there with his mouth open.

Marcin scoffed. "Not all of this money is mine, most is to be deposited for clients." He looked at the clock on his desk. "Probably something I should do today before the bank closes."

"They trust *you* with their money?"

Marcin stood straighter; his shoulders squared as if he was ready for a fight. "What is that supposed to mean?"

Filip shook his head. "Nothing." He took the cash from Marcin.

Catherine secretly wished Marcin would give her a couple of silver coins for Christmas.

"When you get back you can ride home with us in the wagon. I can put your bicycle in the back."

As he walked toward the door he leaned over to Catherine and whispered in her ear. "Goodbye sister. Don't talk to any strangers today, no matter how handsome you think they are."

She felt her face get hot and glanced at Marcin, who was searching in the box on his desk for an old cigar to chew on.

"Don't worry, I won't. My world is full of eyes."

Finally, it was Christmas Eve and Catherine watched as her mother put a handful of fresh hay under the tablecloth to represent the baby Jesus who laid in a manger.

The table had to be ready before the first star was seen. She wondered what Józef was doing and realized she didn't even know where he lived. She thought about the possibility of seeing Józef at Midnight Mass.

Eva stuffed cabbage with mushrooms and rice. "Don't forget to set an extra place setting Mary, there are seven of us at the table and we need an even number of eight." She turned and smiled at Catherine. "We wouldn't want any bad luck to come our way."

"Or there might be an unexpected guest as my mother would say," Mary added.

Filip carried in a stack of wood and set it in the large basket by the cook stove. As he did the smell of a cooling gingerbread loaf reached him.

"It smells so good in here. I'm starved."

He looked at Catherine, who was slicing apples. "Just think, one day you will have a husband and family to do all of this cooking for." He walked over and took a slice of apple from the bowl. "In fact," he teased, "I'll bet I can predict his name." He closed his eyes and held one hand to his head like a fortune teller.

Eva chimed in. "I tried to get Catherine to be part of my Saint Andrew's Day premonition, but she wanted no part of it."

Filip put his hand down and reached for a piece of straw on the table and walked over to the candle lit on the Christmas tree. He held the bent piece of hay in front of it to make a shadow on the wall. "Aunt Eva, what do you think? What letter does this look like? Could it be a D or a J?"

Catherine jumped up and grabbed the straw from his hand. "That's enough, Filip!"

He stepped back and held both his arms up as if to surrender.

Eva and Mary ignored Filip's antics and continued to prepare the table for dinner. Eva placed three round braided loaves of bread, one on top the other and inserted a candle on the top loaf. She then encircled the bottom loaf with tiny twigs of evergreen. Candles on both sides of the loaves completed the table decoration.

Satisfied, she stood back and admired her work. "My mother used to say *kalach* bread decorated on Christmas Eve means prosperity."

Mary approached the table and took the bowl of sliced apples from Catherine. "Filip, it's almost dark outside. Can you go and tell the others it will be time for dinner soon?"

"Yes, I will." He stepped out the door and smiled at Catherine who proceeded to stir the mushroom soup.

After he left Mary shook her head as she set the poppyseed cakes on the table. "I'm not sure if Filip will ever grow up enough to find himself a wife."

Darkness meant the start of Christmas Eve dinner. Everyone took a seat at the table. Before the food was eaten John picked up the *opłatek* wafer from his plate. It was the size of his hand and embossed with the Christmas scene of the Nativity. He held it in front of Mary. "My hope for you in the new year is to wish you good health and much happiness."

Mary broke off a piece.

John continued. "I may not be the best husband always, but I'll try harder."

She smiled but sensed guilt in his voice. "You work so hard, and I appreciate you for that."

She then broke the piece in half and shared it with John, who then handed the wafer to his oldest son Antonio who shared a good wish with Filip. "To my brother, may I always be able to protect you."

Filip then turned to Catherine, who broke off a piece as he said, "Catherine, may you always trust me to do what's best for you." Catherine put the wafer in her mouth and in that moment she believed Filip could be a decent man and one day he will have a wife.

The next person to break off the opłatek was Marcin. Catherine held the wafer up to him as he broke a piece off. "Uncle, I do appreciate everything you have done for me and this orchard."

As he put the wafer in his mouth there was an unrelenting stare. With a subtle wink he said, "Thank you Catherine."

He then turned to Eva. "To the love of my life. I will never let you down." Eva blushed as she took the last piece of the wafer and placed it in her mouth.

"Before we eat, let's have a toast." Eva picked up a silver decanter on the table next to her. "This is Uzvar, a drink the Ukrainian workers taught me to make during their time here." She proceeded around the table and poured the golden liquid into everyone's cup. "It is made with dried fruits and honey."

Catherine loved how Eva was always trying new things.

"Does it have vodka in it?" Marcin asked as he raised his cup to his nose to smell it.

"No." She playfully slapped him on the shoulder.

She raised her cup. "*Nostrovia*—to your health."

"*Nostrovia!*" everyone replied, as they sipped the sweet mixture.

Though the food was plentiful, the celebration was tinged with a bit of sorrow. One war had ended, but the threat of another one weighed on their hearts. Despite the uncertainty, Catherine was grateful to have her family together. Even Marcin looked happier.

After dinner, the presents were opened. Eva had made new candles from her beeswax. Catherine's mother gave everyone a new scarf she weaved on the loom. Filip and Antonio gave their mother a beautiful porcelain serving bowl with two red apples painted on the outside surrounded by elegant green leaves. On the rim of the bowl were the words, painted in deep blue, *God be with you.*

"It's beautiful," she said, wiping her eyes.

Catherine was so wrapped up in the happiness surrounding her she didn't notice the small burlap square tied with yarn in front of her. Eva whispered, "Catherine, that one is for you."

Catherine picked up the small gift and began to unwrap it. Inside was a silver coin. Her eyes filled with tears. Eva gave her a hug.

Christmas day felt like any other day except Catherine didn't have to go work in the city. There were still chores to be done but there was no more talk of her brother's leaving and she finally had her own silver coin. Everyone seemed to be in a good mood as there was plenty to eat. Marcin and Eva left to visit some of Eva's family in a nearby village. Later when Catherine was in the barn cleaning horse stalls and her father was in the other stall milking the cow, Marcin came in with a newspaper for her father. She couldn't help but eavesdrop.

"Look at this headline, John." And he read it.

"DECEMBER 24, 1918: BORDERS STRUGGLES OVER NEW POLISH STATE CONTINUE—ANTI-GERMAN UPRISING CERTAIN."

"Apparently, our men are rising up against the Germans in Poznań."

Catherine heard the newspaper shuffle.

"Look at this picture… it shows men in a truck handing out guns on the street. I thought the war with Germany was over." His voice rose. "Poland had regained its borders. Look at all those Polish flags."

John responded with a frustrated tone. "Poznań is west of Warsaw. Could this area still be being controlled by the Germans?"

Marcin took the paper back. "It's not supposed to be. But obviously the Poles are preparing for a serious uprising."

"But who is organizing this uprising?"

"According to the news article mainly veterans of the Great War and members of the underground Polish Military Organization."

The two men became silent.

John spoke. "Fighting to the north, fighting to the east. This doesn't sit well with me."

"Me, either."

Catherine did not like what she just heard. Her upbeat mood now turned unpleasant like the putrid smell of hay soaked with horse urine. She had an uneasy feeling this was their last Christmas together as a family.

The winter was cold and lonely. The shorter days meant Catherine did her farm chores in the dark. On the days she was at the office, under Marcin's intense watchfulness, she noticed there were many horses being brought in and out of the blacksmith shop. Sometimes she would catch a glimpse of Józef, but he always looked pre-occupied. He rarely stood outside for a cigarette.

Despite the shorter days and colder weather, there was much work for Catherine at the office. More soldiers have been coming through the city to get supplies and creating more business for Marcin's customers. Marcin had gone back to his unpredictable drinking. Some afternoons he would stagger into the office, sit in his chair, and nap for a short time. This made more work for Catherine as he would always put whatever papers he returned with on her desk.

One afternoon after his nap, Marcin spoke with sarcasm in his voice. "I hear your friend is busy."

"What do you mean?" Catherine asked politely, trying not to start an argument.

"It appears the Polish Army has hired his shop to help with their horses—you know, keeping them shoed and ready for battle."

"Oh," Catherine responded, secretly wanting to know where Marcin got his information. *Had he talked with Józef?*

"The Army thinks Józef is too young to fight in the war, but mark my words, soon they will know he isn't."

He had hit a nerve. Catherine stopped writing in the ledger and looked at Marcin directly in the eyes. "Why? Are you going to tell them?"

"Me?" Marcin's bushy eyebrows raised as he innocently answered. "No, I would not want anyone to go to war that didn't have to. I stay far away from that Army."

I don't believe a word you say. She controlled her urge to disagree with him and let his temperament fade.

Just like in years past, the weather during the month of February was unpredictable. There were days of gray skies and dark moods. Other times a light snowfall would unexpectedly turn into gusty winds and heavy snow. On those days Catherine did not go to the city, and she missed seeing Józef.

Laska came to visit on a cold day after church. It was early March, and once again, a soft snow started to fall. After dinner Catherine took advantage of an opportunity to go and sketch while Laska and her parents visited—though Catherine kept her ears tuned.

"I wanted to tell you," Laska blurted, "the soldiers have been visiting our village, going from house to house, looking for men between the ages of seventeen and thirty to fight."

Catherine listened closely. The picture she was sketching, of the loom with a colorful, half-finished carpet Laska had woven, was forgotten now. She set her drawing on her bed and entered the kitchen.

Mother was sitting with her head in her hands at the table and Father was staring at the floor.

A look of terror came over her mother's face. "John, do you think they will come here?"

"Come where? Who is coming?" Filip asked as he and Antonio brushed off fluffy snow from their coats in the doorway.

Laska repeated what she had just said about the soldiers.

"As far as I'm concerned it's settled. Antonio and I need to leave. I've learned if we travel on a steerage ticket, we don't need a reservation; we just buy a ticket at the port and board. There's a steamer that leaves from Amsterdam. We can take the train from the Kraków Główny train station, it stops within a few blocks of the port."

Antonio looked at Filip, who paced back and forth, looking like he was ready to charge out the door any minute. "Do we need papers? What if we get to the port and the ship is full?"

"Antonio, you ask too many questions. If that ship is full, another probably leaves in a few days or a week. If we stay here, we are forced to go to war. Is that what you want?"

The room grew silent except for the clicking of embers in the woodstove. And Catherine felt as if she were helplessly watching her family come apart. Their earlier light-hearted conversations over dinner had escalated to decisions made from fear and uncertainty.

With no more discussion, it was settled. Filip and Antonio would leave within the week.

The morning Filip and Antonio were leaving, they all went to the church and prayed to God for a safe journey, then returned to the farm. It was a quiet morning, and soon it was time for Marcin to take Filip and Antonio to the train station in Kraków. Mary hung her arms around each of her sons' necks and began to kiss and bless them, choking back sobs as if she never expected to see them again.

"Oh, Mother," Antonio moaned, "don't think I will forget your last kisses and blessings. They'll accompany me in good or bad fortune."

Filip just stood there, silent, sullen, his head hung low.

Catherine wanted to shout, "*Don't go!*"—but she knew they had to. Still, did Filip regret his decision? Maybe the soldiers would not come for them.

Antonio pulled away from Mary and lugged his travel bag to the wagon. Filip followed. After a few steps he looked around to his mother once more. John stood next to Mary with his arms around her. She cried out tearfully, "Go with God, and don't forget us." She covered her face and took off inside the house. Catherine walked up to the wagon with her father and gave Antonio and Filip one last hug.

"Promise you will write us, to let us know you're safe."

"We will, Father."

Filip looked one last time at Catherine. "Goodbye, sister. Take care."

Chapter 9

Filip and Antonio were gone, and this meant more work to be done at the farm. There were days when Marcin and Catherine did not go to the city. When Marcin did go, it would not be until late morning after the farm chores were finished. Still, Catherine missed going to the city and having a chance to see Józef.

Despite her own sorrow, Catherine kept her spirits up for her mother's sake. Her mother would complain often of being too tired and she, along with Catherine's father, would go to bed after the night chores were finished. Ironically, Catherine had time to sketch in the evening after her parents went to bed. She often kept the fire going to keep the house warm. As Catherine worked on a design for Józef she found she liked to create pictures from her imagination. Other times she would find something in the house to sketch, like her mother's small statue of the Virgin Mary, or the bowl Filip and Antonio had bought their mother for Christmas. On these long nights she couldn't help but think about her brothers and prayed they had made it to America.

Finally, spring arrived along with a letter from Antonio. The day the letter came everyone sat around the table to listen as John read the letter out loud.

Dear Mother and Father,

I am writing to let you know we have arrived safely to America.

Filip played cards on the boat and made friends quickly with those who had smuggled liquor onto the boat. I had found myself spending many a night sneaking up to the deck of the ship—I would look upon the ocean and stare at the vast infinite space of water. Had I made the right choice?

John stopped reading and wiped his eye.

There was a man on the boat from a village North of the Vistula River in Kielce. His name was Leonek Kruszka. He is a job agent for a paper mill located near the Adirondack Mountains in New York State. He had lived in America for five years and was returning after recruiting men in his village to come to America and work at a paper mill. He convinced Filip to follow him to Pyrites, a town near the Adirondack mountains. His company will pay for the train ticket to get there, give him a job, and a place to live at a boarding house. You know Filip, always making friends fast and willing to take a risk.

Marcin agreed. "Yes, that sounds like Filip." John continued . . .

Before we parted ways, Leonek gave me an address so we can write to Filip. I will share his address at the end of this letter.

As for me I have decided to stay in New York City where there is work on every corner. I have learned of a place called Little Poland in Brooklyn, not far from where the ship came in. I was told there are many jobs for Poles there. Because I am educated I believe I won't need to work in a factory. I may try for a job at one of the four banks located nearby in Greenpoint. Mother, there is even a Polish Catholic Church.

Mary smiled.

The streets of New York City are crowded. There are automobiles and trolley's fighting for space in the streets. The buildings are so tall! It is a noisy place and at times dirty. I will write again soon.

With Love, Antonio

John folded the letter and put it back inside the envelope. Everyone sat quietly with their thoughts. Catherine felt relieved her brothers were in America.

Despite the tensions of nearby battles over land boundaries in Poland, the apple trees blossomed. Songbirds perched on nearby fenceposts sang out their joy to life with their melodies. The warmer weather brought nearby villagers looking for work at the orchard. This meant Marcin could get back to his business in the city.

After she completed the farm chores of milking cows and cleaning horse stalls, Catherine rode her bicycle to town for work. Marcin's afternoon visits to the taverns lingered on his breath, and she was all too happy to not ride in the wagon with him back home. It seemed the time away in the winter, coupled with the vodka from his Jewish businessmen, helped Marcin to forget about Józef, but Catherine had not forgotten about him.

One afternoon in late April after she arrived at the office, there was a sheaf of wild field daisies on the doorstep with a note tied to them. At first she thought someone must have accidentally dropped them until she read the note on the outside—*Let's plan to meet today after the dragon leaves for home.* The attractive flowers with their yellow centers and radiating white petals brought a smile to her face. He hadn't forgotten about her either.

Catherine glanced down as she smelled the daisies when she noticed something on the sidewalk in front of the office window.

Oh my gosh, it's a silver coin! Someone must have dropped it.

She picked it up and rubbed her finger over the top. How long had it been there?

She put the coin in the secret pocket of her purse along with the other coin she received for Christmas. Could this money be a blessing from God?

Quickly she wheeled the bicycle inside to get started on her work.

Just like clockwork, Marcin came in at three o'clock to drop-off the receipts and invoices he had collected. As usual he staggered in, with the smell of his afternoon business meetings. Intoxication on his breath and stale cigar smoke on his clothes. Usually, he would just drop off the paperwork and leave to go home, but today, he plopped in his chair.

"I'm not sure what's wrong with me but I feel tired, and my throat is sore." He crossed his arms and rubbed his shoulders. "I'm also cold, yet it's one of the warmest days of Spring."

Catherine continued to stare down at the page of numbers in front of her. *Probably all of that drinking and smoking.*

She ignored him and hoped he would leave soon. She looked down at the daisies in her purse. She wasn't going to let his foul mood ruin her day.

"Anyhow." His voice became louder. "A couple of the soldiers from France were on their way to the Ukraine war zone and told me a flu is crossing our borders. The French call it the Spanish Flu."

"Maybe you should go home and get some rest."

"Rest? Ha! There is no rest at that farm." He leaned back in his chair and put his foot on the desk. "If I am to get rest, it would have to be here."

She looked at the clock, it read 3:15.

Suddenly he sat up, as if someone had lit a fire under his chair. "Well, I must go. Eva will be worried if I am not home soon. She is anxious to get the garden started."

Thank you, God.

Just as quickly as he had come, he left. Catherine stood up and looked out the window as he disappeared down the street. She glanced over at the new stack of receipts and books Marcin had piled on her desk and then she looked over at the blacksmith shop across the street. For some reason she thought of Filip and what he would say . . . *Catherine, if you want things to change you need to take risks.* Grabbing her purse, she walked across the street to find Józef.

Over the next few weeks Catherine and Józef met for short walks after work before she returned to the farm. Catherine learned he lived in a village named Wiejska just outside of Kraków in Plaszów. Catherine would pass the road of the same name on her way home. She was happy to learn he did not live too far from her.

Once on one of their walks he slipped his arm around her shoulders. "Is it alright with you if I do this?"

She felt his strong body close to her and smiled. "Yes, it's alright."

Suddenly he stopped walking, bent down, and kissed her.

Catherine felt a closeness in spirit between them. They were like two souls yearning for the same thing. Freedom to create.

"I have something for you." Catherine told Józef one afternoon as they sat on a bench in the Market Square. She pulled out a piece of paper from her purse and handed it to him.

"Here is the picture of a design I drew for you."

It was a Celtic type design of interlaced ribbon knotwork.

"I thought you might like to put one of those amber stones inside of it."

"This is beautiful," he said with a smile. "You have captured the pattern of the piece I want to make for this special person."

Catherine blushed. "The design came to me during a gray winter day. My Aunt Eva made a wreath out of apple tree twigs to celebrate last year's harvest and my mother had hung it on the wall. I noticed how the bare branches of the trees intertwined with each other, like a neverending ribbon."

Józef carefully folded the paper and put it in his pocket. "You remembered how I have always admired the art of the Celts. Especially the Celtic knot design from the Middle Ages."

"I have something else for you." Catherine reached inside her purse and pulled out the two silver coins. "These are for you. To make more jewelry."

A look of surprise overcame his face. "But this is your money. I cannot take it."

"You have done so much for me. I want you to have it."

Józef reached for Catherine's hand and gently kissed it. "You have given me so much Catherine. You have kept my desire to create alive over this past winter. I have missed you."

He looked at her with his sensuous brown eyes. Catherine felt the strong bond between them.

"I would like to take you to a moving picture theatre in Kraków. Would you like to go?"

So many thoughts crossed her mind. *How would she manage to be away from the office? What if Marcin stopped by and waited for her to return? How would she explain her absence?*

"If you don't want to go, I understand." He let go of her hand.

Again, she heard Filip's voice in her head… *Catherine, if you want things to change you need to take risks.*

She smiled at him. "Oh yes, I would love to go."

"Thursday we will take the trolley for the 2:00 showing. Meet me at the trolley stop at 1:30."

Somehow Catherine would make it work. She could not risk losing Józef, he was the only one who believed in her dream.

Ironically the sickness uncle felt returned and on Thursday, fortunately for Catherine, he stayed home.

"Don't worry uncle," she told him, "I will get the work done."

The theatre was located at the Main Square of Kraków. As they strolled around the Square Catherine could not help but notice the beauty of the two-level town houses. Every time Józef took Catherine to the city her dream felt more real. She wished to share her experiences with her mother or Aunt Eva but feared they would not understand.

Above the main door of the theatre was a Shakespearean balcony supported by two limestone corbels and three stone pillars with a ram's head at the top of each.

"Here it is, the Pod Baranami Cinema, which also means 'under the rams.'" He took her hand. "But we don't go inside here. We need to go to the side door."

Józef nodded to the large wooden doors as they passed. "Those go to a courtyard."

Catherine looked up again at the rams carved in stone above the door.

As they entered the side door, they found themselves facing a grand staircase surrounded by a gothic hall with stormy gray walls. The entire foyer was full of natural light. She was overtaken by the elegance and artistry as they made their way to the top of the stairs and entered the long, narrow auditorium with elaborate two-tiered, five light, silver wall sconces. After they sat down on the red velvet Pullman seats she looked up at the coffered wooden ceiling. At the front of the room a man sat at a piano facing a wall of gorgeous maroon curtains. Catherine was wide-eyed.

"Did you know this palace is owned by the Potocki family? They are among the wealthiest and most powerful aristocratic families in Poland."

She was just about to ask Józef how he knows all this information when the lights dimmed and the film started to show on the screen. She turned around and squinted her eyes at the light of the projector.

Up on the screen was a picture of a man and a woman under a big hat. The picture read, *Ladies and Gentlemen, Kindly Remove your Hats.* Józef took off his cap.

Catherine was amazed at the large black and white moving pictures before her. The man at the piano in the front did not play any music while a black and white moving picture of a train came slowly inside some sort of metal building. Two men in long coats, each wearing a hat, waited on a platform for the train to stop. Another man straddled the front of the train waving some sort of lantern. More people came onto the platform after the train stopped. Her heart galloped.

Józef leaned over and whispered in her ear. "That's a coal train, see all of the coal piled in the large box behind the engine?"

Catherine nodded.

Words appeared on the screen again.

EUROPEAN IMMIGRANTS ARRIVE SS LEVIATHAN NEW YORK

The screen now showed a large ship with three smokestacks. The scene looked cold and gray. White smoke rose from the stacks.

Józef pushed on Catherine's arm and pointed at the screen.

"See that gray figure on the right?"

She could barely make it out. The picture looked so cloudy.

"That is the Statue of Liberty in New York City."

The image of the ship filled the screen. The crowd in the theater gasped.

Catherine thought of Filip and Antonio. She wiped a tear from her eye.

Will I ever see Filip and Antonio again?

The screen went white and then showed a crowd of men in suits wearing white hats with a black ribbon around each hat, just above the brim. The ship towered over the men on the dock as it pulled closer.

Catherine leaned over and whispered to Józef. "I cannot imagine my brothers on such a huge ship, going across an ocean, to America." She added, "I miss them so much."

Words flashed on the screen once more.

OFFICIAL FILM TAKEN OF POLISH ARMY UNDER ACTION AND SERVICE CONDITIONS IN UKRAINE

A large group of soldiers marching filled the screen. Two Polish national flags waved above a crowd of bystanders. Long guns rested on the shoulders of the soldiers; barrels pointed toward the sky.

A new set of words filled the screen.

CRACK SHOTS WERE KEPT BUSY

Catherine's eyes widened as the screen showed men with helmets who squatted on their knees with the front of their guns balanced on top of downed trees, the butt of the gun pushed into their shoulder. Smoke rose from the barrel of the gun after it fired.

CAMOUFLAGED SNIPERS OUTSIDE OF LVÓW

Armed forces in dark clothing crawled along the ground in a field with short trees and bushes. Their faces covered with a dark cloth.

RECAPTURED TOWNS WERE ENEMY TARGETS

Soldiers ran on a dirt road with abandoned buildings. There was a church steeple in the background. Thick black smoke billowed from the center of town.

Catherine's breath quickened. Her heartbeat sounded like a loud drum in her ears.

RUSSIA ADVANCES FROM THE EAST ON UKRAINE

A fence of twisted barbed wire appeared. Soldiers with gas masks crouched around a cannon surrounded by a wall of sandbags. With two hands they shoved a large, pointed cylinder into the shaft of the cannon, closed the round door and pulled a handle. The men covered their ears as the cannon fired. Lines of combatants ran by a field spotted with dead bodies. The ground exploded! The film showed trenches with three to four dead men piled on top of each other.

Catherine turned her head and closed her eyes.

The screen went black. The crowd of people in the theatre started to murmur.

She leaned over to Józef and was about to tell him she wanted to leave but instead the man sitting in front of the piano started to play upbeat happy music.

"The picture is going to start!" Józef looked over at Catherine and smiled. The projector started again, this time on the screen was the title of the film.

SFINKS PRODUCTION COMPANY PRESENTS

POLA NEGRI IN 'THE POLISH DANCER'

The music coming from the piano played louder.

The happy music and bright white words on the black screen helped Catherine to forget about the war pictures. The story started . . .

Destiny and love can be passionate, unforgettable, and dangerous. If you are not careful with your love, it can bring great disappointment.

In a little town, close to the Polish-Russian border. Pola Basznikow, a beautiful young girl, begins her lessons in life.

The music was toe tapping as the film showed a beautiful young lady with shoulder length black hair, wavy and silky, on a carpet playing with a large dog with big floppy ears. Her dress was short, low cut, and bared her legs. The music changed with the mood of the story. Catherine watched as people talked with no sound. There was drinking and dancing. Men fought over women. Catherine was fascinated by the music and what she saw on the screen.

She also noticed how beautiful Pola was. Her dark eyes and full lips. The beautiful black satin dresses with v-necklines. The way her shoes matched the white and airy chiffon party dress with ribbons and bows at the waist. Pola wore a white coat with soft fur around the sleeves. Catherine glanced over at Józef.

Does he find her attractive? More attractive than me?

As if he could read her mind Józef laid his hand over Catherine's.

During the story there were mansions, deceptions, and heartbreak. It was a story of passion, lost love, and revenge that ended in tragedy for all the lovers.

After the short trolley ride and a quick stop at the office to finish her paperwork, Catherine walked home with Józef. He carefully guided her bicycle along the dirt road between the roots carved by wagon wheels during the recent early summer rains. The fresh air was a welcome reprieve from the crowded and dusty city.

"You were quiet on the trolley ride and now on the walk home. Did you not like the film?"

"Oh yes, I did." She paused. "But I didn't like the visions of war. The images were so real and horrible."

They continued to walk. The blue sky was dotted with fluffy white clouds. She felt his eyes on her. Catherine looked over at Józef as she tucked some strands of her windblown hair behind her ear. "You have been quiet too. Is everything all right?" There was something more to his mood. Had her love story gone wrong?

A smile tugged on the corner of his lips. "I guess like you, I was thinking about the war. All of the horses we have been sent to be prepared for battle . . . the death and destruction."

Soon they reached the road to Wiejska, the place where they would say their goodbyes. Usually with a kiss. The fragrant corn poppies stood high in the tall grass fields; their brilliant red petals fully opened to the late afternoon sun.

"I have something for you." Józef reached into his pocket and hid something in his hand. "Open your palm."

Puzzled, Catherine opened her hand. He laid a piece of jewelry in her palm. It was a perfect replica of the necklace Catherine had drawn. A radiant smile came over her. Inside the interlaced pattern of ribbon knotwork was an amber stone, shaped like a heart.

"I call it the infinity knot. It represents a friendship with no end."

Catherine continued to stare at the necklace. The pendant was elegantly attached to a silver chain with a loop.

"It's beautiful," she breathed, smiling.

"Turn around. Let me put it on you."

She turned to face the field of corn poppies. He reached around her neck and she pulled-up her hair so he could clasp the chain. He softly kissed her neck and she shivered.

She faced him again. "How does it look?"

"Beautiful, like you." He leaned down and kissed her. She closed her eyes, and the kiss seemed to last forever.

"I have something else to tell you." His voice took on a note of despondency, and he looked away far down the road. A small brown tree sparrow chattered in the nearby field followed by the trill of another.

Józef took a deep breath. Catherine sensed something was wrong.

"You know how I've been doing the ferrier work for the Polish Army? Well, they learned about the village I am from and how I am old enough to serve with other young men in my village. I'll be leaving to train for Haller's Blue Army."

"When?"

He looked into her eyes. "Tomorrow.

Her smile hardened and melted into a look of horror. "You'll be going to war? Like the war we saw in those moving pictures today?"

"Yes. I found it hard to tell you. I didn't want to cancel our trip to the movie. They're coming to get us in a wagon to be taken to the training camp Northwest of Kraków."

"What does your mother say? Or your father?" Tears came, followed by a moment of delight. "What if we go to America? Like my brothers did. We could leave tomorrow—"

Józef interrupted. "Catherine, there's no time to flee to America. We would need paperwork, and tickets. And if I flee, the soldiers might do something to my parents or my sisters, and I can't let that happen."

"We could get our tickets at the ship. That's what Filip and Antonio did. First, we go to the church and get our birth records from the priest, then . . ." She could see by the look on his face there was no changing his mind and her heart was breaking.

Józef hugged her then took a step back. He lifted her chin. "Remember, we are connected forever with the necklace. I will be back. I promise."

She hugged him and buried her face in his shirt. She wanted to remember his smell. His arms around her. She whispered, "I will be here waiting. I promise."

Catherine and Józef had created a dream that felt so right, but now it was being taken away.

Chapter
10

The summer heat had taken its toll on everyone. The pigs would not eat which made the food scraps pungent and attractive to flies. Thirsty animals made for more trips to the well, and the longer daytime hours meant less time for sleep. It was lunchtime and Marcin would soon be there to take Catherine to the city for her second job. Catherine didn't know which was worse, the smell of this farm or the stale, humid, heat of an office full of ledger books.

During their lunch of pickled herring and vegetables, her father remarked to Mary, "I'm not sure how we are going to handle this year's apple harvest. Between this flu epidemic in the villages and those young men being sent off to war, we will have little or no help at harvest time." John stood up and stretched his back. "The crop is smaller but large enough where we cannot do it on our own."

"Fortunately, we have not been stricken with the influenza." Catherine watched as her mother stood and scraped her plate into the wood bucket of scraps for the pigs. "But according to Laska, it has reached her village."

"Maybe we shouldn't have Laska come here to help this year with the harvest. Or anyone else from her village."

Mary turned around abruptly. "John, we will need the help. We must trust God it will be alright." She glanced over at the picture of the Virgin Mary on the wall and whispered a prayer.

The sound of a horse and wagon followed by footsteps with heavy boots meant Marcin had arrived. Eva came briskly through the door with a letter in her hand. "I have news! It's a letter from Filip!"

Everyone gathered around as Eva carefully opened the letter so the wax seal would not tear the paper. She handed the letter to John. "Look, there is a picture inside." John held the picture behind the paper as he read the letter.

> *Dear Father and Mother, I want to inform you I have good work. I have work at a paper mill. I have good and easy work. The work is well paid but only if you work steadily. I want you to know I have met a Polish woman named Rose and she is now my wife. And now I send you this letter and the wedding photograph. We were married on June 7, Catherine's Birthday. She takes care of the boarding house where I stay. There are many Polish immigrants here. I am lucky to have her.*

John took the picture out from behind the paper. He looked at it and laid it on the table. In the picture Filip was seated and Rose stood next to him.

"Look at Filip's hair, it doesn't even look like him," Eva exclaimed as she looked over Catherine's shoulder. Filip's hair was flat, slick, shiny and was parted down the middle. His sideburns high. He had on a dark suit with shiny shoes.

Mary picked up the photo. "He does look young and strikingly handsome. Nothing like the boy who lived on a farm."

Catherine glanced at the picture. Rose wore a shear, white veil gathered at the top of her head with a circle of small flowers around her black hair. The veil draped down to her waist over a plain white dress that stopped just past her knees. She had on white stockings and white shoes and held a large flower bouquet with round, puffy white flowers circled with greenery. She looked older than Filip and she wasn't smiling.

John continued to read,

> *I hear from those who get a newspaper in our country there is misery and the war continues. The Polish Army now has over 60,000 men in Lvów. Many poles have perished already. Please write and tell me you are safe. How are the apple crops? The countryside here reminds me of home but with more trees. The*

town where I live has many stores to buy food. We do not need to grow our own. Rose is a good cook like you mother. Love Filip.

John set the letter on the table with glazed eyes.

Mary and Eva stared at the picture of Filip and Rose. "I always thought I would see my sons get married."

Eva put her arm around Mary's shoulders. "At least Filip and Antonio are safe instead over being over here fighting in a war."

"A war that was supposed to be over." Mary added, sounding disgusted.

Marcin spoke. "Catherine, are you ready?"

A feeling of loss came over her. Filip and Antonio were gone and now Józef. But then she remembered something Józef said to her after he kissed her goodbye for the last time. *Whatever you do Catherine, don't stop drawing. Keep drawing and one day we will see each other again. Don't let the dragon blow out your flame.*

"Yes, I'm ready. I just need to go get my bag." With a tall, erect posture she walked to her room. *Today, I'll draw . . . I'll draw for* you, *Józef.*

Later that day when Marcin left to do his usual afternoon errands, Catherine noticed Marcin left the newspaper on his desk. She picked it up and read a story on the front page:

Despite the signing of the Treaty of Versailles in June 1919 at the Paris Peace Conference, which officially ended the Great War and legitimized Polish control over Eastern Galicia, there are still tensions among these newly formed nations. Central and Eastern Europe continues to be torn apart by multiple wars between the new states that had risen in place of the fallen empires.

Parts of Eastern Galicia in the homeland of Western Ukraine have deep historical ties to Poland. The Polish Republic and Western Ukraine People's Republic continue to fight over borders. The Ukrainian people will not tolerate any attempts from Poland to seize the rights to Lviv, a city Ukraine considered its capital.

A cease fire between Poles and Germans in the West and Poles and Czechs in the South have allowed Polish reinforcements from General Josef Haller's

Blue Army, an army of over 50,000 French trained soldiers, to join forces with the newly formed Polish Blue Army to fight the Ukraines. The French want Poland to be a strong ally and help contain a future German threat.

President Woodrow Wilson of the United States sees Poland as a potential "defensive wall" against the spread of Bolshevism, the communist form of Government which began in 1917. David Lloyd George, Prime Minister of the United Kingdom said, "It fills me with despair the way in which I have seen small nations, before they have hardly leaped into the light of freedom, beginning to oppress others."

In addition, the Romanians are ready to fight on the Polish front.

Catherine set the paper down and wept. Would Józef ever return or was he gone forever?

The next few months were a blur of mundane duties. Between her work for Marcin and the never-ending ritual of daily chores on the farm, her neck and body ached. Thankfully, the harvest was finished and soon winter would come. It just wasn't the same without Filip and Antonio.

Central and Eastern Europe continued to be torn apart by multiple wars between the new states of Germany, Poland, Ukraine, and Russia. More than two-thirds of soldiers died from typhus in October. Marcin also told her he read over 10,000 Polish soldiers had been killed.

I pray one was not Józef.

Catherine's heart ached each time she passed the road to Józef's village. She wanted to go there, to see if there was any news, but there was no time.

At Christmas, a letter arrived from Antonio.

My Dearest Father and Mother, I have found work but not yet a wife in America. I do not believe I will return someday or another, and if not I do not mind, because I do ten times better in America than in our country. The factory next to my apartment burned down but I am good. Today I do not need the favor of anybody except God. May God continue to give me health. I read there was a cease fire reached between Poland and Ukraine in Warsaw. But the Polish Army crossed into Zbrucz and occupied Kamieniec. There are rumors the Polish-Soviet war could spread southward. Father, there is no future in Poland, come to America. I can send money for a ship ticket. Enclosed is money for the Holiday. I miss all of you. Love Antonio.

Christmas that year was not the same. Not only were Filip and Antonio gone, but Catherine's mother had been depressed. Eva and Catherine tried their best to keep the home festive with the traditions of baking cookies, honey-spice cakes, and cheese-dough apple cakes but there was no denying the sickness was taking its toll on Mary. She had no appetite for festivities.

The day after Christmas was unusually warm, and Laska came to finish a blanket on the loom. Mary was at the table kneading bread as Catherine stood on a chair and hung freshly washed clothes over a rope stretched above the hot stove.

Mary's face was pale and her eyes were glassy. "Laska, I'm not sure what has come over me. I must have a terrible cold. I'm not able to smell the wood fire and I can hardly hear anything."

Laska stopped the loom and walked over to Mary. "You do look pale. Maybe you should lie down for a bit."

"But there is much work to do, I cannot go to bed at this hour."

Catherine turned around and stepped down from the stool. Her mother looked weak; her normally bright blue eyes were gray. She did not like seeing her mother distraught and wanted to help.

"Yes mother, I can finish the bread and anything else you need to be done. Do as Laska asked; go and nap."

"Laska, I just know something is wrong. I can feel it. I heard an owl hoot through the night last night." Her lips set in a grim line. "My chest hurts and so does my head."

Catherine did not like hearing her mother's superstitions. They would only put fear in her heart.

Laska took hold of Mary's elbow and guided her toward the bedroom. "Come, dear, let's get you some rest."

The next morning Mary did not get out of bed. Catherine made the coffee and set biscuits with honey on the table. Her father appeared. "Your mother is still asleep. I did not wake her." After a quick bite to eat he went outside.

After Catherine took care of the chickens, pigs, and horses she made her mother's favorite tea. She hoped the smell of the fresh orange she cut for the tea from Christmas would stir her but when Catherine looked in on her she was still asleep. Soon Laska came.

"What's wrong Catherine? Where is your mother? Is she still in bed?"

Catherine nodded as she peeled potatoes. Laska went in the bedroom and did not come out right away.

From the room Laska shouted, "Catherine, bring me a rag and a bowl of water."

Catherine watched as Laska wet the rag and placed it on her mother's forehead. The iron bed cradled her mother, who was covered with the bedspread her own mother had made on a loom. In the corner of the room, under a picture of Saint Francis—the guardian of all animals—was a table with an oil lamp. A piece of white fabric hung over the mirror on the wall.

"Laska, why is there a cloth over the mirror?"

"I put it there. It is bad luck for someone to look at the mirror hung in a room with a person who is sick."

Mary barely opened her eyes and muttered, "Oh, Laska, do you hear the children singing and playing outside?" She stopped to catch her breath. "Is the window open? I smell fresh cut apple blossoms... will you bring me some?"

Laska laid her hand on Mary's arm and shushed her. "It's winter Mary, there are no apple blossoms."

Catherine walked over to the bed. "Mother, I'll bring you some. As soon as spring comes. We'll put them in your favorite vase."

Her breathing shallow, Mary smiled at her.

Suddenly Laska's tone became urgent. "Catherine, go and find your father. Tell him it's important he come inside."

Catherine rushed from the room, threw on her coat, and ran to the barn. Puffs of breath appeared as she exhaled in the frigid air. Her father and Marcin were outside when she approached.

"Papa, Laska needs you to come to the house."

"What is it?" He leaned the shovel in his hand on the barn wall.

"It's Mother. She has a high fever and it's hard for her to breathe."

"Should I go to Father Jarek, and get the doctor?" Marcin offered, brushing the hay dust from his sleeves.

"Yes," John replied, his brow wrinkled with worry. "Catherine, you stay here and finish the horse stalls. Then gather the eggs from the chickens."

As they left Catherine made a sign of the cross and folded her hands in prayer. She closed her eyes and whispered the *Our Father*.

After she finished in the barn and gathered the eggs, Catherine hurried back to the house.

"Doctor Laskowski believes it's the Spanish Flu," said John when Catherine came inside.

Laska hung her head with a somber look. And Doctor Laskowski emerged, followed by Father Jarek.

"The flu has spread everywhere. Do your best to keep her comfortable. Let fresh air in when you can. Keep her calm, this is no time for worry or anxiety."

Father Jarek added, "Pray that she fights this and gets well."

Everyone left, except for Laska, who stayed to finish the blanket on the loom. After warming herself by the stove, Catherine decided to go check on her mother. She was surprised to see her sitting up in bed.

"There you are, come sit next to me. Don't be afraid." Her mother's rosary was wrapped around her hand.

Catherine brought her sketchpad to share with her mother, hoping the pictures inside would make her feel better.

"Would you sit over there and draw a picture of me?"

"I would love to." Catherine sat on the trunk near the end of the bed. She captured her mother's beautiful eyes as a smile surfaced on her lips. After she finished Mary was eager to see the picture.

"This is beautiful, Catherine. I know God will find a way for you to use your gift."

Catherine was stunned to hear her mother say that, and she was about to tell her about the necklace Józef had given her when Laska came in with a cup of hot tea.

"Catherine, you should let your mother get some rest." She looked down at Mary whose breathing was raspy and shallow. "Here, I brought you some hot tea to soothe your throat."

Catherine bent down and gave her mother a hug.

"Remember how much I love you, Catherine. Your father and I want only what's best for you," She cleared her throat and she struggled to get the words out, "It's getting close to the time for you to get married and it gives me peace knowing your father has talked to Dominik's father about marrying you."

"Get some rest mother, I will see you in the morning."

But that was not to be.

The next day, Catherine wrote a letter to Antonio to tell him the sad news.

Mother has passed away.

With a heavy heart she wrote the words. She could not bear to write one to Filip and asked Eva if she would do it instead. She carefully folded the picture of Mary she had sketched and included it in the letter to Antonio.

A brisk wind blew against the house, rattling the shutters and reminding Catherine to put more wood in the stove. She looked around the empty house, it felt cold and desolate.

It was then she realized her mother was gone forever. Would her father insist she now must marry Dominik?

Chapter

11

Spring brought the annual return of leaves and blossoms to the apple trees. Today Catherine was up before the rooster crowed. Since the death of her mother, she was responsible to cook and clean for her father who had yet to be stirred by the rooster's second crowing. The farm suffered without the manpower of Filip and Antonio and from the death of the matriarch.

Catherine lit the oil lamp and started a fire in the stove to prepare breakfast. As she scooped coffee from the can her eyes caught a glimpse of a recent letter from Filip. She decided to read it.

> *Dear Father and Catherine,*
>
> *The letter which I received from Aunt Eva grieved me terribly. It is true misfortune and misery from God this has happened to the family. I feel I should come home yet America has been good to me. I do ten times better here than in our country. This town of Pyrites is just like home. There is a river and hills. Father, there is no future in Poland. Come to America. You do not need to farm here; you can work at the Mill. There are stores for food and a moving picture theatre. I can send a ship ticket for both of you. Catherine I have found you a husband to take care of you in America. Please write me back and say you will come.*

Catherine's Dream

My wife Rose is now with child. It brings me great joy to become a father. She would like to meet you. Write back and tell me you will decide to come.

Filip

Quietly she put the letter back on the shelf. Thankfully her father had not mentioned anything more to her about going to America or how Filip found her a husband.

Today, I must find out if Józef is back from the war.

Uncle told her a couple of weeks ago Poland and Ukraine had come to an agreement in which Ukraine gave up the Eastern Galicia Region to Poland.

Catherine heard her father getting out of bed.

I'll take my bicycle today and ride to Józef's village. I need to find out before I'm forced to go to America or father tells me I must marry Dominik.

John entered the kitchen and wilted in the chair, looking downcast. Ever since Mary's death, he often sought the comfort of vodka and the forgetfulness it granted. Marcin had brought him home from the town tavern on more than one occasion. Although her father's irrational behavior left more than the normal burden of farm work on Catherine's shoulders she did not complain. Ironically, she found time to sneak in a sketch of a horse in the field or the geese by the stream. She pictured her drawings of the country being sold to city people who perhaps dreamed of a simpler life. *If only they knew the truth.*

"Coffee, Papa?" Catherine asked as she reached for a cup on the shelf. The early morning sun shined on his forehead and revealed a gleam of sweat on his brow. His eyes blinked owlishly as she set the steamy cup of coffee in front of him. He cleared his throat.

"This morning I will ride to the city with Marcin and take two bushels of the apples from the root cellar to the Kazimierz Market in Podgorze. Also, the squash and potatoes since we have plenty." He took a sip of the hot black coffee. "Make sure you tell Dominik and the village boys the apple trees on the west end near the barn are to be pruned first. I will be back to help with the rest."

There is so much work to be done. The garden needed to be churned, bedding changed, animals fed. How would I make time to leave?

"Yes, Father." Catherine put the biscuits in the oven as a thought came to her.

I'll go after Father and Uncle leave. If Laska or Eva question where I'm going I'll tell them I have a delivery to make.

Catherine glanced at the letter on the shelf. She hoped her father would not see it to remind him of Filip's offer. But this morning his mind seemed pre-occupied. Was he already planning their trip to America or her marriage to Dominik?

The bike ride to Józef's village was long, and neither Eva nor Laska questioned Catherine about her delivery as both seemed to be dominated by their own thoughts. Especially the absence of Mary.

As she turned down the dirt road named Wiejska towards Plaszów, the fields became flatter. The village was along the Vistula River and Catherine noticed many of the homes with thatched roofs were built on earthen mounds or surrounded by manmade embankments. The water looked swollen from the spring thaw and reached up to the lower trunks of the willow trees along the riverbank. Józef once told her, "The river is untamed. Living with the river means you know and accept the rules of the river." Now she understood what he meant.

Catherine scanned the row of homes separated by fences of intertwined willow branches for a wagon like Józef's, but many wagons were in the barn and hard to see. Near the road she spotted a slender elderly woman who showed astonishment but also some delight as Catherine stopped her bicycle to talk with her. She noticed a gap between the woman's front teeth when she smiled.

"Do you know where I can find Tomasz Kowalczyk?" Catherine felt embarrassed she did not know Józef's mother's name.

"Yes, he is the husband of my sister Franciszka." She brushed a string of sand colored hair from her face. "Why do you want to find him?" Her faded blue eyes glared at Catherine.

"I'm trying to find his son, Józef. Do you know if he has returned from the war?" The woman turned her face away and shook her head no.

Catherine touched her hand to her heart. "Has something happened to him?"

"That I do not know. Franciszka waits every day for his return." A curious look came over her face. "Are you a friend of his?"

Catherine felt herself blush. "I am. Is his mother home? Can I talk to her?"

I must know more about Józef. Maybe he has written home.

The old woman pointed toward a house with several cows grazing. "There." She pointed. "That house belongs to Tomasz."

As Catherine stood at the door, her heart pounded against her chest. *What would she say? Did Józef tell them about her?*

A pudgy woman with a baby soft face, a double chin, and charcoal gray hair in a tight bun opened the door. Catherine looked into wistful brown eyes that reminded her of Józef's.

"Hello, you don't know me, but I am Catherine, a friend of Józef's." She continued barely taking a breath. "I work in the office across the street from the blacksmith shop. I don't know if he told you about me but . . ." Catherine turned around and pointed at where she had been talking with the old woman. "A woman on the road told me this is Józef's house… are you Franciszka?"

Catherine's stomach was in knots. *What if this woman tells me to leave?*

"Yes, I am, Józef's mother." She opened the door wider. "Come in, come in."

There was a large wood slab table, and the smell of fish filled the air. Catherine looked over near the stove and saw the large carp laid out on the counter. Franciszka motioned for Catherine to sit down. An unfinished basket made from willow tree reeds sat on the floor. Catherine remembered Józef told her he had sisters, but she saw no one else there.

Catherine found Józef's mother easy to talk with. She received a letter from Józef about how the Typhoid fever had stricken many of the soldiers. He also told of death on the battlefield, but his Legion spared so far.

"When did you receive this letter?"

"About two months ago."

"But so much has happened since then. You haven't heard from him since?"

Despite Catherine's doubt, Franciszka's voice was filled with hope. "Thanks be to God he is still alive. Maybe he will be home soon."

The afternoon sun peered through the window and Catherine realized how late it was. She stood. "I must go but can I come and visit you again?"

Franciszka also stood up and gave Catherine a hug. "Yes, yes, please do." She walked Catherine to the door. "Next time you come, I'll make you a fish dinner."

Catherine smiled, despite her uncertainty if Józef would return.

When Catherine got home, she heard loud voices from inside the house. It sounded like Marcin and her father were having an argument. She stood outside.

"This woman you were with. I recognized her from the Market, how you were always around her, even when my sister was alive." His anger spiked. "I know she has three boys, is she married too?"

Her father's frustrated voice replied. "No, she lost her husband during the Great War. She is widowed, like me."

Rage continued to flow through Marcin's voice. "Is this why you spend so much time in the tavern, so you can rendezvous with her? There is work to be done here."

"I don't have to answer to you."

Unlike Catherine who would cower to Marcin's anger, John continued to fight.

"Her boys can help with the orchard. Zophia is a good cook. I cannot depend on Catherine; Filip found her a husband in America. She would be gone."

Silence followed by a breathless voice.

"*You'd* better slow down. I know she's from the Shtetl village which means she's a Jewess."

"So?"

"So? Your wife is probably turning in her grave."

Next was the sound of a wooden chair being pushed across the floor.

"You need to leave. Get out of here."

"This is ridiculous. I'm not going to lose this orchard to Jews." Marcin continued to shout, but his tone of voice changed. "On second thought Eva and I can move to the city."

The door flew open, and Marcin marched out of the house, his face crimson with fury. He didn't even notice Catherine as he stormed past her.

Her father followed him but stopped at the edge of the stoop. His cheeks flushed as if he had just stepped from a bath. He shouted at Marcin whose long-legged strides already reached the barn. "But it's okay for you to take their money."

Catherine watched as her father rushed back inside, grabbed his hat, and walked briskly the other way toward the orchard.

Who is this woman—Zophia? For the first time Catherine felt alone. This did not feel like her home anymore.

The cold spring, followed by a dry beginning of summer made for harsh apple growing conditions. Soon it would be Saint John's Eve, the longest day of the year, and Eva insisted there be the ritual bonfire to bless the apple crop and mark the celebration of Saint John the Baptist.

The tension had not lessened between Marcin and John. Neither of them wanted to admit they still needed each other.

Many of the local villagers came to participate in the ritual and they passed around a flask of vodka. Catherine learned Dominik was also taken to fight at the Ukrainian border. Their loud voices spoke of an end to the war in Ukraine.

"Now that Poland has secured her border from Ukraine, there are rumors of a Polish-Soviet War near Warsaw. Soon our boys will be home!" The crowd raised their glasses and cheered. With her father surrounded by laughter and Marcin nowhere to be seen Catherine decided this would be a good time to go visit Franciszka to see if there was any news about Józef. She would be back before dark, and anyone noticed her gone.

Catherine peddled quickly over the bumpy road. She prayed the chain would not come off. The fragrant whiff of daisies reminded her of the flowers Józef picked for her last summer.

Franciszka was sitting outside on a chair made from bendable willow branches. There were two young men standing over her. *Soldiers! Was one of them Józef?*

Catherine quickly approached with her bicycle only to be disappointed as she dismounted.

"We did not want to give you this news." The taller one said.

"What news?" Catherine could feel her breath quicken. "Is it about Józef?"

Franciszka drooped her head, her face registering shock.

"Yes, I was just telling his mother about what happened. I am Aleksander. Pawel and I were in the same army as Józef."

She stared at the two soldiers whose field grey uniforms were too big for their frames. Both had no hair under their gray caps, and a sullen look in their eyes.

Catherine gasped. "What do you mean *were?*" She looked over at Franciszka who continued to look at the ground. "Where's Józef? Why isn't he with you?"

"We had been with Józef since the beginning. Most days we would be in a trench with Józef and several others, but then our commander took Pawel and me to another trench about a quarter mile away. This happened before, and we would always return to find Józef telling stories or smoking a cigarette with the other soldiers."

Pawel added, "But then our commander told us a trench of soldiers not far from us were taken by the enemy as prisoners. . . . We prayed it was not Józef."

Aleksander continued. "We were nervous—would the enemy find us?"

He shifted from one foot to the other. Catherine stared at him, open-mouthed.

"It was a long night. The next day we returned to the trench where Józef had been and there was no response when our commander shouted inside. I crawled inside, not wanting to find a dead body, which is something the enemy would do when they found a trench of soldiers… but instead I found this."

He opened his hand to reveal a brass cross with a red and white fabric attached. Catherine bent over and looked at the inscription. *On the Field of Glory.* It was dated 1920.

"General Pick, from the Polish Sixth Infantry Division awarded Józef the Cross of Valour because of his courage on the battlefield." Aleksander wiped a tear from his face. "Józef would always encourage the soldiers to be brave. He would be the first to lead us out of a trench to our next mission. Once, he carried another Polish soldier whose leg had been blown off. Józef did not want to leave him to die alone on the field."

Pawel looked at Catherine. "He would always tell us the war would end soon; we had to fight for our homeland. But he also told me he fought to protect a certain someone back home."

Aleksander handed the cross to Franciszka who stood up to look more closely at the medal.

"I'm not sure if he lost it in a struggle, but I brought it home for you to have."

Franciszka held the cross close to her heart.

The thought of not seeing Józef again sent a wave of terror through Catherine.

"Maybe Józef was taken to another place to fight? How do you know what happened to him?"

"Our commander learned the soldiers in that trench were taken by the Russian soldiers as prisoners and put on a train to Kiev in Ukraine. The Red Army had launched a powerful counter-offensive on the Ukrainian border which forced the Poles to surrender Kiev."

Catherine's body shook. "Then maybe he is still alive." Her voice trembled. She looked at Franciszka whose face was red and puffy from her weeping.

A rumble of thunder rolled in the distance. The darker gray clouds made for a beautiful, blazing sunset, but there was a cool breeze and the scent of approaching rain.

Pawel drew nearer to Catherine. He smelled of stale sweat. "No one knows what happens to prisoners. We have heard many stories, none of them good."

Aleksander shook his head in agreement. "We are so sorry. Our hearts are heavy."

"But how did you escape?"

"We didn't. A few weeks later our commander told us the war was over. Polish troops had left the capital in Ukraine to defeat the Bolsheviks near Warsaw. We were free to leave."

Pawel added, "For all we know Józef was forced to fight with the Russians."

Catherine looked up at the approaching storm, feeling the first light drops of rain. She approached Franciszka and hugged her. "Maybe he'll come home. That medal proves he does not give up."

She grabbed her bicycle and started pedaling. The rain pelted her face. *I don't believe Józef is dead. There is no proof, only hearsay.* A flash of lightening followed by a clap of thunder forced Catherine to shut her eyes. Her clothes were soaked but she didn't care. By now the fire would have ended and her father would have looked for her. But then again, he probably drank too much vodka and was now passed out.

From now on I will be brave, like Józef.

The early summer months were hotter than usual. Likewise, the tension between Catherine's father and uncle grew more heated. They were so concerned with each other they paid no attention to Catherine who does her best to stay out of their way. Catherine was relieved her father has not mentioned anything about Dominik's return from the war or her going to America to be married. She must wait for Józef. Each day she prayed and unwrapped the necklace carefully from the cloth she had wrapped it in for protection.

Catherine felt more determined to draw so she could share her drawings with Józef when he returned. Her bicycle rides to his village on the Vistula River inspired her to capture the calm and serene of the water. One warm, sunny afternoon, when the air was breathless, she took her ledger to the barn, left the door half open and sketched Laska while she sat near the well with the sun on her face. *This one I will call Peasant Woman in God's Eyes.* Catherine found her observation skills more visual and her attention to detail easier to distinguish. She would become an artist... somehow.

She heard an irritated voice behind her.

"I thought you had given up those silly sketches."

It was Marcin, his arms crossed.

She didn't dare close the book to reveal its soft, red leather cover for fear he might recognize it. Instead, Catherine slid it into her bag, stood confidently, and slipped the handle of the bag over her shoulder. She then reached over and picked-up the basket filled with eggs.

She glanced at him. "I was just taking a rest from the heat." She couldn't help but notice his face was ready for a battle. *Had he been drinking?*

"Rest? There is no time for rest." He strode over to the wall and grabbed the three-pronged wooden hay fork. "If you have time to draw, you're not doing enough."

She ignored his comment and headed out the door, thankful the sketchbook was inside her bag.

Laska and Eva helped with pre-harvest cooking for the workers while Catherine continued to help with outside farm chores. Eva had taken over the herb and flower garden. "The soil seems much better here," she said one morning while she tended to the fragrant lavender, and chamomile. When she saw Eva bent over in the garden, she missed her mother. Lately everywhere she looked, something reminded her of Mary. Today she dusted the cobwebbed worker huts who would soon arrive for the harvest. Deep down she knew her mother was proud of the way she had helped her father with the farm. *Why did God take my mother?*

She refused to believe Józef was also gone.

No, she shouted within herself. *I won't accept it.*

But there was no report of him.

As fall grew nearer, news spread the war in Ukraine had ended and business for Marcin became busy again. Catherine was back at her desk to add, subtract, and record numbers. Once again the hard oak chair reminded her to stand, and she walked over to the window to look out onto the busy street. The people who would normally wait for the trolley on the sidewalk were instead forced to stand in the street as the automobiles were double-parked. Earlier she talked with Tomasz who told her he was planning to move the blacksmith shop back to his village. "This city has more automobiles than wagons and horses."

And still not a single word from Józef.

One afternoon in early September Marcin was more annoyed than usual. He drummed his fingers on the desk and meandered to the window as he forked his fingers through his hair for a third time. Catherine tried to ignore him. She glanced over as he crossed his arms over his chest. The reflection of him in the glass showed a look of great bitterness across his face.

"Her name is Zophia Serafin."

Catherine did not want to engage in a conversation, but felt she had no choice. She laid her pencil down and turned around in her chair to face him.

He continued. "She is from the Shtetl Village. Her husband owned a bakery; she would bring her bread and rolls to the market. Your father sold her apples." The muscles in his face grew tense. "I saw her flirt with your father at the market when your mother was still alive. Now that she found out he is a widower she could sink her claws into him and the orchard."

Catherine did not like this conversation. Her body felt rigid.

His eyes narrowed and his teeth clenched together. "She is a Jew. A merchant and a cheater. Not to mention none of those wealthy Jewish boys went to fight for our country. Instead, the Polish Army forced our peasant boys."

He continued to pace back and forth. "And now," he let out a sarcastic laugh. "Now he has asked her to marry him. She will bring shame to our Christian community."

For once, Catherine agreed with his anger. How could her father marry another woman so soon? But then she remembered what her mother told her about marriage. "*People do not marry because of love. It is an arrangement.*"

"Does this mean father would move to the Shtetl Village?"

Maybe this means I would not be forced to go to America.

Marcin let out a large growl of annoyance. He threw his hand in the air. "Ha! Your father would not leave that orchard; she will move there."

Catherine thought of this strange woman, with three boys, who would move into their house. Her brows bumped together in a scowl. "Well, what do we do?"

"Nothing." He sat in his chair and opened a ledger. "There is nothing we can do."

Catherine didn't like that answer and she felt anger rising in her chest.

"I need to go outside and get some fresh air."

She stood and used one foot to shove her bag under the desk.

Marcin opened his mouth to object, then stopped. After she left he looked under the desk at the bag and smiled.

Chapter

12

I t did not take long for word to spread that John Soból would soon be married to a Jewish woman named Zophia Serafin. Because of this news Father Jarek refused to come and bless the apple crop for the upcoming harvest. He told John, "You cannot be a Jew and a Christian at the same time."

Marcin told Catherine he learned at a Jewish wedding the newly married couple had to sign a *ketubah*, a marriage contract that stipulated John's obligations to Zophia. The contract stated Zophia was to be compensated in the event of a divorce or John's death. This meant Zophia would own the apple orchard and it would no longer be a dowry for Catherine or an opportunity for Marcin.

"Why should I do any work for the orchard now?" he said bitterly.

John did not invite any of his family or friends to the wedding.

"I am so confused." Catherine confided to Laska and Eva the day of the wedding. "Why would Papa not want any of us there?"

Eva shook her head. "Who knows why men do what they do. All I know is the need for sex can be one of the most powerful desires of men. This desire is so strong men have risked their life and reputation to indulge in it."

Eva wiped off the small statue of the Virgin Mary and placed it back on the shelf. "Besides, you would be uncomfortable at that wedding. You are a Christian."

"Does this mean Papa will no longer be going to our church?"

"I'm afraid so, but you can still go with us."

Laska interrupted. "Maybe it is time for you to find a husband. Someone who can take care of you. Provide you with your own home."

Catherine thought of Józef. *Was Laska right? How long before Józef would return? What if he never returned?*

Catherine refused to think that way.

Laska continued, "I know of a nice young man in my village. I am sure he would be happy to provide for a pretty girl like you."

Eva agreed. "Yes Catherine, let's find you a husband."

"But I already have someone I would like to marry . . ." She wanted to take back the words, but it was too late.

Laska looked at Catherine with a lackluster smile. "That boy Józef? He is gone—sent to a Russian labor camp. Soldiers never return who have been taken as prisoners of war."

Catherine could not believe what Laska just said. *I thought you supported my relationship with Józef.*

Eva gave Catherine a hug, then placed her hands on Catherine's shoulders. "If Józef does not return, we will find you someone just like him."

But Aunt Eva, there is no one like him. That's why I love him.

After Laska and Eva left Catherine finished pulling herbs from the side garden. The afternoon sun was warm and she wiped a soiled hand across her brow, leaving a small mud streak on her face. Rounding the corner of the cottage, she saw her father beside a small wagon, greeting the woman who would now be his wife. This would be her first-time meeting Zophia.

Catherine waited as they approached. Zophia's hair was luminous and dark. A long, loose braid fell on her left shoulder. The part on top of her head aligned perfectly with the curve of her high cheekbones. An elegant white lace around the collar of her dark dress made her over dressed for farm work and Catherine thought she looked like the film star Pola Negri. Now she understood why her father was attracted to her.

Zophia set her suitcase down and offered her hand to Catherine.

"Hello, you must be Laska. John told me how you come from the village to help with the orchard."

"Oh… no. I'm Catherine, John's daughter."

Catherine wiped her hands over her apron and before she could extend it, Zophia put her hand down.

"Oh." She sounded uncomfortable, "I see your hands are dirty."

John put his hand on Zophia's back and guided her inside the house.

"Come, let us put your things away. Then I will show you around the orchard."

Catherine followed and immediately went to wash her hands. Three young boys came running inside, having apparently jumped from the wagon and gone to explore the barn.

"Madre! Madre!" the youngest one shouted. "Alter told me I have to sleep in the barn alone with the night owls!"

Zophia stuck her head out of the doorway.

"Hush! All of you. I will be right out."

The oldest boy was taller than Catherine, with well-groomed, chestnut brown hair. He had his mother's dark eyes and full lips. Catherine thought him not to be much younger than her. The middle boy had a curious look about him and he stared at Catherine with his expressive eyes.

Wanting to break the awkward silence Catherine spoke first. "My name is Catherine, and John is my father. What are your names?"

The youngest boy's cheeks were flushed from running. "My name is Yehuda. . . . Are there night owls in your barn? Is that where my bed is?"

Catherine couldn't help but smile. "No, your bed is in the room next to mine."

The older boy spoke with arrogance in his voice. "Is that where my bed is, too?" He seemed to have his mother's demeanor. He glanced over at a bed set up in a corner not far from where the stove was. "Or is *that* my bed?"

Before Catherine could answer, her father and Zophia appeared.

"Boys, I want you to go get your things from the wagon."

The boys stood there, looking at the picture of the Virgin Mary on the wall. The middle boy Yair asked, "Madra, who is that?"

"Never you mind, now go!"

Just as fast as they had entered, they were gone.

In the first week of Zophia's entrance into their lives, it was readily apparent two women with vastly different ideas sharing a home would not be easy. Whatever Catherine did Zophia criticized, and the changes were rapid.

Zophia removed all pictures of the Virgin Mary including the small statue of her on the bureau. There were now stringent kosher rules to be followed in the kitchen.

Pots had to be cleansed with boiling water and certain utensils could only be used for specific foods. Meat and dairy were to be kept strictly separate.

Sunday was no longer a Sabbath day. Instead, on Friday evenings just before the sun set, Zophia would bring two candles from the shelf and place them on the table. Her boys would gather and after the candles were lit they all closed their eyes. Zophia said a prayer in Yiddish. Catherine learned this was the start of *Shabbat*, which meant there would be little work done. For the rest of Friday evening until nightfall on Saturday, Zophia and her boys spent the day reading from a Hebrew Bible, known as the *Torah,* and recited prayers. During this time, Catherine and her father would be working out in the barn or tending to livestock.

As she cleaned a stall or fed the pigs, Catherine thought of her mother whose work seemed endless, and there was Zophia, determined not to work at all but to keep her slender, white hands and perfect fingernails utterly clean.

On Sundays, Catherine would still go to church and afterwards have dinner with Eva and Marcin. Her father was content to work on Sunday and not go to church, which seemed odd to Catherine. She had always known her father to be a Christian man.

"Could you pass me one of those *obwarzanek*?" Catherine asked before she ate her bowl of chicken soup. Eva had made them earlier before church and they filled the kitchen with an aromatic memory of her mother's cooking. It was finally time to eat the small, braided circle of bread sprinkled with poppy seeds.

Eva passed Catherine the basket. "I'm so glad you could come for dinner today, Catherine. How are things?"

"Things are . . . different. Zophia has removed from the house anything to do with the Virgin Mary. Mother's pans are gone. The kitchen has only Zophia's cooking pots and utensils."

"What did she do with it all?"

"I'm not sure. She must have put the items in the barn."

Marcin continued to sip his soup, not saying a word.

"I miss mother's cooking." Catherine continued. She felt silly, really, talking about such mundane matters, when more important things were troubling her, but she was determined not to make trouble for her father with his new wife.

Eva searched Catherine's face. "What else do you want to tell me?"

Marcin stopped sipping for a moment. "Eva, stay out of it."

"She needs to talk. I can see it on her face."

Catherine wanted to tell Eva everything, and out it came little by little.

"The older boy, Alter, disappeared a lot when he would be sent outside to do farm chores."

"What is he up to?"

"I don't know. It's certainly not lifting a finger to help."

"And?" Eva prompted, which caused Marcin to shake his head.

"Well, I'm confused about how my father treats *her* so differently than he treated Mother."

Eva's curiosity peaked. "Go on."

"He wants to be alone with her after dinner. He insisted the boys and I go outside to do the chores, which the boys don't do anyway. They would rather play in the barn than milk the cow or water and feed the horses."

Eva shook her head. "I haven't seen Laska around lately either."

"I miss her." Catherine forced a smile. "I just feel lost, like I don't have a home anymore."

I also miss Józef.

Finally, Marcin spoke. "The orchard is no longer your home, Catherine. It belongs to Zophia and her boys. I am through giving my hard-earned money to your father so he can support a lazy woman and her worthless boys."

Don't you mean our *hard-earned money?*

"You should know, Catherine," Marcin continued, "I am now sure about selling this house and moving to the city."

Eva was startled. "This is the first time I have heard this."

Marcin dipped the last of his *obwarzanek* into his bowl of soup, and the look on his face told the matter had been decided and there was nothing more to talk about.

"In the city I would not have my beehives, or gardens." Eva's voice shook with emotion. "I would be far from my family's village." Her face became agonized. "The city is dirty and crowded."

Catherine knew Marcin's temper extremely well, and she did not want to witness it today. She decided to intervene if she could…

"Eva, could I have some honey to bring home before I leave? Mother's honeypot is…" She stopped herself. The pain of talking as if her mother were still alive caused tears to well up, and to stop them from spilling over she picked up her cup of tea and took a sip, then another.

Still, a tension hung in the air.

Marcin brushed the crumbs from his mustache and walked over to pour himself a cup of coffee from the pot on the stove.

"Catherine, I will need you at the office early tomorrow. I just secured a new account, and their books are a terrible mess. You will need to straighten it all out."

"Yes sir." She looked over at Eva who continued to pout.

Eva whispered, "If I were you I would fly from this place as soon as possible. Go where no man is going to make all your decisions for you."

That night, in her room, Catherine lay in the dark considering her situation and how quickly life had turned in directions she did not want to go.

I must make a change. Soon. I feel like my spirit is dying. But how?

Art school seemed out of her reach. She thought about Józef and the necklace he gave her. His promise to come back. She wanted to believe him.

Feeling trapped and alone, she took a deep breath and reached for her shoulder bag to retrieve her sketchbook. But it was gone. Her heart galloped as she frantically searched the bag.

Where is my book? Did I leave it someplace? At the office? Did Marcin find it?

She wanted to rush to Marcin's house and confront him but knew she would have to wait. She rolled over and listened as the crickets chirped. Her thoughts turned to the ledger full of sketches: country birds, city streets, and Józef.

That night she dreamt her drawings came to life with vibrant colors, people stood on the street and admired her art. Art that told a story and made others to see the beauty she saw. When a hand reached over and tore her creations apart, she sat up, breathing hard.

The rooster crowed.

She quickly dressed and crept into the kitchen to grab the egg basket.

"Hello, Catherine. You're up bright and early this morning."

She turned around and smiled. "Yes Father, I want to get an early start. Uncle said there is much to do at the office today. He has a new account."

I need to get there before he does, so I can search for my sketchbook.

"Please tell Uncle I rode the bicycle to town."

"Don't you want any breakfast?"

"No, I'm not hungry." She started toward the door. "Forgive me father, I need to get my chores done so I can leave."

Catherine pedaled hard and fast to town. Her stomach growled and she regretted not eating breakfast. Even one of Zophia's hard biscuits would have tasted good right now. She fumbled with the key as she unlocked the door and immediately went to her desk and searched every drawer. Then she looked under each paper and in the wooden slots.

Where could it be?

Hopeless, she ventured over to Marcin's desk. She kept one eye out the window as she opened drawers and looked under ledger books. Flustered, she went over to the file cabinet and opened every drawer. She looked on the bookshelf of ledgers for anything red. Nothing. The door opened and in walked Marcin.

"Looking for something?"

She bit her lip. If she told him about the sketchbook there was no telling how he would react. Instead, she replied, "I was just straightening up a bit before I got started."

He looked at her with a suspicious eye. "Your father mentioned you were eager to get to work today."

Catherine watched as he took a stack of receipts from his well-worn leather bag and set them on his desk. Her eye caught the safe on the floor.

Of course, that's where he would put it.

"Here, I'll take those." She insisted as he reached into the bag to retrieve some paper bills and coins. He took the key from his pocket and bent down to open the safe. Catherine inched over and purposely dropped a paper on the floor so she could look inside as he opened it. But there was no red sketchbook. Her heart sank, and she withdrew back to her desk.

She had lost Józef again.

A few days later, Catherine came home from the city but did not hear the normal rustling from the pen outside the barn of pigs wanting to be fed. She looked inside the pen, but they were gone. Immediately she ran inside the barn to find her father.

"Father, the pigs are loose." She searched the barn for him. "They are not in their pen."

John was sharpening a scythe blade and turned with a doleful look on his face. "They're not loose. I sold them."

"Sold them? You mean to butcher them? You would always keep a few of the younger ones."

"Zophia is Jewish, and Jewish people do not eat the meat of pigs."

Catherine could not believe how much her father had changed. "Does this mean we don't eat ham or pork anymore?"

He went back to sharpening the blade.

On her way back to the house she passed the empty pen. Although she hated feeding the pigs and getting her shoes filthy, she enjoyed a ham at Easter. Now that small pleasure was gone. More than that, she felt agitated—once again what Zophia wanted dictated her father's and her life.

Her thoughts were interrupted by a bark. She looked over to see a dog tied to the fence near the storage barn. Catherine walked toward the mongrel as its tail thumped the ground.

"Poor creature. Why are you tied up?"

"Hey! Don't let that dirty *Kelev* loose."

It was Alter, the oldest boy, who appeared from out of the storage barn. He was tall like Antonio, but he was nowhere near as robust. In fact, there was a sickly look about him. She learned he had been sick as a young boy and Zophia doesn't allow him to do physical work. Which seemed, to Catherine, he took full advantage of and used it as an excuse not to lift a finger. "That Kelev is a demon. He's bad and dirty."

"Why do you say that? Who told you he was bad? That dog has never hurt anyone." She reached down to untie the rope. "He needs to go back to his village."

Alter charged at her and grabbed her hand.

"Stop, I say!" He jerked Catherine's hand from the rope.

"I don't understand. *Father!*" she called, looking toward the barn, hoping he would appear and put a stop to this madness.

Alter grinned. "Your Padra helped me to find the rope and tie him."

What's happening? Why did Father bring these people here?

Catherine did not want to challenge Alter. He would only tell his mother she encouraged the dog to attack him and that is why he tied it up. Zophia would then accuse Catherine of causing strife in the home. Or her father would say, "it's just a dog Catherine. He will take him home eventually."

Of course, she wanted to leave this place but not because that is what Zophia wanted. She was tired of taking orders from a spoiled brat like Alter or a drunk like Marcin. What kind of father would choose another woman and her family over his own daughter?

Catherine would leave when she decided to. It would be on her terms. When she was ready. *Soon Józef will be back and together we will pursue our dreams.*

She left Alter standing there and headed back to the house to see if Zophia needed help with dinner. Could she find a common ground? She at least had to try, until she could figure out what to do about the disaster her life had become.

As Catherine entered the house, she was reminded of how much she missed her mother's cooking. The kitchen was filled with unpleasant odors of fried onions, cabbage, and fermenting sauerkraut.

Zophia's hands worked quickly as she peeled the pile of potatoes which she then placed in a pot of water. She hummed a tune Catherine was not familiar with and did not acknowledge Catherine after she entered the house.

Catherine noticed a pile of beets for borsch that needed to be tended to and without being told, she prepared the vegetables.

"Do you ever miss living in the Shtetl? Do you have family there? I heard your husband died in the war."

"Yes, I do miss cooking in my husband's family bakery. But once I told them I met your father, they banned me from working there."

Catherine could hear the passion in her voice.

"Gone now is my livelihood! Well, I don't need them. I have John to care for me and my three boys. This orchard will provide for us. We will sell its bounty in their market and these potatoes will help to make good vodka to sell."

If only I had told Mother and Father I wanted to find a husband and live on this orchard. Then maybe none of this would have happened…but God knows I will not stay here now. I will follow my dream of being an artist, and not tend to chickens, cows, and apples for the rest of my life, with Zophia and her sons lording their power over me.

"Well, I know the apples sell well at the market," Catherine said as she handed Zophia the bowl of beets and watched her dump them into the pot of boiling water to cook down.

Tonight, after dinner I'll write to Filip and Antonio to tell them about Father's new family and how much I miss them. And I'll also tell them they made the right choice.

Chapter

13

One morning a week later, as Catherine was getting dressed, she overheard Zophia talking with her father.

"Why is it Catherine can go to the city all day, while I stay here to do all of this work alone. She needs to be here. Does Marcin really need her there?"

Catherine did not want to cook and clean for Zophia and her boys. They were a menace to be around. Always chasing the geese and lying in the hay instead of cleaning the stalls, and they still hadn't stacked the wood her father chopped. During the harvest they complained about having to do work with Gentiles. Alter took Catherine's bicycle without asking and bent the rim when he rode it into the side of the barn chasing the geese. Zophia was angry at the geese—at the geese!—for annoying her son and that evening she vowed to make roast goose for Hanukkah.

It's a madhouse here, Catherine wrote in her next letter to Filip. *You have to help me get away, or I'll go mad, too.*

By the third month of Zophia's "rule"—for she quickly came to rule over all things pertaining to the house and to John—Catherine noticed her father had gained weight. One morning when he tried to object to another serving of Zophia's freshly made loaf of apple kuchen, she regaled him and pushed another big sliver onto his plate.

"Love and bread make the cheeks red."

In December, Zophia was busy making breads and desserts to sell to the villagers for their Christmas Eve feasts. One of their favorite breads was *chałka*, a soft, braided loaf of sweetened bread with raisins and other dried fruits sprinkled with poppy seeds. She sent Alter and Yair to the nearby villages where the sweet-smelling bread sold quickly. They also sold apples and herbs from the garden. The villagers were all too happy to buy from or barter with Zophia's boys, so they did not need to make the long, cold trip to the city market.

"Look Madra, one man even traded with us for some grape juice."

"Grape juice? Let me see."

"They called it 'vish-noof-ka.'"

Zophia took the cork out, smelled the bottle and wrinkled her nose. "This is not grape juice, it's a liqueur." She looked at Alter. "You didn't drink this, did you?"

Yair did not answer.

Alter cleared his throat. "No, of course not."

Catherine knew Zophia believed anything they said.

On a cold ride to the city one early January morning, Marcin's frustration with John reached a boiling point.

"For years—*years*—I've tried to tell your father to sell our goods to the villages instead of just taking them to market, but he wouldn't listen. Yet, he lets *her* do it." His voice had an angry bite.

Catherine listened to his rant and nodded in agreement.

"I told Eva when we move to the city, I'll buy one of those automobiles and we can drive to visit her family anytime. Now that I'll have more money...."

She stopped listening as they passed the road to Józef's village, and her heart felt heavy.

My sketchbook is gone. What if I forget what Józef looked like? How could I have been so careless?

She thought about the last time she saw Tomasz outside of the blacksmith shop and asked him if he heard anything from Józef.

"No, I am afraid not. No letter. Nothing." His face was grim. *"I don't believe he will ever return. When I learned military actions with the Soviets had ceased in October near Warsaw and a peace treaty was signed, I was hopeful. But, here we are at the end of December . . ."* His voice trailed off, leaving all the terrible possibilities hanging in the air.

Then he added, *"His poor mother is hysterical at times, wishing she could give her son's body a proper burial. More likely, he was thrown in a ditch or mass grave somewhere."*

When the wagon was parked in front of the office, Marcin did not move.

Catherine sat staring. Tears stood in her eyes, and she couldn't speak.

"Go ahead inside," Marcin insisted. She waited for him to say, ". . . and start work." Instead, he said, ". . . and get warm. I need to go to the post office. Who knows," he offered, trying to bring a little brightness, "maybe there will be another letter from across the Atlantic."

As she took off her coat and settled at her desk, staring at the piles of ledgers, she hardly dared to hope. She needed something to keep this guttering candle of her dreams . . . her life . . . alive. It felt as if the flame of her spirit was almost out.

She thought about the last letter from Filip, which was two months before. He had written to tell them his wife, Rose, was pregnant with their second child. Money was tight but he felt blessed to have the job at the paper mill. The work was hard, but it paid well. He also again mentioned Leonek, and this time he gave more details.

> *He is the man from the ship who helped me get work here. He's a hard worker and Catholic. I know he will take good care of you.*

> *There is nothing left for you in Poland, is there, Catherine? Father has a new family. And you'll be happy to learn, there is also an art school I've heard of at a college in a town called Canton.*

Where was Canton? He didn't say, but she imagined it was close to where he lived.

> *There are so many opportunities here in America. Say the word, and I will find a way to help you make the journey.*

She felt guilty for not writing back to him.

Marcin had been gone a long time. She looked out the window at the overcast sunless sky. Her hand throbbed from writing the small numbers on the ledger pages, but her hand never ached from drawing. She reached into her bag to get her sketchbook but stopped when she realized it wasn't there.

A church bell rang in the distance.

Maybe Filip is right. I should go to America. But to marry a man I don't know? What if Józef comes back and I'm gone?

109

A knot tightened in her throat. Few had come back from the front. And there was no word at all of him. She blocked from her mind the terrible images his father had created of a cold, lonely grave.

With hands folded tight, eyes closed, and a bowed head she whispered, "Dear God, please help me to decide what I should do."

The apple and plum trees were in full bloom when Catherine's father received a letter from Filip.

> *In her last letter, Catherine told me how uncertain she was about her future. Especially now that you found a new wife. I wrote back and told her about a man named Leonek who would be willing to marry her and bring her to America. He is a hard worker and a good Polish man. We have just learned there will be a new Catholic Church built. This place is booming. Catherine would have a good life here and I promise to protect her. Leonek can send the money to pay for her ticket. I have included a picture of him for you.*

John looked at the photograph. Leonek was clean shaven and wore a collared button-up shirt tucked into his pants. His light hair parted on the side and slicked back with no sideburns. He stood on the stoop of a porch in front of a gray house with white framed windows.

Filip also wrote to say his wife gave birth to their second child!

John knew what he had to do.

Not long after John mailed his answer to Filip, Catherine returned from a nine-hour day in a hard wooden chair. Her back ached but it was time for her to clean the horse stalls and milk the cow. As she walked toward the barn she could hear music being played. Not music to be enjoyed, but loud-out-of-tune-music from what sounded like an accordion but with a much higher pitch. This was followed by a screeching whistle. She entered the barn to find Alter, Yair, and Yehuda in the barn not doing chores but, as usual, playing around.

Alter sat on the milking stool and on his lap balanced a wooden instrument. It almost looked like a violin but instead of strings it had a wooded box with wood keys that Alter pushed as he turned a crank attached at the end of the apparatus.

Yehuda, the younger boy cradled a vessel flute. It was made from clay and shaped like a bird.

When Catherine walked in, they all stopped playing.

"Where did you get those things?"

Alter raked her with contempt as if it was none of her business. "If you must know, I walked to the nearby village and sold some apples and other things." He held up his instrument. "This is a hurdy-gurdy. A Ukraine family left it behind when they went to America and nobody at the village knew how to play it."

Catherine was suspicious. Villagers would be reluctant to trade instruments or toys for apples. "What other things?"

Alter rubbed his hand over the handle of the instrument. "Well, um, some Catholic things."

"Like what?"

"Pictures of the Virgin Mary, a statue . . ."

Yehuda continued to blow the flute while Yair tried to take it away.

Irritation flared. "You had no right to sell my mother's things."

"Why? Your father didn't want them. They reminded him of his first wife."

All the emotions Catherine buried since her father brought these strangers to the orchard poured out.

"His first wife? Those were *my* mother's things. You had no right to touch them, let alone sell them. What if I wanted them?"

He glared at her. "And what would you do with them? You don't have a home of your own. This is our home now. My mother said you're nothing but a poor farm girl who depends on her father to take care of her because she can't find a husband."

A range of emotions flooded through her. Filip and Antonio were gone. The grief from losing her mother and now Józef. Insecurity told her she didn't have a home anymore; this was Zophia's home. She was tired of being a slave to Marcin. She felt out of place; not appreciated or wanted.

But where would I go?

The boys ignored her and started to play with their instruments again. She walked away and kept walking, past the house, over the bridge that crossed the stream, and down the dirt road. The late afternoon sun casted a luminescent glow.

Zophia can get her own cow's milk. Let those boys do it.

111

Catherine wandered down the farm road with no plan in mind—only the plan to rid herself of the frustration. In a half hour, she found herself at Wiejska Road and she stared down the well-traveled dirt road to the river.

She imagined Józef walking toward her. He would take her in his arms and tell her everything was going to be all right. He would support her dream and she would support his. Instead, all she saw was a flock of birds in a blue, cloudless sky.

Consumed with sadness, she sat down in the field of corn poppies, the place where Józef had given her the necklace and told her to turn around as he fastened it, his breath caressing her skin. She could still feel his lips as he softly kissed the back of her neck.

She stared down the road she had just walked. It led to a village woman's life: cooking, cleaning, farm work, survival.

She picked a red corn poppy flower and held it between her thumb and fingers. In folklore, its vivid petals were a symbol of strength and resilience. She looked again down the road to Józef's village and thought about the river—strong and untamed like the people who lived there. If Józef was home he would have come found her. *There's no use going down that road. He's . . .*

Catherine's gaze turned toward the road to the city, a place of uncertainty and opportunity. The way to a school she badly wanted to attend, but oh, how Marcin controlled her and forced her to hide her dreams! She closed her eyes and imagined the flower in her hand as her mother's rosary... how in times of uncertainty the rosary and its prayers would comfort her mother. She made a sign of the cross and pulled the petals off as she recited the Our Father followed by a Hail Mary three times. She looked down, only the black center of the flower remained. With the warmth of the late afternoon sun on her face, she prayed.

Holy Mother, what path should I travel? Do I stay here, or do I go?

As she stood, a stork flew overhead, its white plumage and black wingtips soaring across the warm sky toward the city.

Eva had told her to fly from this place. Was this a sign from God in answer to her prayer?

On her walk home Catherine spotted her father at the far end of the orchard on a ladder against a tree. Seeing him alone reminded her of a better time. A memory of when her mother would be at home and her brothers would be in the barn. These thoughts encouraged her to go talk with him.

She looked up, shading her eyes from the setting sun. "Hello Father, how are the apples?"

John came down the ladder. She wanted him to wrap his arms around her and tell her everything in her uncertain life would turn out alright.

He seemed not to notice her distressed look at all.

"I have news. Here is a letter from your brother Filip. It contains a ticket to America. The war has damaged so much here, and it doesn't seem to be going away. I think it's best if you go to America and marry this man named Leonek. Filip believes he will be a good man to take care of you."

This was not what she expected to hear. Was this God answering her prayer about which path she should choose? Or was this somehow Zophia's doing, because she wanted John and the orchard to herself.

"Catherine, look at me."

"I can't marry someone I don't know. What if Józef survives somehow and comes back?"

"Catherine, I want you to have a future. You must let go of this idea Józef is coming for you." He paused. "You must accept he is dead."

Try as she might, she could not stop tears from sliding down her cheeks, and she wiped them away vigorously. *Face the truth, Catherine*, she told herself bitterly.

"Let me see the letter," she said, grabbing for it.

Inside the envelope was the ticket and a picture of Leonek. She scrutinized the picture. He had light hair, and his face was plain. There was nothing special about his eyes. He had a half-smile, so that was something. Would he be tall like Józef? She did not like men who were shorter than her. Could he be trusted? Can she trust Filip is looking to help her or would her marriage benefit him in some way? On the back of the picture was a message:

Dear Catherine, I will take good care of you. Come to America.

Everything had been decided. She had no choice but to leave. Her brother and father arranged everything. Just like her mother said they would.

Before she left, Catherine knew there was one last thing to do.

"Come in. Come in. I am so glad you decided to come and say goodbye. I have some things for you to take on your trip."

113

Catherine looked around at the large and well decorated room. Eva had a way of bringing nature from the outside in. Of all the people here in Poland, Catherine would miss her aunt the most.

"I have wrapped some biscuits with honey for you. I made some potato pancakes, too. Oh, and here is some cheese and of course apples."

Catherine felt her bag getting heavy.

"Where is Marcin?"

"He went to the city to take care of some business. Sorry you will miss seeing him." Her voice lowered. "Secretly, I think he will miss you, Catherine. That is why he cannot say goodbye."

The thought of Marcin caring about her felt strange. She would not miss his temper or domineering nature.

"So, Catherine, are you excited to be seeing your brothers again? To go and start a new life with your new husband? I am glad you will have a man to take care of you." She kept rambling on. "Make sure you write to me. And send me a picture from your wedding."

"I will. I will." Catherine glanced out the window to see the sun lower in the sky. Reluctantly, she asked Eva a question.

"Did Uncle say anything about a sketchbook he found?"

Eva looked away. "No, why do you ask?"

"No reason…it's just… Filip gave me an old ledger to draw in and now I can't find it."

Saying the words caused tears to well-up in her eyes. Her necklace was also missing. She was certain Zophia, or one of her boys had taken it but she had no proof. Maybe it was for the best if she had no memory of Józef.

"What did this ledger look like?"

"It has a soft, red leather cover and is about this big." Catherine held up her hands and outlined the shape of the book. "I always kept it in my bag, but it's gone." She inhaled a deep breath and let it out slowly. "I believe Uncle took it from me."

Eva looked preoccupied and said nothing.

Catherine picked-up her bag and gave Eva a hug. "I need to go. Good-bye Aunt Eva. I will miss you."

"Wait."

Eva walked over to a bureau and opened the top drawer. "I was looking for an envelope this morning when I saw this. After Marcin left, I was going to look at it more closely but that's when you knocked on the door."

Catherine could not believe her eyes.

"Is this what you were looking for?" Before Catherine answered she dropped her bag and ran over to Eva.

"Yes! Yes it is. Thank you. *Thank you.*"

When Eva handed her the book, Catherine flipped through the pages, relieved to see all the drawings were still there.

"Oh, Catherine," Eva fretted, "I'm so sorry. I didn't know Marcin had taken something so special from you."

Catherine confessed, "Aunt Eva, I thought I lost my dearest dream. Everything I cared about was gone."

"Remember, Catherine, people will always try to take your dreams away. They want us to be miserable like them. Don't let them. Guard your heart. You, too, have something that makes your soul sing. Without *this*," she took Catherine's hand and placed it over her heart, "you slowly die inside."

Catherine closed her eyes and squeezed Eva tight.

"Go to America and make me proud."

"I will, Aunt Eva. I will."

Chapter
14

Catherine had been several days at sea on a voyage to America. The moody ocean's dead calm was followed by endless choppy waves, and the salty air left a taste on her tongue she would never forget. She did not feel hungry since the journey began. The ship's crew forced everyone to suck on a piece of lemon to prevent scurvy. Was it seasickness or homesickness? Once again, Catherine was alone with her thoughts, and she tried not to think about the untamed sway of the boat.

Józef . . . what if he had returned?

She could not bear the thought. Although she was thankful to have her sketchbook back there was something else still missing—her necklace.

Catherine looked around. Exposed pipes and vents were everywhere. So many strange faces stared at her—not everyone on the ship was friendly or could speak Polish. Steerage passengers were prevented access to other decks by metal gates like caged animals. These barriers kept the classes apart like a ranked society. Only when the sun shone on the Atlantic and dried the deck space allotted for steerage passengers could they breathe the fresh air, while spotless-cabin passengers from their spacious deck looked down upon them with pity and dismay. As if it were a sport from the Middle Ages, the cabin passengers threw pennies and leftover meal scraps to the hopeless looking group traveling in steerage.

Forcing her mind away from these discomforts, Catherine let her thoughts wander back to the days before she left Poland and the lost necklace... How the small folded burlap square was gone from under the mattress. A thorough search of her dresser drawers revealed nothing. She thought again about what happened when she went to the main room of the house to confront Zophia . . .

"Catherine, dear, what's wrong? If you are going to be sick get outside." Zophia *turned her back to Catherine and stirred a pot on the stove.*

"I have lost something. Something I put under my mattress. Have you by chance seen it?"

"Why would you think I have it?"

"Because I have caught you in my room before."

"Well, I needed to wash the bedding. I don't want bugs in this house."

"What did you do with it?" Catherine's head throbbed. *"Just give it back to me. I promise, I won't be mad at you."*

Zophia ignored her and walked past to get a bowl from the shelf. With an ingenuous smile replied, *"Catherine, I want you to understand I would never touch any of your things. And I don't appreciate your accusations."* *She scratched her nose.* *"If you will excuse me, I have work to do."*

Thinking of it made her ill. Had Zophia or her boys sold it like a crate of apples?

Maybe it's for the best. Józef was gone forever, and now the necklace. At least I have my sketchbook back. She whispered to herself, *"Thank you, Aunt Eva."*

The ship was overcrowded, and many days there were few available benches to sit on. One morning, she found an empty place next to an older man whose chin rested on his chest. His grayed hair protruded from under his cap. He looked dirty and seemed to be napping. Even though the ship was sectioned to prevent men and women from cohabitating, men wandered and came to the women's area of steerage. Catherine noticed many of the crew members turned their heads when this happened. Steerage was a dark and dangerous place for women and girls, especially at night.

All at once, she felt something on her knee. Looking down, she saw a grimy, blue-veined hand with bony knuckles and fingernails that were cracked and dirty. The lips of the man beside her spread into a smile revealing brown and yellow teeth.

"I see you are lonely on this ship. I can protect you. Poles are not well liked here."

She pushed his hand away. "I will be fine. Please leave or I'll tell the crewman who just came in the room."

The man immediately stood up to leave, not knowing she lied.

In that moment, she realized to make it through this journey she would need to find a friend.

Halfway through the voyage they sailed into a storm, with waves that began to batter the ship. The crew locked the door to the deck area and steerage passengers were forced to stay indoors, which made it feel even more cramped than usual. The closed door did not keep the water from coming inside and the crew member assigned below deck could not mop it fast enough. Eventually he gave up and the growing puddle of water inched its way toward the sleeping quarters.

The next day Catherine met a Ukrainian woman named Viktoriya who spoke Polish. They shared things about their families and prayed together. Catherine learned Viktoriya's husband was already in America and worked at a pencil factory in New York City.

"Why do you go to America?"

"Because of the war between Poland and Ukraine. There is nothing left for me. My mother died and my father remarried. My brothers live in America, and they wanted me to come, too."

Later, she re-read the letters from Filip and Leonek to give herself hope.

I have found a good man to take care of you. He is strong and handsome like me. Pyrites is a boom town and things are different for women in America. Leonek promised to make her happy and wanted to help her attend art school in nearby Canton. You will like it here, I promise.

One day while Viktoriya rested, Catherine took her shoulder bag and went to the woman's dining hall where the scent of lentil soup and boiled fish lingered. She liked to study the paper chart on the wall that showed the ship's location at sea. It gave her hope this journey would end soon.

The boy who would not stop crying and his mother entered the dining hall. Catherine looked at the despondent woman's face who tried to encourage him to drink some water. Once again, he started to sob. The men at a nearby table who were playing cards shouted at the boy, which only made him and his mother more upset.

What would make this boy stop crying? He needs something . . . but what?

The thought of the clay bird Yair insisted she take with her as she stood by the wagon and waited for her father crossed her mind. How the bright sunrise peaked through the clouds and cast a luminescent glow of a male figure running toward her…

"Catherine! Catherine!" His arms waved frantically.

Józef? Could it be? No. It was Yair.

"Catherine, I'm so glad you didn't leave yet." He opened his hand to reveal the flute shaped like a bird. *"Here. I wanted you to have this."*

He forced the clay bird into her hands. As he did he explained, *"I thought about what you said to my brother, Alter. How he should not sell things that don't belong to him. I wanted to give this to you before you left. Here, take it. Hurry, before my brother sees."*

"I don't understand. . . . Why are you?"

"Yair!"

Zophia stood in the doorway with her hands planted firmly on her hips.

"Where is the water? I need it now!"

"Yes, Madre, I will be right there."

"Enjoy your new life, Catherine." He then said something in Yiddish.

"What did you say?"

"Upon you be peace."

He kissed her hand.

She reached into her bag and searched for the clay bird she wanted to throw into the stream but something inside told her to keep it. Could this boy be the reason?

Maybe if I give him the toy to play with he would stop crying.

As she held the clay bird, Catherine watched as a group of men passed by a table of young women and gawked at them. Fortunately, they ignored Catherine as they walked past her and approached the door to the stairway up to the ship's deck. When the first man opened the door sunshine flooded the room, and a reflection caught her eye inside the clay bird. She poked her finger through the small hole and felt something. A chain? Her heart started to pound like a drum in her ear.

Could it be?

She fled to the sleeping area, climbed into a top bunk, and faced the wall. She turned the clay bird upside down and out fell her necklace! She closed her eyes and squeezed it in her hand.

Oh Józef, Józef, I did not lose it. I prayed to find it.

A tap on the shoulder followed by a question in a different language startled her. Catherine did not turn around but nodded her head. Her response seemed to satisfy, and whoever it was climbed back down.

Now what do I do with it? I can't wear it. I will never lose this again.

She sat up and looked through her bag for something to wrap it in and found a piece of wax paper leftover from a biscuit Eva had given her for the trip. Quickly she wrapped the necklace in it, removed her shoe and stuck the folded paper as far as she could inside the toe.

For the first time in over a week, she smiled. A bright, joyful smile. She saw the sun as it shined through the porthole windows. Her heart filled with happiness.

I must go get some fresh air!

The smell of beef tea filled the dining area which meant dinner would be available soon. On her way to the upstairs deck, she stopped and handed the bird to the mother in the dining hall, who sat with the boy on her lap. The woman looked confused, but Catherine insisted as she wrapped the woman's hand around it while pointing to the boy.

The woman smiled, which to Catherine meant *thank you.*

Upstairs the deck was crowded but it would soon empty like cattle at meals by the ring of a dinner bell. Catherine looked around at the people on the deck, some wrapped in the scratchy gray wool blankets as they awaited the return of a life the ship had drained from them. Half of the space was occupied by machinery, ventilators, and other apparatus. She found a spot where she could sit and look out at the open water.

The scene inspired her to sketch. The vastness of the ocean framed by the rusted railing. She was so caught-up in her artistic world when a crewmember approached her.

"What have you got there?"

Startled by his voice she quickly shut her book and looked up.

The smell of a hangover on his breath. His teeth yellowed from tobacco.

"I like to draw and took out my sketchbook." She looked around at the few passengers who remained after the dinner bell rang. They were all men.

"I'm not sure if drawing books are allowed. I may need to take it from you. Unless you can convince me to let you keep it." His eyes seemed filled with lust and ran up and down her body.

Why did I come up here alone? I should have woken Viktoriya to come with me.

"I'm not doing anything wrong. I'm an artist. That's why I am on this ship going to America." She smoothed her skirt and stood up to leave.

A lump formed in her throat. "If you will excuse me my husband is expecting me. I have been gone too long."

He grabbed her arm. "Not so fast. I have not seen you with any man. You are always alone. Are you one of those Polish tramps? What's his name?"

"That's because he's always sick." She jerked her arm away, gathered her skirt and ran toward the stairway back down to the belly of ship. It had been nine days, surely they must be close to America. Right then she vowed not to leave Viktoriya's side again.

One morning as daybreak shone through the porthole window, the ship slowed. A deep rumble awakened Catherine and it proceeded to get louder and louder.

Men from the cabin next door stormed through and several of the women who spoke Polish shouted.

"We are here! We are here! We have arrived."

Cheers echoed from the deck above.

Viktoriya grabbed Catherine's hand, her face no longer pale. "The statue, they see the statue!"

An older woman fell to her knees and made the sign of the cross. Others started to cry.

"Hurry Catherine, grab your bag. Let's get to the deck. We have made it to America!"

Outside the September air warmed their faces. The ship deck was crowded as Viktoriya grabbed Catherine's hand and led her to a spot near the railing.

"Look Catherine, there it is! The statue!"

Catherine stared at the huge metal sculpture of a woman perched high on a pedestal. At her feet, the broken chains of slavery. She wore a dress with many folds. Her hand extended with the torch of freedom. A book cradled in the other arm. Her crown magnificent.

People started to sing and kiss each other but there was no room to dance.

After the boat stopped Catherine watched as well-dressed people from the upper decks disembarked from the ship down a wooden ramp with a handrail of rope. She observed men in uniform help the passengers carry their trunks as they made their way down a long dock towards the city.

As the steerage passengers disembarked there was no one to help them with their belongings. They were motioned by the men in uniform through a gate toward another boat with open sides. Catherine turned to Viktoriya. "Why are we getting onto another boat?"

"We must take a boat to Ellis Island. That is where my husband will wait for me. Then we will be allowed into America. Will your brother meet you there, as well?"

"No, he will meet me at the train station."

"What if you do not pass the inspection to get into America?"

"I don't understand. We are in America."

"Just stay with me. I will help you to understand."

Excited cries filled the air as Catherine and Viktoriya exited the ship. A tall man in a policeman's uniform directed them to go a certain way. On the dock, they passed a man who was disheveled and dirty standing by some wooden barrels as he smoked a cigarette. He stared at Catherine and Viktoriya as he muttered, "Dumb Pollacks."

Viktoriya leaned and whispered into Catherine's ear. "Pay him no attention."

Suddenly the line turned into a group and Catherine felt confused about which way to go. A woman with a blue and white star on her jacket motioned for Catherine and Viktoriya to come towards her. She carried with her a stack of small papers and proceeded to pin one onto their shirts and did not smile. Each paper had a number on it. Catherine did not understand what the woman said and looked at Viktoriya who seemed just as perplexed.

"Maybe the number is the ship number." Catherine said as they were motioned toward another boat with open walls. She remembered Antonio told her in a letter to smile and just do what the people in uniform asked. *Do not draw un-needed attention to yourself and you will be just fine.*

Ahead a man in uniform grabbed and pushed a male passenger who tried to walk past the entrance to the ferry. On the boat most of the seats were taken. Catherine found a spot to stand near the railing and stared at the city skyline. A warm breeze filled the air with the body odor of people around her. Once again she spotted the Statue of Liberty.

"Look Viktoriya, there is the statue again." The bigness of what the statue represented overwhelmed Catherine. She was in America.

"Viktoriya?" Catherine turned around and once again the boat crowded. She had lost sight of her friend.

The fear on the boat became evident as it made its way toward a building across the harbor on an island. Would they be allowed to enter America? Some on the boat referred to Ellis Island as the 'Island of Tears' because if the doctors find you sick they will send you back and you would not enter America.

Catherine did not recognize the language, only the tone of the commanding voice. Body language of fingers pointing and hands motioning to keep walking. She scanned the crowd for Viktoriya, or at least a familiar face from the ship. There were black kerchiefs, white kerchiefs, and men with wool caps. Some of the women carried babies in baskets. Like ants they marched into a red brick building. The ground still swayed like waves beneath her feet.

Once inside the building the shrill shouts of a dozen different languages assaulted her ears. There were large piles of baggage. Some of the passengers did not want to leave their belongings and shook their heads but the men insisted they comply. Men dressed like soldiers opened each bag and trunk to inspect it. Catherine watched as one of them inspected her bag. Suddenly she felt a tap on her shoulder and when she turned around a man in uniform pointed at her purse. She took it off and gave it to him. He searched and found nothing he wanted and handed it back to her. Catherine thankful her ledger was tucked safely inside the secret compartment and the necklace in the toe of her shoe.

Catherine felt tired and hungry. Now she was directed up a steep winding staircase where men in long white coats stood at the top of the stairs and watched over the group. At the top, children were taken from their mothers' arms and made to walk. Catherine thought about her brothers who also went through this maze to be inspected like animals or criminals. As she stood in line Catherine looked up and saw a huge American Flag hanging from a walkway above that encircled the massive room.

A man in a suit stopped Catherine. He studied her face, ran his gloved fingers through her hair, and lifted her chin as he looked at her neck. He reached for her hands and examined her palms. Some of the suited men drew a symbol with chalk on the front shoulder of a few people, but the man with the chalk did not write on her.

A man in line behind Catherine tapped her on the shoulder.

"Do you speak Polish?"

She turned around and was scared to answer him. His light brown hair neatly combed and his voice pleasant.

"My name is Henryk. What is yours?"

"Catherine."

"I am here to bring my sister back to Poland. She wrote to tell me America is hard. Like many people from my village, she does not like the culture here. Not too many speak our language."

The line kept moving as he talked.

"If you are a single woman, you will be looked down upon. There is no work for women, only men. If women do find work it's to cook and clean for others. But there would be something worse than this."

She turned to look at him. "What?"

"As Poles, we are at the bottom of the pecking order. We are considered pigs in a pen. Dirty and smelly. Single women are sometimes forced to be prostitutes just to survive."

Henryk's story weighed on Catherine's confidence. Once again, an uncertain future loomed. What if the man her brother had chosen for her didn't want her? She couldn't be a burden on her brother. How would she survive?

She shook off the man's crude and frightening statement.

Finally, she was near the end of the line. Ahead was a man seated on a high stool with a large open ledger on the desk in front of him. Another man stood at his side. Catherine watched as some of the women who traveled alone were detained and taken aside. As she readied to approach the bench Henryk spoke one last time. "My sister was weak. I hope you are stronger."

Both men motioned for her to come forward. Her heart pounded and she proceeded to the desk with a black walnut top the same height as her chest. The man seated had large bushy eyebrows and she watched as he flipped the pages on the ledger in front of him. Catherine recognized the large sheet of paper from when she boarded the ship in Amsterdam where a man asked her questions and wrote her answers. He looked up at the number pinned to her shirt and Catherine watched as his crooked, ink-stained finger stopped at a place on the paper. Catherine felt a huge relief when the other man, who was an interpreter, smiled at her and said hello in Polish.

"Is your name Catherine Soból?"

She nodded.

"Where were you born?"

"Village of Pomorskie, in Poland."

"What is your birthday?"

"June 7, 1902."

"Where are you going?"

"To see my brother." She was not sure how to say the name of the place she would be going and instead showed the interpreter the address on Filip's letter. He then offered it to the man with the big papers. The interpreter said, "You are going to *Pie-rah-tees*. Which is north, in New York."

The interpreter asked, "Do you have any money?"

She reached into her purse and showed the twenty-dollar bill Leonek had mailed to her. He told her she would need the money to show the immigration officers. Satisfied, the interpreter said, "Go down those stairs to buy a ticket for the train," and he pointed over the desk to her left.

"But I already have a train ticket."

He ignored her and motioned for the next person to come forward.

She turned around to say goodbye to Henryk, but he wasn't there.

At the bottom of the stairs were several booths and more lines. Men who wore round caps with a stiff flat circular top and a short visor stood behind caged windows in the wall. They each had on white collared shirts and black ties. Above them signs with foreign letters. She glanced over at a gate where people embraced on the other side. Loud voices interrupted her thought as a man approached and looked at Catherine's paper badge. He gestured for a woman who wore the familiar blue and white star on her jacket to come over. Catherine remembered this meant she spoke Polish.

"Where are you going?"

Catherine showed her the address on her brother's letter. "To Pyrites, north of New York"

"Do you have money?"

She nodded. But before Catherine could reach into her purse to retrieve her money the woman signaled for Catherine to follow her.

"We will exchange your money for American."

"Oh, I already have American money and a train ticket."

Satisfied, the woman walked Catherine outside to take a ferry to the train station. That is where Antonio would meet her.

How will he know how to find me? How does he know I am here?

The woman stopped to face Catherine and smiled.

"Everything will be good. Here's your ticket for the ferry to the Weehawken Terminal where you will get on the train." Despite the woman's soft voice Catherine's eyes watered from the thought of being alone.

"Let me see your train ticket."

The woman read to her what it said. "New York Central Railroad, West Shore Line to Albany, Syracuse, Richland, DeKalb Junction." She handed Catherine back the ticket. "Just look for someone with a blue star like mine and they will be able to help you get to your train platform. Wait over there for the ferry boat."

"Thank you."

While in line for the ferryboat she could feel the sweat from the afternoon sun trickle down her neck along her backbone. She set down her canvas bag and hoped the boat would come soon. A man and woman stood behind her and their familiar language soothed her.

"Brother, I am glad to be here in America with you. It has been quite a journey."

"Yes, but you are safe now. The war in Ukraine did much damage to our homeland."

"I know. Our brother Vasyklo couldn't come." The woman started to cry. "I feel guilt for leaving him. But he told me to go."

"There, there sister. You did nothing wrong. He would not have been able to enter America. He's crippled."

Her voice grew louder. "Crippled because he was forced to fight for our freedom."

The long-groaned blast of a boat's whistle followed by two short ones signaled the ferryboat had arrived. Passengers on the dock lifted their bags and pulled their children closer to them.

"I know sister, of course he will never be the same."

On the boat Catherine once again caught a glimpse of the Statue of Liberty and she made a sign of the cross.

Amen.

She had made it to America. Her fate in God's hands now.

At the railroad station Catherine searched the strange faces for Antonio.

How would he find me in this crowd?

The smell of coal smoke filled the air along with the familiar sound of the steam engine as it pulled away from the platform.

She looked for a person with the common blue and white star. The clock high above her on the steel pole read 10:21. Her train would leave in about an hour. But which train? Which platform?

Her stomach growled and she remembered the yellow piece of fruit given to her at Ellis Island. They called it a ba-nan-na. Catherine sat on a nearby bench shaded from the covered platform and stared at the odd shaped piece of food. She watched as others peeled and ate the white inside. She did the same and it tasted good.

A woman passed with a light pink cotton short sleeved one-piece dress with a low waistline of appliqued fabric flowers. Another wore a golden cotton brimless hat that covered her forehead just above the eyebrows. Clean-shaven men sported white straw hats with a black sash around the top of a large brim, just like in the movie she saw with Józef. Catherine's pale white cotton button-up shirt and black skirt felt so out of place. She removed her kerchief and wiped her face. She hadn't bathed in days.

Suddenly she spotted Antonio and ran towards him.

They embraced and Catherine started to cry. "I didn't think you would find me! How did you know I was here?"

"The newspapers here tell of ship arrival dates and times. I read your ship would come at six o'clock in the morning and I took the nine o'clock ferry here from the city. Every time a ferry boat would pull-in I would look for you. There would be so many people! I decided to come over to the train platform and there you were!"

He stood back. "Let me look at you." He handed her a paper bag. "I brought you some food and a change of clothes. A woman in the apartment where I live shopped for me. Everything you need is in there." He reached into the bottom of his cloth sack. "She even gave me a pair of shoes for you." He looked down at her feet and set one next to her shoe with the necklace. "Here, try one on. If they fit, I could get rid of your old ones. They look worn."

Catherine looked around. "But I want to change my clothes first. Where can I change?"

"Over there is a woman's bathroom at the end of the building. Let's go get you freshened up and then we can talk."

After she changed they sat on a bench near the platform where the New York Central West Shore train waited to load passengers.

"That's the train you will take to see Filip."

As Catherine ate Antonio showed her a telegram he received from Marcin.

"He wanted me to remind you to not be distracted in America with your silly sketches. You will be a married woman with no time to draw, only to take care of your husband."

Here she was, thousands of miles away from Marcin and he still wanted to control her.

"I know, but my new husband promised to help me become an artist. Filip talked about an art school in a town not far from him. I can be a wife and an artist."

Catherine reached into her bag and handed Antonio the red leather book with her drawings hopeful he would encourage her.

"Catherine, I know you can draw, remember the picture you mailed me of mother? Now there are cameras that can take pictures. There is no need for you to become an artist."

He pushed the book back toward her. "Life isn't about dreams, it's about security. You need a man to take care of you."

She wanted to tell Antonio about Józef and the necklace but instead sat quietly like a scolded child.

"Catherine, it will be good to have a man who can protect you."

"But I have read about the women's rights movement in America. How women can earn their own living and not depend on a man to take care of them." She turned sideways on the bench to face Antonio.

"I could stay in New York City with you and go to art school."

"Catherine don't be a fool. This city is no place for a young, country woman like you. Women who are not married are looked down upon and they end up on the streets."

"*All aboard!*" A man shouted.

Antonio smiled at Catherine. "It's time for you to go."

Antonio embraced Catherine, kissed her cheek, and looked her in the eyes.

"I will telephone Filip and tell him you are on your way."

"Filip has a telephone?"

"No, but one of the local hotels he frequents does and they will give him the message."

Why would Filip go to a hotel?

"Thank you for the clothes Antonio, and the food. I feel so much better."

"Catherine, like you I came to America for a better life. We cannot go back to Poland. Be a good wife to Leonek and you will be fine." He smiled. "America will be your new home. Don't think about the past, it will only confuse you."

"ALLLL ABOOOAAARD! New York Central West Shore to Albany, Syracuse, and points North."

Catherine boarded the train, found a seat near the window, and waved at Antonio as the train slowly pulled away.

Chapter

15

Her last train ride from Kraków to Rotterdam had exposed her to the horrors of war with scenes of burnt forests, killing fields of trenches and barbed wire followed by grassy fields dotted with wooden crosses. Here the trees were green, and the grassy fields dotted with dairy cows. There were no destroyed bridges or cities.

A man near the front of the car lit a cigar, and as the cloud of smoke drifted over her she was reminded of Marcin once again.

All of this was strange. Intimidating. But she squared her shoulders.

I have done the right thing, coming to America.

For most of the trip people were quiet and didn't talk much. Across from her a young man with a moustache and stubble from a few days' growth slept and clutched his suitcase.

Quietly, she opened her shoulder bag to the secret pocket, pulled out the familiar soft red leather ledger, and flipped through the pages of memories. Her memories of home and the new ones discovered on her journey. Towns in Germany destroyed by war. The ship with its frayed ropes, rusted rails, and the trailing smoke of the steamer. The sketch of an older woman in the dining area of the ship at breakfast one morning.

The train slowed, and Catherine looked out the window as it approached a trestle over a rocky stream. The green trees now festive with fall colors, enhanced by the early afternoon sunrays. The hours drifted by slowly and once again it felt strange to Catherine to not know where she was headed.

I will find someone who can help me. God has brought me this far.

She remembered Antonio told her the train would stop two times and her stop would be the third in a city called Syracuse. That is where she would change trains and take another train to DeKalb Junction.

Syracuse was a city of lights illuminated from the late afternoon shadows of a setting sun. The train traveled down the center of the street like a trolley. On each side of the train were buildings and sidewalks. Automobiles quickly moved to the side or turned down one of the intersecting streets. The train slowed to a crawl and Catherine noticed a water canal in the middle of the city that went between two large buildings. A footbridge wide enough for a trolley and car to pass spanned the canal. At the top of one building was a clock tower. A large monument displayed soldiers from a war just ended. There was something about this city that reminded her of home.

At the train station everyone disembarked. Catherine waited to be the last one off the train. The outside air felt cool, and she stopped and smiled at the train conductor in his brass buttoned uniform with a bow tie and brimmed cap with numbers across the top. Like most conductors in America, he probably did not speak Polish, but she hoped he would understand a smile. He stood straight and his face clean-shaven. Catherine prayed he would be in a good mood.

"Hello, could you tell me how to get to my next train?" She held her ticket out and traced her finger over the words. He looked down at her ticket and pointed at another train across the tracks beyond the building, its engine quiet with two passenger cars attached.

As she walked toward the locomotive on the other side of the tracks the smell of coal smoke once again filled the air followed by the huge SNORT of an engine starting. Catherine did her best to not draw any attention to the fact she was a single girl without a travel partner. She wondered how much longer before she would see Filip. She looked around for someone with a kerchief to talk with but most of the women here wore hats or walked with a man. She sat on a bench where someone had left a magazine. Inside were pictures of women with raised hemlines above their knees, short hair, and made-up eyes with bright red lips.

A conductor exited the train and set down a wooden stepstool. He walked to the front of the train to talk with a couple of men who stood by the engine as they smoked cigarettes. Catherine decided to get out her sketchbook as she watched them talk and laugh. The sketch helped her to forget about all she had experienced—a moment without worries or fear.

Once on the train the busyness of the streets disappeared and quickly turned into farmland and pastures of grazing cows followed by swamplands in the distance. The train made several stops where people would get off and each time she would ask the conductor if this was her stop to which he would shake his head. Most times the land was flat but soon the train would struggle to climb an incline. For miles there were areas of dense trees where the only clearing was the railroad tracks that carved through the thick forest. Darkness came and soon the bright dots from scattered homes disappeared.

The metallic squeal of the train's brakes awakened Catherine. Her neck stiff as she stood to stretch her legs. The conductor walked through the car to rouse passengers who were still asleep.

Catherine quickly grabbed her ticket and held it up to the conductor.

"Is this my stop?"

He nodded.

Outside the platform was barely lit and her heart pounded as she searched for Filip. The steam from the train hissed and created a fog of smoke.

"*Catherine!*" His voice soothed her anxieties.

As they embraced a large rush of relief left her lungs.

"Here, let me carry your bag. How are you? You must be tired. Rose has saved some soup and bread for you."

Catherine followed him, not knowing where they were headed.

Before she could ask, they stopped in front of an automobile. He put her bag in the backseat.

"Is this yours?" Catherine could not believe Filip had an automobile. She laughed. "If only uncle could see you now!"

Filip opened the door for her. The seats were smooth black leather. She could barely contain herself as Filip walked around the front of the car. The headlamps from the front of the automobile revealed his blue pants held up with a black belt. He bent over and cranked the engine.

The ride to Filip's house on the dirt road was bumpy and the rumble of the engine loud. The headlamps from the car did little to pierce the darkness. Filip managed to shout loud enough for Catherine to hear the word Leonek.

He shifted the bar on the steering wheel and the engine quieted as he turned a corner. "Where is Leonek? Is he at your house?"

"He will be over tomorrow after work."

Why would he not want to meet me today? I am going to be his wife and I've come all this way.

The children were asleep when Catherine arrived. Rose heated the soup while Filip and Catherine talked about all that had happened since they last saw each other. In the kitchen area was a large black stove with a silver design on each door. It looked nothing like the stove from back home. A long table with many chairs filled the room. On one wall was a stand-alone oak bureau of cupboard doors with large metal hinges. Later she would learn this was called an icebox. Several closed doors lined the wall on the opposite side. Near the entrance was a sitting area with a couch and several soft chairs. A wooden train with a string and some colored blocks were strewn on the floor. Rose walked over to pick them up and placed them in a basket near the couch.

Catherine felt a small thrill of happiness at being with Filip again.

Rose took a seat across the table from Catherine. Her intense brown eyes the color of whiskey.

"I know your father went through a lot. He was fortunate to have Zophia and her boys to help take care of the orchard. Especially since Filip and Antonio left."

Catherine finished the last of her soup. *Was she defending Zophia?*

"Anyhow, I must get some rest. Those children will be up at the crack of dawn."

"I will be in soon." Filip held up his glass. "Give me some more tea, would you?"

"Yes, but you know you have to be at the Mill by seven." Catherine watched as Rose opened a cupboard door, took out a corked brown bottle and poured some in his glass. "It can be a long week with the overtime. And we need the money. I don't want you late to work."

"It's only half-past eleven. I will get plenty of rest."

"Thank you for the soup Rose. It was delicious."

"We are glad you are here Catherine. Your brother told me how unhappy you were in Poland. I hope you will like America, but it can be hard for a poor peasant girl like you." A crafty smile highlighted her rosy cheeks.

After Rose left, Catherine asked, "What kind of tea do you drink?"

"It's a special tea with a special ingredient. It helps me to relax."

"Oh, I see." Catherine reached into her bag and handed Filip the money left over from her trip. He eagerly took it.

"Why did Leonek not come to the train station to meet me? Or come here?"

"He had some business to take care of." Filip swished the tea in his glass and took a swig. "Don't worry, you will meet him tomorrow."

"Tell me more about him. Where does he live?"

"He lives in town at a boarding house with other men who are boarders. He used to be a boarder here but… ah well, that's another story. But once you are married, he will provide you with your own home."

"Before you go to bed, I wanted to show you some of my drawings." She reached into her bag. "Would you like to see them? I am hopeful Leonek will appreciate my art."

"Ha! You still have that old ledger I found for you in the barn."

"Yes." She opened the book past the pictures of Józef. "Take a look."

As Filip flipped through the pages, she shared with him the tales from her journey. There was so much to tell him, and her words would not stop.

Suddenly a door opened, and Rose stuck her head out. "Filip! Do you know what time it is? You must come into bed."

Filip stood and yawned as he arched his back and stretched his arms toward the ceiling. "Yes, I'm coming to bed."

As Catherine laid on the couch, a door opened and shut on the other side of the wall followed by footsteps going upstairs.

Must be a boarder.

She rolled over and stared at the darkness and realized for the first time in weeks there was no movement under her feet.

Chapter
16

Catherine was up before dawn and walked outside onto the porch before anyone else was awake. The early morning air was damp and cool, and a haze floated over the river like smoke from a doused fire. The smell of cooked cabbage lingered outside and when she first smelled it last night, she thought it was from Rose's cooking, but here it was again.

As she looked down the river at the massive paper mill a relentless hum and thump of machinery echoed in the distance. A round smokestack made of bricks towered high into the air with a constant flow of pale, white steam. On the other side of the river the town was overridden with small cookie-cutter houses shadowed by larger square shaped three-story buildings. Every available space looked taken.

Suddenly a high-pitched steam whistle screamed throughout the town. A few of the boarders from upstairs came running outside and down the drive toward a steel bridge that spanned a narrow part of the river.

Beside her, Filip hurried out the door and down the steps.

"'Bye, Catherine."

She watched as his form got smaller and he disappeared into the town.

Back inside, Catherine found Rose pouring coffee into two cups, with one child on her hip while the other child pulled a wooden toy train around the kitchen floor.

"Oh good, there you are," said Rose. "We have much work to do. Soon the boarders will be here for a morning meal after their shift." She set a cup on the table. "But first, coffee."

For a moment, she thought of the grinding life she experienced in Poland. Hadn't she come here in pursuit of her dream wanting to escape that grueling life?

The baby girl on Rose's lap looked at Catherine with her deep brown eyes as Catherine sipped from the steaming cup of coffee.

"This is Bertha. We wanted to give her an American name." Rose broke up small pieces of bread as she spoke, and Bertha put as many as she could in her mouth. "And this is John. . . . Filip insisted his first son be named after your father. Johnny, come over here and say hello to your Aunt Catherine."

The boy pulled a wooden train over and looked up at her. His blondish hair complimented his mouthful of white teeth when he smiled. "Hello, see my train? It goes Chooo-Choooo!" and he ran back around the table.

Rose's voice turned abrasive. "That's enough playing, Johnny. Up here to eat your breakfast."

Catherine took a sip of the bitter coffee as she pushed away from her uneasiness and discomfort. "How many boarders live upstairs?"

"Four. Leonek used to board here but he wasn't reliable to pay his rent, so I told him last spring he must leave. I needed boarders who paid. The farmer who owns this house expects his rent, and if I'm not paid then the money comes from us."

"But he has a job at the paper mill. Where did his money go?"

Rose shook her head as she set the baby down on the floor, took a bowl of dough rising and started to knead it at the counter. "Probably to one of those man places in town where they play cards. Who knows what else? Leonek finds trouble when he drinks. And believe me sometimes this town can be full of trouble."

Catherine watched Bertha crawl toward Rose. "Where would he get alcohol? Isn't it illegal?"

Rose ignored her comment.

"All's I know is I'm glad he doesn't live upstairs anymore." She added, "You do realize Leonek's much older than you, don't you?"

Not wanting to appear uninformed Catherine replied, "Filip told me he is a few years older." Her voice trailed off while she took in what she just learned.

"*Ha*! A few years? More like ten. Sounds like Filip, always stretching the truth." She placed the loaves in the oven. "Well, you're here now so it's water under the bridge, as they say here in America." She looked at the clock on the wall. "Could you tend to the children while I set the table? I expect the men boarders anytime for breakfast after their night shift and I need to go get something from the cellar. I'll be right back."

Rose took a key from her pocket and unlocked one of the doors on the wall.

Why would a door be locked with a key inside the house?

As Catherine sat on the floor and played with the children her inner doubts about Leonek appeared. Filip told her in his letters Leonek had a strong work ethic, and he would be a good man for her. He didn't mention anything about his drinking and not being able to pay his rent.

And what did Rose mean when she told me this town is full of trouble?

All day, Catherine saw Rose working like an ox, never stopping even when she sagged with fatigue. If she wasn't tending to the children, she was cooking. And if she wasn't cooking, she was cleaning or doing laundry in a huge tub outside. As for the rest of the chores, Rose was only too happy to tell Catherine what to do and how to do it—and when.

"You see that bushel of potatoes. They need to be peeled and cut up."

Several men came to the backdoor after the afternoon whistle blew, and Rose told them each to wait outside while she unlocked the cellar door, disappeared for a few minutes, then came back with something in a paper bag.

At dinnertime Rose said, "It's been over an hour since the whistle blew and they're still not home." Three of the boarders who lived upstairs already stopped by to get their dinner pails. "We might as well go ahead and eat without them."

The sound of heavy boots came from the porch along with a bellow of laughter. In walked Filip, followed by another man whose lit cigarette hung from his lips. He was shorter than Filip and wore pale blue, baggy overalls which made him look even more squat.

Catherine thought of a bull—one that looked like he desperately needed to wash—with stubby legs. She caught the smell of machine oil coming from his clothes.

Still, she coached herself, *he may be a good man, as Filip said.* She hoped so. Physically speaking, he was no Józef. More like an unpleasant figure from an old, Polish folktale.

Rose went to get two more plates. "It's about time. How long did you think I could keep dinner warm?"

"Quit your complaining, woman," Filip barked. "We're here now. You're lucky I came home at all."

This was not the brother Catherine remembered. What happened to him here in America to make him like this?

Filip guided the man over to the table, where Catherine had just finished her dinner.

"Catherine, this is Leonek. . . . Leonek, my sister Catherine."

Leonek's breathing was heavy.

Do I smell alcohol on his breath?

His icy blue eyes did not make eye contact as he took a drag from his cigarette. She noticed pockmarked cheeks as he blew out a cloud of smoke toward the ceiling.

After a moment, he studied her body up and down before finally looking her in the face. "So, I get to meet you in person. Filip advertised you quite a lot."

"She is a beauty, like I said, is she not?" Filip announced, smiling.

Leonek said nothing.

I remembered from the picture his hair was longer, but today his head is nearly shaved. Do I see a scar above his left eyebrow?

She stammered. "Yes, I have come a long way to meet you."

Filip filled two glasses with his specially made tea and handed one to Leonek. "*Nostrovia.* Here's to a new life for both of you."

Leonek nodded and they both tossed back the honey-colored liquid—tea kicked up with vodka.

"That's good *Samogon.*"

Catherine looked at Rose as she set bowls of chicken with gravy and carrots on the table.

"Leonek, why don't you take Catherine for a walk," said Filip. "Show her around town before it gets dark."

"What's wrong with being alone with her in the dark?" Leonek grinned, and Catherine caught sight of tobacco-stained teeth.

"Wait, Leonek, what about your dinner?" Rose objected. "I'm not going to keep it warm any longer."

"I'm not hungry. You can eat it."

Outside, the sun was sinking as they walked in silence across the bridge, which was barely wide enough for the automobiles that clamored across it all day. In the near distance, the streets of the town were lined with identical rows of houses. There were two larger buildings on one corner, which made the town look awkwardly unbalanced. Electric poles carried black lines above the roads, which were little more than rutted dirt tracks.

"Filip told me you are a hard worker and a good cook."

"I worked for my uncle in Plasźow, just outside of Kraków—not too far from the apple orchard we lived on."

She watched as a group of young boys chased each other up and down the streets. *Are there no farm chores in America?* She wondered. Certainly, there had to be. *How is it these boys have time to play?*

"I like apples."

She didn't know what to say to that. She thought about mentioning her drawing but thought better of it. Maybe Leonek was a man who appreciated art, but she had no indication of that. Not even a little.

They came to a four-way intersection and Leonek veered left down the main street. A throng of voices poured from the open door of the pool hall. Men stood outside and smoked as they walked by. Next to the pool hall was a store with wide, cement steps, where pumpkins and squash filled tin washtubs. A slightly torn and dingy bed sheet hung from the upper balcony.

"I live in a boarding house next to the Murray Hotel. It's called the Beehive. It has a large porch where we can sit and talk."

The noise from the paper mill had grown louder, and there was an acrid smell in the air.

Seeing Catherine's expression, Leonek said, "Living next to the paper mill takes a while to get used to. Eventually you don't hear or smell it."

She couldn't imagine getting used to this smell and tried to keep an unpleasant look off her face.

"Here we are. Let's sit over here." As they went up the steps, a scrawny man with a hard-bitten face stood just above them on the large open porch. He stared down at Catherine and said to Leonek, "Is this your ship bride? She doesn't look like much."

Leonek reached into his jacket pocket and took out a pack of Lucky Strike cigarettes. Tapping one out of the pack, he struck a match and lit the end of it.

"Now Stanislaw, is that any way to talk about Filip's sister?"

Catherine felt the man's eyes undressing her, so evident by his lustful grin. She folded her arms across her breast and forced herself to be polite. "Hello."

"Have you any idea what you're getting into with this one?" He nodded at Leonek. You're not the first woman he's been with." He proceeded down the stairs.

She was too flustered to counter his remark. Leonek had not *been with* her, nor would he be until and unless they were married.

"Shut up, Stanislaw. Is that any way to speak to a lady?"

"Oh, she's a lady?"

"I said shut up." Leonek turned to Catherine. "Don't mind him. He's a miserable soul, not happy to be here in America."

"Why?"

"He left behind a wife and three children in Poland. He wanted to bring them here, but instead . . ."

"Why doesn't he go back?"

Leonek took a long drag from the cigarette and flicked the ash.

"None of my business, but I hear he's got a bun in the oven with a young girl here in town. Anyhow, forget him. I figured we could get married next week. I told my boss and he agreed to give me and Filip a morning off."

Catherine nearly choked.

"So soon?" she said, when she got her breath back.

"You have a problem with me?"

"No, I just . . ." She didn't know what to say.

"Let's be honest. Filip said you have no prospects back in Poland and your lover was killed. I need a wife. You need to be here in America."

That was it in his mind? *A marriage of convenience?*

Catherine's heart was beating hard, and her stomach was turning.

What has Filip done? Does he think so little of me, to set me up for this?

Leonek plunked himself down on the cement steps.

"Sit," he said.

Instead of running, which she wanted to do, Catherine sat, feeling numb as he told her all about the mill town. How no one needed a car because everyone could walk to work, and the small stores here provided everything necessary to create a home.

"The hardware store sells cloth," he said, "which the women buy to make their own clothes."

Make clothes. On top of everything else? She thought of the shops back home, where she and Józef had seen the beautiful hats she wanted.

Dusk was settling around them.

"Well, it's getting late. I better take you back to the island."

"The island?"

"Yes, the bridge is the only access from town to the other side of the river. People call it an island."

Later as she laid on the sofa at bedtime, Catherine tossed and turned, her mind reaching back.

Samogon. Father talked about it. . . . When the villagers needed extra help they would invite people to a pomoch and serve Samogon. It's like the vodka made by the Jews, only stronger. Sometimes Filip would go and work in the villages until Father put a stop to it.

She lay facing the ceiling and thought about her conversation with Leonek.

He sounded so different in Filip's letters. But what choice did I have back in Poland? She thought of her miserable stepmother and her terrible, spoiled sons. *And what choice do I have now?*

She almost wanted to cry but forced herself not to.

You are here, in America. Make the best of it.

The house was dark and quiet and through the closed single pane window, she heard the familiar pounding and hiss of the paper mill. She wanted to feel something for Leonek, like the first time she met Józef... but this was an arranged marriage. It was not about love.

Once again, my life feels like a bad dream I have no control over.

She folded the thin pillow in half and pulled the blanket close to her chin.

Leonek didn't even ask me anything about myself. Nothing.

Chapter

17

The next few fall days were a balmy 72 degrees. Rose called it Indian Summer and said, "We must take advantage of this time before the coming freezing weather. Winter comes soon here." Despite the fact she had been up at dawn baking, taking care of children, Rose always looked so put together. Not a hair out of place.

"Today's laundry day and I'm glad it'll be warm outside so the clothes and sheets dry quickly." Rose changed Bertha's diaper and handed her to Catherine. "Why don't you take the children outside while I fill the washtub."

This was Rose's idea of a good life. Catherine winced. A warm breeze on washing day and bright sunlight in which to bathe the children.

"Why did Filip take the automobile today?" she asked. "I thought he walked to work. Leonek said no one needs to drive here."

"He and Leonek will drive to the Five-and-Ten in Canton to get some supplies after work. They also needed to stop at the Wallace farm and get us some chickens to take to Syracuse."

"Why would he need to take chickens to Syracuse?"

Rose seemed as though she had become comfortable around Catherine, as the next statement indicated.

"We put chickens in a wooden crate for them to use as a decoy when they take liquor to the city. If the police stop them, all they see are chickens and feathers."

Catherine felt uneasy. Filip and Leonek were smuggling liquor? Were they involved in making it, or just selling it?

Rose seemed to realize she said too much.

"You don't need to tell them—or anyone—I told you this. And it's not important. Getting these chores done is."

There was a soft knock at the front door. Rose opened it a crack and told the man standing there holding out money to go around to the back of the house.

"I'll be right back. Watch that baby; she's crawling toward the stairs."

My God, are they selling illegal liquor in this house? She wasn't positive, of course, but what else could it be, after Rose's revelation. *What if the police come? Will we all be arrested? How can I say honestly I didn't know about it?*

By the time evening rolled around Catherine was exhausted, not only physically but in her spirit, as well. They had done all the household chores and throughout the day, the cast iron stove had to be continually fed with new supplies of wood and the ash box emptied. And between meeting Leonek and Rose's disclosure today, Catherine felt soul sick.

Like a lightning strike to the heart, she realized she was right where she never wanted to be. She fled here to escape the life of a farm woman in Poland and now the only thing missing here was the pigs, cows, and horses.

I am a slave here. And it's even worse, because I'm in a foreign land thousands of miles from anything or anyone familiar.

She went outside for some fresh air, and fight it though she might, tears slid down her cheek.

"Hello girls." Filip whistled as he walked into the house later that day, carrying several stacked cardboard boxes. He was followed by Leonek with a large burlap bag over his left shoulder.

"Beautiful day, isn't it?"

For someone who just worked sixteen hours, he was unusually chipper. They both walked directly to the locked door and waited for Rose to open it.

"Looks like you'll be busy doing some canning this week Rose." Filip turned around with a devilish grin and winked at Catherine.

"As if I don't have enough to do around here." Rose unlocked the door, and she watched the men go down the stairs. "Make sure you put the bag of grain up off the floor, Leonek."

"What are we going to can? I didn't know you had a vegetable garden or any fruit trees."

Rose brushed her hands over her apron and straightened her hair pin. "We do have grapevines, but I'll be filling the jars downstairs. Filip calls it canning."

Catherine was sure her suspicions were correct. There was liquor in the cellar. But how much?

"It's looking good down there," Filip told Rose as he entered the kitchen.

Leonek walked over to Catherine. His eyes were bloodshot, and he reached into his work-stained pants pocket. "I brought you something from the city."

He took out a small bottle, on the label of which was the colorful design of peacock feathers which surrounded some fancy curved letters. Catherine recognized that the letters spelled *New York*.

"It's perfume. You smell like lye soap and boiled cabbage. And sometimes you smell like a baby's hind end." He laughed.

Filip sounded irritated. "I thought you spent all your money on supplies. How did you buy—"

"Why are you questioning? You'll get the rest of your asking price."

Catherine felt a jolt. *Did my brother take money from this man for me?*

"This gift is something I bought the other day," Leonek rushed on.

"Where? The stores here don't sell perfume."

"*What does it matter, you nosy idiot?* It's a gift for your sister who is going to be my wife. At least I know how to treat a woman, unlike you. Do you think your lovely Jenny is going to stick around, the way you treat her?"

Rose stared. "Who is Jenny?"

"She's no one," Filip growled at her. "Why aren't you watching that baby? She's crawling toward the stove."

Leonek reached over and grabbed Catherine's hand. "Let's go outside and leave this couple to fight."

Catherine knew there would be no fight. By now, she realized Rose did what she was told and asked few questions—and certainly asked nothing for herself. She was probably a little heartbroken that Leonek brought her home a gift of perfume. There was no sign Filip ever brought gifts to Rose.

Outside, the sky was ablaze with the fire of a setting sun. They were both silent for a time as they sat outside on the small porch. Leonek lit a cigarette. Smoking seemed to be a constant habit. Even though they had escaped outdoors, his mood was still dampened by the exchange in the house.

Leonek was trying to calm down. "Would you like a smoke?"

Catherine shook her head. The smell of cigarettes or cigars was not something she enjoyed but accepted, of course, as something men did—also some of the bawdier women.

They both watched as a short, barrel-chested man with a full beard walked across the bridge from town. Leonek motioned to the man with his hand to come over. Catherine had seen the man walk toward town earlier while she and Rose were outside once again hanging laundry. Rose had said the house across the drive was also for boarders.

"Jakub, over here."

The man altered his route and approached. "What do you want?"

"You must know by now in America everybody comes here to work. You have not been searching for work but sitting around being lazy."

Jakub looked down at the ground and spat.

Leonek took a drag from his cigarette and blew out a cloud of smoke. "Betty might let you stay without paying out of sympathy or because you're doing something to make her happy, but when I buy her house, which I plan to do, you'll pay fifteen dollars a month. Which means you need to get your butt to work."

"All right, but where should I go for this work? You have seen me at the shops in town. Twice there were advertisements men were needed. I go to those places, but each time they said if they needed me they would send a postcard."

"Excuses."

Jakub removed his wool cap and wiped the sweat from his brow.

"Besides, I talked to Filip. He said he would get me a job at the mill."

Leonek became agitated. "You want to wait for Filip? He's not responsible for you. And he says a lot of things that amount to nothing."

Catherine stared at him. Was he really going to insult her brother right in front of her?

Leonek looked at her. "You don't repeat anything."

"But I am still trying to get acquainted with America," Jakub resisted.

"Baloney. You are worthless."

Catherine sat silent and uneasy as Leonek continued to badger and belittle. Finally, Jakub walked away, and Leonek looked at her again with a hardened face.

"That's how to talk with people when you run a boarding house. Betty is having to leave because of mice like him who don't work or pay. They whine and play on sympathies."

Why would I need to know how to run a boarding house? Catherine thought a moment before the realization struck. She would be like Rose.

Leonek calmed down and lit another cigarette. Then stubbed it out and swore. "I need to go home and get some sleep."

He leaned close and forced a kiss on her lips. His unshaven chin scratched her cheeks.

He pulled away quickly. "I'll set our wedding date soon."

And I, if I am lucky, she thought bitterly, *will get the pox and my face will become scarred and whatever deal you made with Filip for me will be off.*

Several nights later at supper time, one of the boarders, Joe Vielaska, asked Filip, "Where is Leonek?"

"He'll stop by later. He wanted to go home and change his clothes first."

Rose set a steaming plate in front of Filip. "As it happens, Catherine, Joe came from the same village in Poland as Leonek. Well, it was part of Russia at the time, not Poland."

Catherine paused. "Did the two of you come to America at the same time?"

"No. He would come to our village and recruit people to travel here and work at the paper mill. I have only been here a couple of years, like Filip."

"He traveled to your village more than once? Who sent him and paid for his passage?"

"Catherine, you better eat your dinner before it gets cold." Rose insisted, wiping Bertha's hands of the gravy now smeared on the child's plate.

Talking about Poland made Catherine think of home, and how different things were here in America. How there was no cow to milk, instead milk was paid for and delivered each week.

Joe continued. "I suppose they thought we were all just dumb Pollacks—that's what they call us here—and how we'll be happy forever with the peasant wages they pay us." He began to swear.

Filip set his fork down. "You talk this way in front of my wife and sister and my children?"

"I apologize, and I will watch my tongue carefully from now on." He added, looking at Filip, "And I'll be careful not to say the truth about this place, America, where the truth is not always welcome."

After dinner, the men seemed to forget their conflict and went outside to smoke while Catherine tended to the children and Rose cleaned the dishes. Life was so different here in America from what was promised, Catherine mused. On one hand, there was a large porcelain trough attached to the wall with running water, which Rose called a sink. On the other hand, you had to be as careful with what you said as you did back in Poland or risk upsetting someone or revealing something no one wanted known.

Soon, Filip returned with Leonek, who carried the bottom of the backseat from the automobile. Catherine couldn't help but notice, strangely, Leonek's subservient attitude towards Filip as she stacked blocks with Johnny on the floor and balanced Bertha on her lap.

Filip and Leonek went downstairs to the cellar, their loud voices carried through the thin wood floors. Their tone held a hint of aggression. They came back upstairs, and Filip had a mason jar with a small amount of clear liquid.

"Rose, where's the honey to make my special tea?"

Rose continued to stand at the sink. "*Honey*, ha. We are out of your honey. I told you last week."

"Out? We have a big order to deliver. Soon. Where are we going to get more?"

"I'm sure someone in this godforsaken town has some."

"You know we can't sell it without the kick. It takes the bite out. Asking other people will cause suspicion. You'd better figure out something."

Rose turned around; her face was flushed as if she'd been slapped. "Are you blaming me for something you told me you would get from the farmer? I'm not the one who went to the farm."

"She's right, Filip." Leonek laughed. "Now give me another taste of our virgin tea."

Filip glared at Leonek and opened his mouth to object, then stopped. Their sour exchange lapsed into English and Catherine could not tell what they were saying. Something was wrong, though.

Why do they talk in English? What are they hiding from me?

"Papa, papa." Little Johnny could sense the tension in the air, and he walked over to Filip and pulled on his pant leg. "Play with you. Play," he begged.

"Not now Johnny."

"Me play with you!"

Filip's voice rose, with an angry tone in it. "I said *no*, now go away! Take him, Rose, before I swat him."

Johnny started to cry. Rose scooped him up and motioned for Catherine to follow her outside with Bertha.

Once on the porch, she lowered her voice. "I don't like to be around Filip when he gets angry. I am afraid he would hit Johnny for no reason. He has swung at the poor little boy more than once when he's drunk."

Chapter
18

The familiar dong, dong of bells rang in the air as they walked to the church. Leonek waited on the corner just over the bridge for them as he smoked his cigarette. Catherine hadn't seen him so cleaned-up before. His face shaven and clothes clean.

"Good morning Soból family." He walked over and gave Catherine a peck on the cheek.

Filip griped, "What's so good about it? I thought you would be in a damp mood after you lost some of your money last night . . ." He paused. "Money you should have given to me."

Both men doubled their fists.

"Don't worry, you'll get your money."

Catherine waited for Rose as she struggled to push the baby carriage across the dirt road of rocks and ruts until she reached the wood plank sidewalk. It was an uphill walk to the church. As they passed the new two-story brick school and the company baseball field with covered grandstands to sit hundreds of people, Filip and Leonek trotted ahead to talk with a man in a long coat who seemed to struggle as he walked with a woman and five children.

"That's Mary Nego and her husband who walks with a limp. They call him Gimpy. They live next door to the hotel known as Satan's circus, where let's just say, extra-curricular activities happen."

Catherine was shocked to hear Rose talk this way.

At the top of the hill Filip waited as they caught up to him. "Catherine, this is the new church I was telling you about."

The church reminded her of the Zakopane style at the art museum in Kraków with its wooden villa structure supported by a four-foot wall of cobblestones all around the church. A chalet style roof over the stone entrance welcomed the parishioners as they arrived.

Catherine smiled. "It's beautiful."

Leonek placed his hand on Catherine's arm and guided her over to a man who wore a cassock.

"Father Kelley, I would like you to meet Catherine. Soon to be my wife."

He smiled at her with the face of a man with a peaceful heart. "Your brother Filip told me you would be coming to America to marry Leonek." He then turned his attention to Leonek. "When do you want me to marry you two?"

Leonek looked solemn and cleared his throat. "About that, we'll be getting married in Syracuse. Would you help me to arrange a ceremony at the Polish church on Park Avenue, near the new Polish Community Home?"

Catherine looked at Leonek. *Why Syracuse?*

Leonek smiled at Catherine and took her hand. "Filip and I are planning a trip to Syracuse to see my family around the second weekend of October. I want us to be married on Saturday October eighth."

Father Kelley nodded. "I'll contact Reverend Rusin at Sacred Heart parish in Syracuse and let you know his answer to that next Sunday."

"Thank you, Father. I appreciate your help."

Inside the crowded church a carved oak altar with a large cross was enhanced by the kaleidoscopic stained-glass windows. Catherine commented, "I didn't know you had family in Syracuse."

"I don't."

The next Sunday at dinner after church, conversation revolved around the upcoming trip to Syracuse and the wedding.

"What date did Father Kelley tell you?" Filip asked as he filled his soup bowl once more. "Pass the bread would you Catherine?"

"October 10th."

Rose looked over at the calendar. "A Monday? What about work?"

Filip ignored her comment. "I am the foreman. I can take a day or two off. As long as the work gets done my supervisor won't notice we are not there."

Rose shook her head. "I don't like it—usually you deliver on a Saturday to Syracuse. Which reminds me, did you get the ingredient from the farmer?"

Her remark seemed to irritate Filip. "I'm going to have to wait until payday."

She set her spoon down. "What happened to the money I gave you?"

Leonek interrupted. "Father Kelley said that was the only date available in October. There are already two other marriages that day and the rest of the month is booked."

Once again Catherine felt the tension between them and looked over at Leonek whose muscles in his face tightened.

Am I the reason for their tension? I try to help Rose as much as I can; I do whatever she asks of me, and I don't complain.

Filip stared at Leonek. "You know I had arranged a Saturday delivery and now . . ."

"Yes Filip, I know." He slammed his hand on the table so hard the dishes jumped. "But the new date will have to work. My future depends on it."

Johnny started to cry.

"All's I know there are bills to be paid," Rose commented as she shushed the boy and distracted him with a biscuit covered in jam.

Filip added, "Like the payment on that stroller you had to have."

Rose glared at Filip. "How do you expect me to cart these children around when I go to the store?"

"Catherine's here, she could watch them while you go."

"Catherine has enough to do when she moves into the house next door. Besides, I can take care of my own children."

Leonek chimed in. "Yes, Catherine, we are going to take over the boarding house across the way. That's going to be our new home."

Run my own boarding house? How will I have time for drawing, let alone art school?

Rose looked at Catherine. "Don't worry, I can help put you on a schedule like mine. There are only six men who live upstairs."

Only six?

Her heart was sinking. Once again her future would be decided by others, and her dream flickered as if it would be snuffed out.

In just a few days they would all travel to Syracuse for the wedding and as usual, Filip and Leonek did not come home after work for dinner and the boarders had gone into town for what they called the evening entertainment. The children were asleep, and Rose sat in a wooden rocking chair knitting. Catherine looked out the window and stared at the row of white two-story houses across the way whose lights cut through the darkness. To the left were larger structures of hotels and boarding houses with shadows of people on their porches. Rose had told her on the second floor above one of the hotels was a large dance hall where lumbermen with too much time on their hands frequented. But now they would be at their lumber camps cutting trees to be taken down hills of ice to the river leading up to the big spring thaw and the movement of the logs toward the paper mill.

She looked over at Rose who wrapped yarn several times around her index finger while she used two long needles to knit a row of the blanket on her lap. Her fingers worked quickly as she talked in-between counts.

"Our trip to Syracuse is Monday for the wedding."

"Yes, Leonek told me he would take me in the automobile to Canton tomorrow to buy me a new dress."

I am going to ask Leonek about the art school in Canton. He promised to take me there in his letters. But it seems I never have the chance to ask especially since he works so many hours at the mill. Or is gone someplace…

Laughter interrupted her thoughts.

"Leonek doesn't have any money to buy you a dress. He's lying again. You can wear my wedding dress." She measured Catherine with her eyes. "I would just need to shorten it." She went back to knitting. "Besides, nowadays women show more of their legs. I saw pictures in a magazine at the store. They're called 'flapper' girls."

Catherine remembered the magazine she thumbed through at the train station, with pictures of women with raised hemlines above their knees, short hair, and made-up eyes with bright red lips.

"Why would he lie about buying me a dress?"

Rose held her blanket up to admire it. "Because that's what men do. They promise you something to make you feel good." She looked despondent. "Or themselves."

"What about the boarder house across the drive? Is he lying about that?"

Rose gave her a puzzled look. "No, that's truth. I saw Betty at the post office yesterday and she confirmed the day after we come back from Syracuse she would be leaving."

"Why is she leaving?"

"You ask too many questions. What does it matter the reason? At least you'll have your own space."

Rose set the blanket in the large basket of yarn. "I'm tired of waiting for Filip. I am going to bed."

Catherine walked outside and sat on the wooden bench under the window. The crickets chirped in the night air and the paper mill's familiar chug drifted down the river. She looked closer at the house across the drive that would soon be her new home. The two-story farmhouse had a narrow wrap around dilapidated porch supported by wood pillars with two entrances. The wood was painted only by the weather it had endured.

At least I won't have to stay with Filip anymore. I don't like it when he and Rose argue.

Bright stars speckled the night sky and across the river she heard music, loud voices, and laughter. The artificial light from the windows of the hotel with the dance hall were the brightest.

I wonder if Filip and Leonek go there after work? Where else would they be?

She watched as a car's headlamps shined down the main street and turned to cross the bridge toward the house. It pulled into the drive, and Filip exited the car. She said nothing until he reached the porch.

"Hello Filip."

Startled by her voice, he stopped just before the step and quickly laid his hand over his jacket pocket. "Oh, it's you."

"Rose went to bed. I wanted to get some fresh air."

She wanted to ask him if he missed the orchard. Was he happy at the paper mill? But instead, she decided to confide in Filip.

"I'm not sure I want to marry Leonek. Rose told me he lies and does not keep his promises." She sat up straighter and leaned toward Filip. "Has he ever lied to you?"

Filip took a long, slow draw of the cigarette he'd just lit and slowly blew out the smoke.

"Leonek has a lot on his mind and sometimes he gets things mixed-up. He is a hard worker and he'll take good care of you."

"He said he was going to take me shopping tomorrow for a new dress in Canton . . ." Her voice trailed off. She was afraid of the truth.

Filip dropped his cigarette butt on the ground and crushed it with his shoe. "We just found out we work tomorrow so we could have Monday off. This way we don't have to start our shift until Tuesday night. So, if Leonek can't take you tomorrow, it's because of work, not because he lied. I'm sure he wanted to take you for a new dress."

Filip had not heard her. *Should I tell him again my doubts about marrying Leonek again? It's like he's not listening.*

Instead, she said, "America has changed you Filip. The drinking and the gambling. You seem angry. Maybe we should go back to Poland, take your family, I'm not sure I want to…"

Before she could finish, his face became agitated and, like Marcin, his temper flared.

"You're right I'm angry. It's cutthroat here—people hate us Pollacks, just like at home. Especially the German's and then there's the Irish, thinking they are above the law, top of the heap—police, lawyers, judges . . . I'm not going to let them push me around here like they did to us in the old country." His eyes pierced through her. "And now you want me to go back? You want to go back? After everything I have done for you. . . . This is as good as it gets Catherine. You should be grateful."

She had no option but to bite her tongue. Did she want to end up on the street?

"Well, I better get to bed." He stopped at the door. "Don't worry, everything will work out. Trust me."

In the distance a dog barked, followed by another. Something inside told her she was making a mistake, but what choice did she have?

She would make the best of it somehow, she told herself. At least she hoped she could.

Chapter

19

Monday they were all up early and in the automobile before the morning steam whistle of the paper mill. Filip and Leonek filled the backseat with several hardboard suitcases they struggled to carry from the cellar and covered them with the blanket Rose finished knitting days before. The car was crowded, especially because of the crate of chickens in the back seat. The two women barely fit as Rose held Bertha on her lap. Filip, Leonek, and Johnny rode in the front seat. They covered the chicken crate with a burlap bag to keep them quiet. Catherine knew there was liquor in those suitcases.

Suddenly it made sense why they were traveling to Syracuse to marry.

As the car bounced along the dirt road she turned to Rose, "What will they do with the chickens in Syracuse?"

"They'll be used for food at the party after the wedding. The club said if we brought our own chickens they would cook them and not charge us for food."

I thought we were just going to Syracuse to marry, not to have a party.

"It seems strange we are going all the way to Syracuse to marry. Who would come? Aren't all of Filip's and Leonek's friends here?"

Rose let out a peculiar chuckle. "There's a large Polish community in Syracuse. We have been there several times. Don't worry, there will be plenty of people. Just like home, remember? The whole village turned out for such occasions."

At the train station Filip looked at Catherine and smiled. "Next time I see you we'll be at the church. Antonio wanted to come but he couldn't get time off from work."

In the distance, a train's whistle filled the quiet morning air.

"You ladies have a safe trip, and we'll see you in Syracuse."

As they boarded the train it occurred to her why Filip and Leonek would not be going on the train with them. There were deliveries to make.

During the train ride to Syracuse Catherine stared out the lusterless window. She had an urge to run but where to?

The ceremony at Sacred Heart church was scheduled to start at two o'clock. To her surprise, Rose seemed remarkably familiar with Syracuse and knew exactly where to go. When they arrived a nun who introduced herself as Sister Mary directed them to a room down the hall from the majestic Nave which gave Johnny and Bertha time to nap. Rose changed into her new dress and then helped Catherine get ready.

At the bottom of the wedding dress were two colorful rows of satin red and green ribbons. "I wanted the dress to be different than the day I wore it, so after I took the hem up I gave it some color. What do you think?"

"I love it. It's beautiful."

Rose beamed. "My mother used to say never to put red ribbons on a bride's dress. She said it would cause fighting in a marriage. But my mother isn't here, and . . . well, that's just superstition anyhow.

Turn around and look at yourself."

Catherine stared at herself in the mirror. It was hard to believe today was her wedding day. In just a few short hours she would be Mrs. Leonek Kruszka.

Rose looked perplexed.

"Is something wrong?"

"I just wish we had a necklace for you to wear."

"I do have one." Catherine reached inside the pocket of the skirt she'd worn to the church and pulled out the carefully wrapped piece of jewelry—the gift from Józef.

For a moment, two feelings fought within her. One was the love she had felt for this beautiful, artistic young man, which she never really gotten over. The other was a regret she had brought this memento with her on her wedding day. What had she been thinking?

Rose admired the necklace with the amber colored heart-shaped stone surrounded by an intricate design of infinity silver strands. "This is beautiful, where did you get it?"

Catherine tried not to choke up as she answered. "It was a gift from a friend back home." She stopped herself from saying more.

"Turn around so I can put it on you."

Catherine lifted her veil and for a moment wished with all her heart it was Józef she was marrying.

"Who was this friend? Was he someone special?"

Before Catherine could answer, mercifully there was a soft knock at the door and Sister Mary entered. "Father Rusin has returned and is ready for you." She held a large white box. "This is for you. It is from your future husband."

Catherine opened it to reveal a large bouquet of white flare-shaped flowers with freckles at the tips surrounded in a waterfall of greenery. As she removed the posy from the box several long white ribbons unfolded and almost touched the floor. She had never seen such a beautiful arrangement of flowers.

By this time the children were awake, and Rose gave them each a snack from a lunch pail—a biscuit with cherry jam and milk. She glanced over at Catherine. "My bouquet was much larger."

Sister Mary stood back to admire the young Polish princess. "This one is still beautiful."

The Nave of the church was large enough to hold hundreds of people, and the small group who stood and waited for Catherine to walk down the aisle paled in comparison to the massive Romanesque architecture before her. She took a deep breath as she stared at the bright vaulted ivory ceiling highlighted with blue and gold arches and supported by colossal marble piers.

She looked down the long aisle and felt a lump in her throat.

Seeing her, everyone in the small group stood.

How she wanted it to be Józef standing up in front of the altar waiting for her. But it was Leonek.

This feels so wrong.

Once again she felt a pang in her heart and the urge to run.

She also felt a presence beside her and turned to see Joe Vielaska in a tuxedo, his boutonniere a single white rose.

"Leonek and Filip asked me if I would escort you down the aisle." He extended his elbow and smiled. "Is that all right with you?"

Again, Józef's face flashed before her. Handsome, kind, refined Józef, so unlike the man she was about to marry.

She nodded and slipped her arm through his.

As they walked down the long aisle, an organ concealed in a loft above played a soft melody.

In her mind's-eye, she was walking the city streets of Podgorzé with Józef. His arm wrapped around hers as they admired the architecture of the buildings and talked about their future together.

"Your art is beautiful. Just like you."

Leonek had never told her she was beautiful. She wondered if he even knew the color of her eyes.

Up ahead, Leonek stood confidently. His chin raised, and chest out. She couldn't help but feel his dominance as he stepped forward to join her.

Catherine glanced over at Filip, the best man, who watched with a look of satisfaction.

In her mind, she had found Józef in a field hospital, wounded, and dropped to her knees beside his cot.

"Come back home with me, my love—my one and only love—and let's make a life together."

So strong was the image, she nearly had to shake herself to clear her head. This was a terrible time to think such things, when you were about to give yourself to a different man.

The priest spoke the ceremony in their native tongue and, as with all Catholic Masses there was a certain amount of standing up, sitting down, and random kneeling to be endured.

Now, once again, Catherine and Leonek stood before the altar that was covered with a white linen tablecloth. Father Rusin brought the largest candle forward.

"Let us declare your intention before God."

As he lit the candle, Leonek laid his hand over hers.

"My Józef, if only . . ."

Her stomach in knots, Catherine took a long, slow, deep breath.

"Heavenly Father we come before you to thank you for all you have done to help Catherine be the dutiful wife you have intended her to be. Show her how to be a servant to her chosen husband. Increase our faith and trust in you and may your prudence guide her life and love. Bless this marriage O God, with peace and happiness, and make their love fruitful for your glory and our joy both here and in eternity. Amen."

When Leonek spoke the words of commitment to her, she forced herself to remain in the present moment. Maybe there was a glimmer of hope after all. He sounded sincere and, as she looked into his eyes, she wanted to believe this was the right thing.

How light was the thin silver chain around her neck, and how strong the memory it carried. Why had she worn it?

"Remember, we are connected forever with this necklace. I will be back. I promise."

The priest was looking at her with curiosity, repeating, "Catherine? *Do* you take this man to be your husband?"

The true love of her life was gone, and this would seal that fact.

"I do."

Leonek took her hand and placed the slim silver band on her finger. The ceremony ended with another blessing from Father Rusin.

"You may now kiss your bride."

When he leaned in to kiss her, she smiled at him but felt nothing.

As they left, the church bells rang, and they all walked down the street to the Polish Home which was underground like a cellar. A flat roof covered brick walls that extended only a few feet from the ground. People who came to the ceremony promenaded down a flight of stairs through a thick walnut wood door. As the newly married couple trailed behind, they heard a familiar Polish tune from the room below. This was not the wedding Catherine imagined but then again she never thought her wedding would be here in America.

Once inside there was a long hall and to the left was a tavern room where the loud music played the Polish Wedding March. Leonek stopped her before they entered.

"Wait, let me pick you up."

The loud music made it hard for her to hear him. "What?"

Leonek swooped her up and carried her through the doorway. A crowd of men cheered. Inside was a small table for two covered with a white cloth, two place settings, and two small teacups.

Teacups. At least we are not having the liquor Filip brought to Syracuse.

Leonek handed Catherine a teacup and they all raised their arms in a toast. She took a big sip and started to choke. Leonek laughed and told the group, "She has drunk the Devils Candy!" Everyone cheered once more.

Filip shouted, "Now we know who would rule the household!"

"We'll see about that," Leonek said as he put his cup down and waltzed Catherine onto the dance floor for their first dance. The crowd of people circled around them. The smell of cigarette smoke and roasted chicken filled the air.

Filip announced, "Now everyone will have an opportunity to dance with the bride." As if on cue, Joe brought over a tray of teacups. Filip motioned for Catherine to stand next to him as he held out a hat. He shouted, "Who's first?"

What does it matter who I dance with? Let's just get this over with.

The guests once again proceeded to form a large circle around her as the band played a lively tune of polkas. Each of the men danced with Catherine after they contributed to Filip's hat followed by a shot from the teacup. Leonek stood by the bar and waited patiently for each man to dance with Catherine. As is tradition, he made several attempts to rescue her from the crowd but instead they formed a tighter circle around her. Finally, he broke through the circle, placed his wallet in Filip's hat for ransom, and made a hasty exit with his bride from the dance floor.

Filip wandered over with a determined look on his face. "Quite a haul of money to dance with your beautiful bride." He reached into the hat, handed Leonek his wallet, and grabbed a fistful of bills. "But remember, you owe me. Thanks for the payment."

Leonek's eyes widened, and his cheeks flushed. "You'll get your money, don't worry." He snatched the few coins that remained and stuffed them in his pocket. "It's my wedding, and my new bride deserves something nice."

During their argument most of the room had emptied after the man with a stained white apron returned to announce dinner was ready. Catherine went over to get her bouquet from the table.

"I'll see you tomorrow Catherine. Filip is giving me a ride back to the hotel so I can put these children to bed."

Part of Catherine wanted to leave with her. But she had accepted her fate.

Filip approached and took Johnny's hand.

"I'll be back Catherine. Enjoy your dinner."

Throughout the evening guests chanted 'gorzko, gorzko' to make the newlyweds kiss. She looked down at her empty teacup and found herself living in a fairytale of music and laughter.

On the ride back to the hotel after the reception, tension between Leonek and Filip lingered. She wanted to ask why they argued about money but instead distracted her thoughts with the lights along the street. Many of the houses had large windows which enabled her to see their bright interiors and rooms. Some of the homes featured three chimneys and large front porches. The tree lined streets looked so different at night without the normal droves of people and activity of street cars. Despite Filip and Leonek's dispute about money, she still felt excited to be staying in a hotel and then a ride home tomorrow in the automobile. At least the chickens were gone.

As they approached the center of the city, automobiles lined the streets and taller buildings made of brick appeared. They passed the barbershop where Catherine had gotten her hair cut into a bob, like one of the flapper girls in a magazine. Rose insisted for her to be a bride who represented a sign of the times. But the woman at the beauty parlor refused to cut Catherine's hair because she claimed, "It's just a trend."

Rose confided to Catherine, "We can go to the barbershop instead."

Had Leonek even noticed my hair? If he did, he didn't say anything.

Once again she admired the canal through the middle of the city.

"Look out!" Leonek shouted.

Filip swerved to miss a streetcar.

"Darn streetcars—that's what I don't like about this city. Too many of them."

The windows of the stores on the street were full of mannequins who wore the latest fashions for women. It all looked so surreal, the row of streetlights so close together, the colored lights of letters. Filip took a left and found a place to park.

"Here we are, the Mizpah Inn."

She looked at the cathedral like structure with its English style gothic cubed towers and pointed stone carved arches. "Are we staying at a church?"

Filip laughed. "No, there are rooms upstairs." He turned to Leonek. "Take Catherine to your room and meet me at the place next door, you know, on the third floor?"

"Why don't you wait for me here? This way we can go in together."

Filip lit a cigarette. "All right, but don't be long. We need to finish our business. I'll get the suitcase out while you take her upstairs."

Inside the foyer was a maple desk the length of the wall separated by an intricate iron gate from a wide stairwell with a deep oak banister. The carpet was a deep red with a gold leaf design. A glass chandelier hung from the ceiling over a small sitting area of two chairs and a dropleaf table. Leonek tapped the brass bell on the desk, but no one came.

"No matter. I was here earlier. I have our key."

At the top of the stairs was a long hallway with doors on each side. Leonek stopped at door 203 and unlocked it. Inside were two beds separated by a small table. There was a dresser and a desk with a chair near a window. The lights from the street shined through the window like a full moon.

"There's your bag." Leonek pointed toward the foot of the bed.

"Thank you for bringing it here." She laid her flowers on top of the dresser.

They sat on the edge of the bed. Catherine had never stayed in a hotel.

"This is nice."

"Well, I must go with Filip."

"Why? What's he doing? It is late."

"Don't worry, I won't be long."

The sounds of the street outside encouraged her to go look out the window. She looked down and watched a streetcar pass and spotted a woman on the sidewalk in a dark coat with a fur collar who entered a car as it stopped. Something on the desk near the window caught her eye. There on the desk was a fountain pen and several sheets of paper. The pen was the same as the men used when writing on the ship's manifest. She held it in her hand and signed her new name at the top of the paper under the logo of the hotel. The ink was so smooth and dark. Unlike a pencil it could not be erased. She sat at the desk and sketched the eclectic design of the brick building across the street highlighted by the streetlamps and illuminated business signs.

Satisfied with her drawing she left it on the desk to dry and put the extra paper and fountain pen in her shoulder bag.

What luck! I have found some paper, and now a refillable pen.

Catherine removed her necklace and carefully wrapped it in the silver foil and dark brown paper from the chocolate bar she and Rose had shared earlier. If Leonek noticed the necklace he hadn't said anything. After changing into her new night-gown, she laid in bed as the events of the day wandered through her mind. How it all went by so fast.

I wish Antonio could have been here. I wonder which room Rose is in. Did she enjoy the party? Why are Leonek and Filip always fighting about money?

Voices and footsteps in the hall interrupted her thoughts.

I am a married woman. But not to a man I am in love with.

A key clicked followed by the smell of stale cigar smoke. She sat up as Leonek turned on the small lamp by the bed. Glossed eyes stared at her as he hung his jacket from the back of the chair and slipped off his black oxford shoes. His unbuttoned white cotton shirt revealed a hairless chest.

Leonek walked over and stroked her hair. "I meant to tell you I liked your new haircut. It brings out your soft, copper colored brown eyes." Catherine looked up and couldn't help but smile. His pockmarked face smoothed from the dim light.

He took off his shirt and walked toward the window. It was her wedding night, and she knew there would be expectations. Her heart pounded.

He picked up the ink sketch from the desk. "I like this. I see you have talent."

She removed the covers and sat on the edge of the bed. The new soft pink night-gown with bits of lace around the V-shaped neckline Rose talked her into buying made her feel beautiful.

"I'm glad you like my drawing."

With an intimate voice he said, "When we get back to Pyrites, I will take you to Canton to see the art school."

Catherine couldn't believe her ears. Maybe it wasn't a mistake to marry him after all.

He walked over and positioned himself between her legs, lifted her chin and kissed her with his well-shaped lips. The kiss felt sincere—as if he cared about her. Unaware and dazed by the delicate movement of his hands, she let him consummate their marriage. Once again, Catherine sealed her fate.

Chapter
20

I t was just after noon when they all returned to Pyrites. Catherine stared at her new living quarters as they pulled into the drive. She would not be living with Filip anymore. A soft, white smoke that trailed from the central chimney and the familiar drum machinery from the paper mill crept down the river followed by the pungent smell of rotten eggs.

Leonek lit a cigarette and took Catherine's bag. "Let's go inside and see if Betty is still here." Filip, Rose, and the children said little and went home.

She waited as Leonek knocked on the unpainted solid wood door. Now that she was married to Leonek, she hoped that all the growing tension between him and Filip would end. They were family now.

No one came, so he opened it. Inside they were greeted by a large open living area with a well-worn red velvet sofa next to an oak end table which had a small lamp centered in the middle of a white doily. A long table with two benches and a chair at each end separated the kitchen from the living room. The large, cast-iron stove at the back of the room provided ample cooking space. Catherine was relieved to see a wall sink. A board went from the sink to the stove with stacks of large aluminum bowls and pans. Utensils hung below a shelf full of mason jars filled with spices next to a row of canned goods.

Leonek had gone into a room off the kitchen and returned. "She left the bed. That's good."

Catherine's eyes caught a glimpse of something next to the icebox. It was a metal tub on wheels with wooden rollers on top. She walked over to get a closer look and noticed a large iron gearwheel attached to the side with a rubber belt. "What's this?"

"An electric washing machine. It will save you time when you do laundry." He flipped a switch and the rollers at the top started spinning. "After the clothes are washed in the large tub you feed them through these rollers, and it squeezes all of the water out."

Catherine's mind was full of questions.

"Do all the boarders work the same shift?"

Irritation filled his voice. "Some days, some work the second shift."

The brief tenderness he had shown her was gone.

He headed downstairs to the cellar.

Catherine pulled a string hanging from a lightbulb to look at the bathroom. It was small but much better than an outhouse. Back in the main room she noticed the long double-hung windows were discolored from the coal soot and this prevented the sunshine from streaming in.

I wonder what the rooms look like upstairs. I'm not sure I like this arrangement. Rose had only four boarders and now I have six. . . . Rose said she would help . . . but her help is more like giving orders while I do the work.

Leonek came back upstairs.

"Plenty of coal down there." He walked over to the icebox. "Before we know it the boarders will be home for dinner...you need to get cooking. We don't want anyone leaving. Got to keep them fed." He lifted the top. "Lots of ice left. I think the iceman comes on Thursday. Let's see what's inside . . . plenty of food here for at least a few days. What's this?"

He took out a coffee can and inside it was a few bills. "This must have been her stash for food." He put the bills in his pocket and grabbed his hat from the well-worn black walnut table.

"Where are you going?"

"I need to go get the rest of my things from my room in town."

"What about going to Canton? You told me we could ride by the art school."

"Probably won't have time until maybe Saturday if I don't have to work. Plus, you'll be plenty busy around here. We need to keep these boarders fed and rooms cleaned so they pay their rent."

His voice sounded eager. "Besides, I have a surprise for you later this week. I know you will like it."

She wiped the smudge off the window with her hand and watched him start the automobile and drive across the bridge toward town.

She looked around the room once more. Betty was not a good housekeeper. *Why did I come here and think things would be different?*

A few days later Leonek was up early and did not tell Catherine where he was going. He walked to town with a couple of the other boarders. About an hour later when Catherine went outside to empty the ash box, she spotted a horse and wagon coming across the bridge. On the front seat was Leonek with another man. In the back of the wagon were a couple of men and pieces of furniture. Filip stood outside on the porch smoking a cigarette as it pulled up to the house.

Leonek whistled as he disembarked the wagon seat and looked at Catherine. "I told you I had a surprise for you."

"What's this?" Filip asked as he walked to the back of the wagon.

"It's a present for my new bride."

The younger men jumped out and proceeded to unload an elegant long sofa with a satin finish and squared arms framed with a carved reddish-brown wood. Leonek and the other man grabbed a rolled carpet.

"Follow me, boys. Catherine, you wait here."

Filip shook his head and lit another cigarette.

A few minutes later Leonek and the men carried the tattered velvet couch outside and loaded it onto the wagon. He shook the older man's hand, then motioned to Catherine. "Come inside."

Filip followed them inside the house.

Catherine was stunned. The once dull, shabby room had been transformed into a bright parlor.

"Where did you get money for this?" Catherine asked, as she bounced lightly on the sofa's thick cushion.

Filip ran his finger along the intricate carved wood on the arms. "Yes, Leonek, tell us. How did you pay for this?"

"That's none of your business."

Filip slapped Leonek on the back. "Really? None of my business? Don't you have other debts to pay?"

Then Filip said something in English which made Leonek lose his smile.

I don't understand. What are they fighting about? She stood up. "What's the matter? Why are you both so angry?"

Neither of them answered.

"I need to see someone before work. Remember what I said, Leonek."

Leonek followed him to the door. "I've told you, you'll get your money," he said, slamming it shut behind Filip.

Catherine stood there and stared at him. "What do you owe him money for?"

He walked over to the sink and poured a cup of water. Catherine waited for his answer.

"Something . . . something from before you came."

"What?"

"Doesn't matter." He looked over at the clock on the wall. "What's to eat before I go to work?"

She wanted to pursue the question further, but Leonek's face said otherwise. He looked irritated.

"I made a vegetable stew and biscuits."

His mood soured completely.

"Well, serve it up. I'm starved."

December came and Rose told Catherine there would be a lot of snow during the winter months. They would need to stockpile for the winter.

"Even the milkman has a hard time delivering and one year our water pipes froze." Rose explained over a cup of coffee during one of Catherine's visits after dinner on a cool fall evening. "I don't mind the snow, it's the bitter cold that bothers me."

Rose looked out the window at Filip and Leonek who were getting the car ready for a trip across the river. "Big doings in the mill town tonight. The lumberjacks are in town for supplies before the snow flies. I heard the hotels in town are full."

Filip and Leonek came inside and headed straight to the cellar. In a few minutes they returned with hardboard suitcases in hand. Filip walked past Rose and gave her a playful slap on her behind.

"Time to get momma a new pair of shoes."

Rose blushed and snapped the dish cloth in her hand at Filip as he moved quickly to the door. "How about a vacuum cleaner instead?"

Leonek opened the door and motioned for Filip to walk through. "Enough playtime. We've got work to do."

Catherine watched them out the window as they struggled to put the suitcases in the back seat. She knew there was liquor in those suitcases to be sold, but no one ever admitted it to her.

They must think I'm stupid.

She turned to Rose who handed the children some kitchen pans and spoons to play with.

"Where are they going?"

"Oh, you know—just doing things men do." Rose then handed each of the children a sugar biscuit cookie and offered one to Catherine. "Would you like one?"

"These are good. You need to give me your recipe."

Rose laughed. "There is no recipe. These come from a store in town."

Catherine felt embarrassed. She forgot how easy money can make your life in America.

"Anyhow, let's talk about Christmas. It will be here before we know it." Rose opened a drawer and took out a large piece of paper and pencil. She folded it in half and tore off a piece.

Catherine's eyes brightened. Her sketchbook was full, and she needed to get more paper to draw on. "Where did you get that paper?"

"Filip gets it from the mill."

"Do you think Leonek could get me some?"

"I'm sure he could. Filip says it's scrap paper." She sat at the table. "Like I was saying, since your place is bigger than mine, we could have Christmas dinner there. I could have Filip bring some of our chairs over."

"Why? Who's coming? Your table is large enough for Leonek and me."

Rose looked confused. "Catherine, the boarders. We need to make dinner for them, too. The men still need go to work and be fed. The mill never stops."

As Rose talked she wrote a list on paper, and Catherine's mind wandered back to the last Christmas her family was all together. Cooking in the kitchen with her mother and Eva—the tasty breads, pierogies, and sugary desserts. Her father and Marcin setting aside their differences and sharing a meal—the tradition of the *opłatek* wafer.

"What do you think?"

"About what?"

Rose rolled her eyes. "I said Filip could get a couple of turkeys from the farmer. You can cook one and I can cook one here."

"But we don't have meat on Christmas."

"Catherine, this is America, not Poland. People have meat on Christmas. Besides what else would we cook for all these men?" She set her pencil down and glanced over at the window. "Well, it's getting dark. I need to get these children ready for bed. We can talk more about this another time."

"Before I go, can I ask you a question?"

"Make it quick."

"What do Filip and Leonek argue about?"

"What do you mean?"

Catherine looked at Rose. "Does Leonek owe Filip money?"

Rose turned away. "They're arguing because of you. Leonek borrowed money from Filip to bring you here to America."

"I thought Leonek paid for my ticket. Why would Filip need to pay? How much does he owe?"

"I don't know. That's men talk. Whenever I ask Filip, he gets angry at me, so I don't ask anymore. All I care about is he provides money to take care of our family." Rose looked over at Johnny who wiped his sticky fingers on the sofa. "See? This is why everything gets ruined."

As Catherine walked across the drive toward home, she could hear the music and boisterous laughter from across the river. Leonek hadn't even told her good-bye or what time he would be home. Catherine wasn't sure if she liked American culture. Everything was dictated by the clock and money seemed more important than people.

I will need to ask Leonek about the money. Or do I ask Filip? I'm not sure what to do.

The house was quiet except for the murmur of the coal furnace in the cellar. Had Leonek filled the coal furnace? She went over and put her hand on the radiator located under the window. It was still warm.

I'd better go check it before I go to bed.

She did not like going downstairs to the cellar but Leonek told her she must check the stove each morning and evening.

"You can't let that fire go out," he had told her more than once, with force in his voice.

She headed back upstairs and sat on the sofa. The empty dinner pails to be filled for the men's lunch tomorrow sat on the table. Her anxiety about the money owed to Filip surfaced.

Did my own brother sell me . . . for money?

She could not bear the thought.

How could I have been so foolish—to marry a man I didn't know? Yes, that was the Old-World way, but this was America. She had been told things were different here.

She stared at the shelf of pots and pans. The wringer washer.

I need to return to my art. I refuse to be a slave to this life. Somehow, I need to break free.

A few days later Leonek brought her home paper. "I know you like to make silly little scribbles, but don't let your work slack. We need these boarders to help pay the mortgage on this house to farmer Wallace."

Her delight at getting the paper vanished. "Don't we pay rent like the others? I didn't know you owned this place."

"Rent, bought, what's the difference? The point is, without happy boarders we don't have a roof over our heads. So, keep them clean and fed." His jaw clenched. "Do you understand me?"

The days turned into weeks and during the week leading up to Christmas Catherine noticed Rose had more visitors than usual. Word spread she had made Vishnyovka.

"Aren't you worried the police will find out what you are doing?" Catherine had to ask one day after Rose came back from town with some supplies.

Rose ignored her question. "Here is your change. Remember what I told you, keep a few coins for yourself." She nodded over at a coffee can on the top shelf in the kitchen. "See that can? Inside is my rainy-day fund. If I always give Filip change back he never questions the amount." She added, "Men are so stupid. Especially when we give them what they want. Sex."

Her comment startled Catherine.

"I also managed to get us a ham for Christmas. The grocer said they are selling fast, and you know how these men can eat." She pulled several letters from her coat pocket and flipped through them. "Here, this one is for you."

Catherine looked at the address. It was from Eva.

"What's this?" Rose declared after she opened one of hers. Her neck had reddened to her ears. "That idiot Filip. He never made the payment on the sewing machine. What does he expect these kids to wear when they grow out of their clothes? The merchant wants to come and take back the machine."

She picked up another letter and opened it. Her eyes scanned the paper. "Of course, the electric is more . . . $2.15 compared to $2.03 last month." She looked over at Catherine. "Just think what yours will be with six boarders! Plus, your house is larger than mine. You better pray Leonek doesn't gamble away all of his money or you'll be out on the street."

Eager to get home and read the letter she told Rose goodbye. Her fingers trembled as she opened it.

My Dear Catherine,

I pray God has been good to you. We are all well and we hope you are also well. I am hopeful you and your new husband are good. I have not a letter or picture from you. Maybe our letters will cross on the ocean, and I would receive one soon. Marcin wants to move to the city, but I cannot bear to leave nature for a dirty city.

This Christmas we will spend time with my family in the village. Some of the young men have returned from war but many have not. My nephew Franek Stanislaw had been taken as a prisoner, sent to Russia. My sister cries each day. If he is dead, she wants to give him a proper burial. It was reported executions go on like waterfalls. You made the right choice by leaving. May God bless us.

The orchard work is heavy on your father. Zophia's boys help but she insists education is more important than labor. The youngest boy Yehuda has taken favor with my honey and gardening. We spend much time together. He is like a son I never had.

Best wishes. Please write to me. I am sad when there is no news from you. Remain with God. May God help you.

Love, Eva

Catherine read the letter several times. She ran her finger over the violet and buff colored postage stamp with its picture of the crowned white eagle. Her heart ached. The letter from home made her think of Józef.

Could I ask Eva if there was ever any news about Józef? But what good would it do? I am married now.

Christmas Eve and Christmas Day passed quickly. Cooking for twelve men and two children meant there was little time for celebration amongst the women. Rose had brought over her strong, homemade *Vishnyovka* brandy, which she insisted was okay since it was Christmas.

"There isn't a police officer within five miles of here. And if there was, well, they would not arrest anyone on Christmas day."

"Nostrovia." Filip shouted as he raised his glass and the men joined in.

"And a Happy New Year. Here's to 1922." Leonek added, giving Catherine a playful wink."

Rose interrupted their celebration. "Leonek, there is a woman who wants to talk with you; she came to the house when I went over to get the cheesecake."

Leonek set his glass down. "Me?" He grinned over at Filip. "Are you sure she doesn't want Filip? Is her name Jen...."

Filip's smile faded, and he clutched Leonek's shoulder roughly as Leonek twisted away and swore.

Rose eyed Filip with suspicion. "I'm sure. She has two children with her."

Leonek snatched his coat from the wall near the door, followed by Filip.

"Where are you going?" Leonek barked.

"With you. You're not about to make a sale without me."

Catherine stared at Rose, who looked just as perplexed and clearly wanted to change the mood.

"All right, who wants some dessert with coffee?" Rose brought over the tray of cups and put them on the table. "Catherine, get the coffee pot."

Rose brought over the *Makowiec* which was decorated with icing. The boarder who Leonek always belittled named Jakub was the first one to the table and set Johnny on his lap.

"Don't give Johnny any poppy seed cake." Rose insisted as she set a plate of gingerbread cake on the table. "He can have this instead."

Catherine poured each of the men some coffee.

"What did Leonek get you for Christmas?" Stefan asked as she filled his cup.

She cleared her throat; mindful Rose was listening. "He bought me a plush coat with a raccoon fur collar."

Catherine could feel Rose's eyes on her.

The man known as Gorski spoke. "Amazing he bought her anything at all; he's a cheap *dupek*."

"Hey! Watch your tongue," Rose snipped. "Don't talk that way in front of my children."

Gorski raised both hands in the air with open palms. "Okay, sorry."

"What did Filip get you?" Jakub asked, holding his plate up for a slice of cheesecake.

Rose's cheeks reddened. "Nothing. These children are more important."

Gorski laughed. "No surprise to me. He lost quite a bit to me the other night."

Laughter filled the room.

Catherine walked over to the sink to fill the coffeepot with water. She looked out the window to see Leonek, Filip, and a woman with long red hair pulled in a braid, and two children, who looked to be school age, across the drive on Filip's porch. Near the bridge waited a horse and wagon with a man at the helm who wore a large straw hat. Catherine watched as the woman's head drooped as she pulled the children closer to her. The woman touched Leonek's arm several times as she talked.

Leonek forked his fingers through his hair, reached into his pants pocket, and handed the woman what looked to be a wad of folded bills, while Filip leaned against the porch rail and smoked a cigarette.

"Catherine, did you hear me? We need more coffee."

"Okay. Yes. I'm coming."

Much to her surprise, Leonek continued to shower Catherine with gifts. She learned not to share this with Rose or Filip, or they got angry. But sometimes Leonek bragged to a boarder and the gossip would spread. One of her favorite gifts was a pad of paper he bought for her to sketch on along with some new pencils. His initial dismissal and mocking of her desire to draw had disappeared.

"Once spring comes, I promise to take you to Canton and the art school. Until then you can keep drawing."

Her eyes grew wide as she held the thick pad of paper. The cover was red with a star and the number five.

"And here is something else I bought for you. This box of pencils with color." He held it up to her. "When I noticed the picture of a man on the box drawing, I opened it and saw the colored pencils."

Catherine took the narrow box, lifted the cover, and examined each one. A wave of heightened emotion came over her. She smiled and stood up to hug Leonek. "Thank you. Thank you."

"You have been doing a good job keeping these men fed and happy. That makes my life easier."

She put the pad and pencil box on the shelf over the sink. As she did her eyes caught a glimpse of Leonek drinking straight from the jar of milk in the icebox until it was empty. He put the empty jar back in the icebox.

"I do need money to pay the milkman tomorrow."

The light mood faded a little.

"What happened to the money I gave you last week?"

"I used it when I paid him last time; he does come every week. I also mailed a letter to my father…"

He scowled. "A letter, for what? How much was that?"

"Just a few cents…"

She felt confused by his sudden mood.

"Don't spend my hard-earned money without my permission. Do you understand?"

The warmth in her heart for him dissolved.

"I said do you understand?"

"Yes."

I'm so glad I put money in the coffee can, like Rose said. She only hoped he wouldn't find it.

"Tonight, I'm going to win my money back. Then you can pay the milkman."

"But what if you don't? He'll still expect his money."

"Just tell him you'll pay him next week. It's Christmas time, he will be lenient."

The long nights of winter and the isolation of drudgery—cooking, cleaning, and laundry—took its toll on Catherine. On top of that she had missed her menstrual cycle twice.

Chapter
21

"**W**hy are my boots still covered in mud?" Leonek asked one morning as he grabbed his lunchpail from the table. It had been a warm week in early March and the melting snow helped to soften the frozen ground.

"Well, you're the one who wore them in the mud."

"Don't you know it's your job to clean them?"

"I have more important things to do than to clean your boots. Taking care of six men upstairs, cooking, cleaning…"

He scoffed. "You seem to take better care of them than you do me."

At least they appreciate what I do for them.

The long winter and now warmer weather made Catherine want to get out of the house. After Leonek left she decided to wear her new coat and visit Father Kelley.

Once inside the warm empty space of the church her voice echoed. "Hello? Father Kelley, are you here?" The oak pew benches arranged in rows faced the altar on either side of a central aisle. An ambry cabinet stood on each side and held the sacred oils used to anoint parishioners in baptism or give them strength and courage during sickness.

From a door near the altar Father Kelley appeared. Catherine knew him to be dressed in a cassock but today he wore a black suit with his white Roman collar. His short, wavy, coal black hair was parted in the middle and shined from being smoothed down with petroleum jelly. She was glad he spoke Polish.

"Good day, Father Kelley. It's me, Catherine. Filip's sister—I mean Leonek's wife."

"Hello, Catherine, yes, I know who you are." He smiled and his angelic face comforted her. "What can I do for you today?"

She took a deep breath. "I need to seek God's forgiveness, and penance."

They were both quiet as Father Kelley waited for Catherine to speak.

"I am hiding something from my husband. A gift from God."

He encouraged her. "Go ahead Catherine, what is it?"

Her throat tightened. She hesitated. "I am with child." Looking down at her hands, she twisted the silver ring on her finger and continued. "How can I bear children to a man I don't love."

"Catherine, the union of two people in marriage is not always based on love but is a vocation. Love must be learned. As husband and wife, you are to grow together and bring children into the world. God says in Genesis: 'It is not good man should be alone; I will make him a helper fit for him.'"

"But what about my creativity? My love for art?"

"You can serve God as both a mother and creator of art. Let your spirit of creativity compliment you as a mother and wife. You just said children are a gift from God—just as you were to your mother and father."

He opened his prayer book. "Let us pray. Heavenly Father, thank you for this time in your presence. Help Catherine to be called to her married life. Make her strong enough to keep the lifelong commitment of marriage and the procreation of children. I make this prayer in the name of your Son, Jesus Christ, our Lord and Savior, Amen."

God, please forgive me. If I am pregnant, I promise to be a good wife and mother. . . But God . . .

"Catherine, is there anything else you would like to tell me?"

She thought for a long moment.

"No." A tear streamed down her cheek. *How could I tell Father Kelley what I am really hiding is my love for another man? Józef. But he is gone forever.*

"Are you certain?"

"Yes. I accept that God wants me to be a dutiful wife and mother."

"Then let us bow our heads and praise the mercy of God."

Catherine folded her hands once more in prayer.

"Give thanks to the Lord for he is good."

Catherine responded, "His mercy endures forever."

"Go in peace, Catherine. And never forget that your love for art is a gift of God, too.

On the walk home the scrunch of hardened snow reminded her the temperature had dropped. The gray sky refused to let any sunshine through the low hanging clouds. As she approached the main four corners to the bridge the monotonous thud and thump from the paper mill filled the air.

Catherine stood on the bridge and looked down the river at the monumental factory of bricks and blackened glass whose elongated smokestacks churned white clouds of steam. For the first time the smell of rotten eggs did not fill her nose. It seemed her senses were acclimated to the pungent smell of sulfur.

Days later, in the evening, when Leonek and Filip once again went into town to play cards, Catherine decided to visit Rose. She wanted to know about the woman that came to visit on Christmas Day and to confirm a story she overheard about Filip.

"Come in. Sit by the stove," Rose insisted as she opened and closed the door to the eastern winds of winter. "I have just put the children down and was about to make a cup of tea while I do the bookwork for the boarding house." She carried the teapot over to the sink and filled it with water.

Catherine was quiet.

"You look like something is on your mind."

"There is. One of the boarders told Leonek something happened in town last weekend. I was down in the cellar getting some potatoes and they didn't realize I could hear them in the kitchen talking. He told Leonek he was on the back porch at Mary Nego's house." Catherine could feel her throat tighten.

"Go on."

The water started to boil, and Rose went to the shelf above the sink for two cups and a tin canister.

"I overheard Mike tell Leonek he was on the porch with Mary and a few others when Filip came with a gun and shot it off six times. Mike doesn't believe Filip was mad, he was just shooting for the fun of it."

Rose did not seem surprised as she set the steaming cups of tea on the table.

"Do you think Filip owns a gun?"

Rose scowled. "Why are you asking me that? How could you even think that? If he does, he never told me."

Catherine sipped her tea. *Why would Filip have a gun?*

After a long moment, she said, "I have something else to tell you . . ."

Rose patiently waited for her to finish.

"I believe I'm pregnant."

Rose bit her lip.

"Is something wrong? You don't seem happy for me."

"Have you told Leonek?"

"No. Not yet."

Rose stood and walked over to the window. She drew the curtain back and looked out. Then started to pace back and forth.

"What is it? Is something wrong?"

"I don't know how to tell you this. I just learned about it myself." She stopped near the table. Her face lost all its color.

"Tell me . . . what is it?"

Rose looked up at the ceiling and made the sign of the Cross with her right hand. She sat and put her palms around her cup of tea.

"Filip told me something, but if he finds out I told you, he-he would be furious with me." She hesitated. "He might even kill me."

"My brother wouldn't kill anyone." *Why would Rose say this?* Catherine felt nauseous and part of her didn't want to hear what Rose was about to say.

"Do you remember the woman who came to visit on Christmas Day?"

Catherine nodded. "The one with the two children?"

"She wasn't there to buy Vishnyovka like they said." Rose breathed in and let out a long breath. "She was there to get money from Leonek."

"For what?"

"For her children. Leonek is their father." Rose looked at Catherine. "And now you are pregnant with his child."

That night as Catherine sat on the couch and waited for Leonek, so many thoughts blazed in her head.

What am I going to say to him? He's my husband, I need to be faithful to him. Does Filip have a gun? What happened to my brother?

She looked over at the clock. It was just past eleven p.m. Catherine knew she needed sleep; the men would want their lunch pails ready and the ones who worked the night shift would be hungry for breakfast.

I knew having sex could lead to pregnancy, but Leonek assured me each time he would be careful. I thought he understood I wanted to go to art school . . . I believed him.

She stared at the lath and plaster wall.

How am I to go to school and care for a child?

She felt the small flame of her dream flicker.

What was Filip thinking, setting me up with this man who doesn't love me? A man who expects me to cook, clean his boots, and keep his bed warm at night.

A few days later after the boarders finished their dinner, Catherine stood at the sink and stared out the window across the drive toward town. Outside the wind howled. Once again a steady wall of snowflakes stuck to the frozen ground.

Does winter never end here?

She still needed to tell Leonek about her pregnancy, she had missed another cycle.

"Katie, come over here and take a seat. Mike is going to read us the newspaper."

Catherine turned to look at Stefan who stood up and pulled a chair out for her. "Looking out the window won't make Leonek come home."

Jakub chimed in, "Most likely he and Filip are getting hotsy-totsy with some giggle-water."

The others ignored his comment, except for the man they called Kowalski. He too had left behind a wife and two sons in Poland to come to America and make money to send home. Usually, he went to the pool hall after work and often missed dinner. "Or they're at the pool hall on a bender."

Mike opened the folded paper and looked at Kowalski. "Do you want the news or not?"

Silence took over the table as Catherine sat down.

"British troops to resume evacuation of Ireland; Many kidnapped Ulster Unionists are liberated."

Jakub leaned forward. A scowl came over his face. "Who cares about Ireland— or the Irish? What else?"

"Here is something about a clash of German and French soldiers."

Jakub gave Mike a dismissive wave. A look of bitterness swept across his face. "There's another useless story." He turned to the man next to him. "Kowalski, am I right? You're a German Pole. To blazes with those Germans."

Kowalski nodded. "Yes, you're right. Germany wouldn't give Poland its borders—wouldn't even let us speak our language—but we fought back, remember Poznan? *Szczuny!*"

Mike's eyes continued to scan the page. "Here's something. Eastern U.S. in grip of severe cold wave, little relief until Saturday."

Catherine rubbed her hands together. "Yes, it's cold outside. We don't need a newspaper to tell us that."

"Yeah, tell us something we don't know," Jakub smirked, his forehead puckered.

Mike turned to the next page. "Says here we have a new Pope, Cardinal Ratti of Milan."

"Anything about Poland?" Stefan asked as he tapped a new pack of cigarettes on his palm. The package was covered with a picture of a camel and pyramids. He removed the silver foil.

Mike's eyes scanned the newspaper as everyone waited. He flipped to the back page. "I don't see anything."

Jakub spoke up. "Well, if there's nothing else, I'm going to town and win back what I lost yesterday.

"Let's see . . . here's something about a big still found in a New York cellar."

Catherine asked with concern. "Was anyone arrested?"

"No, but here's a headline about five naval officers sentenced for having liquor." His eyes peered at her over the top of the paper.

Stefan let out a long stream of cigarette smoke.

"Here's something for Catherine. It's on an ad for bread." Mike cleared his throat. "Katie, Katie, quite contrary, what'll we have for dinner? I feel all lank, like an empty tank. I'll cave in if I get thinner."

The men all laughed. Catherine felt her face get flushed.

"Mike, you're embarrass'n her."

Mike looked at Catherine and turned the page of the newspaper around for her to see. "Look, it's you, sitting on a loaf of Handley's bread."

Jakub stood up. "C'mon boys, anybody coming with me. Time's a wastin'."

And with that remark, the kitchen was empty.

Catherine had gone to bed alone and woke up to find Leonek next to her, his breathing heavy. As she opened her eyes the lack of sunlight told her it would be another cloudy day. For some reason, her face felt cold. She turned over and tried to bury it in his back but as she moved the blanket the frigid air stung her face. She nudged his back. "Leonek, wake up. The heat is out." He stirred… the smell of his breath reminded her of his late night. "What? It will be fine. Go back to sleep."

"No, it's not fine. It's cold. Did you check the coal furnace before you came to bed?"

He rolled over and pulled the blanket around him. Catherine had no choice but to get up. She turned on the light in the kitchen and walked over to the couch to get her soft wool blanket with orange, brown, and red stripes. The one she brought with her from Poland but could not use on the boat for fear someone would have taken it. She wrapped it around her shoulders and breathed out a sigh.

Her first instinct was to start a fire in the cast iron cook stove. She looked at the table, thankful Mike left the newspaper and she used it to get the fire going. Soon the kitchen area was warmer, along with her mood, and she started a pot of coffee. There was a soft knock at the door.

She was happy to see Stefan, one of the few boarders who had always been kind to her.

"It's cold upstairs; I came down to see how you are doing. Leonek put on a good one last night. . . . Did he make it home?"

Catherine felt embarrassed. How could she have such a rotten husband, and now she was pregnant.

"Yes. Come in. I just made some coffee. For some reason there is no heat—and on the coldest day!"

His smile brought a warmth to the room. "Yes, just like home in Poland. I remember on a chilly day the first thing we did was start a wood fire in the stove." A thoughtful look came over him. "We are spoiled with the heat provided by the coal boiler." He walked over to the radiator and touched it. "Something is wrong, no heat here." He looked out the window over the cast iron coils and in the background the automobile was covered in snow like an igloo against an early morning grey ash sky. "I see smoke from Filip's chimney. He's got heat. You could go over there until Leonek gets the heat fixed."

"I should get started on breakfast for you and the others."

"Catherine, it's Sunday. There is no hurry. We were on the Monday through Saturday shift this past week. Which means today is our day off."

She had forgotten. Every day seemed the same to her: cook, clean, cook, clean.

A cough from the bedroom told Catherine Leonek was up. She handed Stefan a steaming mug of coffee.

Leonek shuffled from the bedroom. He stopped at the doorway and put his arm up in a salute to cover his eyes from the light of the kitchen. The first thing Catherine noticed was his eye. It was swollen half shut and bruised. "What is *he* doing here?"

"What happened to your eye?" She went to the sink and ran a cloth under cold water. "Stefan came downstairs to make sure we were all right. Remember, I told you there was no heat?"

Leonek said nothing and hurried into the bathroom. The sound of him vomiting echoed.

Stefan took a drink of his coffee. "I could go downstairs to see if I can find the problem with the heat. There might be a frozen pipe." He walked over and put his hands over the warm stove. "But you just turned on the water and it worked so we know the water pipe isn't frozen."

He jerked his head toward the bathroom.

"Besides, he doesn't seem to appreciate my company."

Catherine followed Stefan to the cellar door and watched him as he pulled the strings that lit a path down the steep wooden stairs. Stefan hollered back, "Hopefully, I can get this heat working."

"Thank you." She left the door ajar and turned around. Leonek stood there, his eyes filled with suspicion. "I'll have my coffee now. And that baby inside of you better be mine."

He knows. How does he know?

"Don't look so surprised. Filip told me. Did you really think anything you told Rose would stay a secret?"

An uneasy feeling came over her, yet she had nothing to be guilty of.

"Here is a cold cloth, for your eye." She reached toward him to put it on his face. He took the cloth from her and pressed it against his eye.

Stefan yelled up the cellar stairs. "Looks like the coal fire is about out. I'll just need some paper to get it started again."

Leonek glared at Catherine. "I thought I told you to not let that fire go out."

His uncovered eye looked at the shelf above the stove. "Is that the pad of paper I bought you?"

Before she could answer he grabbed it and began to rip out some of the pages.

"Wait! Those are my drawings, don't . . ." But it was too late. He threw the pad on the floor and then pushed by her as he marched down the cellar steps.

Catherine picked up the pad and was horrified to see her drawings were gone. "Leonek, wait! Here, use these blank ones instead!" She rushed down the cellar stairs just in time to see him throw the tightly wadded papers into the coal stove and blow on the orange embers. Catherine watched as the flames erupted.

Stefan looked at Catherine and glanced back at Leonek as he scooped up a shovel full of coal. "At least we found the problem. I'll go back upstairs and let the others know. Glad the pipes weren't frozen, eh Leonek?"

"Tell that yokel, Jakub, he's on borrowed time. The nerve of him accusing me I cheated him from his winnings."

Stefan smirked. "He sure did put a punch to you."

Leonek said nothing and shut the door to the boiler. Catherine started to follow Stefan up the stairs.

"Where do you think you're going?"

Catherine stopped and leaned her head down, seething but containing her anger. "Upstairs to make some breakfast. I'm sure the others are up by now."

Besides, right now, I can't stand to be in the same room with you.

"Seems you have a thing for Stefan. You follow him like a puppy."

A fresh swell of anger rushed through her. Catherine looked up to make sure Stefan had left before she confronted Leonek.

"Like you didn't have a thing before I came here? Why didn't you tell me about the woman on Christmas? That you are the father of her children?"

His jaw tightened. "Are you talking about Teresa O'Connor? She's nothing but a streetwalker. There's no proof those half-breed kids are mine."

She could feel her heart race. "Then why did I see you give her money?"

"What are you talking about?"

"That night. When I looked out the window. I saw you reach into your pocket and hand her money."

"We already told you. She was there to buy *Vishnyovka*. I gave her change."

Catherine looked at his smug face. She felt her eyes well up with tears. "You are lying."

He leaned the shovel against the wall and turned his back to her as he opened the door to the boiler to reveal a yellow fiery flame atop the red coals. "Believe what you will, but I'm telling you they are not mine."

Would Rose have lied to me? I am so confused.

"Hello . . . is anyone here?"

Catherine recognized Mike's voice. "Be right there!" She started up the stairs, glad to leave Leonek in the cellar. Where he belonged. With the dirt and vermin.

Chapter

22

Spring finally came, which meant it was time for the Log Drive, when thousands of newly cut timber logs, thirteen feet long and up to two feet wide, would float down the swollen river toward the paper mill.

Like the lumberjacks, the mill workers were overworked, which meant accidents happened. Immigrants didn't need to speak English to work in America, they were shown how to do their jobs. Longer hours at the paper mill and lumber camps left the men little time for leisure. These dangerous and stressful situations pushed people to their limits, which meant less patience for one another.

Extra hours at the mill meant extra work for Catherine and Rose, and just like the women at the lumber camps, their jobs were to keep the men fed and the bunkhouses in order. Since the men labored fourteen or more hours a day, they were always ravenously hungry. Women either delivered dinner pails to the foreman or some, like Filip, would come and pick them up only to be swayed to have a few drinks before returning to their tedious work. No one could afford to lose their job. The more money Filip and Leonek made from illegal liquor, the more excitement they felt and the more risks they took as gamblers.

One evening, after a long day of cooking and laundry, Catherine walked outside to empty a bucket of dirty mop water and found Filip leaning on the porch railing as he smoked a cigarette.

"Hello Filip, it's good to see you." Catherine sat down on the rustic wood bench in between the two rectangular windows. Her back against the side of the house. She was almost four months pregnant and tired easily.

"I was waiting for Leonek. He owes me something."

Catherine watched as Filip put out one cigarette and lit another. The long hours at the mill aged his once younger face. Wrinkles appeared around the corner of his eyes as he took another drag of the tobacco. He hadn't shaved and gray whiskers on his chin shimmered when he talked. "Rose told me you are with child."

"Yes, it was not planned."

Filip turned and spat on the ground. "Nothing in life ever is." He smiled. "Who would have thought I would have two children?"

She smiled back. "How are they? I haven't seen Rose much."

"Johnny is starting to talk pretty good. He's growing out of his clothes again. Bertha just has a big appetite."

Catherine was about to ask Filip about the money Leonek owed him when she looked down the drive and saw Leonek with Jakub on the bridge. Filip followed her eyes and turned his head.

"Catherine, you better go inside. I've got some business to attend to with Leonek."

"Is it about me?"

"What? No." Filip reached into his inside jacket pocket, unscrewed a cap of something he held in his hand and took a swig. "Nothing for you to worry about."

Catherine went inside but didn't close the door all the way. She stood and watched.

As soon as Leonek was within earshot he said to Filip, "Did you hear what happened to Gimpy?"

"No, what?"

"He got caught in a shaft. He was alive when they found him, but only for a few minutes. Jakub here said about every bone was broken in his body."

Jakub was staring off into the distance, clearly shaken. "He went into the basement to get a drink of water. The water bucket was near the shaft and when he bent down to get it, his collar got caught in the machine somehow and he was whirled and twisted to his death."

They were all silent. Leonek spoke first. "Wonder what Mary will do? She's got five kids. Can't be cheap to feed them."

Filip recovered from his somber mood and snarled, "That reminds me . . . You got that money you owe me?"

"I just gave you some last payday. I'll give more to you next payday."

"That was yesterday."

Leonek took out a pack of cigarettes and offered one to Jakub.

"Seems like you got money to buy cigarettes. I say you quit smokin' and pay your debts."

"Who are you? My mother?"

Filip grabbed Leonek's collar. "No, I'm your banker. And do you know what bankers do to scum like you, who don't pay their loans?"

"What's the matter? Did you gamble your check and now momma's gonna wonder where it went? Your gambling problem is not my problem." Leonek jerked away. "Don't worry, you'll get your money. Even if I need to sell your sister…"

Filip reached inside his jacket pocket and pulled out a revolver. "If you weren't the father of my sister's child, I'd take you out right now."

"You know, one day you're going to do that to the wrong person. . . . I know you're just strutting your ego, but someone else . . ." Leonek shook his head and motioned for Jakub to follow him inside the house.

Catherine darted to the table and started to peel potatoes.

"There's my good bride," Leonek said as he walked toward the stove. "We're starved."

She gave him a half-smile, gripping the potato so her hand would stop shaking.

He looked down at the bowl of salad on the table.

"Ugh, what kind of pig food is that?"

"It's called Waldorf salad. Apples, grapes, celery, and raisins mixed in mayonnaise. Rose gave me the recipe a few weeks ago."

His nose crinkled. "It looks disgusting. You better have made something else besides that."

Jakub tried to lighten the mood. "Hey, Leonek, while we wait for dinner let's have a bees knees and a smoke. I know you've got some here."

Leonek let out a mirthless laugh. "What are you, a cellar smeller?"

"No, I'm someone who gave you a black eye instead of a broken nose. It's the least you could do."

"Can't argue with that logic. Be right back."

Leonek strolled past Catherine toward the basement door and grinned as if he had a big secret. She finished peeling the last potato and carried the heavy pot to the sink. As the pot filled with water, she turned her head toward Jakub. "What's a bees' knees?"

"Just a name for—you know."

Leonek returned with a glass soda bottle filled with an orange-colored liquid. He went to the shelf for two glasses and set them on the end of the table near Jakub.

After he filled them they each nodded and took a swig.

"Ah, that's good stuff. You're lucky I'm in a good mood today despite Filip's demeanor."

Jakub wiped his mouth with the back of his hand. "Yeah? What's got you so happy?"

"Today I told the foreman Filip had been drinking on the job. Remember all the times he left the shop to get the dinner pails? After he dropped them off to the workers he would say he forgot something. But the guys in town told me what he was doing…"

Jakub, who loved to gossip, hung onto every word as he took another drink.

Leonek continued. "On the clock no less."

Jakub's eyes grew wide. "What if Filip finds out it was you?"

"Who cares. Hope he loses his job. Then he would beg me for money like the dog he is."

Catherine sat at the dining room table for a moment and watched Leonek and Jakub talk amongst themselves. Her mind wandered back to a few days ago when she was upstairs changing the sheets on the beds. She heard a loud knock on the door at Filip's house and when she peered down there were two men in uniform. They reminded her of the soldiers back home with their brass buttoned jackets and knee-high black boots which caused their pants to pucker above the knee. A wide black belt held a gun holster. Her heart raced and she was afraid they would come to her door. Instead, they stood in the drive a moment before they walked down to the bridge toward their horses.

She felt Leonek's eyes on her. "What's the matter with you? You look like you just saw a ghost."

She wanted to tell him, but not in front of Jakub, who had a tongue of fire.

"Anyhow, I've got news that would cheer you up. After Easter Sunday is the Papermakers Ball at the Union Hall in town. There is going to be food and music."

Jakub added, "I heard oysters are being served. On a Monday night, no less." His voice lowered. "Joe told me what happened last year when the lumberjacks showed up." His eyes looked glossy.

"Yeah… they did bring some good pipe tobacco."

Leonek poured a little more from the long-necked bottle into his glass. Jakub slid his empty glass over. "We sang and danced till we couldn't walk."

"Doesn't sound like fun to me." Annoyed with the conversation she took a knife and started to cut up the salt pork. She was glad when Leonek and Jakub ventured outside.

A few days later, Good Friday dawned clear and cold. All week Catherine and Rose prepared their homes for the Easter feast. Today, they would make their sweet, braided raisin bread. The loaves took three hours to make. This gave them time to do the long-standing tradition of *Pisanki*, which was a way to decorate eggs for Easter. They used a pencil and hot paraffin to create a design on each hard-boiled egg. Rose talked as they applied melted wax over the designs with a wooden matchstick.

"Leftover raisin bread makes delicious French toast or bread pudding, so breakfast on Monday will be set."

Bertha and Johnny squealed with delight as they helped their mother put the eggs in tin cups of colored water to reveal a dyed egg.

"You're pretty good at creating designs on the eggs, Catherine. It comes natural to you."

Catherine smiled. It felt good to hear someone compliment her drawing skills.

"I am hopeful Leonek and Filip could put their differences aside and we might have a peaceful Easter." Catherine said as she handed Rose another egg.

"Just so you know, I ran into Mary Nego today. The Rushton house in town is having fish dinners tonight so the men would go there after work. Mary told me she would work the dinner to get food for her children." Rose stopped and looked over at Catherine. "Did you know she lost her husband in an accident at the mill?"

"Yes, I heard Jakub tell Leonek."

Rose shook her head. "It's a shame. With five mouths to feed. I can't imagine . . ." Her voice trailed off. "Anyhow, Sunday would be a good day. A day of feasting as Filip would say."

The women ended their conversation with a hollow laugh.

Chapter
23

When Leonek came home that evening he was drunk as usual. He sat on the couch, fell asleep stinking of alcohol, and slid to the floor. The mill was still on overtime and between the long hours and alcohol, he looked in no shape to get up and go to work the next morning. Rose told Catherine Filip had the day off and she expected him not to get home until late. Catherine decided to leave him there, and when she turned off the lamp to go to bed, he growled, "What—don't I even get a kiss goodnight?"

Disgusted by his stale breath, she placed her hand on his shoulder and leaned down to peck him on the head. He then grabbed her arm.

"What kind of kiss is that?" He pulled her down to his face and all she could taste was the sour flavor of a drunken binge. She twisted her arm from his grip as she pulled away. "Ow, you're hurting me."

He used the arm of the sofa to pull himself up. "I saw Stefan tonight. He had nothing but good things to say about you."

Catherine watched in silence as he struggled to stand. She felt no compassion to help him.

"Are you having an affair with him?"

"What? No, of course not. Why would you ask such a thing?"

"I've seen the way you look at him. Talk with him."

"He's just a nice person. That's all." *Unlike you.*

She did not like where the conversation was headed. "I'm going to bed."

"Where? Upstairs with him?" He lurched toward her, grabbed her arm, and this time she could not pull away. With his other hand, he slapped her across the face.

Her eyes filled with tears, and she filled with rage. "What is wrong with you? Why are you acting this way?"

"Jakub told me about the other day. When you had Stefan fix the water pipe under the sink." His fingers dug painfully into her arm.

"That's because I had to keep emptying the bucket and when it gets full it gets awkward and heavy. He was just trying to do you a favor since you were at work."

"Oh, so he was here when I was at work?"

"Could you please let go?" Her heart felt like it could beat out of her chest.

Another sting across her face, this time harder than the first. An energy surged through her, and she pushed his chest which caused him to stumble backward. She ran out the front door across the drive behind Filip's house. Leonek stood in the doorway. "Get back here! Where do you think you're going? Get back here NOW!"

She ran as fast as she could and ducked down behind the chicken coop. The chickens clattered and clucked. Tears streamed down her face. "Shhhhh! Shhhh!" She looked down and realized she had no shoes on.

A light came on inside the house and someone opened the back door of the porch to look for the predator. "What's going on out here?" It was Rose.

Catherine stood up; her body shook. "It's me. . . . Catherine."

"What are you doing outside at this time of night?"

She walked toward Rose and took a deep breath. The tension was gone, for the moment.

"And barefoot no less?"

Catherine hung her head as she made her way toward the door.

Rose stood on the porch with her arms crossed. "Are you all right?"

As they stood on the back porch Catherine felt the light from the kitchen on her face. "What happened to you?" She took Catherine's hand. "You're shaking."

"Is it all right if I come inside?"

Rose led her inside. The warmth of the house felt good. "Filip is asleep. Passed out as usual. Do you want me to wake him?"

"No, please." She didn't want to be rude to Rose or start a fight between Filip and Leonek. "I just need a moment to catch my thoughts."

"Here, put this cold cloth on your face. That's quite a bruise you have there."

Catherine looked at the clock, it was just past one a.m. "I'm sorry to have woken you."

Rose stared at her. "Who did this to you? Was it Leonek?"

Too many thoughts filled Catherine's head. "Leonek is supposed to work tomorrow. He has been late several times this past month and is on the verge of losing his job. If he doesn't go to work . . . then what would we do?" Her brain searched for safety. "We are going to have a baby. If there is no money . . ." She walked over and sat on the sofa. Rose followed, sat next to her, and placed her hand on Catherine's shoulder.

"Catherine, Leonek may have his bad points, but I know he would always find a way to make money." Her compassion quickly turned to anger. "I'm just not sure if he would be a good father…look at how he abandoned his other two children . . ."

Catherine felt the color drain from her face and her body shook with fear. She thought about those two children on the steps at Christmas.

How could a man abandon his own children? What kind of man did I marry?

She felt trapped in a country whose values were hard to understand.

Could I go home to Poland? Not to live with father, or Zophia. Marcin and Eva had probably moved to the city.

"Catherine, why don't you stay here tonight. We can talk about this in the morning." Rose took a folded knitted blanket from the basket near the overstuffed chair. Catherine laid down as Rose spread it over her.

After Rose turned out the lights Catherine closed her eyes and prayed to God, first with the Our Father and then three hail Mary's.

I might as well be alone. I hoped Leonek would be a good husband, but he is nothing but a drunk and a gambler.

A tear streamed down her cheek. Something had to change. But how?

She closed her eyes.

God, thank you for all you have provided for me here in America. I know you will help me find a way where I see no way.

The cold cloth was now warm, and she imagined it as the hand of God touching her. She didn't want to be mad at God.

The sun came up and Filip was surprised to see Catherine on his couch with a purple and red bruise on one side of her face.

"Catherine, what happened to you?"

She sat up, and before she could speak, Rose said, "Your good friend, Leonek. That is what happened to her."

Filip's eyes narrowed and his jaw clenched. "Leonek did this?"

Catherine felt ashamed to look at her brother.

Rose grabbed Filip by the shoulder. "Yes, Leonek did that. Along with going to the shop supervisor and turning you in for drinking on the job." Rose started to cry. "Filip, what if you lose your job? Then what? Where would we go?"

Johnny and Bertha cried out from the bedroom.

Catherine watched in horror as Filip's hangover rage erupted. He pointed at Rose. "Do you know what else that blind pig has been doing? He's been selling liquor behind my back. I just found out last night. One of the men in town told me they liked my new orange flavored tea. I said, 'I don't have any orange flavored tea.' That's when he told me Leonek sold it to him."

He looked at Catherine. "Where is that yokel now?"

"He's supposed to be at work."

Rose followed Filip into the bedroom. "Don't do anything rash. Especially at work. Why don't you wait until he gets home?"

Catherine could hear Filip putting on his belt, and she clutched the blanket, too frightened to move.

He came out of the bedroom, followed by Rose. There was a revolver tucked in his pants.

"Filip!" Rose begged, "don't go. Leave that gun here. *Please!*"

Ignoring her, he put on his jacket and stopped in front of Catherine, his face crimson with fury.

"Don't you worry Catherine. I'll make sure he never hurts you again." His expression softened. "I'm sorry I brought you here." He touched her cheek gently. "What have I done?"

Rose took hold of Filip's jacket. "Don't go to the mill. Nothing good will come of you confronting Leonek there."

He jerked away and left the door open as he stormed down the steps toward the car. Once it started, he jerked it into gear and rocks spun out from under the tires as he drove away.

Rose dropped into a chair and started to sob. "He gets crazy when he's mad. Oh my! What's he going to do?"

Filip had been gone a long time and Catherine knew the boarders would be up and want their breakfast. She went into the bathroom and looked at herself in the mirror. The swelling had gone down around her eye, but a deep purple bruise remained. She lifted her sleeve and saw another black and blue mark on her forearm.

Why would Leonek do this to me?

She splashed cool water on her face and patted it dry. The thought of telling people Leonek hit her made her not want to face anyone. She returned to the kitchen to find Rose staring at the basket of food they put together to be blessed at the church. Rose hadn't said two words since Filip left.

"The basket looks beautiful." She sat down at the table across from Rose and glanced at the clock on the wall, it was almost ten o'clock.

"I know you're worried about Filip. I am too. But I'm sure he'll be back soon. He probably stopped in town to brag about how he put Leonek in his place."

"You should go home. Leonek would be sorry for what he did. Just like all men are."

Rose's remark stunned Catherine. It was as if women in America accepted this type of behavior.

"I suppose you're right." Catherine walked over and gave Johnny and Bertha each a hug and a kiss. "There is much to do before Easter." She added, "Father Kelley said the blessing of the baskets would be at two o'clock. I could stay with the children while you and Filip take the basket."

"That would be nice."

I hoped Filip would be back by now. Why was he not back yet?

When she arrived home the smell of fresh coffee welcomed her. Mike and Stefan sat at the table.

"There you are Katie, we wondered where you . . ." He stopped and stared, his eyes wide, eyebrows raised.

Mike pivoted on the bench. "Jesus Catherine, what happened to you?"

"Just a misunderstanding."

Stefan walked over to her. "Looks like more than a misunderstanding." He looked down at her wrist. "That looks painful, too."

Mike's usual calm voice turned angry. "Did Leonek do this to you?"

"I don't want to talk about it." She went over to the icebox and pulled out some eggs and salt pork. "You must be hungry. Let me fix you something to eat." Catherine could feel their eyes on her. She glanced at the unmade bed in the bedroom and shut the door.

Mike lit a cigarette. "I'm surprised Leonek went to work today. What time did he get home?"

Catherine kept her back to them as the salt pork sizzled in the pan. "I'm not sure. I was asleep on the couch."

"Well, when I see him, I'm going to give him a black eye and a bloody lip. I have no respect for a man who hits a woman, and a quick beating may help him remember."

Catherine set two plates of steaming food on the table.

"While you eat, I'm going to go change my clothes." Part of her was scared to face Leonek and the other part of her hoped Filip told him to never come back.

Stefan and Mike were both standing at the window when she returned.

"What are you looking at?"

"A strange car just pulled in the drive next to Filip's house. Looks like two police officers along with Father Kelley."

Catherine followed them out onto the porch, and they watched as Rose let the officers and Father Kelley inside.

Why would the police be there?

"Catherine, where are you going?" Mike called out, as she charged across the lawn.

A loud scream from inside the house startled her, and she barged inside.

"You! You!" Rose screamed at her.

The officers grabbed Rose as she lunged at Catherine, tears streamed down her cheeks. "*It's all her fault! Get her out of here!*"

Confused and afraid, Catherine shouted back, "What are you saying? What's my fault?"

Mike and Stefan entered the room.

Rose continued to yell. "They told me Filip's dead—*He's dead!*" Her chest rose and fell with rapid breaths.

The officers talked to her in English, guiding her over to the couch, where she collapsed.

Catherine's mind reeled. *Dead? How? Where?*

I'm so frustrated not knowing the language American people speak.

Father Kelley motioned for Mike and Stefan to take Catherine outside.

Catherine refused to move. "What is it, Father? What has happened to Filip?" Father Kelley stared at her eye.

"Please wait outside Catherine. Stefan, take her outside." He sat on the couch next to Rose who sobbed uncontrollably.

Stefan gently placed his hand on her back and guided her out the door. Mike followed closely behind.

Once outside, Joe Vielaska approached them. "What's going on? I was upstairs and could hear the screaming and commotion." His eyes veered to Catherine's face.

"All we know is something terrible happened to Filip." Mike lit a cigarette. "Rose was out of control, blaming Catherine. Father Kelley wanted us to bring her out here so he could calm Rose down."

Finally, Father Kelley and the officers came out of the house.

"Catherine, this is Sherriff Gibson and Sergeant O'Connor. They have a few questions for you. I told them I would translate."

O'Connor? Where have I heard that name?

Catherine looked up at the tall men. She noticed one had a tinge of reddish hair under his Stetson hat.

Is he related to Teresa O'Connor?

Father Kelley turned to Joe. "Could you go inside and sit with Rose until I get back?"

"What happened, Father?"

"I'd rather not say until the police have more information."

The officers motioned Catherine and Father Kelley to the porch away from the ears of Mike and Stefan.

"Catherine, they want to know when you last saw Leonek."

Leonek? What does he have to do with this?

They waited for her answer.

"Last night, after he came home from town."

"What time?"

"I'm not sure. I had fallen asleep on the couch."

Father Kelley gave her answer in English to the officers, and they responded back. Catherine could tell by the tone of their voice they had another question.

"How did you get that bruise on your face?"

Catherine felt too embarrassed to tell Father Kelley what happened. She looked down and didn't answer.

"Did someone hit you?"

She nodded.

"Was it Leonek?"

She hesitated, then nodded again."

"Catherine, Leonek has been arrested."

Arrested? The thought brought a lump to her throat.

"Why?"

"Apparently something to do with Filip's death."

Catherine began to feel dizzy and leaned against the house.

"Leonek has been taken to the jail in Canton."

Catherine felt a surge of fear in her chest. In Poland, men who went to prison did not come back.

Her heart pounded.

My brother is dead and Leonek might be the reason?

"Let's say a prayer for Filip." Father Kelley gently placed his hand on Catherine's shoulders and bowed his head. The officers removed their hats and Catherine closed her eyes.

"Father, I thank you Catherine does not sorrow, as one who has no hope. I thank you she is not alone and is comforted by those who surround her today. God, bless her loved one Filip, who now sleeps in your arms. I ask you comfort Catherine, for you said, blessed are they who mourn for they shall be comforted. Amen."

Catherine watched as the officers left in their automobile and Father Kelley went back inside Rose's house.

Mike and Stefan walked over to Catherine.

"You're shaking," Stefan said, gently touching her shoulder. "Let's get you inside."

Once they were inside Mike locked the door.

Stefan asked, "Why are you locking the door?"

Mike guided Catherine to the sofa. "Stefan, would you get Catherine a drink of water?"

"Maybe she needs something stronger."

"I can't, I'm pregnant," she blurted.

They all sat at the table in silence while Catherine sipped her water.

Mike spoke first. "I don't like to say it, but I could see this coming." His eyes looked at Catherine. "Leonek was arrested by the police. It's obvious he had something to do with Filip's death."

"How do you know?"

"I don't know. I just have this sense."

Stefan agreed. "Maybe I should go into town. Someone might know something."

"We don't need to hear any rumors right now. That's why I locked the door. Filip had many friends."

"And Leonek has a lot of enemies," Stefan finished.

"I need a cigarette."

"Me, too."

Soon all the boarders who lived on the island heard versions of what happened and tried to make sense of the speculations. They were all waiting for Jakub to return home from the mill. Jakub worked in the sulphite room with Leonek. Maybe he would have some answers.

Mike remained at the window. He would announce to the group who came and went across the drive. People like Mary Nego had brought some food with her five children.

"The police are back," he said suddenly.

Catherine bolted to the window, and they watched as Father Kelley came outside and stood at the door of the car and talked with the officers. Then he went back inside and came out with Rose. They both got into the police car.

Joe Vielaska came outside toward the house. Mike opened the door.

"Do you have news?"

"Father Kelley just left with Rose to identify the body. She wanted me to watch her children, but I don't know the first thing about babies. Mary Nego offered to stay with them."

He looked at Catherine. "I suggested she bring them here, but Rose wants nothing to do with Catherine. The minute I mentioned your name, she would get angry all over again."

Mike leaned into Joe. "Where is the body?"

"Still at the mill."

"I need some air."

Catherine started shaking as she prepared dinner. The thought of never seeing Filip or Leonek again made her angry one minute and sad the next. When she took the hot loaf of bread from the oven, her mind was still distracted and she burned her fingers when she grabbed the wrong hot pad.

As she ran her fingers under cold water, Filip's car came up the drive. Hastily, she wiped her hands on her apron and rushed outside. The men had already gathered around the car when she got there.

"So, then what happened?"

Jakub was in the driver's seat, and they all stopped talking when Catherine approached them.

"Jakub, where's Leonek? Did the police let him go?"

"No, the police took him to jail. He's in big trouble." His eyes widened. "Geez, Catherine, what happened to your face?"

"Doesn't matter. Tell me what happened to my brother."

Jakub looked around at the faces who stared intently at him. Normally no one would pay attention to Jakub but now what he was about to say was all they cared about.

"Leonek, Aleksandr, Jerry, and I were in the sulphite room. The pulp still had two hours left to cook so it was hot—all those darn steampipes." He turned to look at Joe. "Remember how we started the mix three days ago?"

"Yeah, yeah Jakub, go on."

"Anyhow, the noise of the logs being ground in the chipper from the barking room for the next batch was giving Leonek a headache. All he did was complain… then Filip shows up, guns blazing."

"You mean he was shooting his gun?"

"No, I mean he was hot under the collar. His face was beat red. Jerry thought Filip was there to take over his shift, so he left." Jakub's eyes turned toward Catherine. "That's when Filip started to yell. Something about he should have never trusted Leonek, especially after what he did to Catherine. There would be no more excuses. He demanded Leonek pay him everything he owed and get out of Pyrites."

The small crowd continued to grow, and Catherine glanced over at Filip's house to see Mary Nego pull back the curtain and look outside.

"Aleksandr and I didn't know what to do. We just kept working, trying to keep out of it. We thought about going to get Jerry, but then we heard Filip say he was going to beat the lights out of Leonek."

"Holy cow." Joe rubbed his fingers through his hair.

"Then there was the sound of a loud crack followed by a thud. We ran over and saw Filip on the floor in a puddle of blood. Leonek just stood there with a piece of metal pipe in his hand."

Catherine felt sick and could not believe her ears.

Jakub continued. "Leonek told us, 'I had to do it. He reached under his coat for his gun. He was going to kill me. I had to do it.'"

Nobody said a word.

"We all just stood there in shock. Filip wasn't moving. Then Leonek tossed the pipe on the floor near the wall and said, 'I better go tell Jerry, and he left."

"Did Filip get up?"

"No way. His skull was smashed open, and he was dead for sure. His brains . . ." Jakub stopped. "It was gruesome. Reminded me of the war, when I was a soldier. Well, once I did see a man lose his leg." His eyes glazed over.

"Anyhow, I need a drink. Anybody been to see Rose to get some, you know . . ."

No one answered him until Joe spoke, "Who's going to tell Rose what happened?"

"Nobody. Nobody better say anything to Rose. She's upset enough. Let the police handle it." Mike stared down the river at the paper mill, the constant *thud* of machinery echoed in the distance. "Let the mill tell her what happened." He spat on the ground. "Can't imagine her seeing that body."

Jakub looked at Mike. "Where is Rose? At the mill?"

"Yes, she had to go identify the body."

"But they know it's Filip."

"It's something they do. Next of kin must identify the victim."

They all started talking again, while Catherine staggered back toward the house, her mind lost in a mass of painful thoughts.

My brother is dead. And my husband killed him?. . . But did Filip try to shoot Leonek? Did Leonek kill Filip to defend himself?

She walked up the stoop and felt a flutter in her stomach, followed by another. She reached down and placed her hand on her mid-section. *How am I going to care for this baby?*

Chapter

24

T he next day Catherine felt exhausted. She had not slept well and the vision of Filip with a gun and Leonek hitting him in the head with a pipe played over and over in her mind.

I need to tell the news to Antonio . . . and our father. They'll be devastated.

She looked over at the cake of babka she made on Friday evening before Leonek returned home.

It was Easter Sunday.

Outside the rising sun cast a rosy hue across the morning sky.

There was a soft knock at the door.

It was Father Kelley with another man who was dressed like a priest yet looked too young to be a man of the cloth. In one hand was a bible and on his robe a velvet tippet attached to his sleeve just above the elbow with a gold cross and fringed bottom.

Catherine hung her head. She felt ashamed to make eye contact and didn't want whoever it was to see the bruise on her face.

"Catherine, this is Reverend Joseph Lauzon. He has been at the Reynoldston logging camps to preach the word of God and stopped to see me last night on his way back to the Diocese in Syracuse."

"Hello Catherine." His voice was strong. "I was sorry to learn about what happened to your brother."

"Thank you."

Her eyes turned to Father Kelley.

"Have you heard anything more about Leonek?"

"He's still at the County jail. Sergeant O'Connor told me last night it looks like Leonek would be there at least a couple more days."

"I don't like this. The police do not keep people unless . . ."

"Don't worry, Catherine. I'll see what I can do." He smiled at her. "But I do have other news. Rose gave me the telephone number to call your brother Antonio, but I thought you would like to do it."

Reverend Lauzon added, "Father Kelley asked me to take you to the Central House Hotel in town and place a phone call to Antonio. He has arranged with the hotel for us to use their telephone."

She thought this was all a terrible mistake—all of it: coming to America, marrying Leonek, agreeing to live in a terrible, gritty place like this struck her full force. She found it hard to breathe.

"What about—" Her throat tightened. "A funeral for Filip?"

"There is no cemetery here, so I arranged for him to be buried in Riverside Cemetery in Canton, not far from Saint Mary's Church."

She turned to Reverend Lauzon. "I will get my coat. Could we go call Antonio *now*? Maybe he would have time to come on the train?" Guilt filled her eyes. "I should have called him yesterday."

Father Kelley went to see Rose as Catherine and Reverend Lauzon walked to town. The only sound was the thumping of the paper mill. The spring log drive piled timbers higher than the roof of the mill. The people here might depend on this mill for their future, but Catherine was not about to let it dictate hers. She was angry, frustrated, and now she was about to go tell Antonio Filip was gone. Forever.

To lighten the mood, Reverend Lauzon told Catherine a story about a bear that visited the logging camp while he was there.

"It broke into the kitchen at night, and when the poor women went in to start making breakfast for the camp at four in the morning, the bear came out from behind. . . ."

She nodded to be polite, but her thoughts were elsewhere. *How do I tell Antonio, and our father? How will I get to the funeral? Will Rose prevent me from going?*

People passing by shot furtive glances and quickly looked away.

Catherine had never been inside the Central Hotel. Inside the parlor was an oasis of lace curtains, an ornate dark blue carpet, and intricate wallpaper. A man with a full beard wearing a brown, straw pork-pie hat sat on a Victorian style sofa next to a woman who Catherine thought too fancy for a mill town woman. She wore a long robe-like dress with laced sleeves. Her long black hair was held up with jeweled combs and smudged mascara from her tears gave the appearance of raccoon eyes. The woman was crying out in English to the man, and Catherine swore she heard her say Leonek.

"I feel sorry for women like that," Reverend Lauzon commented after they walked past.

"What do you mean?"

He cleared his throat. "I mean women who are trapped to have to make their way in the world by doing what she's doing, selling herself to make a buck."

Catherine looked back at the woman whose head was cradled in the man's shoulder.

He stopped to open a door in the long hallway and whispered, "Father Kelley calls this place Satan's Circus."

In the hotel office, Reverend Lauzon placed the call and handed Catherine the earpiece.

"Catherine, how are you? Happy Easter. How is Filip and his family? When my landlord said there would be a call for me from Pyrites, I expected Filip."

Catherine's eyes filled with tears. "I am sorry to make this call, and on Easter of all days, but Filip is not here… He is dead."

"*Dead?* How? What happened?"

To soften the blow she said, "There was an accident at the paper mill. He died instantly."

The telephone line went silent.

"This is terrible news. I do not want to believe it. You are lucky to have a husband to take care of you. How are Rose and the children?"

Catherine wanted to cry but instead took a deep breath. "The funeral is tomorrow. Can you come on the train?" She would rather tell him in person what really happened.

"Tomorrow? No—I cannot get time off from work on such short notice. The bank is busiest on Monday, especially after a holiday."

It was not the answer she expected or wanted to hear. "Not even for your brother's death?"

211

Antonio did not respond.

"I-I'm sorry . . . I didn't mean to sound so harsh. It's just I'm alone here, and—"

"No, I'm sorry Catherine. I'll try to explain to my boss. If I could come, I would. But here people are expected to come to work, even if they are sick."

Suddenly, a woman's voice interrupted them in English. Catherine handed the receiver to Reverend Lauzon who bent down to talk into the mouthpiece. After a few words in English were exchanged he said to Catherine, "Your time is up. You need to say goodbye."

She cleared her throat. "Goodbye, brother. I will write to our father. God bless you. I hope you can come."

"Goodbye, sister. I—" The line went completely dead.

She hung her head and sobbed.

Reverend Lauzon put his hand on her shoulder. "That took courage. At least your brother knows."

Catherine reached in her shoulder bag for her handkerchief and dabbed her eyes. "I wasn't able to tell him I am with child."

She walked across the bridge up to the house as a warm spring breeze dried her tears. Reverend Lauzon offered to walk her home, but she didn't feel like talking anymore.

How could he have been so mad at Filip to kill him? What kind of man is he? I knew he had a temper but this . . .

The sound of the mill's steam whistle broke into her thoughts.

I am thankful for Father Kelley and Reverend Lauzon. If it wasn't for them, I would have no one. They both give me hope and strength.

Soon church let out and the boarders who had to work were home. Despite what happened the day before, Easter Sunday was full of eating and drinking. The ones who wanted to drink went over to Rose's house and the boarders who wanted peace and quiet stayed with Catherine. Stefan was protective of Catherine and stayed with her as she cleaned-up.

"A woman's work is never done." He tried to joke with her before he left to go outside with the others, but all she could think about was what happened between Filip and Leonek. It was as if she expected him to come through the door any moment, and she caught herself saving him a plate.

How can I care for someone who was so mean to me? Who fought with my brother?

"Katie, did you hear me?"

She didn't realize Stefan had come back inside.

"The guys were out there talking. Apparently, Jakub is going to drive Rose and the children to Canton in the automobile tomorrow for the funeral."

"Does this mean I cannot go? Would Rose let me ride, too?"

"Don't worry. Mike talked with a local farmer at church. He offered to give people a ride in his horse and wagon to Canton."

"It's been a long time since I rode in a horse and wagon." They both laughed.

The next morning the boarders gathered by the automobile once again to hear Jakub, who was now the most popular of the group.

Catherine walked over to Jakub. "How is Rose doing?"

"Not good. Better stay far away from her. She still blames you for Filip's death."

The words stung.

"But she must know my heart aches just like hers. We could not know . . ."

Mike looked at Catherine. "We better head into town. The farmer will be waiting for us."

They all started to walk down the drive in a group except for Jakub who walked toward Filip's house.

"Catherine, remember not to say too much to Jakub. He would twist your words. Especially to Rose."

It would be a six-mile ride on the wagon to Canton where the culture of America once again passed before her eyes. Signs were all in English. She spotted moving picture posters on a building with a large marquee sign above the door. The store windows were full of products and clothes worn by mannequins of women. Just like Syracuse, everywhere she looked there was abundance. She remembered on the ship how the immigrants would say, "In America, the streets are paved with gold." No wonder people risked their lives to come here.

The front of the church was crowded as people walked up to give Rose their condolences. Catherine didn't realize until today how many friends Filip had despite his drinking, gambling, and fighting. There were wreaths of colorful flowers on top of the casket. Catherine did not want to cause a scene and decided to sit in the back of the church. She had not met many people since coming to Pyrites, only Rose, Leonek, and the boarders who lived on the island.

"Is it all right if I sit here?"

Catherine looked up. It was Reverend Lauzon. She appreciated his company and slid over.

"It would seem Filip had many friends. How long had he been in America?"

"Only for a few years. At home Filip always made friends quickly." She smiled. "My father used to say, 'too quickly.'" She watched as Father Kelley took his place at the podium. She added, "he always wanted to have a good time."

At Polish funerals there are songs sung to get into heaven. This is when people once again broke down and cried.

After the funeral mass Father Kelley explained to the mourners Filip's coffin would be taken by the undertaker to a vault in Riverside Cemetery until he could be buried. Rose started to sob uncontrollably, and several people went over to comfort her.

Catherine had not cried yet. She was still in shock over what happened. Unlike a death at home there had been no wake, no observance of the body, no time to say goodbye.

"Are you all right, Catherine? Is there anything I can do for you?"

Catherine reached into her shoulder bag and took out the letter she wrote to her father.

"Could you mail this letter? It's to my father . . ." Her voice trailed off.

"Of course." Reverend Lauzon paused. "Catherine, I know you are scared, and confused, but you are strong. Like Filip, you came to America looking for a better life. Remember how far you have come to start a new life. Just like a plant uprooted, you have struggled to adjust. You were taken from one environment and put into another."

She felt a tear roll down her cheek.

He smiled at her. "You have friends here in America, like me. Think of yourself transplanted, not uprooted. The church community is here to help you."

As the church started to empty, people slowed and stared at Catherine as they walked by.

Stefan and Mike stopped when they saw Catherine.

"Are you ready to go?" Stefan asked as he put on his cap.

Catherine nodded as she and Reverend Lauzon stood.

"Thank you, Reverend."

"I'll come by and see you this week. We can talk more then." He made the sign of the cross. "Remember God is with you, Catherine."

No one spoke as the horse and wagon made its way through the tree lined street of large homes on the way back to Pyrites. Her brother was gone, forever. How would her father react to the news? She said in the letter the same thing she told Antonio, Filip died in a mill accident. She couldn't bear the thought Leonek would have killed Filip on purpose. It was as Jakub had said, self-defense.

Catherine looked toward a large open area surrounded by a wrought iron fence with two four-story rectangular brick buildings. An American flag on a flagpole next to a chapel built of gray limestone overlooked a courtyard of well-placed trees. Catherine observed the well-dressed people milling about. A woman with a white cotton dress strolled between the buildings.

She turned to the farmer to ask, but remembered he only spoke English. Instead, she turned to ask Mike.

"What is that place?"

He shrugged and said something to the farmer, who then replied to him.

"Jim here says it is a university."

Her eyes grew wide. "Ask him, is that where the art school is?"

Catherine waited patiently as they conversed.

"He believes they study art there."

Catherine felt happier knowing she had finally seen the art school. It was beautiful. So much space and places to draw. She imagined herself being on the campus.

It occurred to her that if she was going to make it in America, she would need to learn English. God opened her eyes to the fact she could not depend on anyone but herself. At any moment life can change. Filip brought her to America with a plan, but deep down she knew God had a different idea. Above her a hint of blue sky appeared in the clouds.

It had been two days since the funeral and still no word about Leonek. Catherine was getting restless. She knows the ice man comes on Thursday and the milk man on Friday. Did Leonek have any money on him? Surely, he would have given it to the police who would bring it to her. She reached for the coffee can on the shelf and counted the coins. She felt better, there was enough to pay them, at least this week.

After dinner Mike gathered the group at the table to read the newspaper. Catherine was thankful to have Mike translate. She wanted him to teach her English, but he never seemed interested. "I'm not much of a teacher. You need to find another way." Yes, she thought, I would find another way.

Before he started reading he looked at Catherine. "I'm not sure you are going to want to hear what the newspaper wrote. But remember what I told you, a reporter creates a story to sell newspapers."

"It's okay. I want to know what they are saying."

Mike began to translate.

"Kruszka Retaining his Composure. Alleged Murderer Said to Be Glad of Soból's Death."

No one spoke except for Jakub. "He didn't look glad after it happened."

"Keep reading," Stefan demanded.

"Leonek Kruszka, the alleged slayer of his brother-in-law Filip Soból, was recently reported to be on a hunger strike at the jail. Kruszka was rather gloomy, after first taken to jail, though he said to have asserted, 'I'm glad I did it' and on Sunday night refused his supper. Soból, the murdered man, is said by his fellow workmen to have been quick tempered and for that reason difficult to talk to in an explanatory manner for he was quite liable to flare up. Many who knew Kruszka have expressed surprise at his act for he was considered a reasonable man of a quiet easy-going nature."

"Where does the reporter get this information?" Catherine asked after Mike was finished.

Stefan interrupted. "I saw a reporter down at the mill asking questions. He was also at the pool hall."

"Filip did have a temper, but mainly when he drank." Jakub looked over at Stefan. "Was he drunk? You know, the day he came to the mill."

"How would I know? He probably had a hangover. Last time I saw him was Good Friday. He was in a bad mood at the pool hall."

As they bantered, Catherine noticed another newspaper in front of Mike on the table. "Is there another news story?"

Mike picked up the other paper. "Yes, but this one already has Leonek guilty. It mentions you, Catherine."

"Me?"

"Maybe you shouldn't read it in front of Catherine, Mike. We don't need her getting upset, I mean, she is with child."

Jakub's eyes grew wide. "Catherine, you're knocked up?"

"What?"

"I mean . . ." He leaned back to look at her stomach. "You know, a baby?"

She smoothed her dress over her stomach.

"Go ahead, Mike, read the story. I want to know what it says."

All eyes were on Mike.

"The headline says: *Murdered Man's Funeral is Held. Sister, Wife of Murderer Attends but Holds Aloof. Widow of Philip Saben, DeGrasse Worker, Left with Two Children with No Insurance.*"

Stefan spoke up. "Saben?"

Mike set the paper down and shook his head. "That's how these American papers are, they don't even get the names right half the time."

Catherine was shocked. *Murderer? Aloof? This doesn't sound good.*

"Keep reading." Jakub said as he smiled at Catherine. He seemed eager to go spread whatever the story said.

Mike continued.

> *"The funeral of Philip Saben, who was murdered on Saturday by his brother-in-law, Leonek Kruszka, in the mill of the DeGrasse Paper company at Pyrites, was held at St. Mary's Church yesterday morning and the remains were placed in the vault at Riverside cemetery. The funeral was largely attended by the Polish relatives and friends of Saben's from Pyrites, and among them was Mrs. Kruszka, Saben's sister, the wife of the alleged slayer of Saben. Mrs. Kruszka sat in the rear of the church and did not shed a tear, although the rest of the family wept."*

Mike stopped reading and they all looked at Catherine whose knee shook the bench she sat on.

Stefan tried to comfort her, "Katie, we know you were sad. Pay no attention to what the reporter wrote."

This person doesn't even know me, yet he writes my feelings.

As Mike continued to read, her mind became fogged until she heard the words 'marriage to Kruszka' and 'kept putting it off.'

"What did you just read?"

"Saben's sister made her home at his house for several weeks after arriving in this country from Poland and before her marriage to Kruszka. She reached New York on Sept 5th and was to have married Kruszka at once, but it was said by her friends yesterday that after she arrived here, she changed her mind about the marriage. She kept putting it off from one week to the next but in October was finally married. The marriage was solemnized in Syracuse and Philip Saber, his wife and two children all went to that city to be present. The Kruszka's then returned to Pyrites and took up their residence in a house directly across the road from the one which the Saber's occupy. Both houses are located on what is called the "island" and look out upon the paper company's dam across the Grasse River."

Catherine felt so exposed. Her personal life in the newspaper for everyone to see. Her mind started to create all kinds of scenarios. *What if someone mailed this paper to my father? Or my brother Antonio?*

She heard the drum of her heartbeat between her ears and her face felt hot. She turned to Mike. "Who would have told the paper all of this?"

As the men started to talk, another thought crossed Catherine's mind. *The only one who knows all of this is Rose. Why would she share my personal life with strangers?* She had an urge to grab the newspaper and march straight over to Rose's house. Instead, she stood and started to pace back and forth. Then she remembered the bread dough in the bowl still had to be kneaded.

"What else does it say?" Catherine opened a canister and spread some flour on the counter, removed the puffy dough from the metal bowl, and pushed on it with her palms, folding it over and over. Her back faced the men at the table.

Mike decided to summarize the article instead of reading it word for word. "It says Leonek is still in jail, how you and Rose are not speaking, and how Rose's house is nicer than yours."

No one spoke as Catherine divided the dough and formed the two pieces into loaves. She placed the loaves into two greased loaf pans and covered them with a damp cloth to let rise.

"Is that it? Or is there more? What else did Rose tell them?"

Jakub swung his legs over the bench and stretched. "I'm going to the pool hall. Anybody else want to go?"

"Count me in." Kowalski said as he put his cap on and followed Jakub outside. Catherine looked at Stefan and Mike who remained at the table.

Her mind wanted to believe it was all an accident. Maybe Filip had pulled his gun on Leonek . . . but . . . Leonek only meant to stop him. Not kill him. Her head throbbed. None of this made sense. *I thought Rose liked me.*

Catherine removed her apron and washed her hands.

"Where are you going?"

"I'm going to see Rose. She shouldn't have said those things about me."

Mike folded the newspapers as Stefan stood up. "I don't think that's a good idea. Those reporters are probably watching this island like hawks. As soon as they see you go over there, they'll start writing. And then who knows what Rose might tell them? She could say you're just as bad as your husband and want to kill her."

Mike agreed. "She is not to be trusted."

Catherine's eyes filled with tears. "But I can't let her get away with it." Suddenly her mind gave her an idea. "What if I tell the newspaper she sells illegal liquor? How would she like that."

They all stood silent letting the emotion flatten.

"Not a good idea, Katie. Leonek sold illegal liquor too. It would only harm his case and he might never get out of jail."

"Also, Rose could say you did it, too," Mike added.

"The best thing for you to do is keep quiet. Don't give Rose any more ammunition against your husband." Stefan looked at Mike. "Let's go see Father Kelley. Maybe he has news about Leonek."

Before they left, Stefan turned to Catherine. "Promise me you won't go see Rose."

Reluctantly Catherine agreed. "I promise."

Chapter
25

Since the death of Filip and the arrest of Leonek there had been more activity of people near the bridge to the island. Rose and Catherine's lives had become the new circus in town and nobody wanted to miss any altercation between the two women. One evening Catherine noticed Jakub on the bridge with a gander of gawkers after the mill whistle. She could only imagine the tales he spun in his web of deception.

So far Catherine did as Mike told her to do, but one warm day in early May, when the purple fragrant flowers of the lilac bush bloomed, she looked outside and saw Johnny at the edge of the drive playing with his toy train. Despite Mike and Stefan's warnings to avoid Rose, she took one of the cookies she had baked and strolled outside to sit on the porch to watch him. As soon as he saw her his arm waved and he ran over.

"Hello, Cath'rin!"

His wide smile reminded her of Filip.

"Johnny, how are you?" She reached inside her apron pocket. "Would you like a cookie?"

He nodded.

She patted the palm of her hand on the porch step. "Come sit here by me."

The young boy took large bites and looked over at his house. He pointed and said, "That's my house."

"Yes, it is. It's a big house."

"Yeah." He agreed and swallowed. "Big house."

Being around the small innocent boy made her heart sing. She felt a small glimmer of hope.

Suddenly from around the back of Filip's house came a familiar voice. "Johnnee, John-nee, where are you?"

"I here mama, I here!"

Catherine touched the boy's shoulder and gave him a hug.

"You better go to your mama."

"Okay." He hopped off the step and turned around. "You come, too."

She smiled at him.

"Johnny! What are you doing over there?"

Rose stood at the edge of the drive with Bertha on her hip.

Catherine watched as the boy walked toward his mother. "Cath'rin give me a cookie. It's good."

Rose bent down and gave the boy a strong swat on the fanny. "Get up on that porch. Don't you go over there anymore."

The people on the bridge had gotten what they came for.

"Don't be angry with Johnny. I called him over here."

Rose blocked the sun from her eyes with one hand. "I don't care who did what. You stay away from my children."

Despite Rose's angry demeanor Catherine felt compassionate for her and uttered, "How are you?"

Rose placed her free hand on her hip. "How am I? How do you think I am?" Her voice grew louder. "Oh, I don't know. My husband is dead and my children have no father."

Rather than argue Catherine remained silent.

Rose continued. "You just stay over there—away from me and my family. You are nothing but a naive peasant girl. I've always thought that about you."

Catherine felt her temperature rise. Her eyes narrowed. "Your family is my family. My husband is gone too."

"You come from a horrible family. You let your husband be a monster. I had to straighten Filip out. I hope he rots in jail."

Catherine ignored the voice inside her head telling her to go inside, to just step away. But Catherine was tired of being blamed and slandered in the newspaper by Rose. A burst of pent-up energy rose inside her. She stood.

"Why did you tell the newspaper reporter those things about me? About our wedding in Syracuse. You didn't tell them the real reason we went to Syracuse. To sell ille—"

"Oh, shut up. That's nothing compared to what they reported last week. What your own husband told them."

"Why? What did he say?"

"Leonek told them he paid money to bring you here, like a piece of meat. The whole town knows you are nothing but a prostitute. Paid for with a hefty sum of three-hundred fifty dollars."

Bertha started to struggle, and Rose set her down on the ground.

Catherine felt the color drain from her face. Rose smirked, satisfied she won the battle.

"How could my brother have married a nasty woman like you." She swallowed down her frustration.

Rose bent down, picked up a stone, and threw it at Catherine who ducked as it hit the single pane window and ricocheted off onto the porch. The glass now revealed a circular puncture, with cracks radiating outward from the point of impact.

As Rose walked away, people on the bridge began to disperse.

Antonio hadn't come. Filip was gone. Leonek was still in jail.

I can't just keep living here across the drive from Rose. I refuse to go back to Poland. I must take action—but who could help me? Who has the answers?

Catherine started to walk. Down the drive, over the bridge. Up the hill. To the church. It was there she must find the answers she needed.

A horse was tied outside to a fencepost, which meant Reverend Lauzon was there. Catherine pushed the heavy wooden white painted doors open and stepped inside.

"Hello?"

The church looked empty, and the sun shined on the stained-glass windows to show off their magnificent colored glass.

Father Kelley and Reverend Lauzon sat in front near the altar. They hadn't heard her come in as she walked toward them. It was Father Kelley who noticed her first. He immediately stood. "Catherine," he said, with a look of concern.

"Have you heard anything about Leonek? It has been a few weeks. I cannot live with no answers." With an exasperated voice she demanded, "I need some answers."

"Yes. We just found out from Trooper O'Connor Leonek had a hearing today and Judge Casper has agreed Leonek can be released on a bail bond tomorrow until his trial. The charges are manslaughter and not murder. We were just talking about which one of us was going to come and tell you."

A wave of relief rushed through Catherine's veins, but it was short lived. "What is a bail bond?"

Reverend Lauzon spoke. "It is money given to a bondsman who then secures the bail money to a judge."

"How much money?"

"His bail was set at twenty-five hundred."

Catherine's voice raised. "Dollars? Who has that much money?"

"All we know is it was a couple of men from Canton. Did Leonek have friends there?"

She thought for a moment about all the times Filip and Leonek went to Canton, but they never mentioned any friends . . . only business.

"I'm not sure. I mean no."

"Trooper O'Connor asked me if I would go pick up Leonek tomorrow at the jail and bring him home."

Reverend Lauzon added, "We also learned the foreman at the mill agreed to give Leonek his job back to help secure bail so Leonek wouldn't run away."

Catherine took a few steps toward Father Kelley and took his hand. "Thank you. This is good news, right?"

"Yes. Tomorrow I'll bring Leonek home after his bail hearing. But remember, at any moment before his trial he could be sent back to jail. He needs to be on his best behavior." He released her hand. "I just pray he listens to me."

Catherine walked back home from the church with new hope. The charge of murder had been dropped and soon he would be out on bail.

Surely God wouldn't want an innocent man to go to prison.

The shriek of the mill's steam whistle pierced the air.

I'm not sure who these friends of Leonek's are that Father Kelley talked about, but I'm relieved he'll have his job back.

The coffee can was empty.

She walked past the new two-story brick school and heard the laughter of children as they played outside.

Oh no. I forgot to ask if they know when the trial will be. Well, I will find out soon enough.

She crossed the bridge and noticed how the water of the river sparkled from the afternoon sun. Usually, it looked confined and blighted, unlike the river where Józef lived, wild and free, surrounded by hills of green. She stopped and looked down at the shallow water under the bridge where an amber colored glass of a broken bottle shimmered. It reminded her of the necklace from Józef. Her mind drifted.

Had he ever returned from the war, or? And if he had been fortunate enough to live and be set free from some terrible prisoner of war camp, would Uncle have told him I was gone forever?

She closed her eyes and could see his face. His crooked smile and silky loose curled hair. His voice, so deep and soothing.

For the first time in a long while, she felt inspired to draw again. It was as if Józef had spoken to her.

She walked up the dirt drive and stepped onto the porch, the cracked glass window greeted her. The stone Rose had thrown lay on the porch, and she kicked it onto the ground. Once inside, she began to prepare the evening meal for the six men who would be hungry after a long day at the mill. For a moment she missed how Rose and she worked together to prepare the food. Catherine would make the noodles while Rose baked bread. How Johnny and Bertha would be so happy to see Catherine when they greeted her at the door.

Later, as she mixed the dough for biscuits, she wondered how Rose would react once she found out Leonek had been released from jail.

What will the boarders think? Jakub witnessed what happened. Would he fight with Leonek? Did they know who put up Leonek's bail? Why didn't one of them tell me?

She pressed the ridge of a floured tin cup into the dough to cut out perfect circles, which she placed on a baking sheet.

At least the Judge let Leonek out on bail. He must believe Leonek did not murder Filip; it was self-defense.

Her mind flashed back to the morning Filip left in a rage, the revolver tucked in his pants just above the waist.

Leonek is my family now. I need to pray something good will come from all of this.

Catherine's mind was so pre-occupied she couldn't remember if she mixed baking powder in the biscuit dough.

As she sliced the carrots and turnips, the red cover of her sketch book caught her eye on the end table near the sofa. She wiped her hands on her apron and went over to pick it up and put it in her shoulder bag—out of sight from Leonek. Despite everything that worked against it, the dream to become an artist was still strong and she would not risk his angry outbursts to damage her work.

What if I need my drawings for art school? I can't let him destroy them.

Soon, the men were home, and conversation once again filled the supper table. The buzz that Leonek was being released from prison and had his job back spread like wildfire. Catherine was certain Rose must have heard the news. She set the platter of flat biscuits on the table. She had forgotten the baking powder. Stefan asked, "Katie, what happened to the window?"

"Oh, that." Catherine struggled to come up with a reason other than Rose had broken it. "A large bird—like a crow—flew into the glass. Scared the daylights out of me."

"Must have been a very big bird," Jakub added. "You're lucky it didn't come through the window."

"I thought the same thing."

Jakub stared at Catherine with a look of disbelief. "Did it die?"

Catherine didn't know what to say as she put a tub of butter on the table.

Felix, who was quiet and didn't say much, commented, "Back in my country when a bird hit the window, it meant death or something bad would happen."

Jakub smirked. "Guess the crow was a little late."

Mike glared at him. "Catherine, have you heard Leonek will be released on bail?"

"Yes. Father Kelley told me the mill agreed to give Leonek his job back." She paused and looked at the table of hungry eyes who lived to fill their mouth with gossip. "Do any of you know who put the money up for his bail? Father Kelley said it was two people from Canton."

The boarder they called Kowalski spoke. "I know they passed the hat at work. Joe Vielaska started the collection."

Catherine placed a steaming bowl of cabbage soup in front of Mike who added, "I read in the newspaper Leonek had a lawyer and when they went before the grand jury to plead not guilty, the judge charged him with manslaughter instead of first-degree murder." He picked-up his spoon. "They said Leonek's act was not premeditated but was committed in the heat of passion."

Jakub's voice turned razor sharp. "What difference would it make? Either way, he still killed Filip."

Mike leaned over the table toward Jakub. "The difference is Leonek will be out on bail until his trial in June."

"June?" Catherine interrupted. She looked at the wall calendar. That was just a few weeks away.

Mike continued. "The bad news is Leonek will be tried in the county court which means the judge will be James Burke."

Catherine felt a rise in her chest. "Why does that matter?"

"For one thing, Judge Burke has contempt for immigrants, mainly Poles."

Catherine wanted to believe in America things were different. Her mind wandered back to the hierarchy of Poland and the discrimination from Russia and Germany against Polish people.

"What else did the newspaper say?" Stefan asked.

"It said something about how Filip was known to threaten the lives of other people in Pyrites when he drank."

Catherine shook her head. "I don't understand. Where does this newspaper get this information?"

All eyes turned to Jakub.

"Don't look at me. I didn't talk to any of those reporters."

"No, but you'll talk to whoever will listen."

Jakub gave Stefan an irritated look and, like an animal, tore the biscuit with his teeth. Crumbs fell and stuck on his beard.

Soon dinner was done, and the table emptied except for the dirty dishes, abandoned glasses, and crumpled fabric napkins. Catherine cleaned up and thought about the last time she had seen Leonek.

I pray he will be sorry for the way he treated me.

A part of her feared, however, he would still be angry.

Later, as she readied herself for bed, she opened a bureau drawer and reached inside to reveal the necklace Józef made her. She clenched it in her hand like an amulet and held it to her heart.

Why, God? You took Józef to give me Leonek? I don't understand.

The next morning after the men ate breakfast they went outside to wait for Leonek. Although it was Saturday and some of the boarders had a day off, Catherine did not. She stripped the beds and pushed the electric washer tub to the sink. As it filled with water, she cleared the table. The men moseyed outside and stood around the automobile as they smoked their cigarettes and waited for Leonek's return.

Soon, Joe Vielaska came over to join them carrying a paper bag. Catherine knew what was in the bag and she prayed Leonek would not be tempted to drink. The washer finished and she put the wet sheets through the wooden wringers to squeeze out all the water. Catherine carried them outside in the basket to hang on the clothesline at the back of the house.

The sunshine made it a perfect day to dry laundry in the fresh air, and as she fastened each clothespin to the line, she felt someone was behind her. Turning, she saw Leonek.

His face sunken and blue eyes now grayed. He had a buzz cut and needed a shave.

She felt no urge to rush into his arms or to hold or even touch him. And he made no move toward her.

"Hello, Catherine. Father Kelley dropped me off down the road toward DeKalb Junction. I didn't want him to drive through the town or up the drive."

Leonek was once again the stranger she didn't know. Only now he had killed her brother.

"It's good to see you," he said, flatly. Lighting a cigarette, he inhaled, and blew out a white stream of smoke toward the deep blue sky. "And to be out of that God-forsaken hole in the wall."

Her emotions had been hijacked by contempt and disgust, and she hesitated to speak.

"I know you have questions, but first I want to wash up, shave, and put on some clean clothes." He rubbed his head.

"I have some leftovers from breakfast. If you're hungry."

"Yes, I'm starved. I need a home cooked meal."

His lustful eyes went up and down her body. "And that's not all I'm hungry for."

He dropped the half-smoked cigarette to the ground and put it out with his worn leather shoe. He walked past her toward the back door.

If it had not struck her before, it did now. Things would never be the same between them. Filip was gone and she was married to the man responsible for his death. The anger she felt toward Rose directed itself toward Leonek. She hung the last sheet and went inside. For a moment she felt scared Leonek could beat someone to death. What if he became angry with her?

What would he do to me?

She could hear him in the bathroom and decided to make a fresh pot of coffee.

No, I would never make him so angry.

Yet she knew he could become terribly angry. She had seen it repeatedly.

An urgent need to be on her best behavior surfaced to protect the life inside of her.

It took no time at all for Leonek to slip back into his old habits. After the men learned he had come home they all went upstairs. Silence followed by muffled outbursts of laughter told Catherine they were drinking. Part of her was glad Leonek had gone upstairs. Being around him was more uncomfortable than she imagined. She started the evening meal.

After dinner, Leonek passed out on the sofa.

Catherine left him there when she went to bed.

The next morning as Catherine readied herself for church, Leonek sat at the table and watched her. Church became the one thing normal to her. Despite her concerns about his arrogance when she first met him, Reverend Lauzon had become a confidant and gave her hope for the future. But recently she overheard a man tell him after church as she walked by, "What a stupid woman, coming here to marry a man like him."

Would he look at me differently? Being with a man like Leonek?

She looked over and wondered why Leonek had not dressed yet.

"I do want to go to church. Maybe it's best if I avoid people in town." He paused, then asked as she stood at the counter and put jam on her biscuit, "Are you certain you want to go? You will be shunned, being married to an accused murderer."

She turned to him, her face set. "I am used to the stares and whispers. They don't bother me anymore."

Leonek walked over and emptied the cup into the sink. He took her hand and looked her in the eye. "I will show you I am a changed man. They will not send me to jail." He looked down at her stomach. "I have a baby on the way. They will want me to provide for our child."

Catherine wanted to believe him. Had he seen the evil of his ways?

She let go of his hand. "I must go."

"I may not be here when you get back."

"Why? Where are you going?"

"I have something to deliver in Canton. To the men who paid my bail."

Suspicion returned.

"If it makes you feel any better, Joe Vielaska is going with me."

"Rose will not let you take the automobile."

"Ha! Rose knows the automobile is mine. Not Filip's. Besides, Joe parked it on the other side of the house." He pointed out the window. "See? It's not in the drive anymore."

Catherine looked out the window.

How did I not know this? What else don't I know?

Catherine placed her hand on the doorknob and paused for a moment. "Then I will see you later. Tomorrow is a big day. You are back to work, and we need the money."

The church filled with the same judgment as before, only now people stared longer because they knew from town gossip that she was pregnant. Catherine went to sit in her usual seat at the back of the church when she noticed two women seated there. Both had shoulder-length dark hair and wore large, straw Cavalier hats decorated with colorful satin sashes above the brims. She tried not to draw attention to herself as she sat next to them.

"Good day, Miss," the woman closest to her said in Polish. "I am Amelia Dobry, and this is my friend Felcia Hagez."

The other woman leaned forward and smiled.

Catherine felt surprised at their kindness. "Good day. My name is Catherine Kruszka."

Both women nodded in unison, and though she expected them to look shocked and move, instead they continued to talk with her.

"I live with Felcia and help with her store on the corner. Hagez and Hagez." Then her voice filled with compassion, and she added, "We heard of your brother and husband. We are sorry for your loss."

"Yes." Felcia's smile faded. "We are sorry." And to Catherine's surprise she suggested, "Please, come to our store and visit." She paused. "We read in the newspaper your husband went to prison."

Catherine looked down at her shoes. "Yes." She confided to both women, "But he is home now. Released on bail. Until his trial in June."

Once again Amelia smiled. "That's good news. I lost my husband in the Great War. He went back to fight for our country."

"Back? How long have you been in America?"

"About five years. Felcia has been here ten years. First, her father-in-law came and then the rest of the family followed, to help with the store." Despite the sadness in Amelia's emerald eyes, Catherine felt a strong connection.

"You must be able to understand English?"

"Yes. Very well."

Everyone stood for Father Kelley's entrance, as Mass began. As she stood next to Amelia, Catherine felt the bulge in her stomach. She was now five months pregnant.

Without thinking, she whispered, "Would you help me to learn English?"

Amelia nodded. "Yes, we can help you."

Catherine felt relieved they hadn't rejected her. "Thank you. If I want to make it here in America on my own, I need to learn English."

It occurred to her Leonek's confidence that the judge would not send him to prison could well be misplaced.

After Mass, Catherine gathered her things and stood to leave. The other two women did too. Then she noticed a pendant necklace on Felcia with a Baltic Amber stone secured by a delicate filigree silver holder. The Celtic pattern reminded Catherine of Józef and his dream to create jewelry.

"Do you like my necklace? My husband gave it to me for our anniversary. He bought it from a jewelry store in New York City, called *Wasserman's*."

"Yes, it's beautiful."

People started to file out of the church. Catherine felt a sense of calm next to these two women as people walked by and stared at her coldly. She overheard one woman say, "who marries such a terrible man?"

"Goodbye, Amelia and Felcia."

"Come down to the store anytime, Catherine. Don't be a stranger."

She had found new friends.

Chapter
26

Leonek dutifully went to work each day but would not come home on payday until hours after the steam whistle. Catherine felt relieved when he gave her money to buy supplies and pay the milkman. She put a little extra in her coffee can, just as Rose taught her to do.

The next Saturday, Leonek had to meet with his lawyer in Canton, and he invited Catherine to go for a ride past the university, just as he promised in the letters he wrote to her in Poland. She was even more surprised when he mentioned bringing her sketchpad. For the past few weeks, he seemed to appreciate things more, at least a little, such as her love for art, and she started to believe he might be changing.

Outside the courthouse, Catherine waited in the automobile. She took out her drawing pad and stared at the castle-like building with its red sandstone rusticated blocks and two arched doorways. To the left of the entrance, a belfry topped with a small spire. Featured above the doorway in copper were the scales of justice. The flow of her pencil interrupted when Leonek opened the car door.

"The lawyer said my trial would be on Thursday of next week. He was glad to hear I have gone to work and managed to stay out of trouble."

But Catherine knew there were days when Leonek did not come straight home from work. Jakub mentioned Leonek still played cards upstairs at the Central Hotel. All she could think of were the ladies who worked the hotel for men who were willing to pay for their services.

He put his hand on her leg. "I know you are worried, but there is no reason. My lawyer believes I am innocent of murder. He says I acted in self-defense, not in a fit of anger."

A chill ran down her spine at his touch.

On their way home, he stopped the car across the street from the college and they both watched as people walked the well-kept sidewalks.

"I know you wanted to go to art school. We will find a way for you to go."

Catherine placed her hand on her stomach. "But how can I? There will soon be a baby."

He blew out a stream of smoke. "We will find a way." He grinned at her. "Just like I found a way to bring you to America."

On the day of Leonek's trial the morning sun greeted her. She opened the window to a gentle breeze and a cardinal chirped as bright green leaves cast shadows of hope on the yard outside—a new beginning. Leonek stood on the back stoop with a cigarette in his hand. He should have been home before sunrise after working the graveyard shift, but as usual he must have stopped someplace in town.

I pray he hasn't been drinking.

Shortly, Leonek came inside. "Here's the boarders' rent money to give to the farmer. I should be home to give it to him myself, but just in case." He winked at her.

"I thought you paid him last week, on the first of the month."

His brow furrowed. "I've been busy working. I must've forgot."

"I'm surprised he hasn't come looking for it."

He looked over at the wall clock. "We better go. I told the guys we had to leave by eight o'clock to be at the courthouse by nine."

"But I saved you some breakfast. Aren't you hungry?"

"No, I'll be fine."

"Who's coming with us?"

"Mike, Joe, and your *friend*, Stefan."

Catherine ignored his comment as he left out the back door. She put the money in her coffee can, grabbed her shoulder bag from the table and looked inside to make sure her drawing pad and pencils were there. Then she took the lunch pails from the counter she just finished packing. As she did, a glimpse of Filip's house caught her eye. During the few weeks Leonek was home, they managed to avoid Rose. Catherine overheard Joe tell Leonek how Rose had received a small insurance policy pay-out from the mill, but it wouldn't last forever. "Rose could never live within her means. The money will be gone in a couple of months. Mark my words."

They arrived at the courthouse a few minutes early. This gave them all time to stand outside on the sidewalk and say some final words to Leonek.

Leonek pointed to a building attached to the courthouse with bars on the windows. Large numbers carved in stone read 1898. "There's the pigsty jail I was in. Half the toilets didn't work, and we were forced to use buckets in the hall."

Mike looked disgusted. "How many cells are in there?"

"At least twenty, maybe more."

Catherine watched Leonek light another cigarette. This was the first time she heard him talk about the jail.

"No toilets or buckets in the cells and they left the cell doors unlocked so we could use the ones in the hall. Twenty men and six buckets." He spat on the ground. "Disgusting."

In the distance, a church bell started to dong.

"Guess it's time for me to leave." He took one last drag from his cigarette and flicked it onto the lush green grass.

He walked over to Catherine and planted a long, wet kiss on her mouth.

Embarrassed by his forced kiss in front of the others, she pushed him away.

With a glare, he responded. "Is that any way to treat your husband? I'm going to have to straighten you out when I come home."

He had not changed. Was his recent kindness just an act, then, to show what a "good" man he really was?

"If you come home," Stefan added.

Leonek poked a finger into Stefan's chest. "You mind your business."

Stefan slapped the hand away.

"Alright you two," Mike intervened. "Let's go inside and get this over with."

Dozens filled the courtroom—those who despised Leonek for what he did and those who believed he acted in self-defense.

As the trial started, Mike reminded Catherine Leonek could be taken away and put in prison for a long time. She refused to believe him, though. Leonek convinced her he would be a free man and he had changed. Still, doubt crept into her.

Much of the trial was in English, and during these times Catherine would sketch what she saw in the courtroom. Such as the massive white globed chandeliers hung from a twenty-foot-high ceiling or the judge with the bald head and black robe who sat up higher than everyone else.

A man with a light-colored double-breasted suit paced back and forth as he talked to a jury of men, most of them gray-haired except for a farmer who had a mane of dark hair when he removed his straw hat. As Catherine sketched, the man stopped, and with a raised voice lifted his arm as if to strike something three times through the air. Afterwards, he pointed at Leonek and confidently walked to his seat opposite the judge. She watched as the man in the darker suit next to Leonek rose and approached the jury. He only spoke for a few minutes and never raised his voice.

Catherine whispered to Mike. "What are they saying?"

"He said Leonek did what he did to protect his life. Then he said only one blow was struck by Leonek and the other wounds were caused when Filip fell on a pipe nearby."

The thought of Filip on the floor helpless sent a rush of anger through her.

Had Filip suffered? How long before anyone called the doctor?

Another man in a dark blue suit, with round rimmed glasses, took the stand, and the animated lawyer with the loud voice asked questions. Mike remained quiet. Catherine sat there waiting for Mike to tell her something and felt the tension in her chest. Being in a place where she didn't understand the language started to irritate her. She stared at the judge whose lips were the only ones not moving. Finally, the mumbled voices stopped and the man with the glasses stepped down. Catherine finished drawing the judge whose jawline remained taut.

She leaned toward Mike and whispered, "What did they say?"

Mike looked Catherine straight in the eye and said with a stern voice, "Believe me, you don't want to know."

She folded her hands on her lap and took a deep breath.

The sound of footsteps echoed on the wooden floor and Catherine watched a man escort Rose and Jakub to a row of chairs opposite of where Leonek sat.

A wave of guilt overcame her.

If I hadn't come to America none of this would have happened. But Filip convinced me to come. Józef was gone. Filip told me America had a future, unlike Poland.

Sergeant O'Connor, the man with the red hair, took a seat next to the judge. His uniform gave him a look of authority. She noticed he would always turn to the judge to answer a question given by a lawyer. Mike leaned in and listened. At one point the officer became quiet and shrugged his shoulders.

Hearing words she could not understand gave Catherine a headache. Now more than ever she was determined to learn English.

Mike shook his head.

"What's wrong?"

"The lawyer just told the jury there was no gun found at the scene. So there is no proof of self-defense."

"But Rose knows Filip had a gun." Catherine looked at Rose who sat in the front of the courtroom. Her hair pulled neatly into a bun on top of her head. "Would they call her to the stand?"

"I think so. She's sitting next to Jakub who told us he would have to testify."

"Why didn't they have me testify?"

"I don't know."

She watched as Jakub took the stand. At last Catherine would be able to understand because there was an interpreter needed just like at Ellis Island. The conversation went slow, first asked in English then in Polish.

Would Jakub tell the jury he knew Filip had a gun and Leonek would never kill anyone on purpose?

She closed her drawing pad to listen and watched as Jakub raised his right hand, placed his left hand on the Bible, and swore to tell the truth.

"Did you see the accused hit Filip Soból on the head?"

"Yep, me and Aleksandr was there. I saw Filip come in and next thing I knew Leonek raised his arm with an iron bar in his hand and hit him."

"Did he hit him more than once?"

"I'm not sure. I was at my machine. All I know is he hit him."

"Did Soból own a revolver?"

"I heard he had one a year ago but sold it to a man who went back to the old country." Jakub paused and looked at Leonek. "I never saw Filip with a gun. Ever."

Catherine could not believe what she'd heard. *Why would Jakub lie? He knew Filip owned a gun.* Her leg started to shake, and she could feel the beat of her heart against her chest.

Finally, it was Rose's turn. Catherine was shocked when she also said Filip had no gun that she knew of.

"Had your husband drank the night before?"

She shook her head and replied, "I don't know."

"Was there ever a time your husband went to town with a gun and threatened to shoot Joe Adoniskey?"

Without hesitation, she said, "No."

Then Catherine watched as Leonek leaned over and said something to his lawyer who stood and shouted at Rose. The interpreter then asked in Polish, "Did you know of your husband threatening to shoot Mary Nego?"

Before she answered the other Attorney raised his voice at the judge who once again banged the gavel. Rose glared at Leonek. "No. I had influenza then, but I heard about it."

She continued to swear in Polish at Leonek even after the judge slammed his gavel several times. Then she turned to the interpreter and said, "Leonek wanted to get my husband fired. The whole trouble started because of him and his wife."

The interpreter nodded his head and told something to the jury in English. Rose stepped down and blotted her eyes with a laced handkerchief. Leonek's head followed her as she walked by.

"How are you doing, Catherine?" It was Stefan on the bench behind her, with the smell of cigarette smoke on his breath.

"I'm not sure."

"Here, I brought you some water."

She gulped it down and when she turned around to hand him back the tin cup, a head of long auburn hair caught her eye from the back row of the courtroom. It was Teresa O'Connor, the woman who came to meet Leonek at Christmas.

Why was she here?

The next person who took the stand was Leonek. Because he spoke broken English Catherine did not understand everything he said. Once again, she relied on Mike.

"He just told them about how he met Filip and arranged for you to come to America."

Catherine waited for Mike to share with her what else Leonek said. Her instincts told her the jury would not believe anything Leonek stated. Especially since Rose cried on the stand about how because of Leonek she had no husband or father for her children.

Stefan leaned forward and asked Mike a question. "Why does Leonek sound so angry?"

"He's talking about how Filip always ran his mouth and threatened him when he drank. Like the night before he came to the mill to shoot Leonek."

Stefan agreed. "Filip did drink a lot that night."

Catherine interrupted. "What's he saying?"

"The lawyer keeps asking Leonek if he struck Filip more than once in the head and all he says is 'I can't remember.' The judge looks unconvinced."

The morning of testimony weighed on Catherine, and she found it hard to calm her emotions. Her back hurt from sitting for so long. She felt anger building inside of her when Rose turned around and smirked. It was near lunchtime when the jury left to determine Leonek's fate. Catherine, Mike, and Stefan went outside for some fresh air and ate their lunch on the soft green grass from the dinner pails Catherine packed. Leonek had to remain with his lawyer until the jury returned. Jakub and Rose were nowhere to be seen.

Soon Joe Vielaska came outside to tell them the court was back in session.

"Geesh. That didn't take long." Mike replied as they made their way back inside.

In the courtroom Catherine wanted to ask Leonek if he thought he would be going to jail but all she could do was pray. She sat and closed her eyes.

Dear God, you would not leave me alone with child. I know you would not send the father of my child away. Where would I go? What would become of me?

She wanted to believe with all her heart Leonek would not have killed her brother on purpose. As she prayed, the mumble of voices grew louder followed by the familiar sound of the gavel. She opened her eyes and saw Rose hug Jakub. Leonek fell into his chair, hunched over.

"What is it, Mike? What happened?"

She then felt Stefan's hand on her shoulder followed by the words "I'm sorry."

Her face grew warm as she turned to him. "Sorry? About what?" His answer became one garbled sentence. With shock and numbness, she watched as the officer with the red hair walked over to Leonek and escorted him out of the courtroom through a door behind the judge.

She looked at Rose, who had a smug smile.

It's all because of her and the alcohol she made that caused people like Filip to lose control. And she still makes it and sells it. Look what happened to Filip. It wasn't Leonek's fault, it was her fault!

Her chest started to pound; her head spun, and she grabbed Mike by the arm. "Hurry, let's go!"

He picked up his jacket. "I agree. We need to leave."

"No, I mean let's go tell the judge what we know. How Rose sold illegal liquor that made people drink and fight." She pulled on his arm, but Mike would not move.

"Catherine, we can't. The trial's over."

"Yes, yes, we can. Look," She pointed toward the judge who was still seated as he talked to both lawyers.

"Hurry, before they leave."

"Catherine, the trial is over."

"Never mind, I'll tell them." She began to shout in Polish. "He's not guilty! Filip had a gun! It was self-defense! It was Rose's fault. She made the liquor that killed her husband!"

But the judge or lawyers could not understand her. From the looks on their faces, it was clear that all they saw was a woman who lost control of her emotions. The judge banged his gavel several times.

The judge shouted at the officer with the red hair who just returned to the courtroom, and he started to walk toward Catherine.

Mike and Stefan prodded her to the aisle. "Let's go."

"Go? Where? How would I survive in America with no husband?" She let out another wail; her cries echoed off the large glass windows and empty white walls. While Stefan and Mike continued to walk her down the aisle her eyes caught a glimpse of Teresa O'Connor who stared at Catherine and shook her head. Catherine struggled to stop but Mike and Stefan wouldn't let her.

She pleaded with them. "Wait, wait, I need to talk with her."

"Not now, Catherine." Mike insisted. "Let's just get you home."

"But why was she here? I need to ask her."

The bright sunny afternoon turned dark.

Chapter
27

Catherine didn't remember the ride back to Pyrites. When the automobile stopped, Catherine opened her eyes and saw the church. She lifted her head. "What's going on? Why are we here?"

Mike turned off the engine. "You had been so upset after we left the courthouse. We didn't know what to do so we brought you here to see Father Kelley."

Exhausted, Catherine sat and stared as Stefan went inside the church. When Father Kelley and Reverend Lauzon came outside, panic and frustration raced through her again.

She looked at them both with tears in her eyes. "Father Kelley, what am I going to do? He lied to me. He told me he wouldn't go to prison. He had changed."

"Catherine, you are not alone. You still have good people in your life, like these men who brought you here."

Reverend Lauzon added, "God wants you to be strong, Catherine. He wants you to think of your child."

She exhaled. "I know. I'm just scared. My brother's gone, now my husband. What will become of me?"

Father Kelley handed her a cup of water.

"Catherine, remember the story in the Gospel of John? Jesus sat down, weary, needing a drink of water. A Samaritan woman came to the well, and Jesus asked her for a drink. When she gave him the water, Jesus told her, "Everyone who drinks

241

from this water would be thirsty again but whoever would drink from the water I give them," he smiled at her, "they will never be thirsty again."

She handed him back the empty cup, and he added, "When you drink of the water from God, eternal life is yours."

"But how could God have left me so alone? Why did he let Filip die and send Leonek to prison?" She looked down. "Leonek convinced me he was innocent, and God would set him free."

Reverend Lauzon said, "Catherine, right now you are wounded. God has shown you truth; we all have injury to our souls, caused by our own actions or the actions of others. God gives us gifts to show he loves us, but he also gives us challenges—to show he loves us. Because just as Father Kelley said, God always wants us to drink from his well, from his Spirit."

"So, God hurts us to help us?"

Reverend Lauzon nodded. "Yes, so we would drink of his water."

Father Kelley took her hand. "I know you are hurting. But God is calling on you to trust him. He isn't finished with you yet."

Something stirred within her.

"What is it, Catherine? What happened?"

She looked down at her stomach. "The baby . . . it's kicking." Without thinking, she took his hand and placed it on her belly.

He smiled. "That's right, Catherine. God's spirit is there. It's alive. Everything that has happened to you was supposed to happen. As painful as it is, one day it will make sense."

Catherine looked at the faces around her.

"Mike, take her home. Let her get some rest. I'll stop by later with the doctor to check on her."

"Yes, Father."

Once home Catherine stayed in bed. None of the men came for supper. A knock on the door awakened her.

"Hello again Catherine, how are you feeling?"

Father Kelley stood next to a younger, attractive man with light brown, slicked-back hair. Dark rimmed circular eyeglasses accented his light brown eyes. He carried a hard black leather bag secured with a large silver buckle.

"This is Doctor Frank Williams from Canton. Can we come inside?"

Catherine smoothed her tousled hair. "Of course."

The doctor greeted her in Polish, and she felt reassured. He set his bag on the table to open it and put a stethoscope around his neck.

"I would like to examine you. Listen to the baby's heartbeat and take your blood pressure. How many months pregnant are you?"

"I will be starting my seventh month in July."

The doctor nodded. She watched as he put a rubber cuff around her arm and squeezed a ball which made it become tight. She looked at Father Kelley.

"He's taking your blood pressure. To make sure there are no problems."

She felt relieved when the pressure around her arm released.

After taking her temperature the doctor motioned for her to lie on the couch while he listened to her stomach with his stethoscope.

"Everything looks good. Make sure to drink milk," he motioned with his hands, palms down toward the floor, "and slow down and take it easy."

Dr. Williams said something to Father Kelley in English. Catherine waited to hear back.

"The baby should come in mid-September. Do you know what happens when you go into labor?"

Her mind flashed back to a woman on the ship who gave birth. She had started to complain of stomach pain that would come far apart then closer. When her water broke the baby came.

She nodded. "Yes, I know what happens."

Dr. Williams closed his bag. "Once the contractions start to become twenty minutes apart I want you to go to the Canton Hospital. My office is not far from there."

Father Kelley nodded. "I have a car and could drive her." He added, "I will also tell Mike and Stefan in case they need to drive you." With a smile he said, "The doctors here in America have found it safer for a woman to give birth at a hospital, instead of home."

Before they left Father Kelley took Catherine aside.

"If you would like, I can arrange another marriage for you. I could talk to Father Rusin who married you in Syracuse and have your marriage declared null and void because of the crime Leonek committed."

So many thoughts raced through her head. The thought of another arranged marriage made her nervous. Or staying here in Pyrites. She wanted to take some time and figure things out.

"I don't want to upset you, but you have a child to think about."

"I know."

I need to earn some money. But how?

She thought of the ladies she met at church. Maybe there would be a job for her at the store.

As they went to leave Father Kelley stopped and glanced at Catherine's sketchpad on the table.

"Do you like to draw, Catherine?"

Without asking he picked up the drawing pad and started to flip through it.

"Well, yes, but . . ." The memories of Marcin finding her "doodles" overcame her and she felt scared he would ask why she would waste time drawing.

Instead, he said, "Take a look at these, Doctor Williams."

Both the men flipped through the pages. Her drawings of the town from the riverbank, a fox in the backyard one morning, and her courtroom sketches.

Father Kelley smiled. "These are good Catherine. What a special gift God has given you. Stop by the church this week. I may have a project for you."

A ray of hope touched her. She couldn't believe he appreciated her art. Especially coming from a priest, the closest person she knew to God.

The next morning, Catherine felt motivated to get her chores done so she could go to town. The men ate their breakfast and took their lunch pails, all except for Jakub, who they said didn't have to work until later this afternoon.

"Just so you know, Catherine, Jakub is leaving."

"Leaving? Going where?"

"He's moving into town." Mike seemed hesitant to tell her anymore.

"Well, I need to get to work."

Catherine finished cleaning and put the bread dough in a bowl to rise. She looked out the window and saw a wagon pulled by two donkeys. Just as Leonek had said, Farmer Wallace would come for the rent money.

Does he know Leonek went to prison? Will he tell me I have to leave?

She grabbed the coffee can from the shelf and reached inside for the money when she noticed a piece of paper folded between the bills and shoved it into her apron pocket. As she counted what Leonek would have given her to buy food he knocked on the door.

With a smile, she handed him the folded bills. Nodding, he glanced at her stomach. She felt thankful when he stuck the money in his overall pocket and left.

The outside morning air felt cooler than inside the house and she decided to go sit on the porch. While seated on the wooden bench underneath the window, she reached into her pocket for the piece of paper written in English. Some letters looked the same as Polish and when she looked at the signature, she recognized the name as Teresa.

Was this from the woman with the red hair?

Heavy footsteps came down the stairs, and Jakub stopped on the last step when he saw her.

"You missed breakfast," she said, coldly.

"Yeah, I'm on the second shift this week. I don't have to be there until three o'clock."

Catherine looked at his bag.

"They told me you are leaving and moving to town."

He grinned. "To the Central House Hotel."

Her irritation with him was just under the surface. "Oh, that's a nice place. Expensive. Did you get a raise?"

His brow furrowed. "Have you been there?"

"Only for a few moments. To make a phone call to my brother Antonio. To tell him about Filip."

Jakub stroked his beard and shifted his weight from one foot to the other.

Determined to know, she finally asked, "Why did you lie on the stand? You knew Filip had a gun. You saw what happened at the mill." As she spoke, her anger mounted, and she felt her breath quicken.

"Calm down, Catherine. You're making me nervous." He looked at her stomach.

The compassion she always felt in her heart for Jakub hardened. "I'm glad you are leaving. I wouldn't want to care for someone so despicable as you."

He picked up his bag. "Oh yeah? Well, you cared for that no good lyin' husband of yours."

He spat over the porch rail. "You're nothing but a pretender. You're no better than me."

He took off down the drive and over the bridge toward town. The sound of a door closing caught her attention. She looked over and saw Rose on the porch.

How long had she been standing there?

To her surprise, Rose walked toward her.

"Here," she said, thrusting something at Catherine. "This letter came to my post office box, but it's addressed to you. It's from Poland."

Catherine took the envelope and looked at the address written on the back. *Zophia? Why would she write me a letter?*

The awkwardness between the two women kept either of them from saying anything more. Catherine knew Rose heard her outburst in the courtroom.

"Maybe you should go back to Poland. There is nothing left for you here."

She might as well have slapped Catherine in the face, and she turned and walked back to her house.

Once inside Catherine unfolded the letter to find a photo of her father in a casket beside a grave strewn with flowers. Zophia, her boys, Aunt Eva, and Uncle Marcin stood behind it. She didn't need to read the letter to know what it said.

Catherine touched her belly and thought about the life growing inside of her.

Going back to Poland seemed out of the question. She had come a long way to be in America and she wasn't about to let Rose's daggers get to her now. She knew in her heart if things were going to change she needed to change. After all, women in America could even vote. They have a voice. They could work and earn money.

She sat at the table with her sketchpad. On a blank page she wrote:

I, Catherine ~~Kruszka~~ Soból, will become the artist who will earn enough money to provide a home for my child. Then she added: *One day I will marry again, but this time for love.*

She closed her eyes and imagined her dream coming true. She did not live in Pyrites, but on a beautiful tree lined street . . . like the street near the university. She pictured herself riding the trolley to college where she would learn how to create beautiful pictures people could hang in their homes.

From now on, she would read this every night before she went to sleep and in the morning when she awoke.

Catherine learned from Filip a person must take action to change their life. He told her, "If you just sit around and wait for something to happen, it won't."

Catherine knew it was time to act. No one was going to do it for her.

Chapter
28

As the loaves of bread cooled Catherine walked to town and crossed the bridge to the store where Amelia and Felcia worked. Once again the water reminded her of the stream on the orchard back home and brought back memories of a time so long ago. She decided to wear the necklace Józef made to give her the confidence she needed.

She stopped on the bridge to watch the swirl of the water currents and held her face in her hands and started to cry. As she wiped her tears, the chirp of a red cardinal sounded above the constant thud from the mill.

Taking a deep breath, she composed herself.

I must be strong. I am blessed.

She thought of Lady Liberty in the New York harbor.

In America I am free, as the statue declares.

It felt odd to walk through this part of town alone. Usually, she would have been with Rose or gone up the hill to the church. Catherine usually shopped in the store next door to the pool hall but not this one. The freshly painted gray square two-story flat roofed store featured living quarters upstairs and a glass-front store downstairs. On the covered porch crates of apples, tomatoes, and onions were stacked on one side while metal tubs, brooms, and large burlap bags of chicken feed were on the other. A bell jingled when she pulled open the door. A blend of ripe cheese, pickles, cured meats, and leather entered her nose.

Amelia stood behind a glass display case, where colorful candies of peppermint sticks, licorice, rock candy, and lemon drops were displayed. She looked up with a warm smile when she heard the bell and saw Catherine.

"Good day, Catherine. Welcome."

From the floor to ceiling shelves were stuffed with goods. Along the dark board-and-batten ceiling hung pots, pans, lanterns, and washboards. In the center barrels, boxes and tables held a wide array of items.

"You and Felcia encouraged me to stop by. I hope I'm welcome."

"Of course you are. Come in. I will let Felcia know you are here."

Amelia walked behind a long glass display case with teas, spices, and perfectly folded denim clothing stacked on top. No space within the store remained empty.

Felcia appeared and looked cheerful in her cotton dress of blue and white plaid. Catherine smiled at the two women who spoke Polish and knew English.

"I would like to learn English from you. If you still would like to teach me."

Both women smiled. "Of course! You need to speak English here in America."

"And read English," Amelia added.

Catherine looked over at the rack of newspapers by the front door.

"We read this morning in the newspaper about what happened to you at the courtroom."

"What happened to me? You mean to Leonek."

The two women looked at each other. Neither one of them spoke.

"Why? Did the newspaper write something about me?"

Felcia motioned for Amelia to hand her the folded newspaper on the shelf behind the counter.

"They wrote you created a violent scene and howled like a beast."

Catherine felt ashamed. *Why would they write that?*

Felcia flipped through the pages. "Are you sure you want me to read it?"

Catherine waited. She laid her hand on her chest and felt the lump of the necklace.

"The headline reads '*Wife Of Kruszka Creates Violent Scene When He Is Sentenced.*'"

"Violent?"

"We couldn't believe it, either."

"What else does it say?"

Felcia took a deep breath. "The prisoner's wife created a violent scene when she heard the judgment pronounced. Breaking into hysterical shrieks she tore at her hair and clothing. She refused to be quiet and was removed from the courtroom . . ."

The bell on the door jingled and in came a customer.

Amelia smoothed her smock and walked around the corner of the display case. Her voice faded as she greeted the person at the far end of the store.

Catherine whispered to Felcia, "I was upset because Mike and Stefan wouldn't let me go. So I shouted at the judge because Rose and Jakub…" She stopped. "But he couldn't understand me."

"You don't have to explain anything to me. I know how those reporters are."

Catherine walked over to get a closer look at the paper. "And they wrote I howled like a beast?"

Felcia nodded. "Right here . . . '*Mrs. Kruszka is in a delicate condition and after she was borne from the room, her cries sounding almost like the howling of a beast and penetrating the courtroom long after she had been removed from its vicinity.*'" She laid the paper down.

Catherine felt a lump in her throat and remembered why she had come. "I stopped by to see if you would have work for me." She looked down at her stomach. "I need to earn money to take care of my child."

Felcia rubbed her chin with one hand. "I could have you help Amelia stock the shelves and clean, but I wouldn't want you to lift heavy things. Do you have any other skills?"

Catherine followed her to the end of the display case to the cash register.

"I used to do bookkeeping for my uncle in Poland. Accounts receivable, accounts payable, invoices."

Felcia's eyebrows went up. "Well, it just so happens we need a bookkeeper. My husband, Simon, usually does the books, but lately we are busier. His time is needed to find vendors or meet with them."

Catherine glanced at the cash register machine's ornate brass exterior with a marble plate above a cash drawer. The machine displayed two rows of keys. It looked like a work of art.

"The cash register helps us to keep track of daily sales. But we still need to record in the ledger book invoices and tabulate income from the machine."

"Thank you. I will do an excellent job for you."

"I know you will. I have already told Simon about you. We like to help others who are in need."

The person who entered the store, Mary Nego, walked up to the cash register.

"Hello Mary." Felcia gathered the items Mary placed on top of the glass counter and pressed a numbered key to enter a price. When she released the button, numbers on white tabs popped up inside the glass at the top of the machine.

"I saw your children go by earlier on their way to school. Your boy took an apple from one of my crates outside on the porch."

"He wouldn't do that. We have plenty of food at home." Mary looked at Catherine with taut lips. "I'm surprised you're still here."

"What do you mean?"

"Rose told me you would be leaving. Now that Leonek's gone, the men at your boarding house will want more from you than a hot meal."

Mary reached into her change purse and handed several coins to Felcia. "Jakub was smart to leave before you caused more trouble. He came into a large sum of money . . . rumor has it he was paid to lie on the—"

"That's quite enough, Mary. I'm surprised you don't have more compassion for her. She not only lost her brother but her husband, too. Like you."

Mary adjusted her hat and before she picked up the cloth bag from the counter she gave Catherine one more dagger-like glare. "You do know the whole time he was with you he was with prostitutes." She took the bag and turned to leave. "Good day, ladies."

Catherine thought about the note she found signed by Teresa. What did it say?

Amelia walked over. "Pay no attention to her, Catherine. She is what we call 'full of baloney.'"

Their laughter broke the tense mood.

"See you tomorrow morning at eight o'clock?"

"I'll be here."

When she arrived at the church, Reverend Lauzon was at the front with a vase of white trumpet-shaped flowers which he placed on the altar. Sensing her presence, he turned around and his expression softened.

"Father Kelley told me you would be stopping by. He went to the Post Office. I'm surprised you didn't see him on your way here." He stood back and admired the flowers and picked up a paper from the altar. I hope you are feeling better."

Catherine looked down at the floor. "I was, until . . ."

"Until what?"

She told him about what the newspaper reporters wrote and what Mary Nego said.

"Try not to take it personally. Mary Nego is not doing well."

"Oh?"

"The Postmaster suspected Mary has been getting illegal shipments of Gozomo from Chicago and the police went to her house. She was arrested and let go. She told them she did it to support her five children."

"What's Gozomo?"

"It's a medicine prescribed by a doctor with lots of liquor content. Some call it, whiskey."

A cloth he had used to wipe drops of water off the flower vase slipped from his hand to the floor.

Catherine bent over to pick it up, and as she stood, he said, "That is a pretty necklace you're wearing."

Catherine looked down and saw it had slipped from under her blouse and lay neatly on her shirtfront.

"Where did you get it?"

She tucked it back under her collar. "Someone special gave it to me in Poland. I wore it to bring me luck."

"It's beautiful. I've never seen anything like it."

"It means a lot to me."

Father Kelley entered from the side door.

"Catherine, you're here." He set his papers and envelopes down. "I know you were concerned about earning some money and I thought about hiring you to clean the church once a week. I couldn't pay you much, but it would be better than no money coming in." He looked at her stomach.

Two job offers in one day.

"Thank you, Father. This would be helpful to me along with my other job."

"What other job?"

"Mister and Miss Hagez hired me to help at their store."

"I hope they will not have you stocking shelves or lifting heavy boxes. Remember what the doctor said."

Catherine smiled. "Oh, nothing like that. I used to do accounting books for my uncle's business in Poland. They need someone to help with recording their invoices and income receipts. I would be sitting at a desk."

"Well, that's good news." He pressed his lips together. "What about your responsibilities to the boarders?"

"Well, I have one less boarder. Jakub has left."

"Where did he go?"

"To live at the Central House Hotel."

Father Kelley's eyebrows raised, and he looked at Reverend Lauzon.

"Anyhow, I also wanted to ask if you would be interested in an artistic endeavor."

"What sort do you mean?"

He motioned behind her. "See that plain window over there? I would like one more stained-glass window in the church. Would you be willing to design one so I could show it to Bishop Lucia for approval when I see him in Syracuse this September?"

Her eyes first went to the plain, glass window, then to the other beautiful pictures made from colored glass. Jesus at his Crucifixion, the Manger, Saint Francis and the animals, the angels.

"There is a group of stained-glass window artists in Syracuse, called Keck Studios. They make windows for churches and homes throughout America from pencil drawings. I would need your picture by the tenth of September."

The thought of creating a picture for the stained-glass window raised her spirits. "What scene would you want?"

"Whatever one you decide. Use your vision and put it on paper."

The next few weeks seemed to pass quickly. On Monday and Friday mornings, she worked part-time at the store and Wednesday morning she cleaned the church. This meant more for her to do on the weekend to prepare for the week. As her child grew inside of her, so did the money in the coffee can. The ladies taught her how to greet people in English. Amelia flipped through the magazines to show her pictures and together they said the word in English. Felcia let her bring a magazine home to practice. The signs under the goods in the store with prices helped Catherine to recognize words.

"We are proud of you, Catherine. You are learning quickly. When you go to the hospital, this will help you to better communicate with the nurses and doctors."

One hot August day, Felcia's husband, Simon, returned from Canton with a donation from the Red Cross.

"After reading the news story about you and the trial they collected a large supply of secondhand clothing, new underclothing, and stockings. And they will be sending a layette for your baby."

She stared at the box of colorful dresses in the backseat of his automobile.

"Why would strangers give me this? They don't know me."

"But they know what happened wasn't your fault. People feel good when they help others who are less fortunate. One day, you will be in a position to do the same."

On Wednesday mornings while she cleaned the church she would stare at the stained-glass windows. She always brought her sketch pad to draw them so she could get a feel for the design she would create. Reverend Lauzon left to visit the logging camps for a few weeks and Father Kelley was always glad to see her. One day after she finished cleaning, he gave her a Polish newspaper to look at.

"Father Rusin mailed it to me from Syracuse. I thought you might like to read it."

Sitting in a pew, she pored through the paper, reading about a building collapse in Lemberg that killed forty people, followed by a story about two days of street fighting between Socialists and Fascists in Italy.

This paper is full of nothing but sad news.

A headline caught her eye.

ALL HALLERIANS RETURN TO AMERICA

WARSAW—THE POLISH HAVE SECURED THE RETURN TO AMERICA OF ALL SOLDIERS FROM GENERAL HALLER'S FORMER ARMY WHO ARE STILL IN POLAND. THESE SOLDIERS WERE POLES LIVING IN AMERICA. THEY PARTICIPATED IN THE WORLD WAR AND THEN IN THE POLISH-RUSSIAN WAR.

The story made her think of Józef. How he too had gone to fight for Poland but ended up being captured and killed. His dream to create jewelry was now gone forever.

She looked over at the blank window in the church.

Maybe there is a way I can design a window in memory of him.

Later, after the men returned home from work, she shared with Mike what the newspaper said.

"There were also stories about a civil war and bloody battles in Ireland. An Irish leader was assassinated."

"Yes, I read those stories in the American paper. But I came downstairs because I wanted to tell you what I read in the paper today about Leonek."

Catherine wasn't sure if she wanted to hear any more news reports after what Amelia and Felcia read to her following the trial.

"Leonek has been put in solitary confinement on bread and water for starting a brawl in which he almost got a guard killed."

She felt a mixture of anger, fear, grief—and to her surprise, some relief. Was this her way out of the life she was stuck in?

Maybe Father Kelley was right. I need to have my marriage to this man ended.

A knock at the door interrupted her thoughts. Farmer Wallace had come to collect the rent. With a proud voice she said, "Good evening, Mister Wallace."

This time when Catherine handed him the money, he stood in the doorway and counted it. His forehead furrowed.

"Where's the rest of the money?"

Catherine feared he would tell her she needed to leave. She knew the rent would be short due to Jakub moving out and struggled to find the words to explain.

"I have not the dollars . . ."

His voice tightened, "Where is the rest of the money?"

Mike came to the doorway then, and the two men talked in English. Catherine felt relieved when Wallace left.

"What did you tell him?"

"I told him a boarder left, but there would be a new one moving in."

Catherine was shocked. *Why would Mike lie?*

"Why did you tell him there would be a new boarder?"

Mike smiled. "Because there will. A Pole named Krzysztof transferred to my department at the mill. We talked and I learned he lives in town but is tired of living above the pool hall. He has a girl from Poland. He paid for her passage, and she needs a place to live until they can get married. She will be here at the end of the week. I thought it might be a good idea if she moved in to help you." He looked down at her belly. "You are going to need help."

She knew Mike was right. Stefan had been spending much time with her and at times she felt he wanted something more. Just as Mary Nego warned. Father Kelley still insisted Stefan could marry her to help take care of the child. But Catherine wasn't sure if she wanted to stay in Pyrites. This was no place for an artist. She needed to live near a university and refused to live in a place like this where her dreams would die.

What will happen if Wallace tells me to leave? He must know Leonek was sent to prison.

"Don't worry, Catherine. Everything is going to work out. I can feel it." He pounded on his chest in a show of strength and confidence.

She wanted to believe him and forced a smile.

29

The sticky, humid August air greeted Catherine as she walked home around noon from the store. The sweltering sun showed no mercy these past few days. Mr. Hagez had gone to Canton, otherwise he would have given her a ride home. The conversation she overheard between Mr. Hagez and a customer, just before he left, replayed in her mind.

"I hear you have a new employee. I'm surprised you would hire her."

Catherine heard the familiar bell of the register, followed by Mr. Hagez's voice.

"Why? Because she's a woman?"

"No, because she's married to a murderer. How could she have married such a terrible man? Especially one horrible enough to kill her own brother. She must be stupid."

"Your total is fifty-seven cents."

"And now she is going to have his brat. How disgusting."

A pang of guilt ran through her. She wondered if Mr. Hagez would soon fire her.

At the pool hall on the corner, men from the nearby lumber camps with too much time on their hands and money to spend, loitered outside on the front porch. She felt their eyes on her as she walked by. Two of the men visited the store earlier, and Amelia complained after they left about the smell of body odor from their clothes.

As she crossed the bridge, there was a light breeze and she stopped to feel the wind on her face. The river sparkled from the afternoon sun. It was then she noticed the two men from the Pool Hall coming toward her. As they started up the road toward the bridge, she hurried home.

She tried to keep the house cool on this hot August day by keeping the windows shut and shades drawn, but it still felt like an oven inside. An uneasy feeling came over her as she peered out the window. She watched as the two men approached Rose's house.

They knocked on the faded clapboard and, as usual, Rose cracked the door and most likely told them to walk around to the back of the house. Catherine knew the routine like clockwork, and soon they would reappear with a brown paper bag and walk back down the drive toward town.

The house was quiet, but her mind raced. She poured herself a glass of water and glanced out the window once more towards Rose's house. She imagined Filip on the porch and remembered how she would walk over to talk with him. But instead, her heart sank as she stared at the empty stoop.

A stopped automobile on the bridge caught her eye. It turned up the drive and stopped in front of Rose's house. Two men with Stetson hats exited and approached the porch. Catherine recognized them as police officers, and one held an envelope in his hand. As the other officer knocked on the door the two lumbermen appeared from around the corner of the house with their brown bags. When the officers spotted them, the men ran past Catherine's house. Their heavy boots sounded like horse hooves as they ran by toward the river. The two officers were in pursuit, but Catherine knew there are many paths of escape in the woods near the river, and the lumbermen would surely know the secret passages around the mill.

The heat in the house was becoming unbearable. Catherine took her water outside along with a magazine. As she sat on the porch and fanned her face the officers returned empty handed. They banged on Rose's door and shouted inside through the open window. Finally, Rose opened the door, and Catherine watched as one of the officers held up a piece of paper then forced himself inside. The scene reminded her of home and how she would hear stories from Laska of soldiers in uniforms with their weapons, raiding homes, looking for something or someone.

Soon, the door opened once more to reveal Rose with Bertha on her hip as she held little Johnny's hand. Rose spotted Catherine and desperately motioned for her to come over.

What was going on? Where are they taking her?

"Catherine, I need to go with these two men. Would you watch these children until I get back?"

She awkwardly handed Bertha to Catherine.

"Where are you going?"

Rose pleaded. "I'll explain later. Help me with them, please? I was just about to lay them down for their nap."

Catherine smiled at Johnny, who looked confused, and extended her hand. "Come with me."

The boy started to cry when he saw his mother get into the back seat of the car. "Mama . . . *Mama* . . ."

"Shhh. It's okay." She took his hand. "Let's go inside and have a cookie."

She hadn't been in the house since Filip died. She gave each of the children a snack of milk and crackers before she laid them down for their nap. She looked around the spotless house for something to remind her of Filip but saw nothing. It was as if Rose had erased his memory.

The clock on the wall told her soon the men would be home from their shift at the mill. She sat on the sofa for a moment to think about what she would make for dinner but drifted off. Soon the sound of an automobile followed by heavy footsteps on the porch awakened her. When Rose walked in her hair was disheveled and her apron draped over her shoulder. She walked past Catherine to the sink for a cup of water.

"Are you alright? Where did those officers take you?"

She gulped it down, and then with an accusing tone replied, "They tried to take me to jail. Somehow they found out I was selling liquor."

Catherine watched as Rose smoothed her hair and fastened it with a bobby pin.

"I told the judge I did what I needed to do to support my family since Filip died. He told me I better find myself another husband."

Despite Rose's still sullen demeanor now that the men were gone, Catherine felt grateful she was able to spend time with Johnny and Bertha. She waited for Rose to thank her.

"There was something else I wanted to tell you."

Catherine took this as an invitation to step closer.

Rose leaned over the table. "As if having two children wasn't bad enough without a husband, now I will have three."

"What do you mean?"

"What do I mean?" She threw her arms up into the air. "I mean I'm carrying another child. *Another child* with no father!"

Rose walked over to the sink and placed her palms on the edge as she looked down. Catherine tried to find words of comfort.

"Isn't that a blessing? Filip was able to give you another child."

"Blessing?" She turned around, her eyes filled with tears. "More like a curse. No man will have a woman with three children to take care of."

She started to pace the floor and put her hands on her hips. "I just can't deal with this anymore." The afternoon steam whistle wailed in the distance. She continued to talk out loud. "Look at Mary Nego; people look down on her—no one will give her work, and her children are forced to eat scraps meant for dogs."

A cry from Johnny broke into the wave of her rage.

"My children will never eat garbage. I'll do what I must do to support my family. Even if it's illegal."

Catherine knew she should leave, but was afraid to move.

"None of this would have happened if it wasn't for you." Rose started to sob. She was back to attacking Catherine. "I told Filip not to bring you here, but he wouldn't listen." Her rant continued. "'Oh, but you'll like Catherine. She will be a good friend to you. She is such a nice girl.'"

Catherine made her way to the door. She looked out the window to see a group of men crossing the bridge with their lunch pails.

"I better go. The men are home for dinner. Maybe one of them could help you…"

"Help me what? Raise my children? Half of them have a wife and family in another country and the others are nothing but gamblers and boozers."

Johnny cried out and Bertha joined in.

As Catherine opened the door, heat from the humid air came rolling in.

"You have ruined my life. I never want to see you again. Get out of my house!"

Shocked by the hatred Rose spewed, she quickly made her way down the stairs. As she hurried across the drive, dark clouds trapped the sticky warm air below.

A gust of hot wind blew across her face.

Once inside the house, a new thought entered her mind . . . *What if Father Kelley was right and something greater might come from all of this?*

It was a ridiculous thought and she dismissed it.

Stefan was the first inside the house. "Good day, Katie, what's for dinner?"

After a late dinner most of the men went to town, as it was too hot for them to play cards upstairs. Thunder clouds loomed on the horizon. With the house to herself, Catherine settled into bed. The crickets chirped and she could hear the distant rumble of thunder. Finally, a cooler breeze came through the opened window and lulled her to sleep. As the lightening flickered, images of her past flashed into her head. The black and white film footage of war, the death of her mother, a ship lost in the dark ocean in the middle of a stormy sea. She tossed and turned. Soon the rain pattered against the single pane window.

Her thoughts turned to the last time she saw Filip with a gun tucked in his belt as he left the house. The courtroom with a judge who slammed the gavel. Another crash of thunder disturbed her.

She drifted off once more and visioned a red rose in the garden. Its thorns shrouded by dark green ivy wrapped around a trellis. She reached down to pick the flower only to be cut by the hidden thorns repeatedly. Soon her hands were covered in blood. Another clap of thunder followed by a crack of lightening.

Catherine's eyes snapped open to reveal the empty pillow next to her. She listened for the next crash of thunder, but there was none. Finally, the storm passed.

A few days later, Mike told Catherine he would be bringing the new boarder to move in. Her recent encounter with Rose still lingered and now more change was coming.

What if this new man brings more trouble? This town is so full of trouble.

As she finished dressing, there was a hard knock on the door. She was not surprised to see Mike and another man standing there.

"I know it's early, but I wanted you to meet Krzysztof. He's the new boarder I told you about. I asked him to stop by this morning before work."

Krzysztof removed his cap to reveal a bald head. He had a boyish face as he grinned from ear to ear.

"Good day, Catherine. I am pleased to meet you."

"Good day." She glanced at Mike and stepped aside. "Please, come in."

Krzysztof walked around, first toward the bathroom and then by the door to the bedroom. "Mike told me you keep a clean house. I am impressed." He winked at her with his soft brown eyes. A well-trimmed bushy mustache complimented his smile

261

along with the goatee below his lip and Catherine thought it odd how there was hair on his face, but not on his head.

"You only have one bedroom here. Where would my Miriam sleep?"

Before Catherine could answer, Mike interjected. "She could sleep there, on the royal bench."

Krzysztof walked over to the sofa, sat down, and bounced a little. "It does seem comfortable enough."

As Catherine started a pot of coffee, Mike asked, "Would you like to see the upstairs? The other men should be up."

"Naw, as long as I have a quiet place to sleep I'm good; it's got to be better than the noisy hole in the wall I've been staying at." He walked over to the table and started to pick up a biscuit off the plate but stopped. "May I have one of these?"

Impressed by his manners, Catherine responded, "Of course. There are plenty."

"Thanks." He winked at her again.

Mike cleared his throat. "Krzysztof wants to move in today after work. But first he would need to pick up his bride to be from DeKalb Junction. Her train arrives around seven o'clock this evening. I told him we could take the automobile."

"Yeah, I was sorry to hear about your husband and your brother. I met them both at the pool joint. Seemed like good fellas until they got corked."

Catherine looked at the clock and started to assemble the lunch pails.

Krzysztof slapped Mike on the back. "You were right, Catherine's a real cake-eater. Not like bug-eyed Betty where I live now."

"I guess I'll take the compliment. I do like cake."

Krzysztof looked at her and winked again. "I appreciate your hospitality. And I know you're going to like Miriam. She's clever and funny." He leaned into her. "She's the youngest of five brothers and she isn't afraid of men." He looked down at Catherine's stomach. "Wants to have a big family too. Which is fine by me."

It was nearly dusk when Miriam arrived. Catherine had taken a liking to Krzysztof, and she was certain he would know how to pick a good bride. She felt bad Miriam would not have a bed but then remembered how good Filip's sofa felt after sleeping on the plank beds of the ship.

Catherine watched as Miriam got out of the automobile. A colorful shawl of blue and green with embroidered red poppies wrapped around her face. Her long dress looked to be made of heavy cotton with a red stripe on the cuffs and down the front. Krzysztof carried her large knapsack on his shoulder. Catherine opened the door as they neared the back stoop.

Miriam gazed back at her with green eyes highlighted by the few faint freckles on her cheeks. She looked to be not much older than Catherine. With a strong, friendly smile she said, "Hello Catherine. Thank you for letting me stay here with you. My name is Miriam Shatsky."

Krzysztof set her bag on the floor near the sofa. Catherine tried to make it an attractive bed with a white sheet and Leonek's pillow. Her orange and red striped blanket from Poland folded neatly at the end.

"Oh, a real place to sleep. Not like those hard beds on the ship. What a ride, I'm beaten." Miriam looked around. "This place is nice."

Her eyes landed onto Catherine's mid-section. "Krzysztof told me you were expecting a child. . . . I'll say you are."

"You must be hungry. I saved you some leftovers from dinner." Catherine dipped a ladle into the pot on the stove and filled a bowl. "I hope you like pork stew."

"Like it? I love it. Back on the farm we raised cows, and every fall my father would trade for a pig from the villagers." She walked toward the bathroom. "But first I need to clean up."

After dinner they all sat and talked. Catherine learned Miriam and Krzysztof were from Kielce. They spoke about the Great War and how the Russian military was extremely brutal toward Jews in their city.

"Before the war there was no strong authority, and we were always victimized by one military force or another. Many Jews populated to Kielce, which helped my father's business, but brought with them the Russian military."

Krzysztof added, "The Russian military was deeply suspicious of Jewish people settled in the war zones and at times forced removal of entire Jewish communities."

"That was why many Poles like Krzysztof wanted to come to America." Their eyes met. "He promised to bring me here."

"Krzysztof told me you had brothers; did they leave too?"

Miriam became quiet. Krzysztof put his hand on her shoulder.

"Miriam's family raised cattle and sold them to the Jewish butchers. During the Great War, Poles accused the Jews of being Bolshevik and urged others to boycott

Jewish owned shops and businesses. Then one night a Pogrom was started by the Red and White Russian armies."

Miriam looked at Catherine with tears in her eyes. "Because we served the Jewish businesses, we were also accused of being Bolsheviks. But my father was just trying to take care of his family." She took her fabric napkin and dabbed her eyes as she continued. "My father told them not to go."

Catherine could hear the fear in Miriam's voice. "What happened?"

"There was a gathering at the Polish Theatre to celebrate our independence. Many Poles, including three of my brothers, rallied behind the Jewish leaders. Soon a group of soldiers entered the auditorium and began to search for arms, driving Jews towards the stairs where a double line of extremists, some armed with clubs and bayonets beat the Jews as they were leaving the building. My brothers tried to escape but outside the Jews were assaulted by the right-wing mob again. The soldiers started spitting fire into the groups of people who tried to flee. My two oldest brothers, Wladislaw and Feliks, were among the dead."

Catherine felt confused. "But the war ended. Poland had gained its independence..."

Krzysztof answered, "The Pogrom activities did not stop with the liberation of Poland. That's when I told Miriam I needed to leave for America, and I would send for her as soon as I could."

This was the same time Józef was sent to fight . . . only I would never see him again.

Miriam turned to Krzysztof and smiled. "I am grateful to be in America. Away from the violence."

Chapter
30

The next week Catherine was thankful for her new friend. Miriam was fascinated with Pyrites and how immigrants from other nations could get along. There was no fear of soldiers coming to cause fighting. At first Catherine didn't talk much about Leonek or what happened to Filip, and whenever Miriam would ask her about how she came to America, she would change the subject. But eventually she shared with Miriam her story to which she replied, "Don't let other people's opinion of you define who you are." She looked up at the ceiling and made the sign of the cross. "God has a plan for you, I can feel it." She smiled. "Look, he already brought me here."

One afternoon after Miriam finished making what she referred to as "her grandmother's Fasolka a La Polonaise" or green beans with breadcrumbs, Catherine sat at the table with her sketchpad and colored pencils.

Miriam finished wiping the last of the dishes. "What are you working on over there?"

"It's a drawing for Father Kelley. He asked me to design a new stained-glass window for the church."

Catherine stared at the page. "I was troubled by what to draw but then it came to me in a dream. I decided to draw the Immaculate Heart of Mary."

Miriam glanced over Catherine's shoulder to look at the sketch of a heart on fire encircled by thorns. Around it was a ring of red roses. A sword pierced the flaming heart. "I like the heart, but I think it would be better if Mary held it in her hand." She walked over to face Catherine and posed. "You know, like this."

Catherine thought for a moment. She didn't have a picture of the Virgin Mary to use as a model. "I need a person to draw. . . . I know, how about you?"

"Me?"

"Yes, get your scarf and wrap it around your face. You can be the face of Mary."

"Oh, I don't know, I'm not free from sin."

"But your face is angelic. Would you at least let me try to capture Mary in your face?"

Reluctant to agree, Miriam went to do as Catherine asked, and returned.

"Sit over there, in front of the window."

After Catherine was done drawing, she turned the sketchpad and showed it to Miriam.

"I like it." She chuckled. "Who would have thought I would end up on a stained-glass window in America?"

Krzysztof and Mariam brought a harmony to the boarding house. When Farmer Wallace came to collect the rent, he was pleased all the money was there. When he saw Miriam, he tipped his hat to her.

"I thought for sure he would have asked why you were here."

"I know. I meant to go into the bedroom when he arrived, but you opened the door before I could hide."

"He probably thought you were a visitor. Besides, there's no reason for you to hide. All he cares about is his money."

Catherine's due date was fast approaching and soon she would be a mother. The thought started to weigh on her. She was thankful to have Miriam's help but knew once she and Krzysztof married they would leave.

With one less boarder, the rent money would be short. I can't keep living like this, hand to mouth, but what should I do?

Miriam sat at the table and peeled potatoes while Catherine prepared to go to Canton with Stefan in the automobile. She wanted to get some last-minute supplies before the baby came. But first she would drop the drawing off to Father Kelley, and she prayed he would like it.

"I met Rose today."

"Oh?"

"Yes, I went outside to walk down by the river. I thought about making a fishing pole to catch something. Trout maybe. Perch . . . something I would do with my brothers back home." She took the pan of potatoes over to the sink. "Anyhow, she accused me of trespassing. Said I wasn't to cross her yard again."

"She came outside just to threaten you?"

"No, she was in the backyard hanging sheets. That little boy of hers is a cutie."

"What did you say?"

"I told her, 'I don't believe this is your yard. It belongs to Farmer Wallace. I pay my rent just like everyone else and this is my land just as much as yours.'"

Catherine held her stomach as she let out a hearty laugh.

"You should have seen her face. She just looked at me bewildered." Miriam expressed a look of shock and held her mouth wide open.

Stefan came in from the back door of the kitchen.

"Are you ready, Katie? I've got to be back by two o'clock. I need to win my money back from last night's card game."

Miriam asked Catherine, "How far is Canton?"

"About six miles from here. I like to go to the five and ten. We need to stretch this money as far as we can."

"Five and ten?"

"It's a store where everything's less than ten cents."

"Well, we better get going, Katie."

Catherine picked-up her shoulder bag along with a handful of cloth bags. "I need to stop at the church first to give Father Kelley something."

Miriam walked with Catherine to the back door. "Don't let that baby bounce out of you."

"I won't. I'm not due for another two weeks."

At St. Paul's Church, Father Kelley was outside with Reverend Lauzon engrossed in conversation.

Fear and doubt filled her.

Will Father Kelley like my drawing? Maybe I don't have talent after all. Will he have changed his mind, and tell me I am better off to end my marriage with Leonek and marry again to provide for my child. After all, how can I be a mother and attend art school?

"Well look at you, Catherine," he said, as she approached. "I haven't seen you in a while. You look like you're about to burst."

Catherine felt her face flush.

"Not yet, Reverend Lauzon. I still have two or three weeks."

She followed Father Kelley into the church.

"I have those drawings for you."

"Excellent. Let's see what you've done."

"I decided to draw the Immaculate Heart of Mary."

Father Kelley took the paper and scanned it with his eyes. "What made you choose this picture?" He then handed it to Reverend Lauzon.

"I liked how the Immaculate Heart's fire illustrates the burning love Mary has for God the Father and for her Son. I thought of Mary's heart, surrounded by thorns, and pierced with a sword to remind us of the sorrows she endured silently." Catherine looked up at him and thought, *Just like me.*

"I also liked how you have shown Mary carrying the heart in her hand. The gesture suggests Mary wants to give her heart to the one who is viewing the image."

Reverend Lauzon smiled at her. "The face of Mary in this picture, surrounded by rays of light. Did you envision Mary in your mind? The drawing seems so real."

"Thank you. I sketched Krzysztof's soon to be wife Miriam. She posed for me."

"You have captured Mary well. I'm sure Bishop Lucia will like it." He looked at her. "Are you all right Catherine? You look pale."

"Yes Reverend." She looked down at her protruding stomach. "I'm just not sure what will happen to me and this child. This was not the life I imagined." Tears rose in her eyes, and she fought to hold them back.

His expression changed to one of concern. "Remember, Catherine, those who flourish in life face misfortune and experience many heart-breaking struggles before they succeed." He took her hand.

She drew in a deep breath and managed to smile. "Well, I must go. Stefan is waiting for me."

The ride to Canton lifted Catherine's spirit. The leaves were beginning to show their colors, and the farms they passed had a bounty of fall vegetables for sale near the road.

"We will stop and get some of those vegetables on our way back home." Catherine gleamed as the warm fall day shone on her face. As they passed the university, she once again imagined herself walking the campus. After they were done shopping Stefan remarked, "You have been quiet since we got to the store. Is everything all right?"

Catherine tried to convince herself the ache in her back was from sitting too long in the automobile, but now it radiated to her stomach.

"I'm not sure, but I am having some pains. It's probably from the automobile ride."

"When did they start?"

Catherine thought for a moment. "I woke up this morning with a backache, but now it seems worse."

Stefan finished loading the bags in the back seat. It was then Catherine realized her undergarment was soaked.

She looked at Stefan. "We'd better go to the hospital."

"Are you sure? You mean . . ."

"Yes, I'm sure."

When they arrived at the hospital, an empty wooden table with a single chair greeted them. Catherine hobbled toward another wooden chair against the wall. Her contractions had started.

"Hello? *Hello?*" Stefan's anxious voice echoed down the hall.

Finally, a woman appeared dressed all in white with a hat too small for her head. She spoke in English, and Catherine recognized the words she heard so often from Amelia in the store. "Can I help you?"

Stefan explained in Polish and pointed toward Catherine. The woman immediately grabbed a chair with large, spoked wheels that belonged on a bicycle and guided Catherine to sit in it. Although her back throbbed, she managed to do as the woman wanted.

The nurse motioned for Stefan to sit and wait as she wheeled Catherine down the hall.

Catherine prayed Stefan wouldn't leave.

Catherine's delivery was quick and, to her relief, easy. The hospital staff thought Stefan was the father, and invited him to see Catherine and the baby. When Stefan entered the room, Catherine was drowsy after her labor and could barely keep her eyes open.

"Hello Catherine, they said I could see you for a few minutes."

"Thank you for bringing me here. I wouldn't have wanted to have this baby in a boarding house."

He looked around. "Where is the baby?"

"The nurse left to clean her up. They wanted me to rest so I can feed her."

Stefan smiled. "She?"

Catherine nodded. "Yes, I have a daughter."

The nurse who could speak Polish appeared with a clipboard. She looked at Stefan and then to Catherine.

"Is this the father?"

Before Stefan could answer, Catherine said, "Yes."

He stared at Catherine, surprised, and she told him with her eyes, "*Please don't tell her the truth.*"

The nurse smiled at Stefan. "I am Miss Ethel Pinder. I came from Russia, where I led a band of Red Cross Nurses."

"Miss Pinder told me she escaped from Siberia on a train, and that's when she met her husband. He was an American Commissioner to Russia."

She looked surprised. "And you remember me telling you this. How kind of you." She looked at Stefan. "Then at Vladivostok we were separated. I met him again when I returned to the United States. He is a graduate of Cornell University, here in New York."

"I see." Stefan looked at the clock on the wall and fidgeted with coins in his pocket.

"Your wife will need to stay in the hospital overnight. You can come pick her up tomorrow around noon."

Catherine watched Stefan walk to the other side of the room and prayed he wouldn't be angry with her.

"Yes, I can do that. Tomorrow is Sunday and I don't have to work."

"Where do you work?"

"At the DeGrasse Paper Mill, in Pyrites."

"All right then. We will see you tomorrow. But before you go, do you want to see your daughter?"

Stefan took a handkerchief from his pant pocket and wiped the sweat from his forehead. "Okay. Yes."

"Are you alright?"

"Me? Oh, yeah. Just nervous."

"Most new fathers are."

Stefan glanced at Catherine with a pleading look.

She could see in his eyes he wanted to leave.

"It's been a long day for Stefan. Maybe he should go home and get some rest."

"Yes, rest. Sounds good. Goodbye Catherine."

"Bye Stefan, see you tomorrow."

Awkwardly, playing his part, he bent down and kissed her forehead. Then his footsteps faded quickly as he walked down the hall.

Nurse Pinder pulled a chair over and sat next to Catherine. "He certainly was in a hurry to leave."

Catherine nodded. "Like I said, it's been quite a day."

"Do you know how to write in English?"

Catherine shook her head.

"Well then I will have to fill out this birth registration for you."

"Your first name is Catherine, what's your maiden name?"

"Soból"

"And you live in Pyrites, correct?" She finished writing and stopped. Her eyes met Catherine's.

"What about the father, the man who just left, what was his name?"

Catherine paused for a moment. She cleared her throat.

"His name is Stefan, Stefan Janowski."

God, forgive me. I promise to tell my daughter the truth one day. I want to protect her from Leonek.

"Catherine? Did you hear me? Have you decided on a name for your daughter?"

She thought for a moment.

"Mary. I want to name her Mary."

The nurse smiled at her and started to write again. "Mary Janowski it is."

The hospital provided Catherine with a large basket to take Mary home in. On the ride back to Pyrites Stefan bragged, "Mary must have brought me luck."

"What do you mean?"

"Luckily, I didn't get to the Pool Hall until late. By then most of the men had been drinking too much and couldn't tell if they had an ace or a deuce. I won my money back and then some."

When they returned home, Stefan offered to carry Mary inside the house. Miriam opened the door before Stefan even reached the porch.

"Bring that baby right inside." She held her hands together as if she was praying. "Oh, isn't she beautiful. Look at all the hair!"

Stefan set the basket on the table as Catherine carried in the bag of gifts from the hospital. The Red Cross provided Catherine a layette for the baby along with other bags of clothes and diapers.

She handed a bag to Stefan. "Would you take these over to Rose?"

"For what? She doesn't have a baby."

"Not yet, but she told me she is with child."

"By who?"

Catherine didn't answer right away to give him a moment to think.

"Oh…Filip."

Catherine nodded. "Yes, she is having his child in January."

"I'm sure she will be grateful, although, she probably won't admit it." He smirked as he took the bag of clothes from her. "I'll be back to see if you need anything else."

Miriam leaned over the basket and smiled at Mary. She exclaimed, "I have more good news! Krzysztof and I have set a wedding date! Father Kelley told us at church today he can marry us on September 30th."

She looked over at Catherine. "What's wrong? Aren't you happy for me?"

"Oh no, I mean—yes, of course. Krzysztof is a good man. . . . It is good to see someone marry for love. That is something I always wanted."

"You will find love. Don't give up." She grinned. "Stefan seems to care much for you."

"Yes, well . . ."

But I don't love him.

"Anyhow, we have a wedding party to plan." She wandered over and looked out the window at the backyard. "Let's have an outdoor celebration right here in the yard." She spun around, her face filled with joy. "What do you think?"

"I think that's a fine idea."

"We could have music, and dancing. I've always wanted a wedding celebration."

She pranced around the table and sang a Polish wedding song.

"ONE HUNDRED YEARS, ONE HUNDRED YEARS,

LET US LIVE, LET US LIVE,

A HUNDRED YEARS, A HUNDRED YEARS, LET US LIVE

ONE MORE TIME, ONE MORE TIME,

LET US LIVE ONE HUNDRED YEARS!"

As Miriam sang, Catherine's mind wandered. Although she was happy for her friend, she felt sad about her leaving.

How will I care for these boarders and a baby?

It all seemed overwhelming.

Is this the life I wanted or am I living the life I feared I would be trapped in back in Poland?

Three days later, Catherine had a visitor.

"Hello, Father, come in."

"How are you feeling? I just returned from Syracuse and heard you gave birth. I came to see her." He walked over to the basket on the sofa and sat down next to Mary. His presence comforted Catherine.

"I'm doing well. Thank goodness I have Miriam here to help me. I'm glad you stopped by. I wanted to ask you about baptizing Mary."

He continued to smile at the new life next to him. "Hello Mary. My, you are a beautiful one." Father Kelley reached into the basket and took her tiny hand. "She has so much hair. It almost looks wavy . . ." He stood and walked toward Catherine who started to knead the bread dough.

"Do you think she will have curls?"

His comment made her think of her own grandmother, how her hair was naturally curly.

"That would be nice. Would you like a cup of coffee?"

He sat at the table and reached for a freshly baked sugar cookie. "Yes, and one of these."

"Miriam made those."

He looked around. "Where is Miriam?"

"She went to visit with Amelia and Felcia. They are going to help her make a wedding dress."

"Ah yes, a wedding and a baptism. God is good."

Catherine forced a smile as she set the cup of coffee in front of him.

He reached for the sugar. "I have news for you."

"Oh?"

"Not only did Bishop Lucia love your drawing, he told me about a Polish couple who are looking for a live-in housekeeper."

Catherine pressed her lips together. *Not another arrangement.*

"I told Bishop Lucia how well you take care of this boarding house and how good of a cook you are. We could also have Mrs. Hagez write a letter of recommendation for you."

"You want me to go to Syracuse and live with strangers?"

"Unless you marry Stefan. Then you could stay and make a life for you and Mary here."

Catherine did not like either of these choices. Father Kelley took the last sip of his coffee.

"Would you at least consider it? You would have a place to stay until you find another husband."

Later when Miriam came home, Catherine shared what Father Kelley had proposed.

"What did you tell him?"

"I didn't give him an answer."

Miriam's eyes lit up and her face filled with delight. "Do you know what this means?"

"No, what?"

"It means Krzysztof and I could live here and run the boarding house. I really like this small town. Everyone is so friendly . . ." She reached across the table and cupped her hands around Catherine's. "You could start a new life. You told me more than once this place has no future, only bad memories. Just think, no more Rose or mean looks." She gripped Catherine's hands once more. "Catherine, you must take a chance!"

On the wedding day, the blue sky was dotted with fluffy white clouds. The trees were decked in golden, amber, and scarlet leaves. A logger Krzysztof invited brought his fiddle. Mr. and Mrs. Hagez provided a bounty of food they insisted didn't sell and they would need to dispose of anyhow. Krzysztof had many friends in town including the lumberjacks who would soon leave for their camps in the Adirondacks. The yard was full of conversation and happiness.

"I am going to miss you, Catherine."

"Yes, you have been good to me, Stefan."

"Could you believe how the hospital thought I was Mary's father? I wonder if Leonek knows he has a daughter." His eyes met hers. "I would be a good father to your daughter, and I would take care of you."

"Stefan . . . I . . ." She told him about her decision to leave Pyrites.

He looked at the ground. "Can you at least give me your address, so I can stay in touch with you?"

"Yes, I can do that."

Catherine went inside to check on Mary, and Reverend Lauzon followed her.

"Father Kelley told me about your decision. You must be looking forward to leaving this mill town—and all the memories from it."

"I'm not sure how I feel. I am happy things have worked out for Krzysztof and Miriam, but I am not happy about what happened to my brother . . . or Leonek." She glanced at the basket on the bed. Mary was swaddled in a deep pink cotton blanket—comfortable, safe, and secure. "But part of me is glad to leave this place."

"As you should be. I know of the family you are going to live with."

"You do?"

"Yes. When I was in Syracuse they would come to church at Sacred Heart. Halina is the Godmother to an artist who created a famous architectural style from Poland. Have you ever heard of Stanislaw Witkiewicz?"

The name did seem familiar.

"He is known for the Zakopane Style."

The name created a memory of her and Józef when he took her to the art museum in Poland.

Why didn't Father Kelley tell me this?

"Yes, the Bonzenta's fled Poland before the Great War and planned to go back after the troubles were over. But his wife wanted to do theater here in the United States and they ended up staying." He smiled. "For someone like you, Catherine, with your gift of observation and drawing, being with them would be good for you."

Catherine looked out the window at the crowd of people who linked arms and formed a circle around Miriam. She watched as Miriam removed her headdress and placed it onto the head of one of the girls who then picked a man to dance with them in the circle. Catherine remembered the passing of the veil was the bride's way of offering good fortune to girls for when they marry one day.

It's up to me to create a future for my daughter. It seems impossible, but perhaps God will find a way for me to become the artist I know I am meant to be.

The thought warred against a feeling inside her; the time for dreaming had passed. Why could she not let her desire go?

The rising sun cast a rosy hue across the sky as Father Kelley drove Catherine to the train station in DeKalb Junction. Ironically Leonek's car had been repossessed just before the wedding.

"Were you able to say goodbye to Rose?"

"I wanted to but when I tried to see her after the wedding I knocked and knocked but she wouldn't open the door. I think she was angry about not being invited. But I'm sure the sale of her liquor made up for it."

He agreed. "Rose can certainly hold a grudge."

When they arrived at the station a large group of people waited on the platform for the train.

"Before I leave, can I ask of you a favor?"

"Of course, Catherine. What is it?"

She reached into her shoulder bag and retrieved the folded piece of paper she found in the money Leonek had given her. "What does this say?"

His eyes scanned the paper.

"It says: '*I should have filed a bastardy bond on you a long time ago. My father said you are a Bolshevik. You don't care about a proper family life; you are nothing but a stupid Polack. Thanks to my uncle, you will rot in jail. Signed Teresa.*'"

He handed it back to her.

On the train ride to Syracuse, she crumpled up the paper into a tiny ball and threw it out the window. She was fully ready to begin her new life.

Chapter
31

At the train station in Syracuse Catherine searched the crowd for a tall, slender man in a suit and tie. The problem was there were many tall men in suits. Then she remembered what Father Kelley told her. *"Karol Bonzenta wears dark-rimmed pince nez glasses and has a well-groomed, thick mustache."*

She spotted a man who fit the description. He held the palm of his hand over his eyes as if he were searching for someone.

That must be him.

She cautiously walked into his view, and he started toward her . . .

"Miss Catherine Soból?"

She smiled and nodded, relieved Father Kelley had used her maiden name. She wanted no ties to Leonek Kruszka.

The man removed his felt Fedora and extended his hand toward her. "It's nice to meet you. My name is Kount Karol Bonzenta, but you may call me Kount Bonzenta."

Kount? Is he a part of Polish nobility?

"Miss Halina Mikeska awaits your arrival." He looked down at the brown leather suitcase in Catherine's left hand and at the basket with Mary she held tightly in the other.

"May I take your suitcase? And the canvas bag off your shoulder?"

As he spoke, his eyes transfixed on her, and Catherine felt awkward. She wanted to wear her comfortable cotton polka-dotted dress for the train ride, but Miriam insisted she put on one of the outing dresses from the box of clothes the Red Cross had given her. It was a maize crepe dress and it swished and swayed when she walked. Now she wondered if the long neckline was inappropriate.

She stammered. "Yes, thank you." She slipped her Coker bag from her shoulder and handed it to him.

His face softened as he looked in the basket at Mary, who didn't seem to be bothered by the chaos and the hiss of steam from the stopped train. "Please follow me."

As they left the train platform, the memory of when she first came to America flooded her mind. How excited she was to see Filip, yet fearful of her future. Here she was, one year later, back in Syracuse. Filip was dead, her husband in prison, and now she had an infant daughter.

She followed Mr. Bonzenta toward the most luxurious automobile she had ever seen. It was olive green trimmed with a black hardtop and fenders. Unlike Leonek's automobile, this one had glass windows all around. He opened the passenger door to reveal soft, tan wool upholstered seats. For a moment she felt like a queen, getting into a carriage.

As he put her things in the back seat, he commented, "This automobile is a Franklin. They are manufactured here in Syracuse." He took a step back and guided Catherine to the front seat. "Here, let me hold the basket until you get seated."

"Thank you." Despite feeding Mary on the train, she sensed another feeding would soon be needed.

As they drove to the house, Catherine was thankful Mr. Bonzenta liked to talk and this helped to ease any tension she felt. As he turned the automobile down a side street off the main road, majestic trees framed large two and three-story homes. The next turn was a one-way street where a lush green lawn separated the homes on the other side.

The automobile stopped in front of the first of five homes that all looked the same except for their different colors of gold, tan, and sage. Each had a spacious porch enclosed with balustrade rails and a corner polygonal tower topped with a bell-shaped roof. She looked up at the second story where another porch below a front gabled roof featured carved designs in the wood. The chalet-style overhang looked like the Zakopane Style Reverend Lauzon had mentioned.

It seemed the Bonzenta's were well off, but Catherine remembered how in Poland rich people treated servants as second-class citizens, especially women. *Would I be relegated to a room in the attic or some small outbuilding?*

The auto door beside her opened and interrupted her thoughts.

Mr. Bonzenta extended his hand and took the basket off her lap while he offered his other hand to help Catherine out of her seat. She felt herself blush as he steadied her exit. She was not used to being treated like a lady.

Inside the home the elaborate ornamentation continued. The large, open parlor displayed oriental carpets and wooden furniture with velvet cushions. To the left, a dining area and straight ahead was a library separated by a velvet fringed portiere. A brass nine light chandelier complimented the high tin ceiling and set the stage for the interior opulence. Catherine had never seen such richness, and she couldn't help but feel out of place,

"Halina, where are you? Miss Catherine Soból is here."

A song-like voice echoed from beyond the dining room. "I'm here, I'm coming . . ."

Mary started to fuss, and Catherine knew she either needed a change of diaper or needed to be fed. There seemed to be plenty of privacy in this home. She took Mary in her arms and shushed her when a tall, slim woman who looked like she just stepped out of a magazine advertisement appeared. Fair skinned, she was god-dess-like with her wavy, silky, shoulder-length chestnut-brown hair, that was slightly grayed near the temples and softened her high cheekbones. An elegant, violet silk dress with vertical pintucks complemented an hour-glass figure, and Catherine could not help but notice her dark, seductive eyes.

"Hello, Miss Catherine, I'm Halina Mikeska. It's a pleasure to meet you." Her voice calmed Mary and the coral orange lipstick she wore made her smile even more enchanting.

"What a beautiful child. Do you need a place to comfort her?"

"Yes, she needs to be changed and she may be hungry."

"Of course," she motioned for Catherine to follow her towards the dining room to the kitchen and down a short hallway. Kount Bonzenta talked as they walked.

"You will like it here, Catherine. Our last housemaid met a man at one of our social events and left to get married. When we met Father Kelley, he told us about you and your work ethic. His news came just at the right time."

Halina opened a dark walnut door to a room where natural light from behind the curtain of a large window tried to shine through. The bed had a simple flowered cover-let with a dark walnut headboard. In the corner was an armchair upholstered with olive green velvet fabric next to a small coffee table with a bronze tripod metal-based lamp.

"This room was to be used as storage, but we made it into a bedroom for Kamila. She found it easier to be near the kitchen since she was usually the first one up." She opened the curtains to reveal a backyard garden whose once green shrubs had turned a fiery red. The vines on the trellis were still green and fall flowers displayed colors of yellow and orange. "It has a window, so it just made sense."

Kount Karol added, "Besides, the bedrooms upstairs are being used. Halina wanted a place where we could host parties and have overnight guests. She also needed a room to showcase her costumes."

Costumes?

"Down the hall across from the pantry is a bathroom with a clawfoot tub. Just come out when you are ready. The Kount and I are about to have our afternoon tea with caramel biscuits made at a local bakery. Since it is a warm fall day, we will be out on the veranda."

"Thank you."

For the moment, she stood in the center of her room, feeling joy and relief.

What would come next, she had no idea. But for the moment—*this* good moment—she felt a rush of gratitude to God.

The next few weeks were spent getting to know one another. If the Kount and Halina knew of her past they hadn't said anything. Mrs. Mikeska was impressed with Catherine's English language skills, and she took a special liking to Mary. "Once I had a child, but . . ." Her eyes filled with tears, and she took a deep breath.

"What happened?"

"My son was born out of wedlock and taken away from me."

Catherine didn't know what to say, so she remained quiet as she set the table for dinner.

One afternoon over tea Halina asked Catherine about her love for art and how she planned to use her talents. This is when Catherine shared her sketches with Halina.

"Oh my, I can see how your drawings have developed over time."

"Thank you."

"I am intrigued by your dream to go to a university and learn art. I have a good friend who teaches art classes at Syracuse University. Her name is Adelaide and I'm certain she would be impressed by your drawings." She paused and looked at Catherine with a doubtful expression. "But how would you pay for an education? Do you have anything of value to sell?"

"I do have a necklace. But I'm not sure it's worth anything."

"What is it made of?"

"Silver with a stone of Baltic Amber."

Halina stood and went over to a desk near the parlor. She returned with a newspaper. "You reminded me about an upcoming jewelry exhibition at the Syracuse Museum of Fine Arts. Perhaps Kount Bonzenta could take it there to see if anyone might know its worth."

When the day came for the Art Show, Halina insisted she stay home with Mary while the Kount and Catherine went to the exhibit. "I'm sure the jewelers will have questions and who better to answer them than you." Then she added, "Kount, I would like you to invite the artists to our home afterwards. The bakery truck is going to bring little cakes. Catherine, you will need to put together the small sandwiches and serve coffee when you return. Like you did when I had guests over after Kount and I attended the opera house show last week."

"Yes, I would be happy to do that."

The exhibition displayed paintings and sculptures alongside ceramics, jewelry, tapestries, and wall hangings. As they walked around, Kount Bonzenta had much to say. "Previously, this Museum displayed work by local artists, but since I became part of the Board of Directors, I reached out to some of my friends in New York City to showcase their fine jewelries." Catherine nodded, but she was too mesmerized by the exhibits to pay attention.

As she walked around admiring the artwork a drawing in a glass display case caught her eye. She stopped and stared at a piece of jewelry next to it. She could not believe her eyes. She turned to tell Mr. Bonzenta but he stopped to talk with another man.

Can it be? How is this possible?

It was the drawing she created for Józef. Next to it was a replica of her necklace along with several other pieces made with Baltic amber.

A voice carried from around the corner—a deep voice. So familiar, yet she hadn't heard it in so long . . .

She crept toward the conversation. A tall man's back was to her. His curled brown hair was tamed with shiny gel. There was no mistaking the form or the voice.

Standing so close behind him she could have touched him but did not—she could barely speak the word, "Józef?"

The man turned and their eyes met. Her breathing seemed to stop and the ember of passion she had buried surged into a living flame.

"*Catherine?*" he said in a hushed voice. "Oh my goodness . . ."

He lunged toward her, wrapping her in a full embrace. Burying her face in his suit jacket, she held him tightly and could not let go.

She had so many questions, and he must have so very much to tell her.

He took a step back, his hands still on her shoulders. "Look at you! All your uncle would tell me was you had gone to America to be with Filip. I thought I would never see you again."

He pulled her close and hugged her once more, and she closed her eyes, floating in the waking dream of this moment. It was as if they were back in Poland, in the field of scarlet poppies, but this time Catherine could feel the eyes of strangers on her.

He lightly touched her head. "You cut your hair. I love it."

A confident and slender, attractive young blonde woman, with white satin anklette pumps approached them. Her overly made-up smokey eyes stared at Catherine, and immediately she hooked her arm inside Józef's elbow.

In English, she asked him, in a cool voice, "Józef, who is *this*?"

Józef replied in Polish. "Tiffany, this is Catherine—the one from Poland who designed the necklace for me. I never thought I would see her again—and now, here she is!" He opened his arms toward Catherine, who stepped back a pace and forced a smile.

Kount Bonzenta came over and extended his hand to Józef and said something in English. Tiffany smoothed her hair and smiled at him. As they talked, Józef glanced at Catherine, his eyes said so much more than his mouth could say.

Kount Bonzenta was pleased when he learned it was Józef who created Catherine's necklace. "I have invited Józef Kovarik and his fiancé Tiffany Wasserman to the house for the after-party. I told them they could ride with us."

Kovarik? Had Józef changed his name?

As if he could read her mind, Józef smiled at her once again, which made her heart melt. "When I came to America to work for Mr. Wasserman, he suggested I make my name more American. He said it would help me to sell my jewelry."

Wasserman. Where had she heard that name before?

Catherine remembered the pendant Mrs. Hagez wore when she first met her at the church when Tiffany added in Polish, "My father is a well-known jeweler in New York City. We moved to America last year but then my mother became ill with tuberculosis and my father sent her to a sanatorium in the Adirondacks." She unsnapped the silver button of her soft grey sheepskin envelope sized purse and reached inside for an embroidered handkerchief, which she used to dab the corner of her eye. "Shortly afterward we received word my mother died."

Tiffany took a deep breath. "At the same time my father discovered Józef in Kraków. We had gone back to Poland to be with family and to get more agates and amethysts for my father's business in New York City." Her eyes turned to Józef. "He installed a wrought-iron gate for my uncle. My father was impressed with the design and asked Józef if he would be interested in designing jewelry."

Józef looked at Catherine. "It was like a dream come true."

"But then Józef introduced my father to Baltic amber, and now it is our best seller." She laughed with delight.

Somehow, Catherine felt there was something missing from this story.

Kount Bonzenta responded, "That's quite a story." He pulled a gold pocket watch from his vest pocket. "We should get going. Halina is expecting our arrival."

Outside, brown leaves danced down the cobblestone street and swirled in circles from the cool fall wind. The streetlights shined on a familiar building across the street. Catherine recognized the Mizpah Hotel where she and Leonek stayed after they were married. She was reminded the past would always be present. How would she tell Józef what happened? Besides, did it really matter? He was engaged to be married.

Mr. Bonzenta insisted Tiffany sit in the front seat near him, and she was more than happy to oblige. As they conversed in English, Catherine could not take her eyes off Józef—*Józef!* In that moment, she knew that what they said was absolutely true. There is no other love like a first love, and all the feelings she had for him came back. What she wanted was to be lost in his eyes and in his arms.

And there sat Tiffany. And there lay all the years and events between when she had fallen in love with him and this bittersweet moment.

"I thought you died in the war," she said, trying not to let herself choke up. "I was at the house with your mother when Pawel and Aleksander came to tell us." She turned away and stared out the window at the canal. The neon lights of the nearby hotels and businesses created a colorful shimmer on the water as the automobile crossed the bridge. She couldn't find her voice again to finish.

Tiffany laughed as Mr. Bonzenta continued to tell one of his many stories. Józef laid his hand on top of hers.

"I know. My mother told me. "I-I don't blame you for leaving."

"What did happen to you?"

"After being captured I traveled for at least three months with other Polish and Ukraine soldiers by train from camp to camp. The Russians would interrogate us. The wounded soldiers were given treatments and forced onto other trains." He paused. "Some called them 'death trains' but I was one of the lucky ones. Most of the others died of cholera. I couldn't wait to get back to you. One evening, there was only two of us left and we came up with a plan to escape before we would be sent to Siberia, to never return." His voice became quiet, and he whispered, "The love I felt for you kept me sane."

She still could not believe he was here. Next to her.

But why was he telling her this, piercing her heart, when he was engaged?

"When I finally made it back home, I went to your uncle's place and all he told me was you had left for America."

Kount Bonzenta turned off the automobile. "Looks like the others are here before us."

Inside, Kount Bonzenta escorted Józef and Tiffany to the library where the guests congregated. Halina rushed over to Catherine holding a tray of cookies. "I had just laid Mary down when the guests started to arrive. I need you to assemble the finger sandwiches and serve coffee."

"Yes, ma'am."

"Catherine, are you all right? Were you able to find the value of your necklace?"

"No . . . I mean, yes."

"I can't wait to hear."

Once in the kitchen, Catherine took a moment to look in on Mary. She looked so soft and sweet as she lay sleeping, oblivious to the life she was now a part of.

How I wish things had turned out differently . . . but—she took hold of herself—*I am thankful for my daughter.*

A faint smell of cigar smoke reminded Catherine of Marcin.

Why didn't he tell Józef where I was? No matter, if he had known I went to America to be married, he wouldn't have come to find me anyway.

As Catherine served the coffee, she could feel Józef's eyes on her. But when she looked over, it was Tiffany who looked intently at her as she sat at the table next to Józef and sipped from her teacup.

How do I tell him I am married and have a daughter?

She was so confused yet happy to see him. Was this a cruel joke God was playing? Saying goodbye to Józef again would be another knife in the heart.

Catherine hurried to check on Mary once more. Satisfied, she quietly closed the door. When she came back to the kitchen, there was someone waiting for her.

"You startled me! Can I help you with something?"

"I wanted to save you a trip and bring you my cup."

Tiffany walked around the large kitchen looking at the colorful floral patterned Italian tile and stained-glass window above the breakfast nook. "Beautiful place. How long have you lived here?"

Fearing Mary would wake, Catherine started to assemble a new tray of sandwiches so she could walk Tiffany back to the Parlor. "Not long."

"Józef said he knew you from Poland. You are the reason he creates jewelry. Like my father, he designs jewelry for its beauty, rather than its monetary value."

As she talked, Catherine became more aware of an irresistible aura coming from Tiffany—charm and loveliness. She understood how Józef, or any man, could be attracted to her.

"Józef and I are to be married soon. Maybe we should invite you to the wedding."

"You are lucky. I always wanted to marry for love."

Her pretty face became serious. "Love? Oh no . . . Józef will marry me because my father said so." Her mood changed. "My father has always controlled me. Even now, telling me who to marry so I can keep his business. Women cannot own a business but a man can . . . my father told me I must marry so my husband would own the business. Once my father is gone, I would need someone who can maintain my comfortable life."

She set her teacup in the sink.

"If Józef wants to continue creating jewelry to sell, he needs my father's help. Once we are married he will inherit my father's business." She beamed. "I am the ticket to his dream."

Catherine re-tied her apron and picked-up the tray of sandwiches. "What are you trying to say?"

"I see the passion he has for you. He does not love me. I know that. But I could learn to love him. Afterall, he is good looking and does make beautiful jewelry. Isn't that what we want as women…income and security?"

She helped herself to a cheese sandwich from the tray and took a small bite. "I guess I could learn to love him."

Catherine set the tray back down and peered into Tiffany's eyes. "I know what it's like to be married to a man you don't love. To marry for the convenience of money and security, like the marriage my brother arranged for me. You are unhappy and miserable. You always feel there is something you are missing. That is no way to live." She knew she should stop but kept going. "A woman needs to find a husband who cherishes her for who she is, not because of some arrangement. I now believe we deserve love."

"There you are," Józef interrupted. "I wondered where you went."

How long has Józef been standing there?

He looked even more handsome than the day Catherine first laid eyes on him. Catherine had all she could do to not beg him to stay.

"Kount Bonzenta has offered to take us back to the hotel. Besides, it's late and our train to the city leaves first thing in the morning."

"Yes, we should go." She brushed the crumbs from the front of her dress. "It was nice to meet you, Catherine. Don't forget, the invitation still stands."

Tiffany slipped her arm inside of Józef's and pulled him out the door, but not before he glanced quickly over his shoulder, a look of loss in his eyes.

"Goodbye, Catherine."

She could barely get the words out. "Goodbye, Józef."

Chapter

32

After Józef left, Catherine's heart ached, and she felt a deep, painful loss. How could God have brought him here, only to take him away?

Unlike Mary, who was content to eat and sleep, Catherine could not. All she could think about was Józef. She looked at the necklace and was reminded of the story Józef told her about the poplar trees in Poland weeping amber tears, and now she was crying her own tears.

Why did I let him leave? I should have told him I loved him. But he seemed content to leave with Tiffany.

She walked out to the veranda where the harvest moonlight made the garden look as if it was daylight. The tall phlox cast their shadow on the white fence. A small noise from the kitchen broke the silence of the night.

"I thought I heard a noise down here. What are you doing up?"

"I guess it was the excitement of the evening. That was quite a party."

They went back inside.

Halina pulled up a chair across from Catherine. Her carmine red silk robe accented wide sleeves and a mandarin collar. On the front were two dragons embroidered with silver silk floss that shimmered. "Yes, we do like to entertain. I hope you were able to enjoy yourself. Mary seemed to sleep right through it."

Catherine stared out the window at the big silver disk in the night sky. She didn't want to be rude but wanted to be alone.

"What's wrong, Catherine? You look so sad. Kount shared with me your necklace has value and was designed by Mr. Kovarik, who you seem to know well."

"Yes, I did know him well . . . back home in Poland. I thought I would never see him again after he left to fight in the war. That was why I came to America, to start a new life and pursue my dream of becoming an artist."

"The same reason I came to America, to pursue my dreams."

"But you told me you were already an actress in Poland. Weren't you living your dream?"

"My biggest dream since I was a child was to play Shakespeare in English. When the Kount and I fled Poland and came here to sit out the Great War, I was able to perform in the theatres. My dream had come true. We planned to go back after the troubles were over, but that was not to be. So, we settled here."

Catherine sat up straighter.

"When I first came to America, I worked hard to learn English. I was determined to live the life I longed for." Halina walked over to the window and looked out at the garden. She then turned around and started to pace, as if she was on stage, there was a fire in her voice. "Life is always moving, Catherine. Life is challenging work. It is pain. It is a thousand times better to suffer fighting for what we want than to stay asleep."

She touched Catherine's shoulder. "Father Kelley told me of your sorrows and your desire to become an artist. I will not live forever and if I can help someone like you live your dreams, I promised God I would do it." She added, "We must do it, for Mary."

Four days later, there was an early morning knock at the door. Catherine was up with Mary and had just fed her. She thought it was the milkman, and she opened the door to greet him, with the child in her arms. Instead, Józef was standing there.

"May I come in?"

Her heart started to race.

"Of course. I was just about to make some coffee."

"And who is this?"

Silence fell. Catherine was numb with the reality of what was happening before her eyes. She hadn't expected to ever see him again.

"This is my daughter, Mary."

"You didn't tell me you had a daughter."

"I thought you were going back to New York City to be married. I saw no reason to tell you."

There was a pained look on his face.

Halina walked in and said nothing when she saw Józef.

"Good morning, Miss Mikeska. I can leave if you want me to. . . . I know it's early."

"No, no," Halina quickly responded, "here, let me take Mary, you two have much to talk about."

She winked at Catherine and took the baby.

"We will be upstairs."

When she was gone, Catherine and Józef stood there, each waiting for the other to speak first.

"Would you like a cup of coffee?" Her hand shook as she removed the cups from their hooks.

"Yes, thank you."

"I can't believe you are here."

"Neither can I."

She carefully handed him the cup.

"Tell me about Mary. She is beautiful."

Catherine told him everything: how she came to marry Leonek in marriage of convenience, the bootlegging and drinking, the ongoing arguing that eventually led to Filip's death, and Leonek being sentenced to prison.

Józef said nothing. She couldn't tell if he was angry or in shock.

"So, you're married? And Mary is his daughter? When is he getting out?"

Catherine was at a loss for words. She felt so embarrassed and ashamed. He had come back to her, and she would not blame him if he wanted nothing to do with her.

Instead, Józef took her hand. "I didn't survive being a prisoner of war by giving up. I know somehow we will work this out. But today, I need to find a place to stay and a job. Luckily, my jewelry is still on display at the museum. I must go get it before they ship it back."

"There is a Polish Community Home not far from here, near the church down the street with the two tall steeples. Kount Bonzenta goes there often. I'm sure they will know of rooms available."

As Józef approached the door to leave, he turned around to look at Catherine. It was enough to remind her Józef was right, they have come this far, he would be back.

Catherine heard nothing from Józef for a few days, but Halina remained hopeful.

"I'm sure he is busy looking for work. Who knows, maybe he started a job already. There are many factory jobs here in Syracuse.

This did not make Catherine feel any better. "But Józef doesn't deserve to work in a factory, he needs to create his art, his jewelry. I wouldn't want him to give up his dream for me."

The next day, a telegram arrived for Catherine from Stefan. That was all Catherine needed—Stefan coming here, wanting to marry her. Too nervous to open it, she handed it to Halina.

As she scanned the message, her eyes grew wide and her mouth fell open but no words came out.

"What does it say?"

Halina read it out loud.

LEONEK STARTED A FIGHT WITH A GUARD AT THE PRISON STOP

HE WAS SHOT AND KILLED BY A PRISON GUARD STOP

Catherine felt a shock of horror . . . and then an unexpected surge of release. Although she never wanted to be with Leonek again, the thought of him being killed in such a cruel manner brought grief.

"Do you know what this means, Catherine?"

Catherine walked over to the large picture window and looked out at the street. It was the end of fall and the trees once filled with life stood empty and bare.

Halina followed her. "It means you are free from Leonek. He is not your husband anymore. You are free to be with Józef."

Her mind flashed back to the thought she had in Pyrites of something greater coming from her pain and suffering. God had reunited her with Józef.

Yes, I must tell Józef, but how?

Where was he? Had he gone back to New York City?

Later that morning, Kount Bonzenta offered to go to the Polish Community Home to see what he could learn.

In two hours, Halina became concerned when he didn't come home for afternoon tea. "I do hope no news is good news."

Finally, he came home and confessed, "A man at the Polish Home told me Józef came there to inquire about hotels in the area as well as jewelers. He usually came back for a bite to eat, they said, so I waited."

Halina reassured Catherine. "At least he is still here."

Catherine's grief at the news of Leonek's death subsided. The truth was, to him she was just a household servant and a bed partner.

"Did he come back? Did you see him?"

"Yes. We sat and talked. He loves you, Catherine, and wants to be with you. He told me about his concerns and how he had been praying to God for an answer. I listened without saying a word. I smiled and told him about the telegram. He said, 'You mean, God answered my prayer with a telegram?' We both started to laugh."

Catherine and Halina both gave a hearty laugh.

"I invited Józef over for dinner tomorrow. He wanted to come right now, but he made a choice as to which jeweler he was going to give his talents to in Syracuse and had to go meet with them. Then he grabbed his coat and white straw hat and told me he hadn't felt this happy since leaving the prisoner of war camp."

The next evening Halina set the table with her finest dinnerware, which she called Syracuse China. Catherine prepared a special Polish dinner of Golabki, made with minced pork, rice, mushrooms, and onions wrapped inside cabbage leaves. Kount Bonzenta managed to have some brown honey put away for an occasion such as this. Dinner was full of hope for a new future.

"To Catherine and Józef! May they live one hundred years!"

The toast took Catherine back to her wedding day. Her brother's smile as he raised his teacup.

Józef put down his cup. "Catherine, are you all right?"

"I just can't believe you are here, and we can finally be together."

Kount Bonzenta agreed. "Yes. How was it you managed to leave your arrangements with Miss Wasserman and her father? He is a powerful man."

"The ride back to New York was quiet. She barely spoke to me. Then when we arrived, she told me to go back to Syracuse and be with Catherine. She did not want to be with a man who cherished another woman in his heart. I told her I had an arrangement with her father, and he would be furious, but she said, 'I will tell him we had a terrible fight and I want nothing more to do with you. I don't want my father telling me who to marry. I deserve a man who loves only me.'" Then she told me, "'Now go, before I change my mind!'"

Later in the evening, they talked about marriage, and Halina insisted they get married right there, outside in the garden.

"The garden will be in full bloom by June."

"I'm not sure if I can wait that long to marry Catherine, but I do need time to save for a place where we can raise Mary."

Halina reiterated. "Catherine, I told my friend at the university about your drawings and how you designed a stained-glass window made by Keck Studios. They are willing to let you come to school. I can help with Mary while you pursue your studies."

"And together we can design and create jewelry to be sold right here in Syracuse," Józef added as he raised his glass.

Later, after Józef had gone, while in her room alone with Mary, Catherine flipped through her soft red leather ledger. As she reflected on the moments of her life she came across a piece of folded paper. Tucked inside was the note she had written to herself in Pyrites after Leonek was gone.

> *I, CATHERINE ~~KRUSZKA~~ SOBÓL, WILL BECOME THE ARTIST WHO WILL EARN ENOUGH MONEY TO PROVIDE A HOME FOR MY CHILD. ONE DAY I WILL MARRY AGAIN, BUT THIS TIME FOR LOVE.*

Acknowledgments

Thank you to my publisher, Morgan James Publishing, for believing in me and my story. Also, for W. Terry Whalin, who said those famous words I will never forget, "Send it to me," and to my author team at Morgan James. I appreciate your guidance and support with this book.

Thank you to my writing coach, David Hazard, who I met during an online workshop through View Arts in Old Forge, New York. He taught me the importance of storyboarding, outlining, and how to create character and plot arcs. Also the importance of the rock in the river.

I am beyond thankful for the thoughtful advice from my critique partners and early readers that helped make this book stronger. Thank you to my dear friends: Ashley Logsdon, Jim Ripper, Frances Drost, Grace Pettman, Nancy Roberts, Susan Montgomery, Pam Holbrook, Kathleen Bradley, Sandra Swierczek, Christine Smith, Lorraine Morganti, and Marilyn Higgins. A special thank you to Dan Miller and my tribe at the 48 Days Eagles Community for your continued support and encouragement.

To my newfound friends at the Syracuse Polish Home, who I would have never met if I didn't write this book. Thank you for your knowledge of Eastern European culture and support. I am forever grateful and proud to be part of your community. A special thanks to Marta Chmielewski who helped me translate letters written to my grandmother from Poland.

As a historical novelist, I am thankful for those who preserve and promote history. I would like to express my gratitude to the organizations that helped with my research when writing this book: Onondaga Historical Association, St. Lawrence County Historical Association, Syracuse Polish Home, Canton Historical Association, Potsdam Public Museum, Adirondack Experience: The Museum on Blue Mountain Lake, the Pastoral Administration at The Roman Catholic Church of Saint Mary in Canton, New York, and to the Sacred Heart of the Basilica in Syracuse. Also, the countless online databases of historical records.

To my family members for their memories of Catherine. You helped make this book possible.

Most of all, I would like to thank my husband Chris, who supported my dream of telling this story and becoming a published author. To you, I will be forever grateful. I love you.

Finally, I am grateful to you, my readers. Thank you for spending time with my characters and for your continued support. I hope you enjoyed this story as much as I enjoyed writing it. May all your dreams come true.

About the Author

Roxanne Bocyck began her publishing career by writing feature stories for two weekly newspapers in her hometown. At age forty-four, she attended Syracuse University as a post-traditional college student, where she earned her Bachelor of Arts degree in Writing and Communications, all while working and raising a family. She chronicled her experience as an adult returning to school in a blog and was featured in Syracuse University's ad campaign for part-time studies. Roxanne was an honoree of SU's Writer's Distinction Program, and her professor, Steve Parks, featured her story, "A Capitalist Fairy Tale" in the book *Pro(se)letariets* by Parlor Press. Her poetry also appears in *Working: An Anthology of Writing and Photography*, published by Syracuse University Press. Roxanne is a teacher at heart, passionate about helping women overcome fear and doubt to pursue their dreams. She wanted to share this story to encourage everyone to nurture their dreams and never give up. Roxanne lives in Syracuse, New York. For more information visit roxannebocyck.com.

A free ebook edition is available with the purchase of this book.

To claim your free ebook edition:

1. Visit MorganJamesBOGO.com
2. Sign your name CLEARLY in the space
3. Complete the form and submit a photo of the entire copyright page
4. You or your friend can download the ebook to your preferred device

Morgan James
BOGO™

A **FREE** ebook edition is available for you
or a friend with the purchase of this print book.

CLEARLY SIGN YOUR NAME ABOVE

Instructions to claim your free ebook edition:
1. Visit MorganJamesBOGO.com
2. Sign your name CLEARLY in the space above
3. Complete the form and submit a photo
   of this entire page
4. You or your friend can download the ebook
   to your preferred device

Print & Digital Together Forever.

Snap a photo

Free ebook

Read anywhere

Printed in the USA
CPSIA information can be obtained
at www.ICGtesting.com
JSHW020222141023
50184JS00002B/14